Stay

JANE BAILEY

ORION

First published in Great Britain in 2023 by Orion Fiction,
an imprint of The Orion Publishing Group Ltd,
Carmelite House, 50 Victoria Embankment
London EC4Y 0DZ

An Hachette UK Company

1 3 5 7 9 10 8 6 4 2

A CIP catalogue record for this book is
available from the British Library.

ISBN (Paperback) 978 1 3987 0500 5
ISBN (eBook) 978 1 3987 0501 2

Typeset by Input Data Services, Bridgwater, Somerset

Printed in Great Britain by Clays Ltd, Elcograf S.p.A.

www.orionbooks.co.uk

For all the tender maids

Chapter One

Every weird family is weird in its own way. I should have spotted straight away that this was a weird one. Instead – given the state I was in – I just thought it might be a bit of fun. Rage made me reckless. When I stepped off that ferry at Dover, it wasn't really the encroaching pandemic I was escaping, although that was definitely creeping off the ferry behind me. Reluctantly, I was going home – until my card refused to pay for a train ticket. Home was still where I was heading when I stood by the side of the road coming out of the port. We'd done it in Italy when we'd been stuck for a lift, and now I was fearless, my arm like gold in the March evening sun as I extended my thumb.

The car looked a bit boho, and the family in it seemed interesting, then intriguing, then seriously crazy. And only later, sinister. But that spring of 2020 was crazy for the world at large. It was easy to get lost, to lose contact. And I was angry with Luke and Lotti and my father. All of which made what happened possible.

I always thought betrayal would be more uniform, like a perfectly square slab of something bitter that you could cut into chunks and work your way through, bit by bit, and then you'd be done with it. But it seemed to be eating me instead, nibble by nibble, reaching further and further into the deepest seams of my self-worth.

I imagined shooting Luke, then gunning Lotti down for good measure. I'd wished him on the ferry with me, so that I could shove him off the back and watch him disappear – shocked – into the foaming wake. But, yes, I know. Adrenaline fuelled by rage. It could never end well.

If I think about it too much, I'll have to admit that a lot of the anger was with myself. Being blind to hideous betrayal is just about forgivable; but blind to such emotional stinginess, happy to take such tiny crumbs of attention and tell myself it was enough: that's the worst kind of pathetic. I failed to see Luke's true intent, when all the while he was feasting greedily on my last teenage year. Part of my job was to attribute cleverness to him, too in awe of him to see that he was just older than me, fairly bright but unoriginal. I do feel shoddy about leaving without giving any explanation to Lotti's boyfriend, Tom, though. He was a good friend to me. He was the only thin membrane between Luke's contempt for me and my contempt for myself.

I thought I was having a good time, but now I come to take a good long look at it, it was Luke telling me I was having a great time, like he was doing me a favour as I trailed round Italy after him. But that misses the point. What did he actually give me, apart from low self-esteem and repeated bouts of cystitis? What did he get from me? Well, that is the issue: he used me for something I didn't even guess at. They both did.

The police were intrigued by how I came to be embroiled with what came later. It's simple, really.

*

English drivers seem far more wary of a girl on her own than Italian drivers. For over an hour, no one stops or even toots their horn. I refuse to imagine what would happen if a lone male driver pulled over and there was no Luke skulking in the bushes, waiting to share the lift.

Fucksake. Why on earth am I heading home anyway, since home is the last place I want to go? And I don't know how I'm going to face my father after what *he's* done. So when Marcus pulls over in his cliché of free spirit – a flower-painted Land Rover – and his wife Mimi rolls down the window, I take one look at the faces of their children in the back and I don't hesitate. I assume this is a picture-book happy family and ask where they're going.

'Gloucestershire.'

'That'll do fine. I'm heading for Cornwall. Drop me off somewhere.'

The older girl, who must be about twelve or thirteen, gets into the very back seat to make way for me. I take it as politeness, but after a while, I realise she probably wants to be apart from the main body of the family to listen to her music. The little girl sits behind her father, so I sit behind the mother, who twists her head around the seat to look at me, very directly, as if reading something important in me. It's hard to see much of her, but her hair is long and brown and streaked with auburn, and her eyes are so pale that they seem almost colourless.

'I'm Mimi, by the way, and this is Marcus.'

Marcus lifts a hand off the wheel and waves, and I see his smile from the side. His arms, stretched out to the wheel, are brown and velvety with dark hair. The thought of making conversation right now is pretty horrifying, but probably the best bet. My head is a cage with tigers in it. I can't hang about in there for too long.

'I'm Caitlin,' I say.

The little girl is staring at me with big eyes. I'm not great around kids. I smile, but she seems coy.

'Who's this?' I look at the soft toy in her lap. She holds it out to me and I take it, examining the floppy arms and legs. It eyes me with tenderness, the gentlest smile sewn on to its muzzle. The best smile I've had in days, actually. A donkey. 'Well, Donkey, what's your owner called?' I make the toy whisper in my ear. '*Dizzy* – what? Come again? *Dozy* – no, wait,' I make the donkey agitated and come back for another whisper. '*Oh*, that's a nice name.'

The girl swings her feet back and forth, beginning to smile. 'What did he say?'

'Daisy.'

'That's me! I'm Daisy! How did you know?'

It's written in felt pen inside some little trainers on the seat between us. I put the toy back on her lap. 'That's one clever donkey you have there.'

'Henna!' shouts Mimi, leaning round the seat again. Pale blue. Her eyes are pale blue.

'*Henna!*' shouts Marcus at the girl in the back.

'*What?*' Henna takes an earplug out and sounds annoyed.

'Caitlin, this is Henna.'

'Hi.'

'*Henna?*' says the man.

'What?'

'Say hello to Caitlin.'

'Hello, Caitlin.' She says it in such a sing-song voice that it's clearly filled with sarcasm. She sullenly puts the earplug back in.

'I apologise for my daughter,' says Marcus, without looking round. 'She's thirteen.'

'It's her *hawmans*,' whispers Daisy, very softly.

'I see. Well, that explains it.' I wink at Daisy, and she smiles back.

I can see Marcus grinning again. 'She'll be all right when she's twenty-three.'

'Oh God. I've got four years to go myself, then.'

'You're nineteen?' asks Marcus, turning slightly now, so that I see his friendly face. 'You at uni or something?'

I explain that I'm taking a year off. This isn't strictly true. Actually, it's not true at all, but I don't want to tell them that I flunked my A-level grades hanging out with Luke. I don't even want to think about that. But he keeps asking questions now, so I change the subject by asking Daisy how old she is. She replies very quietly: 'I'm five and I like your bracelet.'

'Thank you. It's just a cheap old thing.' I slide the bracelet off my wrist and put it on hers, and she seems awestruck.

4

So sleepy. I close my eyes and wrestle with a longing for home. The salt wind rushing in from the sea, rocking the little boats and bending the trees into submission; the ragged choughs around the cliffs, the air filled with the screams of gulls and children and fierce scents of seaweed and ozone and chips; the retreating tides leaving warm rock pools, jewelled with weed and anemones; the tingle of woollen jumpers over cold, salt-sticky skin; the grit of sand stuck between toes and tumbled out onto doormats and floors; and inland, the endless damp of winter, the grey, racing clouds, gravelly rain and herringbone walls bright with moss; then the greenness of it all in the lanes, bringing in the gentle ice-cream jingles and grass strimmers and curtains billowing out through summer windows, and old men sitting outside pubs remembering how it was when shoes were a luxury and everyone knew your name.

After a while, Daisy whispers loudly, 'Mummy! She's *asleep.*' Her little hand is stroking my arm, and comes to rest on my hand, which she takes silently in her own and holds all the way to Membury service station.

'Caitlin! Caitlin, wake up.' It's Mimi. 'We're at Membury services, on the M4. If you're heading for Cornwall, here might be a good place – or Bristol – but it's getting dark. It's a bit too dark to be standing by the side of the road on your own.'

'It's okay. I'm used to it.'

'I don't think it's safe.' Marcus has come round to my side of the car and opened my door. He could equally be a hippy or someone who models chunky knitwear leaning on a windswept sea rock. Now he leans on the door frame and I can smell the sweet, musky sweat from his armpit and see the folds of his rust-coloured T-shirt stretch diagonally across his chest. I picture his bare skin, just beneath the cotton. His head is a mass of brown curls falling sideways as he looks in at me. (Pebble beach. Donegal knit.) 'Why don't you come with us to Gloucestershire tonight, at least? We can set you on your way tomorrow.'

'Yes!' says Daisy, suddenly animated. 'Come back with us!'

The sun has gone. All the lights from the service station give off a cosy glow against the gloom. I'm still churned up, but a little less so than before. Darkness has cut the throat of the day and left a long red wound on the horizon.

After a coffee and a sandwich, during which Mimi insists I go back with them, I'm already giving in. I don't even want to see my family at the moment – especially Dad. I check my phone: three messages from Mum asking if I'm back safely. I'll text her to say I am, but later, and that I'm staying a night or two in Gloucestershire with friends. I don't see why I should rush back, under the circumstances. I'm quite glad they're worried about me. They should be. So I push a bunch of euros at Mimi and say, 'Only if you let me pay for the sandwiches and the drinks. Sorry, I've only got euros.'

'Yay!' says Daisy.

And that's how it was decided. I simply slung my rucksack on my shoulder and climbed back into the car – and into the life – of perfect strangers.

Chapter Two

I drift into sleep, disturbed only by the sensation of someone – presumably Daisy – playing with my hair, and later placing a coarse blanket over me.

Silence jolts me awake much later as the engine is switched off. It's pitch black outside, and the artificial light inside the car makes me squint.

'We thought we'd let you sleep,' says the woman, after opening the door. 'You were so tired, poor love.'

I lean forward, trying to get my bearings. *Mimi*, I remember. I once had a hamster called Mimi. The others are bundling luggage off the car, and slowly I crawl out to join them, not done with sleep but trying to heave it off. 'Can I help?'

We're in woodland, as far as I can make out from the light of the car, in some sort of small clearing by a low stone wall.

'Thank you. We're all done,' says the man, putting an arm around my shoulder. *Marcus*. That's it: *Mimi and Marcus*. 'Let's get you into bed. You've been out like a light.'

I can't fight it. My body is like lead. I would have been happy to curl up again in the car or at the foot of a tree, but the prospect of a warm bed is too good to turn down. 'This is so kind of you. I'll be on my way in the morning, don't worry.'

'Stay as long as you want – unless you're in a hurry to get somewhere.'

I'm certainly not that, but hope it doesn't show. I mutter

something that trails off, and follow the family down a steep wooded path in the darkness, eyes on the torchlight that dances ahead, held by Mimi. Marcus has his hand on my back now, shepherding me gently down the slope, and I'm confused by this, trying to remember if there had been something between us before I'd fallen asleep; and then, realising there'd been nothing, wondering at this hands-on approach of his, and at my slight thrill at his proximity.

Suddenly, several squares of amber light give shape to a spacious stone house tucked into the lap of the wooded incline we've just descended. Its back is nestled against a sloping field, with another rising slope in front, but from the side, as we approach, its outline stands out sharply against a sky now stippled with stars.

'Welcome to Amberside House,' says Marcus at my shoulder. We walk through a cold utility area hung with cheeses in muslin bags, into a wide flagstoned kitchen with a clutter of objects hanging from the ceiling. And alongside the endless colanders, saucepans, tea towels and fat bunches of herbs, there dangle home-made *objets d'art*, ranging from macramé and corn dollies to wonky papier mâché animals. I stand and marvel at the room like a child, breathing in a fascinating mix of odours which are suddenly dominated by cigarette smoke and patchouli, as a gravelly voice arrives to greet us.

'The travellers return! Hey! Welcome back.'

It belongs to a shaggy-haired woman in jeans, who puts her arms around each of them in turn – and then me, after she's been introduced. ('Our damsel in distress,' he calls me.) She feels bony and wizened, although she can't be more than forty. The woman's eyes take me in and fix briefly on Mimi; what does this mean? Is it something to do with Marcus's hand on my shoulder? Does she think I'm a threat? *As if.* Mimi is perfect, and I'm a slab of lard by comparison. But it bothers me. I hate catching those exchanged glances. They always mean trouble. I won't think of Luke now, though. Italy is behind me.

'I trust everything went smoothly on the journey front?' she asks them.

'Wonderful, thanks. All well here, Suze?'

'All good. And I've got some news. There are two more—'

Marcus interrupts to explain that Suze has been keeping an eye on things while they've been away, and that she lives in Gloucester with her boyfriend, Arrow. *Arrow?* I must have betrayed some sleepy confusion, because he lifts a tabby cat abruptly out of Daisy's arms and says, 'Daisy, take Caitlin up to Bryony's old room straight away. I'll read you a story after.' I note this, and I see that the promise delights her.

The oak stairs have a strip of threadbare reddish carpet running down the centre. Daisy charges up them and gives me a running commentary. There's still a shyness about her, but now she seems excited. She flings open a bathroom door to reveal an old-fashioned toilet with a wooden seat, ceiling-high cistern and a long pull-chain. Damp is bubbling under the lilac-painted plaster high up on the walls, and the bath – which stands on four rusted clawed feet – has seen better days.

'That's Violeta's room,' she says, pointing to a door opposite. 'She's . . . um . . . Remainian and really nice, and down there is Mummy and Daddy's room and I'm . . . here!' She opens a door and leaps inside, turning a circle with her arms out to her sides like a wildly enthusiastic estate agent.

I put my head around and see a patchwork bed covered with animals, walls covered in pictures of animals, and paper creatures dangling from pieces of string. Almost asleep on my feet, I attempt delight: 'Lovely!'

'And you're up here with Henna.' She gallops up another flight of wooden stairs, at the top of which is a passage with three wooden doors leading off it in a row. She points at each one: 'Henna . . . You . . . Bathroom.'

My door opens on to a simple room with muted blue walls, a low oak-beamed roof and a single wooden bed. The little girl bounds in and tries to find special features to point out. She flicks on the bedside lamp. 'A lamp!' She points to a pot of dried flowers on the windowsill: 'Lavender!'

Where does she get her energy from? I drop my rucksack on the floor and yawn.

She smiles at me and then lunges forward, throwing her arms around my hips and kissing my T-shirt. 'I'm glad we met you!'

I stroke her chaos of curly hair, a little overcome with the affection in her wide blue eyes. 'Well, I don't know where I'd be now if you hadn't. It's really kind of you all.'

Footsteps plod up the stairs and Henna walks towards us across the narrow landing. Her thin legs are pale as driftwood in her shorts. 'Goodnight,' she says, and hovers.

'*And . . . ?*' whispers Daisy.

'And sleep in peace. I'm sure you will.' She goes to push open her bedroom door without the flicker of a smile.

'Thank you, Henna. You, too.'

I undress with relief and sink into the bed, considering briefly trying to find a T-shirt to act as a nightie, since the warmth of Italy and a bed companion have become even more of a distant memory now that the chill of an English night has drawn in. But as soon as the stiff cotton of the sheets meets my skin, I switch the lamp off and drift into dreams.

I'm woken by a soft sound and a slit of light. Suddenly aware that it's the bedroom door creaking open, I sit up swiftly. It's still dark, still night, and only a dim glow from the lower landing lights the shadowy figure in the doorway, who now approaches.

I catch my breath, but say nothing. I've become used to dark mornings, glaring sun blocked out by heavy Italian shutters, but the light from beyond the door looks artificial, so it can't be time to wake up. I can't tell if I've been asleep for hours or just minutes.

The figure sits on the edge of the bed and puts a hand on my bare arm. For a bewildered moment I think I might still be in our flat in Florence, and that Luke has come to say it's all been a joke, a send-up, and now everything between us will be all right again. But the smell is wrong.

'Don't worry,' says Marcus. 'It's me.'

He leans forward and puts his arms around me, squeezing his naked torso against my own.

Whoa!

I catch my breath again and loathe myself for giving a small embarrassed laugh.

'What is it?' he asks in a low, amused voice. 'Not used to being hugged?'

I stutter something, trying to make him out, my eyes becoming accustomed to the dark. He's wearing jeans and no top and smells of soap. How is he imagining this will work, with smiling Mimi just downstairs? My first inclination is to cover myself, but I don't. He has shocked me, and made me confused or indignant or something – I can't say what. I leave my breasts uncovered as a challenge. What's he going to do, surrounded by his family? I feel like provoking him, knowing that he can do nothing. It gives me back some control.

'I'm sorry,' he says gently, stroking my shoulder. 'I didn't mean to frighten you.'

Knobhead. Even though I don't voice the word, it helps to replace the other things I have no words for: a resinous scent when my nose was plunged deep into the hair behind his ear; the way his torso fits into mine; the brief holding of my shoulders with a pressure both firm and light as air, thumbs rubbing the curve of them. Strange things I have longed for so much they are as familiar as memories, though dizzyingly new. The word I don't say, scathing and decisive, fills my head and covers all these startling things like a convenient dust sheet. Knobhead. Who does he think he is?

But. Oh.

Oh, God.

'Um . . .' I say awkwardly. 'But . . . Mimi?'

He laughs lightly again. 'She'll be up in a minute.'

'What?'

'To give you a hug, too.' He pushes some hair back from my eyes. 'Don't worry. It's what we do here. We always hug everyone before we go to bed. We all do it – to wish our friends peace and to give them sweet dreams.' He leans forward and kisses me very tenderly on the cheek. 'You see? That didn't hurt, did it?' He gets up and walks to the door. 'Sleep in peace, Caitlin.'

He's got to be taking the piss, surely. Although maybe it really is what they do here, and that was why Daisy expected something more from Henna earlier: a hug for the new guest, perhaps?

I'm still trembling after Marcus when the door opens again, and Mimi does indeed come over and repeat the procedure, only this time it's a simple hug and peck on the cheek.

'Sleep in peace, Caitlin, and welcome to our home.'

She sits there for a while, gazing at me in the darkness and smelling slightly differently of the same soap. Then she folds her hands gently over mine and says, 'You are very welcome here.'

And I'm certain that Mimi is smiling.

Chapter Three

A slice of sunlight coming between the thick curtains works its way onto my face, and I wake to the sound of someone moving about quietly downstairs. Outside, a blackbird is making a noise, as if defending its territory from a predator. My phone is in my rucksack, so I don't bother looking at the time. I creep into the bathroom and splash my face with water. The bath has a shower attachment, and I hose myself down, not wanting to disturb Henna if I run a bath. I long for a good, long soak. The shower in Avignon – where I spent my last few days – gave out a dribble, and I haven't had a proper bath since Florence.

The house seems empty. There's a hollowness to it, as if it might magnify each small sound. Despite the thin carpet on the stairs, the sense is of stone and wood. The flagstones, when I reach the hallway, have a welcome solidity after so much train and ferry travel.

As soon as I step outside, I can hear Daisy humming somewhere. A blond track winds off to the left across a field and disappears behind bushes. To the right is the steep path up to the woods where we parked last night. Straight opposite the house, beyond some gravel and a flat unkempt area that could have been a garden, a bank rises, grassy and lush, to a barn which is surrounded by beech trees, and higher up again there is a ragged seam of gorse bushes stitching the sky to the land.

I turn and look up at the front of the house. The main body of it is symmetrical, but the window frames – what you can see of them – are painted in alternate shades of blue, mauve and pink. The walls are a pale Cotswold stone, but seem to be supported by a creeper with leaves as big as place mats and alive with small darting creatures; unkempt trellis is broken off at the corners and coming away from the wall in places, wadded behind with more creeper. A climbing rose has meandered all the way up to the eaves, which are smudged with the remains of old swallows' nests. By the front door sits a stone Buddha with moss growing out of his head, a barbecue made out of broken bricks, and rows of random wellington boots. Off to the left is a rainbow-painted outhouse, and against it leans a paint-spattered easel and a selection of folded wooden chairs, rotting and knitted together with cobwebs. A little way in front of the house is a swing-chair with broken wicker spikes coming out from it like hedgehog quills. It seems a different house from the grand one I walked into last night. This one has an air of neglect, as if children have been allowed to look after their parents' house for the summer.

Back inside, I walk into a dining room off the hallway. It has a long wooden table and a high stone fireplace. I picture women in sandals making corn dollies around it. I'm still alone in the quietness when I see Mimi through an archway, standing at a kitchen counter, kneading some dough.

She turns slowly, as if she has waited for a moment to absorb my presence first.

'Caitlin!' There are those eyes again: startling, pale and blue. She smiles warmly, but her eyes are assessing me somehow. There's something about me she's appraising, but I can't tell what. 'Come and sit down. Coffee? Did you sleep okay?'

'Like a log. And yes please – but don't go to any trouble. Wait for the others.'

She tosses her hair back and laughs, leading me into the kitchen. 'The others have long gone. I popped in to see if you might be ready for breakfast, but you were out like a light.'

'Oh, I'm so sorry! What time is it?'

She peers at an old-fashioned clock on the wall behind me. 'Nearly ten. But don't worry. You must've needed it. Now, what can I get you? There's bread and jam – damson or plum. There's muesli, yoghurt . . .'

I'm mortified. I don't want to be any trouble. In fact, I was hoping, as I nodded off to sleep, that I might impress these people enough to get them to let me stay on a bit. Then I won't have to face my family. They mentioned it last night, but I didn't really believe they were being anything but polite. I especially need to impress Mimi, because I'm not sure if she's picked up on her husband's rather flirty behaviour towards me. I want to be her friend.

'Please, I really don't want to be any trouble.' But she places in front of me a basket of wholemeal bread, cut in giant chunks, a slab of yellow butter on a dish and a selection of jams. The kettle is purring loudly and she scoops coffee from the drawer of an old coffee mill into a cafetière.

'Coffee okay? I'll join you.'

I nod, and watch her movements at the counter as she replaces the little wooden drawer of the coffee mill and pours water onto the coffee. The smell is wonderful. She's wearing jeans and a berry-coloured cotton vest, and her figure is perfect. Or perhaps it isn't perfect. It's the way she moves that's perfect. Every action is smooth, as if she glides on ice. Her burnished mahogany-brown hair is wavy and almost waist-length. I can't work out her age, but I think she's beautiful.

Opposite me, she watches. I know I have to make conversation, otherwise she'll start to ask me about myself and I'll have to talk about everything that's happened, and I really don't want to do that. Not any of it.

'So,' I say, spreading a hunk of bread with jam, 'is this a working farm? Do you keep animals and that?'

'Oh no, not any more. We did have a cow once, and until

recently a couple of goats and a few chickens. But nothing now.'

'Ah. So, what do you . . .?'

'Marcus has some polytunnels and does . . . market gardening.' She flashes me an intense look. 'And I run a nursery.'

'A nursery? What – for plants?'

'No, small children. Well, babies, mostly. It's quite "niche" actually. It's for those professional mums who need to go away for periods of time – a few days or a week, maybe – and need to leave their babies somewhere safe.'

'Oh, like a . . .' I want to say 'like a dog kennel service', but stop myself, as that would sound as if I disapproved. It actually sounds like a good idea, if you like babies, which I don't. 'That sounds like a good idea.'

'Well, it can be quite lucrative, actually. *However*, looks like that's all about to change.'

'Oh?' I stuff a large piece of bread and jam in my mouth, so she'll have to do the talking.

'Oh, you won't have heard the news either, then? We've been away for a two-week holiday, so we had no idea what was going on. We stayed in a run-down old house in France – lovely place – and we never listen to any news while we're away. But anyway, on the radio this morning we heard that the schools shut down on Friday.' Seeing me raise my eyebrows, she explains further: 'All of them. Primary and secondary. All the schools in England. And nursery – with a few exceptions.'

This is no surprise. We'd left Italy because of the pandemic, and fears that we wouldn't be able to get out if we didn't go soon. And then when we reached France – where I stayed just a few days – the virus was already starting to take off.

'There is one baby I'm expecting. We can still take the children of health-care workers, so . . .' She passes me a different jam to try, but I shake my head. 'And I also help vulnerable women, when I can. So people come and go.'

'Oh. What, like women in danger?'

'That's right. We try and help them get back on their feet and give them some independence.'

'Oh, wow. That's . . . good.'

She's watching my mouth as it's chewing. It's as if she's an artist examining a model to draw. I focus on the edge of my plate, unsure where to look.

'Um . . I was wondering . . . before I set off for home . . .' She widens her eyes, encouraging me. 'This is really rude of me, but could I have a bath?'

She relaxes into a broad smile, like a mother whose child has successfully read a whole sentence for the first time. 'Of course! You go ahead. Have a good long soak. The bathroom next to your room is best. I'll bring up some fresh towels and some of my lavender soap.' I smile, and thank her. 'Oh, and there's no need to leave today. Wait until tomorrow at least. Have a look round the farm after. I know Daisy was longing to show you. And play with you.'

'I'd like that.'

'I should warn you, she'll want to plait your hair. You may have to succumb.'

The bath is sublime. Although I have to say, the home-made soap is a bit shit. It turns to slime on contact with the water. The room is cool, though: tiny, with a sloping roof. I lie in its curiously electric-blue bath and face towards the exposed beam and the little window which is flooding the space with sunlight. Days of grime float away in the hot suds. I close my eyes and breathe out a long sigh, hoping to eject everything that's happened. But as soon as my lids drop, I see Luke standing on the platform at Avignon station, where we parted unceremoniously. I had pretended I was just going to Paris for some time out and I'd thrown a few things in my rucksack – as much as I could carry. He knew, though. I could tell from that pained look and the need to defend himself one last time with a cutting parting shot: *You don't know everything about your dad, you know.*

17

I could've told him that. Even Dad doesn't know everything about himself. Or much at all. I was afraid Luke would stop me from leaving if I told him it was for good. I was afraid – or I hoped, maybe – that he would convince me it had all just been a silly misunderstanding.

With a giant towel wrapped around me, I decide to review the contents of my rucksack, fearing the worst: a few pairs of knickers, no spare bras, one pair of socks, a long skirt, a pair of jeans and a few wrinkled T-shirts. Not even a jumper, and it's quite nippy in England. I rummage in my toilet bag and find a travel alarm, one of my gran's handkerchiefs, a kohl eyeliner, my toothbrush, dental floss and mosquito cream. I look for my contraceptive pills, but can only find the empty strip I used up before the trip. That means my period will start in a few days and I doubt I even have one spare pad. I must've left the pill packet back in Avignon. Fucksake. Still, I won't have to worry about producing spawn of Luke any more.

There's a mirror on a small chest of drawers and I try not to catch sight of my untameable hair. I've remembered a wide-toothed comb, although my little pot of hair gel is dangerously low. I sit on the bed and sigh. I should at least phone my parents and tell them I'm back safe. Not that they're expecting me, but under the circumstances, they might be worried about me being unable to make it home. Fishing around for my phone, there's a flood of relief when my fingers feel its familiar shape at the bottom of the bag.

Three text messages from Mum. Hmm. Nothing from Dad. Like he'd care. There's a saved voicemail from Mum, too: *Caitlin, call me when you get this . . . Caitlin? There's talk of last flights and ferries from France soon. Just come home as soon as you can, love. We'll pay, if there's a problem. Just get home, love.* There's a strange scuffling noise, as if my mother hasn't quite learned how to end a call yet. Or maybe she had something else to say, but decided against it. Does she know? That is the million-dollar question: Does she know about my father?

It's not fair to punish Mum by not phoning. It's not her fault, after all. I'll phone my sister later. This evening. Or text. Maybe I'll just text Mum. Then she can't persuade me to go home. The signal's not good. Shit. I might as well get this over with:

Mum I'm back in England. Staying for a few days with friends in Gloucestershire.

Of course, I don't know if I'll be invited to stay a few days, but at least this means there's no expectation of my immediate return. I picture Mum's worried face.

Back soon, I add. Although I know I won't be.

Chapter Four

I follow the sound around to the right of the house and see Daisy coming in and out of view on a tree swing. She's talking to herself now, happy and self-contained. How wonderful to be five years old and swinging from a tree.

'Want a push?'

She looks up and smiles.

'What's this?' Daisy holds the locket which swings from my neck as my torso leans forward.

'A locket. It belonged to my granny.'

She frowns. 'I don't like locks.'

'A locket, not a lock.' I steady the swing. 'Look, it opens. See?'

She inspects the tiny picture of my Granny Rostock. 'It's an open-it, not a lock-it!'

'Yes, I guess it is. In fact, it doesn't lock at all. It just closes. Try it.'

She snaps it shut and open a couple of times. 'I wish I had a granny.'

I push her gently on the swing.

'What do you grow on the farm?'

She looks over to a great field behind the house. 'Those are Daddy's polytunnels. They're not very interesting. There are vegetables in the first one, tomatoes and . . . um . . courgettes. Some mushrooms. Some carrots. Some . . . other stuff. And the other polytunnels are full of weeds.'

'Weeds?'

'Yes. Daddy grows weeds and turns them into . . . balls of weed that people want to buy.'

'I see.'

'That's Cliff over there, who helps. And that's Arrow.' Two old hippy guys appear from one of the polytunnels. 'He's the boyfriend of *Sooze*. And there are all the other places. That's Mummy's office.' She gestures to the rainbow-painted cabin. 'That's boring. And that's the barn over there. We're not allowed in the barn, but there's a bed in there and lots of cushions and stuff. I know, because me and Henna have been in, though we're not allowed.'

Now I'm curious to see the barn. Maybe I'll be allowed.

'I see. And do you have any friends living nearby?'

'No, we don't have people living nearby us.' She gets off the swing and bends down to two plastic lions standing between the roots of a tree; she covers them over intently with handfuls of rough grass and loose earth, not satisfied until they're completely buried. I look about and see that the house is in a wide but shallow valley, and there is nothing to see but sheep dotted on the sloping fields and woodland in the crevices. 'There is a house way, way, up there, and Surfer Joe lives in it.'

'Surfer Joe?'

'And his weird friend Cal. I haven't met Cal.'

'What's weird about Cal?'

'He's dangerous. Daddy says.'

'Dangerous?'

'Yes. He's . . . um . . . annoyed. Surfer Joe says so.'

'A *nerd*,' comes Henna's voice from nowhere. 'A nerd, not annoyed.' She is sitting reading behind the swing tree. 'And Joe thinks everyone who reads is a nerd.'

'Oh, I see. So, tell me about Surfer Joe. What's he like?'

Daisy thinks about this. 'I don't know. He's a policeman. He arrests people and stuff.'

I continue to push the swing gently, my eyes on her little hands, the nails dark with earth from burying her lions.

Chapter Five

At lunchtime we sit on benches at the long oak table in the dining room. We have couscous and hummus and Mimi's nice rye bread, and then there's yoghurt with honey. Violeta joins us, and I see that she's very pregnant. She seems to be a sort of cleaning lady or au pair or something. Or perhaps she's one of Mimi's vulnerable women. My hair is down, loose and damp, and there are the two gross hippy men – Cliff and the younger, slightly less decrepit Arrow – chewing with stained teeth and studying me. It's awkward eating in front of strangers, and I hope Mimi won't watch me again. I don't want them asking me questions, so it's good to have a bit of quiet banter from Daisy, who has brought her colouring book to the table. She's the entertainment, like a radio we are all listening to. When she pauses to fill her mouth, I fill the silence.

'So, Mimi, that's an interesting name. Is it short for something?'

'Miranda. But when we started going out, Marcus called me "Mimi", and so it sort of stuck.'

Henna scowls at her plate, perhaps not wanting to think of her parents being lovey-dovey. And for some reason, the thought of Marcus calling Mimi by a pet name for the first time conjures images that make me slightly sick.

'And Marcus? That's quite . . . classic.'

'Posh,' says Henna, unexpectedly. 'He's from posh stock.'

'Oh.' I don't know what to say next.

'So, Caitlin . . . that's an Irish name, isn't it?' asks Marcus, ignoring her.

'Cake-lin,' says Daisy to herself.

'Yes, you spell it like this . . .' I write with relief in Daisy's drawing book with purple crayon, and she copies it.

'Caitlin. Caitlin,' says Daisy, colouring around it in pink.

'Yes, my grandfather's Irish. On my mum's side. Grandmother's Cornish, though.'

'And your dad's side?'

Shit. I try to take deep breaths. 'Just Cornish, I think.'

Mimi reaches out to stroke my hair, which is rapidly turning into coils. 'A true Celt, then. How strange. Your hair is so . . . exotic.'

I could swear this is the preamble to the where-are-you-*really*-from question, but I can't believe they would care less. Still, I don't tell them that Dad was adopted, and that he has no idea who his dad was.

'I think it comes from my Cornish grandfather.' A bit of a betrayal. But betrayals seem to be all the rage right now, so I don't care.

'Ooh, do you have a Cornish surname?'

'I do. Polglaze.'

'Polglaze? Like that author . . . um . . . hang on . . . Trevik Polglaze!'

Here we go.

'You're not related?'

I try not to sigh.

'Are you? You are!' Marcus puts his head on one side. 'I loved that – what was it? *The Women* . . .? *The Wooden Women* . . .?'

'You don't read books,' mutters Henna, under her breath. 'You just saw it on the shelf because Mum bought it.'

Marcus ignores her.

'*Women of Wood*,' I supply.

24

'Yes! Brilliant book. Gosh, who'd've thought! So he's your father?'

I bite the inside of my cheek and nod. I'm almost sweating with repressed anger, and hope it doesn't show.

'Wow,' he says. 'It must be wonderful to make a living writing novels.'

'Yes. I imagine it would be.' A globule of spite breaks through the surface of my skin. 'If he did . . .'

'You mean he doesn't?' Marcus looks genuinely confused. 'I swear it says it's a bestseller on the cover.'

Daisy gets up quietly and stands behind me. It's as if she can tell I don't want to talk about him, and she begins to plait my spiralling hair. Nobody tells her to sit down. It's all very laid-back.

'Well, he won a few prizes, yes. The money doesn't go very far, though, if you think of a living. Might've lasted two years, I suppose. Then there were the translation rights and royalties for a bit, and he was riding high. Everyone wanted him at their literary festivals. Then he had to write another one. And he couldn't.'

'Oh. I assumed he'd done a few.'

'A couple more, but they were shit.' Henna smirks at her home-made lime yoghurt. I must stop this. We have an unwritten rule in our household that we never run Dad down to outsiders. Not just because his image is important, but because we're proud of him. We love him. It's just that now, after what he's done, it's hard to love him. I don't know what to think any more. This is no one else's business, though. 'I'm sorry.'

'No. Don't worry. It's fascinating. So . . . how does he make a living?'

Good question. He goes into his 'study' every day with a bottle of whisky and looks at his laptop. Sometimes he taps out a little story. Sometimes he gets invited on writing retreats as a tutor, and then he gets the most promising students to come on his special tutorials at home. My father has an uncanny knack of knowing when a student has an untapped genius for writing fiction. He can tell by looking at their tits. In the case of men, I'm guessing it's by the extent of their adulation. They stay in our barely converted barn and Mum has to cook for them after a long day at work. He charges them lots of money and pretends he can find them an agent.

'He does a lot of tutoring. He's very good at it.'

Daisy is working a chunky plait over the top of my head.

'So,' says Mimi. 'You're not too happy at home, I take it?'

'That's an understatement. I do miss my little sister, Dani. Danielle.'

'How old is Danielle?' asks Daisy, perhaps not wanting a rival.

'Fourteen.'

Danielle, five years younger than me and can do no wrong. She gets A grades for practically everything at school, and plays the violin and cello and piano like a concert musician. And only fourteen. And beautiful. That's the first thing people say about her. Even before they drop down and worship at her feet for her musical prowess, or her very grown-up conversation, in which she uses words like 'didacticism' and 'tautological'. I've looked them up. I've forgotten what they mean now. But that's the thing: she remembers. *Fourteen*. Fucksake.

'Well,' says Mimi, 'if you *would* like to stay away a bit longer, we'd love to have you here.'

'Yay!' says Daisy. Henna rolls her eyes.

Henna reminds me of myself at that age. Not that we appear anything alike. She is pale and fragile-looking, whereas I was always somehow too obvious – solid and helplessly clumsy, taking up more space than I wanted to. But Henna, with her mousey hair and freckles, is a creature built for camouflage. Still, there is something in her that I recognise, some fear or anger, something I can almost catch the tail of, but it keeps darting out of my grasp.

'We've actually had a little chat about it,' says Marcus. 'Now the schools are in lockdown, they're talking about online lessons at home and . . . well, we don't want that, and the children don't have iPhones, so . . . we'd really appreciate a home tutor. It might be just the ticket for you, before you head off to uni.'

'Oh, I couldn't . . . I'd be . . .'

Marcus raises his hand as if he's telling a dog to sit. 'It wouldn't be much. But if you're not happy going home . . . just to tide things over. They're talking about a few weeks, or a couple of months at most. Really, you know . . . a bit of reading and writing with Daisy, some basic maths with Henna . . .'

'*Very* basic,' says Henna. 'I hate maths.'

'Well, you know, reading, writing, keeping them ticking over. You wouldn't have to do any housework. Violeta helps out when she can, although she's leaving in a month or so. But, you know, if you don't want to go straight back, we'd love to have you. You seem to like children.'

'Oh, I do.' This isn't strictly true. I don't know any children – not really. The ones screaming on public transport get right on my tits. If the kid on the ferry had kicked the back of my seat any more, I would've taken him out. 'I love children. I don't know about tutoring, though.'

'Just a week or two? Think about it.'

'Think about it and say *yes*,' says Daisy, already convinced that this is the right thing to happen next.

They think I'm accomplished because Dad's an author. They think I've read loads of books – and it's true, it is part of our family tradition to read a lot. Everyone reads a lot except me. I just can't get into it, but I'm still expected to enjoy it, because everyone else in our happy family does. But it might be good for them not to know where I am. I wish I didn't love Dad so much; I wish he wasn't the one person I've always felt closest to. He's always been my rock, the man I've always known would take a bullet for me. I can't bear the thought of him lying, but hearing his excuses would be even worse.

'Provided you can spell and count, you'll be fine,' says Mimi, touching my arm. 'You're not dyslexic or anything, are you?'

'Oh, no.' This isn't strictly true either. I am dyslexic. I got extra time in my exams for it and everything. I try not to be offended. 'Actually, though, dyslexics are teeple poo.'

Mimi looks bewildered, but Marcus laughs, Daisy folds up with giggles because I've said 'poo', and I see Henna smile at her plate.

Chapter Six

I go outside to see if my messages have sent. They haven't, and the battery is low. I should've asked for the Wi-Fi code. I look up the valley. It's stunning. Luke'll be wondering why he can't contact me. That's some consolation.

Luke. I lean my head against a wall. *Oh God*.

Dad had selected him and Lotti from one of the residential writing courses he'd been tutoring on, somewhere in Devon, and he offered them places on his own 'bespoke' course at our place. We don't exactly have a converted barn. It was once a barn, but it hasn't really been converted. It's waterproof and heated. It has three rooms – two study-bedrooms and a library with a couple of old sofas – and there's even an outside loo, but the bathing and eating facilities are all at our house. Which means Mum has to cook for them, and we have to eat with them and hear their literary chunterings (more tautological didactic subtext and so forth), and Mum has to wash their towels and buy crates of wine to service the creative brain cells. Fortunately, they always slink back to the barn for more chuntering and a few more bottles as soon as the meals are over, but it's quite a pain, having to have our privacy intruded on like that a few times a year. Especially when you're trying to revise, as I was when Luke and Lotti came in May.

In fairness, Luke and Lotti weren't like the other students. For one thing, Luke seemed to want to talk to me. He seemed to enjoy my company and laugh at my jokes and follow me out to the garden with a couple of glasses for me to share a drink with him. And I just wanted to spend all my time with him because I thought no one would ever love me again like he did. He was the first boy ever to make me feel interesting. The first one ever to kiss me. My first proper sex. My only love-making. My one and only. Luke.

For another thing, Lotti was far more friendly than any of the other females had been on these little mini-courses. I force myself briefly to remember how she wasn't at all up herself, and she used to joke with me and say she liked my clothes and my taste in music. She was like the cool friend I'd never had. I liked that she wasn't like this to my older sister, Erin – or to Dani. Just me. Luke only lived in Truro and Lotti in Exeter, so we stayed friends. Luke and I spent loads of time together that May. He was practically living at our house, and we did it everywhere – my bed, the woods, the back of his car, the sea, in the bushes at the Lost Gardens of Heligan. (Magic.) Don't suppose Erin or Dani will ever do that. But I'm not going to think about that.

I must phone home.

I walk around the house to see if I can get a better signal, and bump into one of the old hippies: Cliff.

'Oh, hi. Where's the best place for a signal?'

He seems to scowl at me. 'Back up by the woods or on the ridge.'

'Thanks.'

He takes a deep breath. I turn to go but he grabs my arm. 'This isn't for you.' I look at his brown hand on my arm and he removes it. 'You need to go! *Leave!*'

I can't read him. He could be concerned, or he could be hostile.

'How do you mean?'

He points a finger at me. 'Get out of here while you still can. Just *get out!*'

The words cut so sharply it's as if he's chiselled them into my skin.

Chapter Seven

I'm about to climb the path up to the woods, when a voice calls after me. It's Marcus, offering to show me around. I realise I'm shivering a bit from Cliff's words, and I rub my bare arms to hide it.

'You chilly?' he asks. 'I'll wait while you put something else on. There's no hurry.'

'I don't have anything with sleeves. Packed in a bit of a hurry.'

'Wait here.'

He disappears into the house, and I wander slowly back towards the front door. I see him through the hallway, taking the stairs two at a time.

He's panting a little when he comes back, holding out a jumper. 'There you go. Right. This way first, I think.'

The pullover is massive and the sleeves fall way past my fingertips. It's made of something very soft – cashmere, maybe – and gives off an interesting mix of scents I can't quite name. The act of giving me something to wear that is so obviously his seems a tender one; I am wrapped in him. I follow him round the side of the house, looking at everything he points out, swinging the long arms in a sensual free fall. Not sure what I'm falling into, but I'm gloriously, recklessly passive, and don't care.

I follow him into the first polytunnel, and he explains, like Daisy, that they grow vegetables here. He shows me each type of vegetable, as if I'm interested. Now, with this enormous tent of a jumper, I'm sweltering. I just want to get out.

'We're mostly sowing at the moment, of course. But you can see the salad rocket coming along, and some of the spinach is ready, and spring onions.' I continue to sweat. God, I hate polytunnels. It's like the Eden Project back in Cornwall, which also made me gag to escape the one time I went. And like with those bio-domes, I want to find this interesting but I really don't. '*And*,' he says, pushing his hand into some greenery, 'look at this.'

He holds out his fist, but doesn't open it.

'What?'

'Open your mouth.'

'Why?'

'Do as you're told,' he says, grinning.

So I do. He examines my parted lips carefully as he slowly places a tiny strawberry inside them. *Fucksake.* What a cliché. As he does so, he looks very directly into my eyes, and holds the look. Green eyes, he has.

'It's hot in here,' I say, the soft jumper having turned into a hoard of damp kitchen scourers hell-bent on squeezing me to death; I start to take it off, but he places an arm on my sleeve to stop me.

'Okay, no more polytunnels. Let's show you the terrain.'

As soon as we're outside, I ask casually what's in the other polytunnels. He turns to look at me, trying to work out if I know, and whether or not I'll disapprove.

'Something more lucrative than spring onions, I'm guessing?' A smile is playing around my lips, and he smiles, too.

'Come on,' he says, grabbing my hand, and taking me up the sloping field in front of the house. The hand-holding startles me. His authority seems to grow with each step he takes up the grassy slope. With each step away from her? Or closer to the barn? It's hard to say.

When we reach the top, he stops and points out to me the things we haven't visited down below: the rainbow-painted cabin (Mimi's office); a stone building adjacent to the house (an old 'apple store' – Cliff's accommodation); some more outbuildings near the polytunnels (accommodation for whoever comes to help with the harvesting). There is also the barn, just to our right, but hidden by trees.

'It's beautiful,' I say.

He takes in a deep breath, and we stand, gazing at the view. With its blinds half down and front door ajar, the house looks like a drowsy old lady, lids drooping, in her armchair.

'So . . .' He takes in another deep breath. 'You packed in a bit of a hurry?'

I say nothing.

'Something you want to talk about?'

Why would I? 'Nope.'

'Caitlin, you're with friends. You'll see. But take your time. There's no rush.'

The confidence of this man is gobsmacking. But perhaps if you're gorgeous, the self-assurance is easy. Then I remember that he promised a bedtime story to Daisy. He's a good daddy, at least.

'What's up there?' I ask, pointing to the only scrap of footpath I can see, up to the left from where we're standing.

'Oh, that leads to the woods and Joe's house. He's a friend of ours. A policeman, actually.'

'Surfer Joe. Handy.'

I don't look at him when I say this, but I can see him glance at me in my peripheral vision. He lets out a sound of contentment. We stand for a moment, taking in the green valley stretched beneath us.

'Is this all yours, then?'

'Yeah. It was my dad's old hippy colony, back in the day.'

'Are your parents . . .?'

'Dad died twelve years ago. And my mum . . .' he sighs heavily, '. . . at some point.'

'Oh.' I must look alarmed, because he breathes out a laugh.

'She left when I was four.'

33

'Left?'

'Went off with another man. A carpenter who lived here.' He's trying to make light of it with an upbeat voice, but when I look sideways at him his jaw is a little clenched. 'Yeah. Cliff's mum brought me up. She said my mother loved me, that she'd come back for me. She was certain she'd come back for me.'

'Did she?'

'Nope.' It seems final, but then, in the quiet space I leave he says: 'I thought of going looking for her when I was about fourteen, but Dad explained that she'd died. Cancer or something. I'll never know.'

'Oh, God.' I'm not very good with death and stuff. 'I'm sorry.'

'Don't be. It's all in the past. I barely remember her.' He almost chuckles. 'I clearly didn't matter that much to her. *Anyway*, this is Amberside, and you're very welcome.'

'Thank you. It's beautiful.' Poor man. We listen to the birds singing in the trees around the barn, letting the awkwardness melt away. 'Where's the nearest town?'

'We're in the middle of nowhere. There's not much here.'

'You're kidding. This is Gloucestershire. It must be riddled with towns.'

'I forget – you're a Cornish girl. Quoits and tin mines and loud seagulls. Well, there's a couple of large towns.' He points vaguely in different directions. 'But we're not that close to either of them.'

'Small towns?'

'There's Nettleford, a good few miles up that way. But there's not much there.'

'What do you do, then?'

'There's a post office in a village nearby – Ribley – and a Co-op. We mostly go further afield to big supermarkets when we need to, though. Waitrose.'

'Nice. I thought it unlikely you grew your own avocados.'

He places a hand on my shoulder, close to the base of my neck. As I've put my hair up, his palm touches my skin. This is an extraordinary thing to do. I haven't given him any permission for this intimacy. But it's not threatening, just mildly confusing. Perhaps, if I were a bit older or more confident, I would say something. Perhaps I would gently – or indignantly – take his hand away. But I'm nineteen years old and not very sure about anything any more.

I like the feel of his hand, though. I think of all those dark remembered nights with Luke in Florence, hot and clammy in a bed shared with his back, or else with his snorty breath too close to my face for sleep. Sex with Luke was sweaty, functional and abrasive. At best it was character-building.

Did he ever feel anything for me?

I like hands. In Florence with Luke, we lived on the second floor above another flat which was above a hardware store. The owner lived in this flat with his wife, and every week you could hear the sounds of their love-making coming up through the ceiling. He would call her, *Oh, tesoro! Oh, stellina mia!* And she would whimper with such pleasure that it was hard not to stay mouse-still and listen. The first few times we heard it, Luke and I made jokey comments about it, but it wasn't too long before I was listening to the sounds alone, lying beside his turned back. *Oh . . . stellina mia!* There was so much gentleness in his murmurings, so much love, and he never once stopped until she cried out, long and low: *Oh . . . ti amo, ti amo, Berto!* And then, after a few moments, there would be the rhythmic creaking of the bed board until he subsided in more outpourings of love.

I used to wander down into the hardware store just to see him. Umberto Tiraboschi was a solid man of about fifty, with a short neck and a bald head. I would invent things I needed so that he would walk me along the shelves, showing me options. A floor cleaner, perhaps, or a dustpan and brush. I would examine the folds of his neck as he lifted the items off the shelves. Then I used to like to watch his hands as he gathered the items on his counter: large hands with dark hair and pink, square nails. I was in awe of those hands – how they had brought so much pleasure to Mrs Tiraboschi, how they had made her cry out *Oh . . . Ti amo!* How they had persisted, tenderly. For all she was plump and shapeless, I longed to be Mrs Tiraboschi, just to know how it would be to experience so much love.

So I stand there, allowing the warmth of Marcus's skin to melt into mine, sensitive to the slightest change in pressure, thinking of Luke's lack of affection – thinking of men in general – and willing his hand to go further so that I can see what I would think about that. A bleep tells me my messages have sent, despite a low battery.

The half-closed eyelids of the house make it suddenly sensuous, its mouth ajar not with sleep but with desire.

Daisy is waiting for me when we get back. She wants to play. She has a look of such joy when she spots me, that my heart is suddenly full.

'Do you know, um, Caitlin, that children aren't going to school tomorrow or . . .' she spins round in a circle, arms outstretched, 'maybe . . . *ever*!'

'I think you will, but not for a few weeks, anyway.'

'We're not ever going back. Daddy said. We stopped at Christmas.'

I think she's got this wrong. 'Are you sure?'

She looks at me, confused. 'I don't have to get up and walk up to the car every morning any more, but I don't get to play with friends or even *see* any because they live far away and . . . and . . . So I do get sad.'

We're standing near the compost heap, and I idly take some potato peelings from it and place them carefully on the ground.

'What are you doing?'

'We'll have to make you some friends, then.'

I pick two yellow celandines and place eyes underneath the potato-peeling curls, and she quickly cottons on. Before long, he is a curly-haired boy with cabbage-leaf hands and apple-core knees. We make the knees bend and he runs, arms outstretched, on the patch of grass in front of the house. Daisy decides that he needs a sister, so we set about gathering bits and pieces: sticks and cardboard, beech-nut shells, broken flowerpots, primroses, half a rotting deckchair, and so on. Henna comes up and stands watching us, biting the side of her nail, as if deciding whether she hates me or not, and that it's too important a decision to get wrong.

By teatime we have five children, wild and dancing. Henna has made a dog that leaps after them, although she hasn't spoken a word to either of us. I like the dog: it's chasing a yellow ball made of half an empty grapefruit, and it radiates energy. I tell her this, but she frowns and says it's nearly time to eat. It's like success, though, and it goes to my head. I can do this. I am Maria for the von Trapp family.

The circumstances that brought me there made me reckless; those children who needed me, and the ethereal Mimi and Marcus, had a weirdly compelling effect on me. Only later would I see that this was a perfect storm.

Chapter Eight

BBC Radio 4 is playing as we all sit down to eat. It seems that Boris Johnson is going to announce a 'lockdown' tomorrow evening, after which no one will be allowed to travel, and we must all stay in our homes except for essential journeys to the shops or to help the vulnerable. We mustn't have contact with anyone who's not in our household, and if we pass anyone, we must maintain a two-metre distance.

Mimi turns the radio off and brings in a giant dish of arborio risotto. For the first time since arriving at the house, I feel a sense of panic. What if this goes on for ages, like in Italy, and I'm stuck here? I don't like the idea of having no choices.

'I think perhaps I should head back tomorrow,' I say.

'Why? It's only for three weeks.' Mimi takes my plate and serves me.

'But they said it would be reviewed after three weeks, so it might be longer. Look at Italy.'

'We won't get it as bad as Italy.'

'What makes you say that? It has brilliant hospitals. And they were warning us – they warned us to go while we still could, because the whole of Europe's going to be in lockdown soon.'

'That's just scaremongering.' Marcus hands round some salad. 'Three weeks tops. Why not stay here for three weeks?'

I catch Cliff giving Mimi a look. Maybe he just wants some risotto. But he glances at Marcus, too. He creeps me out.

'Yes – please do, Caitlin.' Mimi says this so warmly that I don't doubt her sincerity.

'*Stay!*' commands Daisy, with unusual volume. 'We all want you to stay! Mummy, she's staying!'

'My mum will worry. I really think I'd better get back.'

'Phone her. Tell her you're here and being looked after.'

As soon as we've finished the risotto, I take my phone out of my jeans and try to text Mum.

'There's no signal,' I say.

'It's a bit dodgy here,' says Marcus. 'You can get a signal up the field, where we were earlier.'

'What about your Wi-Fi? Could I get your password?'

Mimi touches my hand. 'We don't have the internet here.'

'What?'

'We don't have any need for it.'

And then, I see it, unmistakably this time: a look passes between Mimi and Cliff. They hold it so firmly it's like a tightrope between them. I hate that. Exchanged looks. They are always a sign of being shut out. It's what started everything off in Italy. A look between Lotti and Luke. Well, no, it was a phone call from my older sister, Erin, that set the wheels in motion. But there were a lot of looks after that, brief and dangerous and all excluding me.

I glance at the text again. The battery is very low. 'Can I borrow a charger? I thought I'd packed mine in my socks, but it isn't there.'

When it's charged, I'll walk back up the field and telephone Mum. She'll worry herself sick otherwise. Whatever I may think about things now, she does love me, and I don't want her to have any more on her plate.

Marcus looks at Mimi. 'We don't have a phone charger, I'm afraid. No phones either.'

'No *phones*?'

The silence at the table seems uncertain, as if the very air is waiting for me to digest this news, worried about my reaction to it. I understood that the kids didn't have phones, but what the . . .?

'But what do you do in an emergency? How do you contact anyone?'

'There's a payphone in the hallway. It takes coins, but we have a bag of pound coins on the shelf. It works. You can ring from there.'

I rub my forehead. I can't believe this. It's as if I've just been told that babies are brought by storks after all. It's very quaint, but utterly mad. How can anyone live like this? This is an absolute deal-breaker. I can't live without a phone.

'There aren't,' says Henna, looking up warily. 'Any pound coins. I took them to school at Christmas.'

'All of them?'

'There were only two! I used one for non-uniform day and one for Miss Wilkinson's present.'

'Oh, well,' says Mimi, calm as you like, 'there are definitely some ten pence pieces. It takes those, too.' She reaches her hand across mine again and says gently, 'Don't worry, Caitlin. You'll get to speak to your mum.'

Mimi's voice seems to come into its own when tenderness is called for. A bit like Bambi's mother.

'God, it's so *embarrassing*,' Henna mutters into her gluten-free blueberry clafoutis. 'It's like living in the Middle Ages.' She addresses Marcus, her voice rising: 'Can't you see how *weird* we are? No one else lives like this. *No one!*'

She gets up and walks out, clearly afraid of a backlash. Good move, Henna. That's what I would've done, too – cleared out before the backlash. At least she's a normal teenager.

Mimi calls out to her, but Marcus pats the air in front of him, signalling to her to leave it. 'I apologise for my daughter,' he says to me, and I remember him saying that in the car when I first met them. If I *ever* have children – which I probably won't – I will never apologise for them.

*

I know what will happen if I go home now. Luke will turn up a few days later. He won't want to be stuck in France indefinitely with no work. He'll be heading back to his family, and he'll try to stay with ours. He'll want to 'explain' things, put his side of the story. I'd like him to wonder where the hell I am. At least with no phone I can imagine Luke ringing and texting me endlessly, begging me to contact him. I can picture his rising anxiety as the rectangle of light shows him all his unread texts. That's the sort of mean maggot I am.

I should warn Erin. And I can't tell Mum about him. Not yet, anyway. And how can I begin to have a private conversation with Mum, standing in this hallway? As soon as I can get to a shop I'm buying a charger, even if I have to go up to the top of the valley each time I make a call or send a text. That's if I stay. To be honest, I'm torn.

I help clear away the food and wash up. I assume there's no dishwasher, since they seem to have a back-to-basics lifestyle, but there is one – and a massive washing machine and tumble dryer in the utility area off the kitchen. Daisy is told to go up for a bath, but she wants me to read to her after. I see it as a trial run for me. If I stay, this is the sort of thing I'll be doing, so I'd better see what it's like.

There are plenty of picture books to choose from, and I read one about a naughty cat. She strokes my arms as I read, and plays with my hair. I know she isn't going to let me go. I used to read to my younger sister, Dani, and she would never let me go. I used to have to extricate myself in stages.

'Snuggle down, now,' I say, kissing her forehead.

'Will you sing me a song?'

'Time to sleep, now.'

'Just *one* song. One little *tiny* song?'

I lie down with her and sing 'Ned of the Hill', which my gran used to sing to me. Two plastic baby lions hidden inside the pillowcase stick into my head. I examine them. Daisy reaches for them, urgently.

'I'm keeping them safe,' she whispers.

I put them back in their refuge and wait until Daisy's breathing is slow.

When I get up to leave, she murmurs sleepily to me with her eyes closed, 'You won't go away, will you, Caitlin? Stay and be with us . . .' Then she opens her eyes and reaches for my hand. 'Please.'

And there is that sense of elation again, the dangerous charm of being needed.

Chapter Nine

Downstairs the grown-ups are lounging about on the long, sagging sofas in the living room, and Cliff is rolling a spliff. When I join them, we form a sort of circle. Surfer Joe has arrived with his girlfriend, saying it's the last time they'll be allowed to meet like this, all together. He's far younger than I expected – midtwenties perhaps – and his girlfriend is even younger, and very pretty and smiley. Violeta gets to her feet and embraces everyone goodnight – exhausted, poor thing. I notice that Henna holds on to her tightly when it's her turn for a hug, and gives Violeta a warm smile. So it's just Cliff and Arrow – the two hairy hippies – Mimi, Marcus, Joe and his girl, Henna and me. Marcus sits cross-legged on the floor now, tuning his guitar, and asks Cliff for a song. He declines modestly for a while, then sings 'Whisky in the Jar', which gets us all joining in, and sparks the pouring of whisky for everyone. The spliff is passed around, and I pass it straight on.

'You don't approve of weed?' asks Marcus, after we've applauded the song.

Arrow makes a jokey sound of astonishment, as if I'm in real trouble now. Actually, I'm tired of pretending to fit in all the time. I'm done with that. Six months of trailing around after Luke and Lotti with her boyfriend, badgered into doing things I wasn't keen on, shamed into trying new things I was reluctant about so I could appear to be 'fun'. Now I'm going to be myself.

'Just makes me feel sick. And I don't like smoking.'

'You don't mind if we do?' asks Cliff. There's no hostility coming from him at all now. I think I just read him wrong.

I say of course not, as he rolls another joint. The veins on his hands stand up like mountain ranges and the skin on his forearms is like roast chicken. His cheeks look as though a child has been let loose on them with a red biro. I imagine he was one of the first hippies: ravaged by sun, drugs and alcohol. He was never going to age well.

Marcus starts to play some chords and then sings 'Streets of London'. *Jesus*. He really isn't very good, but I've always loved this song and my throat aches as we all join in the chorus. All the lost and the lonely. It's an excuse to look at him, at his brown arms, his bare neck, his long feet, his strong, sinewy hands. He closes his eyes when he sings. He has all of the sentiment, if not all of the talent, and I look at the whisky I've been given and take a sip to hide any lip-wobble I might betray.

Surfer Joe volunteers his girlfriend to sing, but she becomes coy.

'Do you get much surfing in so far from the sea?' I ask.

Stella, his girlfriend, smiles and he giggles.

'Well, Caitlin, I do like to sail the silver surf when I can.' His hair is fair and scruffy and his eyes are a bit red. I realise he's been on the dope since before they arrived. He giggles again and Stella nudges him. I'm so stupid. The dumb idiot, just like I was in Italy with Luke's cool friends.

Stella has taken such care over her appearance: long hair all carefully waved, make-up faultless, nails subtly manicured. I imagine her spending hours in her room, choosing the under-stated bohemian outfit she's wearing, deciding on the nail varnish. This giggling dopehead has no idea how long she has prepared herself for coming out with him.

'Well, I'd like to hear you sing, Stella,' I say.

She smiles, dusts some imaginary fluff off her skirt, and gives a sweet rendition of 'Your Song': first verse and chorus, then tapers out. We all cheer, but Joe seems to have dozed off.

Arrow says he has to sort out the new developments with Suze, so he's heading off, and he can give Joe and Stella a hand up the path if they like, given that Joe is unlikely to be able to walk home soon. Mimi ushers them out across the hallway, and she and Arrow speak in low voices for a few minutes by the front door before she returns. When she does, she sits on the sofa behind Marcus, fondling his neck and hair when he sings again. It's as if they're posing for a portrait. There's something incongruous about Mimi's actions, and an indifference behind her eyes, but I know she'll look up in a moment and see me watching her, because she already knows that I am. I have to look away. As I do, I see Henna leaning against the door frame. I smile slightly, and she very nearly smiles back, but doesn't quite make it. I know how it is with Henna, I think. She hates herself so much that she needs everyone else to hate her, too, to justify her own self-disgust. Then at least she is right about something.

When Marcus finishes his next performance, Henna mutters that she's going up. She embraces everyone in turn, and when she gets back to the door to leave, she says, 'You should get Caitlin to sing. She was singing to Daisy earlier. She's good.' And then, just before she disappears up the stairs, she adds, 'Better than you anyway, Marcus.'

Now they are going to insist I sing and I'll be a disappointment because I'm crap. I really am.

They're pushing me now. Come on, come on, please. *Please. It's only in front of the three of us.*

I try a few strings on Marcus's guitar, draw in a deep breath and sing a song about a young girl being forced to marry the laird she doesn't love, but then escaping with her true love, Jock. I can barely get out the last line: *She's o'er the border and away with Jock of Hazeldean.* Perhaps it's the idea of friction with one's

45

parents, or the thought of love with obstacles, I don't know, but I am an emotional wreck. I think I'm doing a good job of hiding it, though.

Mimi tries to pour me some more whisky, but I cover my glass. I am not going down that path. I refuse to sing another song, saying I don't know any more. This isn't true. I have spent my teens collecting folk songs in a pretty nerdy way, inspired by Gran. All the women on Mum's side of the family sang songs, and I could spend weeks singing through them all, but I don't want to hear my own needy little voice right now.

We sit and listen to Marcus some more, and then Mimi has to go to her 'office' for something before bedtime. Probably more good work for the vulnerable. She kisses us all, and when she's gone, he sings 'The First Time Ever I Saw Your Face'. Between looking at the frets of his guitar, he raises his eyes and fixes them on mine. He is ridiculously good-looking. He knows he's getting to me. I'm such a pushover. The ego of the man, though. *Jesus.*

When he's finished, he gets up to use the loo. I'm left alone with Cliff and his greasy white ponytail.

'Nice singing of yours, there,' he says. I shake my head, but thank him anyway. He looks at me urgently then, a grim, frightening look. 'You're still here,' he says, pointing at me. 'You've got to go. You have to go.'

Surely he's joking. Nope, he definitely isn't. He might as well have slapped me. His look stings.

'Why?'

'This place isn't for you. Do you hear me? It's not for you. Get out of here!'

Marcus comes back and Cliff embraces him, saying he must be off, too. Then Cliff puts his arms around me briefly, stinking of stale smoke. Perhaps he thinks I'm not cool enough about the dope farm. 'Night night, folks. Sleep in peace,' and he's gone.

As soon as I'm alone with Marcus, I realise that I need to sort my thoughts out before I ring home. Cliff's remarks have made me all jittery, and I'm flushed and confused about Marcus as well. He's on the other side of the room, opening a drawer. I watch his hands and imagine them on my skin again.

Chapter Ten

'Look, I can only find three ten-pence pieces, I'm afraid.'

I thank him, and explain that I'll wait until everyone's in bed to make the call, if that's okay. I've never used a payphone before, but it looks straightforward.

'Of course. Give yourself some privacy.'

He disappears upstairs. Alone in the hallway, I lift the receiver and try to put the coins in the slot. It won't let me. I dial the number and hear it ringing. Good. There is my sister Erin's voice: 'Hello?' and a terrible beeping sound. I push the coin in. 'Hello?' she says again. 'Aunty Jean?'

'Erin, it's me.' Since Gran's gone, Great-Aunty Jean is the only person who rings our landline any more, but she doesn't do it from a payphone. 'Look, I'm back in England safely. Will you tell Mum I'm staying with some friends in Gloucestershire for a bit—'

'Gloucestershire? Aren't you coming back for this lockdown? Hang on, I'll get her . . . *Mum?*'

'No, wait! Erin—'

She's gone off to find her. I can hear the old familiar sounds of my family home, picture the scene as Erin goes halfway up the stairs, calling, or else she has gone into the kitchen where Mum is making a list for tomorrow, feeding the cat, wiping the surfaces.

Erin and I always used to dread being like our mother. As soon as we were out of childhood, we started to become repelled by the way she carelessly exposed her scaly white shins or her wobbly upper arms. We were appalled by her domesticity, at the way she talked to herself, addressing the kitchen taps or the oven. And although we had luxuriated in their proximity as small children – the soapy scent of them – we were mildly disgusted by the sight of her reddened cheeks without make-up or the creviced skin of her upper chest. We did get to be proud of her, what with her becoming a school counsellor and everything, but there was something about her flopping along the school corridor in her flat shoes, with her greying hair in a long plait, looking like someone who knitted lamppost covers, that made us slightly cringe at the thought of classmates spilling their troubles to her and seeing her at close range.

The beeping starts again. I fumble with the coins and drop one. I push the other one in, just as my mother arrives on the other end.

'Caitlin? Caitlin, where are you?'

'England. I'm just ringing to say I'm back safely and I'm fine.'

'Thank goodness for that! I'll put the heating on in your bedroom.'

'No, I'm in Gloucestershire, and I'm going to stay here for a bit to do some tutoring – some home-schooling – for the children of friends.'

'What friends? How did you meet them?'

I hesitate. I can't tell her I hitched a lift with them. 'On the journey back from France.'

'Is Luke with you?'

'No. He's still there. And Lotti. I think they're coming back soon, though. We split up.'

I wait for her exasperation. I gave up university for him, as she kept reminding me. Sometimes when I was in Italy, I thought that if I died of coronavirus, she would just be cross – cross that I'd disappointed her yet again. Dying like that, without a degree or anything.

'Oh, Caitlin. I'm sorry.'

49

Beep, beep, beep . . .

I crouch down and crawl over to the skirting board where the last ten-pence coin lies. I shove it in the slot just in time.

'Mum? You still there?'

'Yes, sweetheart. Listen, you must come back. *Come back.* Please, Caitlin, listen to me. There's going to be a lockdown, and although they're saying probably three weeks, that's only to begin with. It's likely to be that again – and more. It could be months. People are saying three months – or even six. Just think. And you will be *stuck* there. It's not as if you'll be able to change your mind if you don't like it.'

'I know, Mum, but I'll be fine. They're lovely. Two little girls.'

'Who are these people? What's the address?'

'I'm not sure. Oh, wait . . . Amberside House, near Ribley.'

'Wherely?'

'*Rib-ley.*'

'Right. Ribley. Are they paying you?'

'Yes – we haven't negotiated yet. I expect so.'

'You expect so? Who are these people?'

Beep beep beep . . .

'Okay, bye, Mum.'

'Caitlin, come home while you can. You know nothing about these—'

The line is dead. I put down the receiver, trembling.

I'm still trembling when I get into bed and turn the light off. I lie there, remembering Cliff's words: *Get out of here.* If it wasn't offensive, then it was a warning. I probably should go. *Just come home.* And I should go tomorrow, before it's too late. *You'll be stuck.* I don't know anything about these people. *Who are these people?* But little Daisy, stroking my arm . . . How could I leave her? *You won't leave us, will you?* And Marcus looking at me, singing, '*The first time ever I lay with you . . .*' The whisky is making my mind muddled. I'm so tired.

There is a gentle, single knock on the bedroom door, and it opens. Marcus comes in and sits on my bed. I know it's him. I have to fight off the thought that I want it to be him. But I don't move.

'Caitlin?' he whispers. 'Caitlin, we didn't say goodnight.'

He leans across me and kisses me on the cheek. Then he gently strokes the skin he has kissed. This is ridiculous. *Knobhead*. But, for reasons I can't understand or want to, I am on fire. I can smell the faintly woody scent of him, the same one I get notes of in his jumper.

'Goodnight,' he says.

I say nothing. I'm concentrating on breathing, like a drunk trying to walk in a straight line. When he reaches the door, he looks back, then closes it softly behind him.

Okay. Right. That's that then. I either go tomorrow, or I stay and tell him what's what.

Good. That's decided.

I reach out for his jumper in the bedside drawer and take it into bed with me. I drift off to sleep with it pressed to my nose.

Chapter Eleven

I wake up with a familiar dampness between my legs. My period has started. I reach for my rucksack but can only find one squashed tampon. Not even a solitary, dog-eared sanitary pad. Fucksake. I make a mental note to ask Mimi if she has any spare, although I'm a little anxious about asking her, for some reason. Perhaps she disapproves of them. Probably hand-stitches them out of cut-up pieces of organic cotton T-shirts. Reusable pads. *Pre-loved. Yuk.*

I automatically pick up my phone to check the time, but it's dead. Then I remember the little gift Gran gave me before she got really ill. She had slipped it to me just before I left on a school trip to the Lake District. It was an old wind-up travel alarm of hers, and I didn't have the heart to tell her nobody used travel alarms any more, least of all wind-up ones. I took it with me when I left for Italy. 'A girl always needs to know what time of day it is, and I notice you don't wear watches any more.' It folds into its own red case, and I open it now and wind it up. A twenty-pound note falls out. I haven't opened it since she gave it to me, so I've never thanked her. It would've been for my school trip.

The clock gives a satisfying clicking sound as I turn the key until it can go no further. Then it produces a quaint tick-tock. I place it on the little chest of drawers next to my bed and smile at it. It even has luminous hands. I think of Gran's hands, and of her doing semaphore with her arms for me here inside this little clock. It doesn't need Wi-Fi or anything. Just like Gran. I'll have to find out the right time in order to set it, though.

I take out the handkerchief she gave me, too, embroidered with roses and my initial. I lay it out on the bedside table and place the travel alarm on top. There's something in the careful stitchwork that breaks my heart a little. I touch the soft perfection of the satin-stitch petals. Every tiny stitch seems to be speaking to me, but I don't know what they're saying.

After a shower I make my way down to the kitchen in time for breakfast, but people seem to be finishing. Violeta is already rinsing some plates at the sink, and the *Today* programme on the BBC is coming to an end. Seeing me, Marcus smiles broadly and holds my gaze. Then he gets up and says, 'Must be getting on with work.' He grabs hold of some keys on the table. 'Caitlin, I hope you decide to stay with us, but if you choose to go, just come and find me, and I'll drive you to the station.'

And then he's gone.

I'm a bit stunned. I can hear Daisy pleading with me to stay, as if the idea that I might not is an entirely new one she's never heard about. Mimi offers me muesli, and both Henna and Daisy take themselves off to the 'snug' (which I will discover is a posh word for their playroom or small TV room) on the far side of the house, beyond the living room, to watch something on television and to wallow (in the case of Henna, at least) in not having to go to school. Mimi sits down opposite me, and I hope she's not going to watch me eating again.

'Mimi,' I say, hoping to deflect her close attention from my chewing, 'can I ask you a huge favour?'

'Of course,' she says. So gentle. I wish I could bottle her gentleness. It's like nothing I've come across before (Bambi's mother aside). She tilts her head, waiting, inviting.

'Um . . . do you have any spare sanitary pads? Only I've started, and I forgot to pack them.'

'Of course. I'll go and get you some.'

53

And to my delight, she gets up to find them, leaving me to eat alone. Before she disappears, she rubs Violeta's shoulder affectionately and tells her to go and put her feet up. Then I watch as she heads through the utility area towards the back door, her long, wavy hair almost down to her waist, her movements graceful.

Do I already know that I'm going to stay? The way Marcus left me last night . . . If he had studied how to make me want him to degree level, he couldn't have done a better job; and then to offer me a lift out of here: a master stroke. Not that I want anything to happen between us, except in my head, because I'm far too fond of Mimi. And I would have to ask him for the train fare. I like the idea of tutoring the girls: a sort of governess. I'm going to be a governess with a wind-up clock and an embroidered handkerchief and an employer who melts me with his eyes. They both do. But Cliff's warning still freaks me out. What's the worst that could happen? The announcement of my tragic death would make Dad realise what a selfish shit he'd been, and Luke and Lotti would be forced to examine their actions and feel sorry. Or better still, I would blink out of a coma to see their blurred, ecstatic relief. Well, Dad's. I don't give a toss about Luke and Lotti.

When Mimi returns with a packet of pads, I thank her profusely. I feel safe here, looked after. Although there's still the threat of Cliff.

'I get the impression that Cliff may not be too keen on me.'

'Cliff?' She frowns, genuinely confused. 'Really?' She waits for me to elaborate, but I'm afraid to, in case he's a really close friend. Besides, she already seems to have worked things out. 'Oh! Don't mind Cliff. I'm afraid he smokes far too much dope. It makes him paranoid sometimes. He comes out with all sorts of rubbish. Honestly. Best not to pay any attention to him.'

Her relaxed smile reassures me. That's all I needed to know. And it's only for three weeks. I can go home when the lockdown is over. While she makes me fresh coffee, I address her back: 'Oh,

I've decided I'd like to stay and help home-school the girls, if that's still okay.'

'Oh, Caitlin, that's wonderful. Thank you. They'll be so pleased.'

'But there is one thing . . .'

'Go on . . .'

'Well, I need to get to an internet connection, somehow. If I stay, there's something I need.'

'Oh?' Her ice-blue eyes find mine as if she is almost plugging in a socket. It reminds me of the little magnetic connection wire to my laptop at home. Having found my eyes, she is straight into them with that same imperceptible little hop.

'Yes. I . . . um . . . I need to order a prescription online. I've run out of something.' What I really want to say is that I can't possibly live without knowing how I can have access to the internet some-where, sometimes.

'Oh, I see. Is that anything we can help you with? I have quite a well-stocked medicine cabinet.'

'Oh no. I . . . um . . . well . . . I really probably need to email my doctor – or get my sister to email my doctor. It's a repeat prescription.' She gazes in her other-worldly fashion, as if I'm suggesting a flight into space. 'I think I left my contraceptive pills in Europe. I don't know. But you see, I've run out.'

She laughs. 'Oh, don't worry. You won't need them here, anyway. And didn't you say your boyfriend was still in France?'

'Well, you're right, I won't need to worry about *that*, but . . . I suffer from very heavy periods and . . . um . . . bad skin and . . . Well, I would just like to keep going with them.' This isn't entirely true, but I'm irritated that I need to justify myself. 'So maybe, you or Marcus could drive me up to a chemist or . . . somewhere I can buy a charger and get an internet connection?'

She puts her head on one side once again and smiles. 'What brand name do you use?' When I tell her, she says, 'That's the white ones, isn't it? Or is it the yellow ones?'

'White.'

'That's it – white. Well, don't you worry, I have plenty of those – at least three months' worth, I think. Lydia – she was here before Violeta – left a whole load behind. I'll just check they're not out of date.'

I thank her, but feel slightly cheated out of a trip to make contact with the outside world. I go off to find the girls.

Daisy is hanging upside down on the sofa in the snug, her feet over the back of the seat cushion and her head lolling over the front. They're watching a trashy cartoon and Daisy says it's better upside down. Henna is sitting on the sofa with her bony knees drawn up, and clasping a booklet of Greta Thunberg's speeches on global warming in her stubby fingers. Could be she's got a crush on Violeta. I've seen the way she looks at her, and it's how I used to moon over our cool postman when I was her age. I was a particularly sad case, though.

Henna says that kids at school have been set lots of work to do by their teachers, but it's all online, so she wouldn't be able to do it anyway. I ask her how she downloads the music she listens to in the car, and she says she doesn't.

'It's an old iPod. I can only listen to what's already on it.'

A pair of lions are trapped under an upturned jar on the windowsill, and Daisy sees me looking.

'Mummy and Daddy Lion are in prison,' she says softly.

'Is Donkey going to rescue them?'

'No.' She folds her lips together. 'They need to think about what they've done.' Then she slides backwards onto the floor and says, 'What are you going to teach us?'

Their expectation suddenly fills the room like a massive airbag, and all my vague, heroic plans of things to do get squashed against the walls.

'Well . . .' I swallow. 'First off, I think we should get some air in our lungs. So we'll go for a walk. You can show me where we are.'

'We're not allowed further than the top path,' Henna says.

'Yes, but you're with me.'

'It's dangerous up there,' says Daisy.

'Well, we're going to explore. Come on, get some good shoes on.'

More than anything, afterwards, the police grilled me about the barn. The barn and the ridge and the woods. Of course, I knew everything by then – or thought I did.

Chapter Twelve

It's grey outside, and I have to rely on Marcus's pullover, but I have a tough pair of Doc Martens that have seen me through Europe. I go looking for a book to press some flowers in, but there seems to be a dearth of hardbacks in this house. And the only novels – including my dad's bestseller – are on a very short shelf in the living room. Henna says they were all bought and read by her mum. Eventually I find a cookbook about lentils in the kitchen, and grab two giant elastic bands from a little bowl of hair scrunchies and odds and ends, and stuff it all in a reusable carrier bag that's hanging on the back of the kitchen door. I take some kitchen towel, too, for good measure. My aim, of course, is to locate wild flowers and press them, so that at least there will be something educational to show for our escapade.

Off we set, up the wooded path we came down on the first night. I'm interested to see where this leads: there must be a road somewhere up here, and I can get my bearings. We eventually reach the level ground where the car was parked up, but there is no car there. A narrow, rough track, barely wide enough for a vehicle, winds up through the woodland, and I'm tempted to follow it.

'Where does that go?' I ask Henna.

'Just up to a little road. There's nothing up there. Just fields.'

There's a rusty little gate in a stone wall, and I make a mental note to come back and explore by myself soon.

I feel a sudden homesickness for England, even though I'm here. It's as though I've just been struck in the gut by the relentless greenery of it, the damp smells and the birdsong. Winter has already retreated, and the white stars of wood anemones carpet the woodland floor. Making our way along the path, we see clumps of coltsfoot and primroses, and the girls take samples of each, more eagerly than I'd expected. We place them gently on kitchen paper and clamp them between the pages of *Take Any Pulse*. I hold the book together with the elastic bands.

We go on our way, sniffing the air like foxes. Catkins swing on hazel twigs and butterbur is already emerging on its stout, hollow stems. Into the book they go. Following my lead, we break off the path and wade through densely packed ivy and bright leaves of wild garlic beginning to push up through the earth, to forage the secrets of tree-stumps and hidden roots. We step over fallen tree trunks, frilled in leathery fungus, and gape at the gloriously emerald moss.

It's lovely to see the two of them so absorbed in their foraging. As we come out of the woods, Henna spots some wild daffodils and goes to pick a bunch. I suggest maybe just one or two, but Daisy whispers loudly to me, 'It's for the *grave*,' as if I should know what this is, so I nod, Okay.

We are high above the house now, and cut across the top of the valley, from where Marcus showed me the view. Rabbits bound around in front of us and magically disappear in plain sight. Out here, the hawthorns are already in full leaf, but the buds of other trees create a green, stippled effect among the pale mauve-brown of their winter branches. In a few days they will just erupt, and we'll wonder how they did it without us noticing.

Henna suddenly takes a path down to the right, and we follow her.

'Wait . . . Where . . .?'

'She's going to the barn,' says Daisy in slightly hushed tones, as if we are heading to a slightly hallowed place. Things seemed to be

59

going unexpectedly well, but now my control of the situation has gone slightly off course – rather like Henna.

We arrive at a compact copse of beech trees, and inside is the stone barn with a rickety-looking double door, painted in flaking ox-blood red. One of the doors is slightly lower than the other, making the latch slope down on one side at a serious angle, and the wood is rotting. Henna unlatches the door and goes inside, while I point out some more primroses to Daisy just outside. She looks up at me with something like trepidation when I beckon her in through the door, and reaches for my hand.

Inside is a bohemian hideaway. Coloured floor cushions, a Primus stove and an old spinning wheel line one side of the barn, and two large, old-fashioned wardrobes lean precariously against another. A veined ceramic sink sits under a high window, and a cupboard next to it is stacked with pillows, jars, a kettle and other discordant objects. At the far end of the barn is a low double bed – or possibly one mattress on top of another – covered in cushions, giving the look of a student room. Above it, on the wall, are some posters of otters and landscapes. Lying on the bed is Henna.

There's something strange about Henna. She clasps her wild daffodils on her chest like the stone statue of a dead knight on a medieval tombstone. She stares up at the rafters without moving a muscle. Daisy and I stop a couple of metres from the bed and gaze at her, as if waiting for something to happen. The fusty smell of the place conjures up tombstones, too. And on closer inspection, the brightly coloured cushions have stains and water marks on them. The place is damp. The clouds in the rafters are cobwebs that have thickened over decades. There are gaps in the roof where light beams in, and bird droppings have covered some of the wooden beams like snow.

I'm trying to absorb the meaning of all this when Henna slowly sits up, swings her legs over the side of the mattress, and walks serenely out of the barn like a bridesmaid with her bunch of flowers.

'We're not allowed to open the wardrobes,' says Daisy, twisting a key and opening a wardrobe.

We peer inside together: towels. Piles of old sheets and towels. They look melded together, and I know that if I were to lift some up, they would be heavy with damp.

Disappointed with this find, Daisy tries to open the next one, but it's locked and keyless. I lock the other wardrobe, and as we turn to go, Henna is standing inside the barn door, watching us. She looks ready to go, hands in pockets. I notice she no longer has the flowers and deduce that 'the grave' must be not far from the barn. I make a note to go in search of it on my next walk.

At four o'clock I tell Mimi I'm off out to stretch my legs. She tells me that we're eating at six, so not to go too far.

'Sorry,' she smiles. 'You go as far as you like, of course. I'm just saying . . .'

I suddenly remember what the prime minister said on the radio. 'Oh God. I think we're only allowed one walk a day, with these lockdown rules.'

She laughs. 'I won't tell anyone.'

I make my way out of the front door and go straight up the bank towards the ridge. There's no one about as I veer off towards the copse of beech trees which hides the barn. Once there, I circle it, looking for the grave. I can't see anything, so I circle the barn again, and then walk in bigger loops around it. The trees on the far side give way to scraggy grassland with clumps of gorse. I follow a little sheep path, barely a foot wide, and find myself heading back up to the ridge. Turning, I look back down at the house, but it's hidden by the trees. It can't be far, this grave, because Henna was barely gone a minute or two. I sit down and scan the terrain below me: the gorse bushes, the trees, the barn. Then I see it: just the edge of a speckled stone sticking out from behind a bush. I make my way down from the path and head towards it. There, with a small bunch of daffodils laid at its base, is a lichen-covered stone.

You couldn't call it a slab; more of a boulder. On its flattest flank, someone has carefully carved:

Thea + Kitty

2015

The weather on this limestone has widened and softened the carved lines, making it look more ancient than it is. Thea and Kitty. Pets, perhaps. The daffodils are limp already. I'll ask Daisy at some point. Or perhaps Mimi. Henna certainly seems too invested in Thea and Kitty, and I don't want to upset her.

I make my way back along the ridge to the woodland we walked through yesterday, and when I reach the little clearing, the Land Rover is there again, parked up. I look towards the track. It can't be far to the road.

Almost immediately, a house appears off to the left. It's made of greying Cotswold stone with stone roof tiles dappled in lichen, like all the houses round here. It is small – a cottage really, but with a spacious garden all the way round, enclosed by a waist-high stone wall. This could be Surfer Joe's house. It's a square building, and sits contentedly in its bushy space. A path leads up to a yellow front door in the side of the house, which is facing left; a little further on there's a small, elderly red car on the far side of the house, as if a drive leads off to a road somewhere. A cat is slumped on the low wall in front of me. I recognise it as the cat that lolls around Amberside, and begin to stroke him. He squirms on to his side and exposes his tummy, as if wanting a rub, but when I touch it, he whips out a paw and bats me away. I look about, embarrassed, as if someone is watching me. There's no one here. Then I glance up for some reason and see that there's a dark figure in an upstairs window, looking at me. It's not Joe, and he doesn't look away when I see him. I turn on my heel and go back the way I came.

I hope I've made the right decision staying at this place. It's five o'clock. Lockdown has begun. There's no going back now.

Chapter Thirteen

Mimi is in the kitchen, kneading dough or something. It's only seven o'clock in the morning and no one else is down yet. It's been a few days since lockdown began and I've been getting worried about my phone. I need to charge it up or buy a new charger. I've no idea where I could get one, as only 'essential' shops are open, but perhaps a big supermarket.

'Um . . . when are you next going shopping?' I ask.

She turns and smiles. 'You're up early. Let's see. Marcus might go this afternoon.'

'Can I go along? I need a few things.'

I notice the slight hesitation.

'I'll see. I don't see why not.' Perhaps she's worried about me being alone with Marcus.

'Maybe the girls would like to come too?' I suggest.

She makes a slight noise to imply possibility, and thwacks the dough down hard on the work surface. 'Filkins is in the living room. You should introduce yourself,' she says, without turning round.

'Who?'

'Filkins.'

For some reason the name conjures up a manservant with a limp. *I fixed the missing tile, mistress. Will you be wanting me to saddle up the grey mare?* But I'm getting used to their hippy-dippy names, and so go through the dining room, cross the flagstone hallway, and enter the living room tentatively, expecting another skin-ravaged, ponytailed ex-band member.

There's no one there. I look around, then poke my head into the playroom at the far end. No sign of anyone.

'He's not there,' I say, returning to the kitchen.

Mimi is washing her hands at the sink. 'He was there just now.' Grabbing a dishcloth to dry her hands, she walks ahead of me, through the dining room, across the hallway into the living room. She looks about and frowns. 'How odd. Oh, well . . .' She moves over to the old red velvet curtains, as if someone might be hiding behind them. 'There you are!'

I peer over a sofa and a long-haired tabby turns his head nonchalantly towards us. I let out a chuckle of relief. He's the cat from the wall yesterday. Perhaps he recognises me, too. Filkins stands up and stretches his back legs out behind him like a wheelbarrow. I go over to stroke him. This time he lets me.

'He's not ours,' she says, 'but he spends a lot of time here. He belongs to Joe's housemate. The girls fuss over him so much, he sort of commutes between the two houses.'

I take to Filkins straight away. He lets me rub him under the chin and starts up a heavy purr. I can have no idea, of course, just how important he is going to be in the way things turn out.

After breakfast I'm far too awake to want to sit about tutoring the girls. They're pleased when I suggest an early walk to stretch our legs before we work. I say 'pleased': Daisy is eager, Henna looks relieved.

We put on our walking gear and head up the slope to the ridge. I want to turn left, past the barn, and explore a different direction. Daisy chunters away. Dare I ask who Thea and Kitty are? Probably best not, for the time being.

Ahead of us is a glorious valley. The fields are bright green in the morning sunshine, and look stitched to the hillsides with hedges and drystone walls. Sheep are dotted all over, and the sound of lambs bleating rings out for miles. Nestled in the distant vale are clumps of trees and the stone-tiled roof of a far-off building. From its chimney comes a thin banner of smoke.

'That's Foxes Haye,' says Henna, seeing me squinting at it. 'It's a farm. I've been there before.'

'Have I been there?' asks Daisy.

'No. It was before you were born. The farmer let me hold the lambs.'

'I want to hold lambs. Can we hold lambs today, Caitlin?'

'Well, let's see. Let's see if we can find the farmer. There are certainly plenty of lambs about. Looking promising, I'd say.'

With the added motivation of lamb-holding, we make the remaining distance in forty minutes, coming down from the path through a series of kissing gates.

'You can't let the next person through the swing-gate without a kiss,' I say, with mock indignation. 'I can't believe you didn't know that!'

Daisy is happy to throw her arms up at me and give me a wet smacker on the cheek. Henna flares her nostrils and gives her sister a dry peck, but only because Daisy pushes against the gate until she does.

We follow a wider track now, until we get close to the farmhouse. Almost at once we see some lambs, and Daisy rushes forward as they gambol over to push their muzzles through the fence. They lick our hands and circle our fingers in their warm wet breath. The air smells muskily of sheep dung, but the mothers are all in the next field with their offspring, sending out the odd low-bleat admonishment, but looking fatly proud nonetheless. These two lambs are penned off, motherless.

'You found my little orphans, then,' says a man, coming up behind us.

'They yours?' I say. 'I hope we're not trespassing.'

'You're fine, my love. You stop there as long as you like.'

Daisy turns and looks up at him. 'Are you the farmer? Can we hold them?'

Henna rolls her eyes and seems to shrink with embarrassment. But he hasn't stopped smiling since meeting us, and says, 'Course you can. Tell you what, would you like to feed them? It's coming up to feeding time. You can help me make up the milk. I'm Geoff.'

'Did their mothers die?' asks Henna, suddenly anxious.

'No, love.' Geoff, who is making his way to a door in a stone building, beckons us to follow, which we do. We enter a fusty outbuilding, stacked with hay bales and plastic tubs of powdered milk, pails full of feeding bottles, sacks of unknown farm-like substances. 'Sit yourselves down.' He gestures at the hay bales, and makes his way to a little worktop with jugs, a kettle and some weighing scales. 'I've half-filled this jug with boiling water, see. It's too hot at the moment, so I'm adding some cold.' He turns on the tap at a metal sink set in the worktop, and adds some cold water to his measuring jug. 'Now, I'm going to put this thermometer in.' He turns to Daisy and says, 'What's your name?'

'Daisy.'

'Well, Daisy, I expect your mum uses a thermometer when you're ill, doesn't she?'

Daisy nods, fascinated.

'Now I know roughly how much water to add to make this the right temperature, but it's got to be 40 degrees. You want to check that for me a moment?' He hands the jug to Henna, who takes it on her knee and studies the thermometer solemnly. 'Meanwhile, I need to measure 200 grams of lamb milk-replacer. See this?' He stands back so they can both see the tub from which he is scooping powder onto the scales. 'Can you count to two hundred, my love?'

Daisy folds her lips together, perhaps wondering whether to fib about this, but honesty wins through, and she shakes her head in frustration.

'No matter. Come over here and tell me when the pointer reaches this number here.'

'How's that water temperature, Henna?'

'It's . . . 41 degrees – no, almost 40.'

'That'll do nicely.'

'How did you know my name was Henna?'

'I remember you from when you were a kid. You've changed, mind. Quite a young lady now.'

Henna blushes, and bites her lip to stop herself getting carried away by a smile.

'Right, read off how many mils of water you got in that jug, Henna, love.'

She holds the jug up steady before her face. '800 mils.'

'Lovely. Here we go then. Up you come.' When both girls are at the counter, he pours some of the water into another, larger jug and adds the powder. He whisks it a bit, and then asks each of them to whisk it some more. 'Right, what temperature is that now, Henna me girl?'

'It's . . . 39 degrees.' She waits. 'Yes, 39 degrees.'

'Excellent. That's just right for the lambs.' He pours the milk into two feeding bottles and fastens on the teats. 'Come with me.'

Henna and Daisy have a lamb each, and the farmer shows them how to let the lambs stand and lift up their heads before holding the bottle to them as upright as possible.

'Keep the head up, that's the job. And don't cuddle them while they're feeding. They can get a clot like that. That's it.' The lambs gobble and slaver all over the place, nudging their heads as if they can't get enough. 'Well, look at that. Two naturals!'

I wish my phone was charged, so that I could take a picture to show Marcus and Mimi. I want them to see what a good job I'm doing, under the circumstances, of providing educational experiences for their two offspring.

'Oh, hang!' says Geoff.

'What is it?'

'I've only gone and forgotten about social distancing, haven't I? I'm really sorry.'

'Shit. Me too. I think it's going to take some getting used to.'

'Can we cuddle them now?' asks Daisy, when all the milk is gone.

'Oh yes. Cuddle away, gently. They'll like a bit of affection.'

'Why aren't they with the other lambs, if they still have mummies?'

'Their mothers rejected them. It happens sometimes. They won't let them feed. They nudge or kick them out of the way. It's pitiful to watch. The kindest thing then is to take them away before they get hurt.'

You can see Daisy's heart melt as she hears this, and even Henna wraps her arms around her lamb. I think her eyes have reddened, and I watch the delicate pink seam of her hair parting as she bends her head, quenching herself on being able to give this little creature something it so desperately needs from her.

'Oh,' I say. 'You don't have a charger I could borrow for a bit?' He looks confused, as if I might have just asked him for a raging bull. 'A charger. Just for a few minutes?'

While the girls are playing with the lambs, he takes me back into the outhouse and unplugs something from a socket on the counter. 'This do?'

I look at it. It must be an old charger or something. 'Do you have an iPhone charger?'

He bites the inside of his cheek, thoughtfully. 'I got a Nokia.'

'Oh. Don't worry. Thank you, though.'

We go back outside and watch the girls from a distance.

'You know,' he says, 'it only seems yesterday she was a little kid, that Henna. Come up here with her mother, she did, to see the lambs.'

'You met her mother?'

'Oh yes. Lovely woman. Lovely. I suppose that must've been

Daisy she was carrying then. Fit to drop, she was. But so lovely. I forget her name now.'

'Mimi.'

'Ah, could be. Summat hippy like that. How old is Daisy?'

'Five. And a half.'

'Lord. Nearly six years ago. Time flies. But that would be about right. What about you? You another sister?'

'Oh, no. I'm Caitlin. I'm their . . . sort of tutor or, you know, nanny kind of thing. I'm staying at their house.'

'Things . . . all right over there, are they? Only, I heard . . . well, not much for a while, actually.'

'I've literally only just arrived.' *What? What has he heard?*

'Oh, well. Mark still running it as a "community", then?'

'Um . . . I'm not too sure. I suppose.'

Mark?

Before I have time to think about this, or to ask him what he's heard, Daisy comes running over and asks what the lambs are called.

'They don't have any names, I'm afraid. Wonky-left-ear and Wonky-left-ear's sister is all. How'd you like to name them?'

Minutes later, we have agreed to hand-rear Sausage and Freedom. Geoff says he'll bring them down to the house tomorrow, if we get agreement. He gives me his phone number. 'Signal's a bit crap out here. That's my landline I've written there.'

We start the walk home with a spring in our step. I only hope I've done the right thing.

'Bye, Geoff!' calls Daisy.

'Bye, girls!'

The two of them run on ahead, Henna like a little girl again. I feel ridiculously proud. When I turn back to wave, Geoff shouts, 'I'll await your call! Give my regards to Mark and Mandy!'

Chapter Fourteen

The girls come with us on the shopping trip, perhaps hoping they can persuade Marcus to let them have the lambs. I can't tell whether Marcus is irritated by their presence or not. In my fantasy, he wants to be alone with me, but the way he avoids looking at me on this journey does nothing to feed this idea. It's not a real fantasy, anyway. Just a lukewarm one. I don't fancy him or anything. He's not my type. Too old; too full of himself. Way too good-looking, anyway. I do like seeing his hands on the steering wheel, though: large and tanned, the arched thumb stroking the inside of the wheel from time to time. But shit, they're only hands.

'Can I ask you something?' says Marcus. I don't say he can, but he asks anyway. 'What was it made you want to leave your boyfriend – and your friends – in such a hurry?'

Please, not this.

'Like I said, we had to get out of Italy in a hurry – there really *is* a pandemic, you know – and . . . we didn't all agree on what to do next. We had a bit of a falling-out.'

'Come on, then,' he says. 'Spill the beans.' I say nothing, but turn my head away from him to look out of the window. 'Let me guess – boyfriend trouble. He was seeing another girl.'

'No!' I turn and see him raising his eyebrows, with a slight smile, surprised perhaps at my abruptness, or pleased that he's got a reaction and therefore thinks he's right.

'I'm close, though, aren't I? Betrayal of some sort.' He nods, as if

I've agreed with him. 'It's always betrayal that gets women so riled up. Or else you betrayed him. You ladies are such fickle creatures, aren't you?'

You ladies?

'Oh, *please!*' I try to summon up my derisive voice. 'You're such a . . .' He's such a complete tool. 'Look, I just don't want to talk about it, okay?'

'Okay.' I know he's looking at my profile, to see how close he's got. 'I'm sorry. Really.'

We watch the arches of trees slide seamlessly by in a corridor of budding foliage. Henna has her earphones in and Daisy is singing a made-up song about lambs, trying to find something to rhyme with Sausage.

It wasn't your average betrayal. Not sure that I know anyone else it's happened to, or anyone I could share it with, not without dragging people I care about down with me.

I really thought I was making something of myself. *Something*, anyway. Nothing special, just the beginnings of an identity. Not that trailing around Europe after my boyfriend was anything to be proud about in most people's eyes, but it was a first for me in a lot of ways. First time I'd travelled abroad without my family, first time I'd made a decision of my own that went directly against their advice, first time I'd had a boyfriend.

'Tell me about your family.'

'Well. My sisters are both extraordinary. My older sister, Erin, is doing a PhD in microbiology. She got four top grades at A-level, and boys have always been obsessed with her. So much so that Mum used to get tired of having to pretend Erin was out when they turned up. My younger sister, Dani, is a complete prodigy.'

I'm not jealous or anything. She's just so effing perfect. She's pretty, musical, clever. But what pisses me off is the way everyone tiptoes around her like a baby. You mustn't upset Dani, don't be too harsh, too critical, too exclusive. Don't make a noise, you might wake the baby. Seriously, she's *fourteen*. And of course, all this recent crap is just going to fuck things right up. She's so sensitive, I expect they're rolling her up in cotton wool right now. Mum has probably called in a counsellor for her. It really grinds my gears. If they'd just leave her alone, she might even be normal.

'I've never come first at anything,' I tell him. 'Never had even one piece of work displayed on school corridor walls, or won any awards. Unless you count the Award for Best Attendance when I was eleven. I couldn't even go up and receive it from the head-teacher because I was – exceptionally – absent that day, in A&E with a dislocated finger – genuine. Apparently, when my name was called out and I didn't go up on stage to collect my piece of laminated card, everyone had a good laugh at my expense.'

He smiles. 'You're too hard on yourself.'

'Honestly, I'm supremely untalented.'

He laughs. 'And you're tutoring my daughters.'

'Okay, I'm not totally shit. If I'd been born into a different family, they'd probably be really proud of my average grades, my adequate guitar playing, my clunky singing, my lasagne. Mum says I'm beautiful, but that doesn't really count. She has to. She's my mum and has these mum-filters in her lenses that make anyone she loves totally adorable.'

He laughs again.

'She kept on at me to work harder at my exams, said I wasn't putting in the time. She was right, of course. That was when I'd met Luke. He and Lotti were last summer's "discoveries".'

He's beaming, delighted to hear me open up, but I won't be telling him much more.

'Luke and Lotti?'

'Yeah, these two students of Dad's. Luke and Lotti both had jobs teaching English as a Foreign Language in Florence from September, and Lotti's boyfriend was going along with them to find a job.'

'So you fell in love with Luke.' He says it like a statement, as if it was predictable.

I frown. 'We hung out. So when my exam results came through and it wasn't looking likely that I'd be following Erin into microbiology, or any other ology, I thought I might as well take up Luke and Lotti's suggestion to go with them. Dad wasn't keen. Mum said I must promise to reapply for university in the January, and I promised. (And I forgot, actually.) Not that they had any leverage over me.'

I was eighteen. An adult. And I was travelling to Europe with my boyfriend. My very own.

'You sound like a woman who knows her own mind.' *(That's what you think, mister.)* 'I like that.'

Weirdly, we pull up in a village and he unclicks his seatbelt.

'All out, then. Or do you two girls want to stay in the car?' They do not. But this isn't Waitrose or Sainsbury's. This is a village Co-op store. He turns to me. 'What's the matter?'

'I thought we were going to a big store?'

'This'll do. This'll have everything we need.'

'But I need a phone charger.'

'Well . . . why didn't you say?'

'I did. That's why I wanted to come – partly.'

He holds up his hands in defence, and apologises. 'I'll take you to a big store next week.' He smiles at me then, eyebrows raised in a sort of supplication. 'Forgiven?'

I do my best to smile, but I'm so pissed off with him. He knew this was important to me. He *knew*. If the girls weren't with us, I'd challenge him about it right now.

We trail around the store, trying to follow red arrows on the floor, which are designed to get people walking in one direction. There are circles on the floor as well, at two-metre intervals, to let us know when we are too close to other shoppers. The experience is trying. We keep having to wait while some old guy examines the labels on tuna fish or beans for what seems like an age, before we can get to the next aisle. The girls keep trying to change direction and cut though the displays, but there are ribbons across the gaps preventing this. We're all caught in a tiny maze, only we can't go back the way we came.

Marcus reads from a short list, which has clearly been written out in Mimi's loopy handwriting. Pathetic. He seems like a little boy dependent on Mummy. I want to tear the list out of his hands and tell him to use his own common sense. In fact, I'm pretty sure Mimi knocked up this list just to enable us to go to a tiny supermarket. The items we need are deliberately general: cans of chopped tomatoes, milk, canned tuna, yeast, rice, butter, flour, eggs, toilet roll. None of her posh stuff. We get everything except for flour and toilet roll. There seems to be a run on toilet roll. Commentators on the news have been speculating about the British people's obsession with stocking up on this essential in times of crisis. We buy packets of tissues instead, but there is no flour of any kind.

'I don't suppose you have any phone chargers?' asks Marcus at the counter.

The girl behind the till looks at him as if he's simple. 'What? Here? No, sorry.'

'Do you know anywhere near that might have one?' I ask.

She pulls another face. 'Cheltenham? Go to an Apple Store. Though they'll be closed with this virus. Online's your best bet, I'd say.'

Well, of course. If I could get online. I thank her. I can't help thinking Marcus only asked her this stupid question to show me he'd done his best. Which he hasn't. We take the bags back to the car, and Daisy spots a set of swings in a field; she and Henna set off towards them without a backward glance. Clearly this is a familiar ritual.

'Fancy a drink?' says Marcus.

I follow him down the street and spot a red plastic storage box on the pavement, jammed full with books. A handwritten sign says 'Help yourself'. I saw boxes like this on the way to the shop earlier, outside people's houses. It seems to be a feature of lockdown. I crouch down and examine the treasure. Without the internet, I'll need all the help I can get, and this is a real find. There are all sorts of school revision books, some early reading books, and several novels. I take as many of the school books as I can carry and give Marcus a handful of novels to hold. He insists on going back to the car to drop them off first.

We make our way to a pretty stone public house called the Lamb and Flag. The porch is decorated with hanging baskets trailing with flowers, but the heavy oak door is shut.

'Oh, the pubs are closed,' I say. 'Of course they are.'

He turns away from the door, right into me. He places his hands on my shoulders and stares at me. Then he kisses me, very gently, and I let him. His lips, held soft and wet against mine, send some kind of opiate winging through me to dull my brain and fire up my groin. His skin smells of split logs, and I want to slobber into his neck. He draws away and looks steadily at me again. I look back, trying to hold his gaze.

'What?' he says.

'What?'

'What just happened?'

I want to burst out laughing. What happened was what he made happen. He wants to pretend something magic happened, to make fun of me. But I don't want to break his spell. There we go: his spell. I'm believing it myself now. Well, I can't fault his technique. Corny, but effective. I open my mouth to say something – anything – to make it clear I'm not fooled by this – I'm not getting mixed up with a married man's antics – when he cups the side of my face in his hand.

'Caitlin.' I mean, he looks dead serious. Oh God, he really does. 'Meet me at the barn on Monday afternoon.'

Then he steps back to let me exit the porch, and after I step out onto the pavement, he places his hand on the small of my back, in that way male presidents usher female politicians, as though they are small animals or children. Part of me wants to yell at him to stop taking the piss, but the touch is confusing me, is another dose of something hideously powerful. Before I can say anything, Daisy comes running up with Henna behind her.

'A man told us to get off the swings! He said we can't play there any more because . . . because of the crone . . .'

'Coronavirus,' says Henna.

'Of course,' I say. 'The playgrounds are all closed. That's a shame.'

Imperceptibly, Marcus has removed his hand. He says we'd better get home.

'But it's not fair!'

'Well,' he says, striding back to the car, 'at least you'll have your own lambs tomorrow.'

'*What?* Yay! Daddy! Daddy! Yay!'

We don't see him smiling, as he is ahead of us, until he reaches the car and Daisy leaps on him for a squeeze. I watch her envelop him in her arms and I can feel every inch of cotton T-shirt and the flesh behind it that she is touching. I have to turn my eyes away. Henna climbs in the back seat and belts up.

'I can't wait to hold Freedom again,' she says.

I can tell she's already feeling the lamb's warm woolly body in her fingers.

I can't look at Marcus on the way back. What's he playing at? He has a wife. Fucksake. Mark and Mandy. Is she really called Mandy? Or did Geoff, the farmer, just remember 'Mimi' wrong after I'd said it? This curious longing makes no sense. He's a dick. Anyway, I'm going to ignore the ache in my loins. That's what Mum called our vaginas once, and we always joke about it. Our loins. Mine are on fire, engorged and longing. Because of this stupid, stupid man who thinks he's God's gift, but is actually just a total twat. But undeniably gorgeous. Maybe he just smells good. Some subliminal animal attraction. I close my eyes, trying not to think about that kiss and the remarkable tenderness of it. When I open them, there are his taut, brown arms, his broad hands gripping the wheel.

When we bundle out of the car and wander down the path, he grabs my arm gently at the elbow and says, quietly, 'Two.'

I make as if I'm not bothered, as if I haven't been wondering all the way home about the timing of this rendezvous I'm not going to keep.

Chapter Fifteen

It was Erin's phone call that did it. Both calls. Sometimes you can remember exactly where you were and what you were doing with a phone call, and this was one of them. We were about to go out: me, Luke, Lotti and her boyfriend, Tom. I liked Tom. We'd just started getting into quite a thing busking together. He'd got himself a proper permit and everything. I started going along as his assistant, sometimes pretending to be a bystander and throwing euros into his guitar case. Then he got me singing, too. I thought I'd die of nerves at first, but he started me slowly. He had me singing along with him, softly to begin with, so soft I was barely mouthing the words. Then every now and then he would stop halfway through a verse and let me continue, pretending he'd forgotten the words. It's amazing how confident you can get very quickly, when you realise no one's ever going to see you again, and they're not going to throw things at you, and they're most likely not really listening; you're just providing a backdrop to their walk in the sunshine. Once he got me playing a fiddle someone lent us. I'm not very good compared to my sisters, but everyone likes a bit of Irish fiddle music, especially in Italy. It had been our first week of full-time busking together. Tom made me feel good at something. Because, let's face it, tagging around after Luke in Italy while he taught students English and I washed plates or, at best, waited on tables, didn't do great things for my confidence. Tom didn't have a degree either, but somehow it seemed to matter less with him. He always had his music, and that was something Lotti admired about him. There was nothing for Luke to admire about me – except my father, of course.

So when my phone chimed, I was just admiring my new hair up-do in the bedroom mirror and feeling excited that the evenings were getting warmer. I was anticipating the stroll through the piazzas, the enticing smells of cooking, the intrigue that I might hold for Lotti and Luke now that I spent my days with Tom and had half of Florence looking at us.

'Caitlin, are you sitting down?' Erin's voice had sounded odd on the phone.

'Why?'

'Sit down. Are you alone?'

'Well, yes. But not for long. We're about to go out.'

There was a brief silence, as if she was thinking. 'Look, you'd better hear this.'

'What?'

'I've just been speaking to Dani. She's been acting weird for ages, but Dad had a go at her and she's been in tears all day and snapping everyone's head off. Anyway, I got her alone and she told me.'

'What?'

'Last summer, before you lot went off to Italy, when Luke and Lotti were doing their "writers' retreat" with Dad, Dani went over to the barn to ask where the keys to the shed were, and there was Lotti, naked from the waist down, straddling Dad on the sofa.'

There was a sudden sense of being pulled off balance, like when you're standing at the shoreline and a wave crashes in and then sucks back again, covering your feet in wet sand; a sense of being dragged by a giant magnet.

'Jesus! What was she . . .? What was he . . .?'

'I know! Apparently Dani couldn't see his face, just her great looming arse from behind.'

My pulse was crashing like waves.

'Oh, God! Stop!' This could not be true. It could not. Not Dad. 'There must be some mistake. That's not like Dad at all. I mean . . . is it?'

'That's what I thought. But Dani saw it, Caitlin. She saw it.'

I thrashed about for ways she might have got this wrong. It was hard. There was no corner to pick up, nothing to grab hold of.

'There has to be some kind of innocent explanation,' I tried.

'Like what? She said what she saw.'

Dad would *never* do something like that. Never, ever. I knew there had to be a mistake, some kind of misunderstanding.

'Well . . . was he a willing participant? Or d'you think she just overwhelmed him?'

'Well, all I know is it's really messed Dani up.'

'*Fucksake!* Was it definitely him?'

'She recognised his Marks and Spencer's lumberjack shirt.'

No. No, no, no.

'The one Mum got him?'

'Yes, the bastard!'

The blood was thumping in my chest. 'Oh . . . Erin . . . this is awful. This is shit. I just can't really believe it. And Dani's known all this time and she's said nothing?'

'I know. She didn't know what to do. She wanted to tell us, but she thought we'd tell Mum and then Mum and Dad would split up.'

'Does Mum know?'

'Not yet. I don't think so. That's partly why I'm ringing. What do you think we should do? Should we tell her?'

Luke opened the door and told me to get a move on.

'Okay, I'm coming, I'm coming. Just hang on!'

'Sorry,' said Erin, 'I didn't mean to ruin your evening. I wasn't sure what to do.'

This was so unlike Erin. She always knew what to do. She never asked my opinion on anything.

'Well, I think she deserves to know. She can get the real truth out of him. I mean, if I were Mum, I'd want to know, wouldn't you?'

'But it'd break her heart, Caitlin.'

'Sounds like it's going to get broken anyway. And maybe he can explain what really happened – if there's an innocent explanation—'

'Oh, Caitlin—'

'It's *possible*!' Surely there was an innocent explanation. 'Okay, I mean, either way, you'd want to know, wouldn't you? Otherwise, she's living a lie. Imagine how she'd feel if she found out we all knew and hadn't told her.'

'I suppose . . . do you think this is the first time? He's been having gorgeous young students at the barn for a few years now.'

'*Lotti?* Gorgeous?'

'You know. Ample in the balcony.'

'You know we're about to go out with Lotti and Tom? Christ! I don't know, Erin. Mum may already know. Can I call you when I get back?'

To think of all those meals my mother made them, these gorgeous wannabe writers. To think how she picked them up from the station and changed their sheets and washed their towels. To think how many hours she'd spent reading Dad's drafts, suggesting an idea here, cutting something there, a tactful rewording that wouldn't offend someone they knew. To think of all the years she'd cheered him up, boosted his ego, driven him to unfrequented bookshops and made small talk with the half a dozen waiting fans, trailed after him to dismal literary festivals or to occasional bright overcrowded ones where the queues for his book signing snaked out of the book tent and round a park, to literary prize dinners where he forgot to introduce her when he spoke to other authors or journalists, where she was lucky if she got a free vol-au-vent without wearing a lanyard.

I let it all churn inside me as we went walking through the golden light of a Florentine evening. I tried not to look at Lotti's breasts (not unlike the waiter) as she held the menu in our chosen trattoria. How could I possibly broach it with her? How could she have done this to Tom? To my mother?

The day after I found out about Lotti and Dad, I remember how I had come down from our flat, and Signor Tiraboschi had spotted me mooching red-eyed outside his shop and had invited me in.

'*Ma, cosa c'è, poverina?*'

He sat me down on a chair near the back of the shop and I started to cry. I cried because he gave me a peach and cut it up so carefully with his big hands and put it on a plate. He asked me if it was man trouble, and I nodded, because it was too hard to explain. He asked (I think) if the man had hurt me, and I nodded, because I was hurt, but he must've understood something else, because he swore between gritted teeth.

'*Che cazzo! Poverina!*'

It struck me as a good word to use in anger: *cazzo*. Full of hiss and spit. I saved it up for later use. I felt safe there, with Signor Tiraboschi and his hardware. He nodded reassuringly as I ate each section of peach, seated in front of a row of boxes containing different sized screws.

There'd obviously been some kind of mistake. It just wasn't possible to go from loving my father the way I did to seeing him as contemptible. It was like asking you to leap from one side of a stream to another, without offering any sort of footbridge.

Chapter Sixteen

The time passes that weekend only because of the lambs. Geoff brings them down the twisty farm track across the fields on the left of the house, and we all go up to his truck to meet them. The girls can't wait to get their hands on them, and Mimi, Marcus and I help Geoff bring hay and plastic cartons of feed up to the front of the house. To the right of the front 'garden', opposite Mimi's colourful hut–study, is the remains of a goat-pen with a grass enclosure. This is where they will stay, and Henna asks Geoff anxiously if it's good enough for them.

'It's perfect, Henna, love,' says Geoff, and makes sure they have everything they need.

Then he runs through a list of things with Marcus and Mimi. I feel like a child, like Daisy and Henna, now that Geoff is with the real adults. I stand foolishly, holding one elbow, looking at the girls play with the lambs. Then I hear him ask something about the older one and Mimi lowers her voice and I hear the word 'briny', and then I hear him say 'Their mum', asking after her or something, and Mimi lowers her voice and I don't hear what she says. I catch something like 'Daisy's ours.'

Then Geoff turns to me and says, 'But any road, you have any problems, just ask this young lady here. Caitlin knows what to do, don't you, my love?'

I smile, grateful, and nod. 'Well, if I don't, I'll come and ask.'

'Right you are. Bye, Daisy! Bye, Henna, love!'

We leave the girls with the lambs and follow him back up to his truck to wave him off.

'"Henna, love",' says Marcus, when we get back to the lamb pen.

'Henna, love!' says Daisy in a deep voice. 'Oh, Henna, love!'

Henna scowls. I look at my feet, because Marcus expects me to smile.

'Come on, Daisy-love, Henna-love,' I say. 'Let's go and heat up some water and show Marcus-love how to make up feed.'

Henna shoots me a curious glance, and I wink at her. She seems satisfied I have restored some invisible balance in her favour.

I manage to convince the girls we have some work to catch up with, and the rest of the weekend passes in a blur of bleating, trigonometric ratios, the Oxford Reading Tree and measuring sheep milk-replacer. It's so idyllic on one of our little walks up to the ridge and back along through the woods, and the girls are so relaxed, that I venture to ask about the thing that has been bugging me for days.

'Whose is the gravestone? You know, the one near the barn?'

But a blackbird gives an alarm call at just that moment and I don't think they hear me.

When Monday arrives, I'm a bag of nerves. I'm not going, of course, but I'm intrigued to see what Marcus will do when I don't turn up. Then again, I'm intrigued to see what will happen if I do. I imagine lying on that cold, clammy mattress with him, and someone walking in, like Daisy, say, and then Mimi finding out, and me being packed off home in the middle of this pandemic. Or stuck here, with Mimi not speaking to me, Cliff growling at me, Daisy devastated. Of course I won't go, but I find I've made some comprehensive lesson plans that spill over with worksheets into the afternoon, to keep the girls inside. Just in case I were to take a notion to stroll up to the barn at two o'clock to investigate what that knobhead is up to.

The weather is glorious, again. Every day of this lockdown has been beautiful. After a quick lunch in the kitchen, when I don't catch his eye once, Marcus disappears. The girls prepare the lamb feed, warming up the bottles they've made earlier. We sit and play with Freedom and Sausage in the sunshine. I push my nose into their greasy, lanolin-rich wool, breathing them in, admiring their dogged attachment to life when everything has been set against it.

'You okay?' says Henna, hawk-eyed on me.

'Fine. Got a bit of a headache coming on. I think I'll get a bit more fresh air. When I come back, I want you both to have finished your work, okay?'

'Can we stay out here a bit longer?'

'Of course.'

I go back into the house and look at myself in the little bedroom mirror. I have a spot coming on my chin. I knew I would have something like that. Clearly, I can't go. I clean my teeth in the bathroom and have a quick wash. In this light, the spot hardly shows. I roll some deodorant under my arms. Luckily, I still have some. Mimi uses crystals or something, and it may work on her but it doesn't on me. She made me try it, and I sweated like a pig all day.

I check the travel alarm: 1.57 p.m., which is a lopsided *V*. (I picture Gran with her arms up.) I could go. I would arrive a bit late, which would be good. Not being keen. I could just slip away now, go the other way up the bank, through the woods, so that I don't pass the girls. Anyway, what's wrong with them seeing me? I said I was going for a bit of fresh air, didn't I?

I don't go directly up to the barn. I go out through the front door, walk past Mimi's study, past the lamb-pen and up the path into the woods. I cut back across the top of the woodland to the ridge, follow it casually, then drop stealthily down towards the barn in among the trees.

No one is here. I look about, put my head in through the flaking ox-blood door. No one. I call out, softly, timidly. No one answers. Louder.

Nothing. I go back outside, humiliated. My heart is pounding. My mouth is getting dry. Okay, I'm not having this. I start back up to the ridge, and I'm panting, just as a voice comes from the trees.

'You came, then.'

I turn, angry with him, but relieved as well. Swallow.

'I knew you would,' he says.

'I'm not staying. I just came to tell you—'

He reaches out and takes hold of my hand. 'Please. I'd like you to stay. Just come and see this.'

He makes his way to the far side of the barn, taking me with him, making sure I mind out for brambles. I'm curious, so I follow. We arrive round the corner at a pile of rusting iron stuff, old bits of farm machinery, plough heads and brittle old horse tack. To my astonishment, he loops around behind it, takes out his keys and opens a door hidden from view. Before I can react, he puts his fingers to his mouth and gives two loud whistles.

'I'll explain,' he says. 'Come on.'

I follow him through the hidden door, up some stone steps. We come out into a long thin room, almost the full width of the barn in length, but narrow: no wider than the length of a bed. And there is a bed – a double one, covered in dark red cushions, velvet and cotton. There's a rag-rug on the floor, a bedside lamp (there's electricity here, then), and an old wooden cottage door with a black latch. I look about, admiring the dry old wooden beams that slope massively into the space. This is a slice of the barn roof, after all, and it's almost as veiled in cobwebs as the main barn roof. I examine the cracked oak and the ancient wattle and daub, for all the world as if he has just shown me a house to buy, and not led me into a secret annexe whose main item of furniture is a bed.

'Where does that go?' I point to the door, then go to open it.

'Just a cupboard.'

'Why's it locked?'

He sighs. 'Look, what I'm doing here . . . it's not very legal, in case you hadn't noticed, and I keep all my . . . stuff in there. All my contacts, dealings and so on. So if anyone comes snooping – anyone from the law or anything . . .'

'What – like Joe?'

'Yeah, well, he's safe. I provide him with his stash. But anyone else. And I make sure no one else comes this way too often either, which might attract attention to it. I mean anyone – even the girls.'

'And how do you do that?'

'Ah, well, that's the thing. I have a signal. I whistle.'

'Okay . . .'

'Everyone at Amberside knows the signal. It means "Keep away, everyone". So no one will come up to the barn if I whistle a couple of times, like this.' He puts two fingers to his mouth and gives two piercing whistles. 'We could make that our signal, too, if you like – but *three* whistles.' I must look a little confused, because he adds, 'For you and me to meet here.'

'Oh.'

'Visitors aren't interested in looking up towards the barn. It's completely hidden by trees. Especially this little bit of it . . . I bet you didn't spot it when you came up with the girls, did you?'

'How did you know that we . . .?'

He leans against the wall with one foot propped against it, watching me. A slow smile spreads across his face. 'You must know.'

'Know what?'

He pushes himself off the wall and comes to stand in front of me, closing the gap slowly. He puts his hands on my shoulders and massages them softly with his thumbs, inspecting my collarbone, my chin, my lips.

'You intrigue me. I'm always fascinated to see what you're doing.'

I can't hide my beating heart, my quickened breath. 'Well, what I'm doing now is going back to your daughters.'

'Of course you are.' His hands stop. I think he's going to move away, but he stands very still, looking at me. My loins are in trouble. They really are. He leans his forehead on mine. 'Let me touch you, Caitlin. What are you afraid of? I won't hurt you. Just let me touch you – nothing else.'

'You're a married man.'

Loins: 4, moral fibre: 6.

He laughs. 'Who said I was married?'

'Aren't you?' Hope tempts me with a thin thread to hold on to.

'Good grief, no! Why would I be married?'

'You've got children. And Mimi – you love her. She loves you. You're together.'

He smiles at me, sympathetically I imagine. He strokes my chin.

'Mimi and I . . . Mimi and I, we have a totally open relationship. We see who we want. We don't *belong* to each other.'

There's my mother peeling earthy carrots one time and saying to a tear-stained Erin: 'When a man says he and his wife have an "open relationship", it's bollocks. He means *he* has an open relationship.' That was when Erin's heart got broken the first time.

'That's bollocks,' I say. 'Anyway, I've heard you two.'

'Heard us?'

'Making love.'

This isn't strictly true, but I've heard the odd moan at night. It could be Violeta trying to get comfortable with her swollen legs and belly. Anyway, it'll test him out. He says nothing, leans in very close and, just as gently as the other day, he kisses me.

'Don't be afraid. It's okay.' He kisses me for a very long time. 'It's okay . . .'

We kiss for ever. He pushes his hand down my spine, down, down over my buttock, slowly, slowly, lifting it, his other hand creeping underneath.

Loins: 9. Moral fibre: 1.

Chapter Seventeen

God, I'm such a different person now. Life here is so different from life with Luke. We didn't do anything too *English* when we were in Italy. It was frowned upon by him and Lotti. Sometimes I would long for cups of tea, but I could see it was easier to drink coffee or a cool drink, even if it didn't always hit the spot. When in Rome and all that. But Luke took to disowning any English habits, and if we were with people from other nationalities, he would take great pleasure in ridiculing everything English: our poor diet, our queue-forming, our hilarious politeness, our pints of beer, hopeless dress sense and drunken rabble-rousing. He would snort with laughter at any man crossing his legs and baring an inch or two of flesh between his sock and trouser hem, because he was bound to be English. He claimed – on these occasions in front of other people – to be three-quarters Irish, as if washing his hands of his Englishness, as if anyone with the misfortune to live on an island in places suffixed with 'shire' was a bit simple or uncultivated. I'm sure there's something lame about people harping on about their racial content (half Scots, a quarter African-American, an eighth Asian, 20 grams of butter, a little dash of nutmeg). Seriously, who gives a toss? Like being born in Truro and educated in a school in Somerset doesn't make him about as English as bad teeth. Sometimes Lottie's boyfriend Tom and I would make each other cups of tea, just for the hell of it, and doggedly hunt down Newcastle Brown Ale or Marmite. I reckon I came away with more Italian than Luke, because waiting at tables and busking gives you a better grasp of language – and a better selection of swear words – than teaching the future continuous tense in English, or photocopying Beatles lyrics. Why she had to go I don't know. Ah, but you do know, Luke, if you think about it. Suddenly you're not half the man you used to be. (And that makes you . . . what? Less than three eighths Irish?).

When I say Luke was my first love, it's not, strictly speaking, true. I mean, I was truly in love with the young postman for years when I was thirteen. Six months, at least. Like I would be all jittery for hours before he was due to arrive – and I only saw him on weekends, so it was quite a chunk of my free time. I wrote poems about him and letters I would never send. Or blank letters I sent to myself, so he would have to come up the long lane to our house. Three times I wrote dummy letters to made-up addresses and spent money on stamps and everything, just so I could run out after him and ask if he could put my letter in the post for me. His hands were surprisingly feminine and he had a disappointing voice close-up and smelt of chip fat, but I still adored him. I'd invested too much in him to let go.

And Luke being the first sex thing is pretty much true, but not. I mean, I had done stuff, and had stuff done to me, just not anything you'd call making love. The guys at school were always on at us to do stuff for them. They watched porn every spare moment, and even in class when they could get away with it. So they all had these warped ideas of what we liked. They thought girls got off on giving them random blow jobs, or being partially strangled and treated rough. They thought we were ever-ready for sex, and that so long as they were thinking about it, we must be, too. Like if they caught your eye when you happened to be nibbling the end of a pencil, they were convinced you were thinking it was their cock, and you were giving them a coded message and coming on to them. And they were giving us ratings all day, every day, as if we wanted to be rated on their stupid scales, as if we should be grateful for being a five rather than a three, as if we might just go up to a seven if we made the effort and tried not to gag in the bike sheds, or let them push their grubby, dirt-rimmed nails up us. So, not really making 'love'. But none of the girls escaped it, although I was wiser to their game than most. For a long time, I thought other girls did enjoy it, and there was just something I didn't get; but gradually I realised they were all thinking the same thing, all feeling inadequate and trying to be loved.

What a waste of education. Videos about putting a condom on a banana didn't teach you anything, except how to put a condom on a banana.

I know I block stuff out. It's not just me, though. The thing about stuff in the past is this: we kind of just scrub everything up. I mean, anything that doesn't quite make sense – or doesn't flow – we edit. We clean it up. We polish it, and present it as a finished piece. Like Dad's novels, like complicated dreams we recount as a simple event. And there's another reason we get rid of the messy bits – the real bits that seem too complicated or not too pretty – and that's what other people might think. Because really, it wasn't love at first sight with Luke, or even love at all. I mean, in my head it was, so I suppose that bit was real, all that love-drug madness. But it didn't last long. Sex was crap. I pretended to like it with him, because I wanted to like it. And then there are the bad things – the boys at school who groped me, who I would say I didn't give consent to; the truth is I may have fancied one or two of them. Not that I wanted to be made to do the things I did. I didn't. But I did want something romantic to happen, and *because* I wanted that, I may have led them on, and that's the bit you can't say to anyone, because that makes you into a slut. You led them on, you may even have wanted to lie in a field and be gently made love to, but you didn't reckon on their cock stuffed in your mouth without so much as a kiss first. The whole sex thing with girls is never straightforward. Consent is a tricky one. You don't always know what you're consenting to. You don't know the *quality* of the act until it's over, and too late to say 'No thanks'.

But the thing about Marcus is this: he makes me feel right, invulnerable, as if no blunder I can make will stop him thinking the best of me. He changes the colour of my thoughts. All my thoughts become the colour of that spring: bright, burgeoning, new and unstoppable.

Chapter Eighteen

How gloriously the sun does shine
How pleasant is the air
I'd rather rest on my true love's breast
Than any other where.

May erupts like the sun coming out from behind a cloud. It's as if I can feel the earth's energy, its supreme effort to better itself compared to the day before. I want to congratulate it.

During these balmy weeks of lockdown, I'm happier than I ever expected to be. Perhaps it's following so closely on all my gall and anger, but the greening of the trees puffing out all around, the heady hawthorn blossom everywhere, the full flood of unstoppable spring . . . It all conspires to lift me up, while at the same time drugging me into a helpless lovelorn stupor.

I enjoy my new role as 'tutor'. I actually might be getting somewhere with them – especially with Henna, who is so unresponsive to everyone else, except possibly Violeta, who is quite affectionate towards her. I'm given so much freedom in what I do with the girls that I barely notice the trap closing in on me.

I take them walking every morning, usually before 'lessons', to wake us all up. I find myself singing about May mornings, and surprise myself with how many songs I know. Granny Rostock used to remember any song if you gave her the first line or two.

She could remember ballads that went on forever like that. Which is strange, really, as they all seemed to begin the same, with a May morning, birds singing, and a fair maid walking. My lovely gran. She had an Irish grandmother as well as a Cornish one, so her head was full of all the folklore of these islands. I think of my dear, departed gran as I sing. I think of her neck when I did her hair in later life. Up under the back of her thinning white hair, her neck was peachy, as smooth and unwrinkled as a young girl's, and seemed as soft and innocent, too.

'Sing me a song, Gran,' I'd say as I wound her white floss around rollers.

'Give me a nibble,' she would say, when she wanted to say 'start me off' but couldn't remember how to say it. And it was easy. *As I was a-walking one morning in May* . . . And off she went, with any number of variations with that line alone, and if I varied it to *It was one bright May morning* . . . there would be another dozen possibilities. She couldn't remember my mother's name, or what the kettle was for, but she could remember the details of a fair young maid's downfall and lament the powerlessness of women through the ages. She reminded me of the gas hob at my parents' house. Some days it just wouldn't ignite, and you would press the ignition switch over and over, and just get a ticking sound. Other times it burst into a bloom of blue flame. Mum had the knack, but I never got it. Everyone found it hard to ignite Gran, in the last year or so of her life, but I knew.

They all have pretty much the same plot, these songs.

Setting: May morning; birds singing, flowers blooming.

Characters: Young maid a-walking; young man a-walking to see the flowers and take the air.

Action: A-walking. Young man spies young maid. Tempts her with promises (fine silks/satins/scarlets/beds of feather). He shags her (whether she is won round or not). He gives her a 'green gown'.

Result: She thickens round the waist/her apron strings no longer 'hang low'. Nine months later, he doesn't want to know/

says he has a wife and children three/chooses a girl with gold in store/goes off to sea.

Consequence: She laments the fate of young maids everywhere – *A warning take by me . . .*

They are all a sort of parable, but not told by Jesus. They all tell the same story: don't trust young men. A wonder Gran ever got married.

Some of them have cheery endings. A young maid falls for a man, but resists him because she is promised to another who has been gone seven long years, only to discover this is the very same man returned for her (*seven years do make great alteration*). In other songs, a maid just rejoices in her lovely young man (*I love his cheek and I love his chin / I love the furrow that he ploughs in*), presumably before the waist-thickening bit. In others, the singer laments the back-breaking work at a factory or loom, although Gran, from rural stock, knew few of these. Others relate deportation to Australia, soldiers gone to sea and never returned, lovers enlisted to fight for the king, cruel parents who don't agree with a daughter's reckless choice of lover. There are only a couple that Gran used to sing, where a young maid gets her own back on a rake. There's one with a lovely tune, and I sing it to myself while out with the girls.

> *A fine young man it was indeed*
> *He was mounted on his milk-white steed*
> *He rode, he rode and he rode all alone*
> *Until he came to Lovely Joan . . .*

'Go on,' says Daisy.

> *"Good morning to you, pretty maid,"*
> *"And twice good morning, sir," she said*
> *He tipped her a wink, and she rolled her eye*
> *Says he to himself, "I'll be there, bye and bye."*

96

'Then he took off his ring of gold
"My pretty maid, do this behold
I'd freely give it for your maidenhead."
And her cheeks they blushed like the roses red—'

'What's a maidenhead?' asks Daisy.

'It's . . .'

'It's sex,' says Henna.

Daisy frowns, uncertain.

'Do you know about sex?' I ask.

'Um . . .'

'Mimi doesn't tell us anything. But I told you, Daisy. It's when a man puts his willy into a woman, and seed comes out, and one seed grows into a baby inside the woman. Remember?'

'Oh, *that*. So he wants her to have a baby?'

'No,' I say.

'Why does he want to do it, then?' asks Daisy.

Henna shrugs.

'It feels nice,' I say.

'Not for her,' says Henna.

Now Daisy is looking confused.

'It can,' I say. 'It can feel nice for her, but he has to kiss her and cuddle her and that first. And he has to woo her.' I can see her open her mouth to ask about wooing. 'It's like . . . it's nice for her if he treats her well, sings her songs, gives her flowers, writes her poetry and stuff. Maybe if he takes her out somewhere nice like . . . the cinema.'

'But they didn't have cinemas in olden days, did they?'

'No. No, I don't think he's interested in wooing her at all. I think he just wants to whack it in and be on his way.' Moving swiftly on. 'Anyway, a maidenhead is another word for maidenhood. Like womanhood, or childhood. Before you had sex in those days you used to be called a "maiden", and afterwards, you weren't a maiden any more.'

I'm thinking of Henna saying that Mimi tells them nothing. I may be on thin ice if I explain too much.

'So then what happened in the story?'

'Well, she tricked him. As he made for the stooks of hay, she leapt on his horse and she tore away. And she doesn't give him his horse back, either.'

'Why not?' asks Daisy.

'Well, because she felt trapped. He wasn't giving her a choice, so she felt trapped. And usually in folk songs, women have no choice, but she gave herself a choice, and she escaped.'

We are out on a walk along the ridge. We've reached a spot that's become a regular viewing point, looking down on Amberside and out across the valley. I sit down with Daisy, and Henna slopes off from here, as she usually does, through the gorse bushes, to visit the grave. I sing Daisy a different song with a lovely tune, called 'Searching for Lambs', about a maid who from her home had strayed (also on a May morning), in which nothing bad happens.

'Whose grave is it?' I ask, when Henna reappears.

'My mother's,' she says, plucking at some grass.

'Hang on, so . . . Mimi isn't your mother?'

'No. She certainly isn't.'

'She *is* my mummy,' says Daisy as if I need clarification.

'And Marcus? Is he . . .?'

'No way!'

'I'm so sorry, Henna. About your mother.'

'It's my baby sister's grave, too. Mum died in childbirth.'

'The baby came out already dead,' Daisy explains.

'Oh. That's terrible. You must've been devastated, Henna. How old were you?'

'Eight.'

'Eight! To lose a mother and a sister at the same time!'

'I lost two sisters.'

'Two?'

'Bryony. I lost Bryony last year as well.'

'She ran away,' says Daisy.

'She didn't run away,' says Henna. 'She escaped.'

I remember Geoff saying 'Briny'. I measure my next words carefully, because there seems to be a lot going on here, and I want to pick up the right thread.

'Tell me about Bryony.'

Henna selects a fat blade of grass and blows on it between her thumbs to make a squawking sound. 'She was clever and funny, and Mimi and Marcus didn't like her having a life outside this place.' She squawks again. 'She knew more than either of them about saving the planet. She was like Greta Thunberg to their Donald Trump. And she showed them what hypocrites they were, with all their shite about being self-reliant. And then she got pregnant and Mimi wouldn't let her have an abortion.'

'What's that?' asks Daisy.

Henna says nothing, but takes a big, irritable breath.

So I say, 'It's like, if you find you're expecting a baby and you don't want to have a baby, then you can take a tablet to stop yourself having one. Or you can have a little operation to stop yourself having one.'

'Oh, that's good. Because I don't want a baby yet.'

'Well . . .'

'Anyway,' says Henna, 'Bryony decided she didn't want the baby, so she escaped to get an abortion. Just packed a rucksack one day and went, just before Christmas – the last day of term.'

I can see that she's welling up a bit, and having trouble keeping her lips still, squishing them this way and that. This is the most I've heard her speak since I arrived, and I don't want to stop her. We sit in silence for a while, contemplating the valley.

'Do you know where she went?'

'She wouldn't say. She said if she told me, she was afraid Mimi and Marcus would get it out of me somehow, and she didn't want to burden me with that. Said they had no right to make her keep the baby if she didn't want it. They weren't her parents or anything.'

She throws the blade of grass away. 'She's coming back for me, though. She said she'd be back for me, but it might take a while.'

I put my hand on her leg and give it a pat. 'I'm sure she will, if she said so.'

'I don't want you to go,' says Daisy, looking genuinely troubled by this news.

I pluck a fat blade, try to place it tightly between my thumbs. It seems to rest there flaccidly. I blow anyway. The sound emitted is like a long, low fart, and they both laugh. Well, Henna smiles. It's a start.

'It sounded like a fart!' Daisy is giggling. She's happy because I'm laughing, too, so she says it again, liberated. 'Fart! Fart!'

'Stop it,' says Henna. 'That's an ugly word.'

'Do you have favourite words?' I ask.

'Meander.'

'Perambulator,' I say.

'Dribble,' says Daisy, still laughing.

'That's a good one.'

'Blossom.'

'Lollop.'

'Scamper.'

'Squirrel.'

'Maidenhood.'

We see Cliff sauntering into the house by the front door, clearly ready for lunch.

'Lunch,' says Daisy, getting to her feet.

I pick up a blade of grass again.

'Wait! You have to wait for the lunch-call of the lesser-spotted Clifford bird . . .' I blow, long and low, and the crude sound rings out across the valley. I hear Daisy spluttering with giggles on one side of me, and from the other side, where Henna is, I hear a muffled laugh. I'm so pleased with myself. I'm practically Julie Andrews.

*

That was part of the problem. I was so pleased with my new-found popularity that I let Henna's word 'escape' slip away unnoticed. The very word that had been key to my song about Lovely Joan, a strange word for Henna to use. I let it get buried in the laughter, like Daisy's lions: covered over so I could no longer see it, not have to think about it. I just let it escape my notice.

Chapter Nineteen

Lunch starts off in a happy mood.

Henna: Globule. I like that word.

Me: Nimble.

Daisy: Wobbly.

Me: Elation.

Henna: Crustacean.

Daisy: Borshan.

Mimi: *What?*

Daisy: It's what you have when you don't want a baby – a borshan.

We are sitting at the long table over lunch. The look Mimi fires at Marcus is like a missile, so fast you could miss it. But I don't. The eyes focus on me next, and I look away.

'Flotilla . . .' from Henna, in an attempt to defuse things.

There's a gaping hole in the banter, during which we can all hear the washing machine on its spin cycle.

'Can anyone join in?' says Marcus. 'Parallelogram!'

But I'm sure I haven't heard the last of it, and I'm right.

She waits until I'm alone with her in the kitchen.

'So, what exactly have you been teaching the girls?'

'Oh, well . . .' What does she mean? She hasn't exactly given me a syllabus. 'Well, some maths and English. Reading for Daisy.

A bit of science – mostly environmental.' I get into my stride. 'Some art, obviously, and—'

'And sex education?'

'No, we haven't done that.'

'So why is my five-year-old talking about abortion?'

Her eyes on mine are icy. I can't hold the look, even though there's the trace of a friendly smile about her mouth. Somehow that makes it even more scary. I feel slapped. What would an experienced person do now? Mum always says this thing about small children, and I repeat it.

'Well, I've always believed that if children are old enough to ask a question, then they're old enough to get an answer.'

Mimi leans with her back against the kitchen counter, and now she strokes her chin as if making a caricature of someone considering a complex issue. 'So, let's see . . . My five-year-old asked you what abortion was, did she?'

'Well . . .' This isn't fair. *In case you hadn't noticed, Mimi, she has a sister who's thirteen.* 'Actually, yes. It must've come up in conversation.'

'In what context?'

I don't like her in this interrogator mode. I don't like this at all. 'I can't remember.'

She comes and stands against a chair, clasping the back of it. She looks at me, head tilted, and speaks slowly, as if I'm simple. 'What do you mean, you "can't remember"?'

I'm actually almost afraid of her now, and devastated. She's invited me to educate her daughters with no guidance whatsoever, and now she's being mean.

'No. Is it an issue? I'm guessing you don't believe in abortion?'

'No, we don't. It's wicked when there are so many people who can't have children.'

She's very emphatic, slicing the air with her certainty. And I'm interested in her use of 'we'.

'I'm very sorry.' I swallow. 'If . . . if there are any topics you don't want me to mention, well . . . maybe you could write them down, so that I know.'

'Well, I would think it was common sense. We don't want either of them to have any sex education, thank you.'

I'm spinning. Nothing is what I thought it was at all. Mimi seems so at one with nature, so liberal-minded. 'Well, to be fair . . .' I don't want her to hear my voice wobble. 'I mean, if they were at school, they would be learning things – in age-appropriate ways, of course.'

She seems to take the idea by a pair of tweezers and hold it up for inspection with a look of mild disgust. 'Yes, but they're not at school. We don't want them to be exposed to everything the system would like to ram down their throats.'

'Oh.' She stands up tall and turns her back to me, as if my 'oh' is a jab I've landed with a sword. Maybe this is, after all, some sort of cult. What is it in the outside world they're not allowed to be exposed to? 'So . . . um . . . what else should I—?'

'Was this Henna?' she asks, wheeling round. 'Has she been asking about abortion? She's not . . . is she?'

'No, I'm sure she's not. I don't think she has a boyfriend, does she?'

'Not if I can help it. Well, she won't be going back to that school, anyway.'

'Why not?'

'She told you about Bryony, I suppose.'

'Yes. Now I think of it, that was how the topic of abortion came up. But it's surely not fair to punish Henna for that, is it?'

Angry with me, she does something I find quite sinister: she smiles.

'Punish? Of course not. We're just going to keep her out of danger. We want to bring both of them up in a loving, stable way. None of this sex and gender and minority nonsense.'

It's a blocking smile. She is clipped, jagged. Despite the shock, I'm almost relieved to see the sharp edges of her. She wasn't quite believable before. Now she's getting interesting. Perhaps she knows about Marcus kissing me. My indignation falters. I really do want her to like me.

'Okay. Well, I'll be more careful in future. I'm sorry, Mimi.'

She smiles. 'That's okay. I'm glad we've cleared the air.'

> *My parents they have brought me up*
> *Like a small bird in a cage*
> *And now I am in child by you*
> *Not fifteen years of age.*

Chapter Twenty

'I don't even know your surname.'

'Archer. Like Cupid.'

'Marcus Archer.'

He has certainly shot an arrow into me. We're lying in his den, fingers entwined, naked and sleepy. My nose is in his turf of chest hair.

'Do you think Mimi knows? Are you sure about her not minding?'

'Of course I'm sure. Would you like me to tell her?'

'No. No need to do that.'

Why do I object, if I believe him?

Then he turns to me and says, 'Come on, then. What did poor Luke do – or not do – to deserve losing you?'

'It's not important.'

'It is to me.' He props himself up on an elbow and looks mock-serious. 'Perhaps I don't want to make the same mistake.'

'Don't you?'

Then he strokes a coil of hair off my face and looks suddenly anxious. 'No, Caitlin. I don't.'

My blood fizzes. I swallow, trying to digest his inexplicable desire for me. *Me*. He's looking at me so intently, I know I need to say something, but I can't imagine what. Not the truth. Not yet.

'You're nothing like him. I promise.'

He lies back down and breathes out. 'So . . .?' He walks his fingers over my belly. 'What was he like? What did he do wrong?'

I have to give him something. 'He was pompous. I didn't see it to start with. I thought he was clever, using all this posh vocabulary—'

'You go for that, do you? The erudite young man?'

'No.'

'Good-looking, then?'

'Not especially. He was okay.'

'Funny?'

'Not especially.'

'You're really selling him to me.' He's making comical faces now, as if he's confused, as if he's all ears for the magical secret attraction of Luke.

'He was . . . interesting. And he was interested in me.' I'm beginning to sound needy. 'He got on well with my family. Really well. He just sort of fitted in, and . . . he was heading off to Italy with Lotti and her boyfriend, like I said, and asked me to go along. So . . .'

'He represented adventure.'

'Yes. Yes, I suppose that was part of it. But I was . . . I did fall for him. Or I thought I did. I'm not sure if there's a difference.'

He waits, nodding slightly at the ceiling.

'And I guess he just started irritating me. He was teaching English at a cool place in Florence, and I was tagging along doing shit jobs. I got fed up. It's no fun being eyed up and down by men every day, all day. And cleaning hotel rooms was no better. And I don't know, somehow he didn't seem so clever any more, and I got fed up with the way he spoke. All posh, but with a little annoying quirk. Like he would say "interestud" instead of "interested", and "excitud" and "educatud".'

'Oh, like Tony Blair?'

'Who's he?'

'Oh God! I can't believe you're so young! Now I feel—'

'I'm kidding. Fucksake. I was alive when he was prime minister. Anyway, I don't know if he spoke like Luke. It was as if Luke was trying too hard. I know it sounds petty, but it got right up my nose.'

'Poor guy. Is that all?'

'No. I told you my dad had tutored him and Lotti. Well, he was forever asking about him. *Have you heard from your dad? Has he sent my work off to his agent yet? Has he heard anything? Has he said anything about me?*'

'You felt he was just using you as a connection to your father, and your father's influence?'

I didn't want Marcus reaching this conclusion. It was okay if I said it, but it was ugly hearing it from him. Because that's exactly how I felt. If only he knew the rest.

I'd broached the thing about Dad and Lotti the same evening as Erin's telephone call. Despite all my resolve to think it through, it was bubbling up out of control, and when Lotti went to the toilets in the trattoria, I followed her. I waited for her to come out of the cubicle and watched her while she washed her hands.

'You okay, Caitlin? You've been a bit funny all evening.'

'Just had a phone call, before we came out. Seems my little sister saw you and Dad.' There was silence. Just the sound of running tap-water. '*At it.*'

She froze, and stared into the mirror, then down at the taps, as if she couldn't face herself.

'What did she see?'

I raised my eyebrows. 'The works.'

'Oh God. Look . . . it isn't . . . it wasn't what you think. I wasn't trying to . . . I really do like him, your dad. I really care about him. But I didn't throw myself at him, or anything.' She looked at me, holding her wet hands helplessly in front of her as if she was about to play the piano. 'I wasn't the only one. I'm sure.'

That broken wave sucked me back to the edge of the sea so urgently that I looked down to see if my feet were sinking under wet sand. But what I saw was my brown feet in their market-stall sandals, and at right angles to them were Lotti's sparkling toenails in her open-toed red suede shoes.

'You mean . . . it's a Harvey Weinstein situation – he preys on his students with the offer of fame?'

'No. But I didn't throw myself at him. He was willing. He was really willing. Please don't tell Tom.'

True, then. True, then. True.

'Why not? He's living a lie.'

'He's not. I love him. I love Tom.'

'You betrayed him!'

'Please don't tell him.'

'And you betrayed my mum. What about her? Didn't you think about her?' I sounded shrill and scary, even to myself.

'Well, *he* didn't. He seemed to imply they had an understanding.'

'*Seemed to imply?* She cooked for you, for Chrissake. And what about Dani? She's scarred for life. How do you think she feels, seeing her dad underneath your naked arse?'

'Oh, God! Stop! We thought it was . . . we heard a door close. We thought it was Luke.'

I stood there, shaking my head, incredulous.

'Does she know? Does your mum know? Oh, God.'

'I don't know.'

I wanted to slap her. No, punch her. I wanted to take a swing at her and stop her whiney, self-justifying mouth from shaping words. Instead, I slammed into a cubicle and sank down on the seat, free to sob for the first time since I'd heard the news. She called through the door, pretending to care, and I called her a disgusting parasite. She tried to make excuses for a while longer, and then, faced with my tirade of angry wailing, she said, 'Well,

Luke's no better. He's just as much a parasite as I am. He'd do anything to get published. He's a world-class arse-licker. Why don't you shout at him?'

I don't remember how I explained away my blotchy face when I got back to the table. I know it was noticed, because Luke mentioned it when we got back. I told him exactly what had happened, and he was furious. He ranted about our bedsit, kicking furniture and slamming cupboard doors.

'She's such a sly bitch! Not that it'll make any difference, because her writing's crap. She doesn't have a clue how to edit. And she hasn't got an original idea in her head. Honestly!'

'Aren't you worried about Tom?'

'Of course. She has no scruples. The little whore. I bet she's heard something back from his agent.'

'And Mum?'

'Yes, that, too. No respect. None. God. If she's heard something back from his agent and I don't . . .'

It was pathetic. The next morning Tom asked what had happened between Lotti and me in the toilets to upset me so much.

'Didn't she tell you?'

'No.'

I'd been awake all night, trying to work out the best thing to do. Weirdly, the person I longed to ask advice from was Mum. Should Erin tell Mum? Or was Dani's instinct to keep the family together the right one? Should I tell Tom? Or would it break his heart? It would be better all round if Lotti did the telling, but how could I let him trail around after her, fitting in with her plans, loyally rejecting the advances of girls who stopped to admire him in the street, while I knew she would never do the same for him – while I knew he would make very different choices if he knew how easily she'd betrayed him? Because that's what she was doing to Tom: she was *stealing* his choices. That's what no one tells you about betrayal. It's a theft. It takes away the choices you would have made if you'd known; all the opportunities you turn down are stolen from you. And the betrayer justifies their lies by telling themselves it's a kindness to prevent a broken heart. Ha!

But my torment over what to do and Luke's ranting were interrupted by a new imperative: we had to get out of Italy. The mounting news about a coronavirus overwhelming Cremona and several other towns in the north had started to spread its panic southwards. Florence was talking about being isolated, so we were next. Luke made some phone calls and announced that we could all go and stay at a friend's flat in Avignon for now, as his friend had paid until the end of the month but was going home to England in two days' time. In an almighty rush, the four of us packed our bags and caught the train to Milan, and from there the overnight connection to Avignon.

It was a long, miserable journey of avoided glances. Everyone and his dog was getting out of Italy, and the areas between the carriages were stuffed with people sitting on their luggage. The air was thick with sweat and anxiety. It seemed a highly dubious trip to take in refuge from an airborne virus.

I tell Marcus now about the train journey. I tell him about the cockroach-infested flat we inherited from Luke's friend in Avignon.

'Oh, well, at least you had somewhere to go to. Even if it was a bit ropey.'

'Yes.'

He imagines I came home from France ahead of the others because of the cockroaches and because of Luke's irritating ways. I don't tell him about the next phone call from Erin, and what she told me about Luke. I don't tell him how Luke followed me to the train station and pleaded with me in a self-justifying way. How quite a few people were looking at us curiously. I wanted to scream at Luke in French to *fuck off*, but all I could remember was how to ask the way to the tourist information centre.

'I think he scores a few points for organisation, poor chap. He got that accommodation sorted for you.'

Yeah. Sortud.

Chapter Twenty-One

My lessons are pretty basic. I get through the Oxford Reading Tree with Daisy as slowly as I can, but she's a fast learner. I stall her by getting her to copy out the sentences herself, but it only seems to speed up her progress. Fortunately, she likes the pictures, and spends whole hours copying and colouring them. And although she's softly spoken, when she plays with her plastic animals there is much shouting and pleading going on. Zebras, elephants and horses have noisy adventures, escapes and hangings. The lion family have a fairly violent ongoing soap opera.

Call it guilt, call it ingratiating myself, but I suggest it might be a good idea for her to make something for Mimi. Daisy looks stumped.

'What does Mummy like more than anything?' I ask.

'Making posh food with pretentious names,' says Henna, without looking up from her dissertation on sustainable energy.

'How about a cookery book, then?'

Daisy nods and sets to work. Over the next few weeks, she makes a drawing of everything her mum cooks, and collects the names of the dishes. She starts with 'vanilla semifreddo with chocolate soil', because she likes the name. She works quietly.

Henna is a different matter. I started off convinced she was the sort of girl who might know the national flag of every country of the world for no good reason, but I think she may have hidden depths. She always starts off sullen, but when she gets into something she becomes diligent, sometimes even passionate. The books I brought home from our Ribley trip are a godsend. She likes the history, because we cover votes for women, the Second World War, the Holocaust. She's big on oppression and justice. I give her the copy of Anne Frank to read, I plod through the science and maths, but it's the geography that she loves the most because there are loads of topics about the environment: the rock cycle, the carbon cycle, pollution, recycling, the atmosphere and the climate. She wants to save the world, and I think she might.

I usually start the girls' morning with a walk, and what is just outside their door is breathtaking. The trees are all puffed out and the sheep on the distant hills are lazing in the shade at the edges of the fields like pale moth grubs on a green carpet. It's May, and there are so many of my grandmother's May morning songs threading through my head that I can't help singing.

> 'As I was a-walking one morning in May
> I spied a young couple a-making the hay
> And one was a fair maid and her beauty shone clear
> And the other was a soldier and a bold grenadier.'

'Then what happens?'
'Oh, the usual.'
'What's the usual?'
Better not go there.

> 'As I was a-walking one morning in May
> I spied two fine lamblets a-chomping the hay
> And one was called Freedom and her beauty shone clear . . .

'What rhymes with "clear"?'
'Ear!'
> 'And the one they called Sausage . . . had a wonky left ear.'

We make up lots of verses to many different songs, and get back to the house with lungs full of grass-scented air, giggling, and our shoes coated in pollen.

I swear, I'll be making play clothes out of curtains next.

After our walk, I usually spend the rest of the morning with them on their topics, and the afternoons lying on my bed preparing for them. I'm okay if I stay one step ahead of them all the time. Filkins has taken to keeping me company in the afternoons, and I leave the door ajar for him. He lies curled up at my feet, as tabby as a mackerel, and his presence tells me I'm accepted, even though he doesn't really belong to this household. Sometimes, if Marcus has pre-warned me to listen out for the triple whistle, I lie in wait, almost trembling, jittery with anticipation. And when it comes, Filkins stretches out his long, furry limbs, eyes me with mild exasperation, and moves into the warm patch I have left.

I'm totally amazed by what Marcus does to me. I mean, in some ways he's such a dinosaur, so insanely primitive. But when he kisses me . . . when he touches me . . . he makes Luke seem like a robot in comparison. When I hear his views on anything – pretty much anything – I just blot them out. I can't hear him say patronising things about Henna, or things about 'You ladies', or explain to me (really badly) why global warming exists. Some part of my physical, animal self, filters out this side of him. Some primeval link to my sex respects his skill at connecting me with his. This sensual side is a thing apart. A parallel path that veers off suddenly and takes me with it; that allows me to let go, to tune in to this other, ancient track. He makes love to me with kisses and raw words and gentleness, always with physical strength just below the surface: unused but on display, in case I should have any doubt that this path must become a tightrope walk, this venture into abandon. It could go either way. Carefully, with a certainty that is almost insolent, he takes his time, stroking, ever more daring, as my longing grows, until what escapes me is a roar like something from a lion on an African plain, building up from deep in the pit of my belly, unstoppable. I am the first ever woman on earth.

It's not long before I'm seeing myself in a fantasy future with Marcus. Not seriously, of course, just toying with the idea. I somehow come to replace Mimi as the prima donna of Amberside, and Marcus and I have the master bedroom as our own. We make love a lot, all over the place, and he can't live without me. He wants children with me before he's too old, but I say he must wait. We have Daisy and Henna, and they love having me around, and I make sure they get a chance to go to school, and meet other kids. And I take Henna off to see Greta Thunberg at some venue or other, and she gets to meet boys – or girls (seeing the way she looks at Violeta, that may well be where she's at). Anyway, I'm a successful parent without even having to give birth. I see my parents coming to visit but they wouldn't approve of the dope factory, so I get Marcus to give up the weed and we grow tomatoes and cabbages and shit, and have a few sheep and hens.

Mimi is really nice to me now, and shows me how to make some of her top recipes. She's definitely more cordon bleu than eco-friendly, though, and I have to stifle a smile at her preserved lemon petals and her nasturtium pesto. But she's back to Bambi's mum all over again, and I surprise myself how I can laugh with her in the kitchen and block out the fact that I'm sleeping with her man. I think it may be because she genuinely doesn't mind, but I can't bring myself to broach it.

I do have to get Mimi out of the way, though. Even though it's just an idle fantasy, it gets stuck with her in the picture, and I can't progress it. I've tried imagining a threesome with her, but it wouldn't work. Her mini-hips and lean limbs and perfect complexion don't go well on their queen-sized bed next to my beached whale of a body. And if he so much as touched her, I couldn't bear it. No, she has to go. She confesses to being not interested in men, and is happy for me to be with Marcus. But wait . . . then she'd be happy to stick around. There's nothing else for it, so I have her crushed by a passing tractor up on the road. She doesn't see it coming and it goes straight over her. No, it hits her head, and she dies instantly. I wouldn't want her to suffer. I admire Mimi, I really do. She just has no place in this fantasy and has to be removed as painlessly as possible. Marcus is devastated, but only briefly, because he gets to eat beefburgers and play computer games (we get the internet set up).

I don't really want Marcus as a lifetime partner. I really don't, but . . . but somehow . . . I don't know, this dreaming is taking over. We just go floating around in sunshine together, an utterly gorgeous couple (in my fantasies I'm always utterly gorgeous). I think I've been drugged by spring. All that wild garlic in the woods has touched my brain. I wish I could talk to Erin about Marcus. I'd like to see her face when she realised he fancied me. *Me*. Because whatever else she'd think about him (not too bright, a big kid, full of himself but harmless), she would have to admit he's pretty drop-dead gorgeous.

Living with Luke revealed my raw neediness; first to other people and then, at last, to myself. I felt like a dried-out sponge when he wasn't beside me to plump me up with his ideas. But here I am, oozing with my own ideas now. Occasionally, I try out the idea of having children with Marcus, of being pregnant with his baby. But the thought doesn't last long. It's the sort of ridiculous thing some girls do to provoke something in their lives, and I'm not going to be like that. Sometimes, out of fear of seeming boring, I do stupid things, things that aren't like me at all, in a kind of desperate attempt to find out who I am. But I'm beginning to find out now, without resorting to anything stupid.

My father's search for an identity, according to Mum, all stems from being adopted. He feels like an alien who doesn't know where he belongs. I always found this a bit hard to swallow: he belongs with us, doesn't he? Aren't we good enough? His drinking, I can see now, is a thirst for his sense of self. We have all been afraid of his drinking, growing up, and learnt early on that covering for him if we found his secret hiding places – a bottle of Jameson's under the cistern lid, a few bottles of wine in the spare tyre-well of the car – was not doing him any favours, however much we longed to please him. We saw that to help him in his pursuit of alcohol just ended up with more yearning. His drinking was an endless sadness. Unlike other people we knew – Mum, Erin, our neighbours, our Uncle Aaron – drinking did not make him amusing or just a little reckless. Drink makes our dad change personality, and you never know which one you'll get. Sometimes he will murmur his sorrow and you can almost comfort him; other times he hisses out pure venom like a cornered animal. At these times he might look at you as though he has no idea who you are, or as if you are his arch-enemy and not to be trusted, and that is where our own family terror lies.

The thing is, he can create all these amazing characters, (*nuanced, multi-faceted*, characters that *breathe*, the reviewers say), and yet he can't do the same for his birth parents. As far as he's concerned, his father must be a cardboard cut-out psychopath, having got a young girl pregnant outside marriage, (and therefore he must've coerced her, or forced her, and therefore clearly he was a rapist), and his young mother – however much of a victim she was – and he does like to see her as an innocent victim, with no sexual desire whatsoever, for some reason – clearly took one look at him at birth and saw the psychopath who had raped her and wanted nothing to do with his baby. If she had a warm heart, it turned cold at first sight and she rejected him. For all his talent, he can only come up with clichés for his unknown parents. It becomes exhausting trying to suggest anything else to him.

Maybe his books give him a form of identity. Perhaps he hopes to see something of himself emerging from the pages that people will comment on, and tell him what they see. Perhaps he hopes to see himself in the adulation of his students, like Luke and Lotti. I think Mum understands that, and gives him a lot of leeway. But he must know there is nothing authentic to be had there. He told us once, at the family table, that he feels a fraud when his students sit there open-mouthed in wonder at his most trivial of anecdotes, so he must know that they have no idea who he is. And maybe that's why he feels comfortable in the role: because deep down he finds himself to be a fraud, or at least, he mistakes his lack of identity for a false one.

Chapter Twenty-Two

I wake up one Saturday to the birds singing like mad and a pain running through me. The sun is slicing through the gap in the curtains, hitting the wall opposite like a magic door. I crawl out of bed to the bathroom, and my chest starts aching along with my belly. I must be going down with something. What if it's the virus? I've no way of contacting home.

I've asked Marcus a few times now about the charger. He promised we could go to a big supermarket and see about getting one. I've even suggested he could ask Joe to buy one online for me. I've reminded him so many times now, I think I might ask Mimi about it instead. I could ask her for the postcode here, too, because I might try writing. Not that I have anything to say to Mum – I've been trying to block it all out – but I would like to hear if she knows about Dad yet and what she has to say. And as for Dad . . . Maybe it's fairer to let him put it in writing. Not that I want to be fair, but I'm not sure I could even speak to him on the phone. I'd like to hear his take on it, though.

Ow. My chest hurts. I find Mimi in the living room and tell her I think my period is about to start. She frowns.

'Well, it's not impossible. People do get little bleeds when they change pill. It's a different level of oestrogen, perhaps. And what I've given you is a continuous mini-pill. You really do have to take it at the same time each day.'

I have the distinct sense that the pieces of furniture – the sofas, the low tables, one or two of the older floor cushions – are exchanging knowing looks, and that whenever I catch them in the act, they glance away.

'Do you have some painkillers?' I ask. 'Paracetamol or anything?'

'Of course.'

I follow her across the hallway, through the dining room and into the kitchen. She indicates for me to sit at the table, cuts some bread from a loaf and pushes it in front of me with the jam.

'Where is it hurting exactly?'

'Actually, my breasts are hurting. And I think there may be a lump. I don't know. I'm sure it'll go.'

She must think I'm a hypochondriac. She raises her eyebrows and puts her head on one side.

'Want me to do a quick check?'

I wasn't expecting that. She goes to a cupboard and pops some painkillers from their blisters. She puts them on the table in front of me.

'Take these, and when you're ready, just pop upstairs to my room and take your top off.'

She looks me straight in the eye, and I look away. She knows. She knows about me and Marcus, and she minds. She wants to see my body. She wants to see what all the fuss is about.

'No, it's okay. I'll be fine.'

'I am a qualified doctor, you know. I've seen it all before.' She puts her hand on mine as I swallow the second tablet. I try not to think she may have poisoned me. 'Come on – it'll put your mind at rest.'

She replaces the bread knife in the knife rack. She has already decided this will be her weapon of choice, and she'll examine me now to work out the best ribs to stick it between for my heart.

I follow her meekly up the stairs to her bedroom. Their bedroom. It is a celebration of them: their colours, their core values. It smells of sandalwood or something, and all around are batiks and tapestries on the walls in warm reds and ochres. The bed is huge.

Good. They are not plastered together all the time. But the bed is clearly centre-stage, an important statement of their union, the place where they come together. *Bad.* I try to work out which side he sleeps on, but she pats the bed that they share and turns away to close the door as I take off my T-shirt and bra. She turns back and looks at me, steadily in the eyes.

'That's it. Lie back and put your arms behind your head.' She rubs her hands together and looks down at my breasts. She places a hand steadily on the side of one breast, then palpates the other side of it. She studies them both carefully, pressing them with the flat of her fingers, then again in small circular motions. She feels around my nipples, and as she does, she looks at me, and I have to stare up at the ceiling. 'Any pain here . . .? Here . . .?'

'Just there.'

'Show me.'

She takes my wrist and guides me. Her skin is cool. I know mine is hot. There is sweat prickling on my scalp and under my arms.

'I think that's normal lumpiness. Breast tissue can be quite lumpy. It's all movable. There's nothing static here – nothing I'm worried about.'

'Good.' I start to sit up, swinging my legs over the side of the bed. It's a patchwork of reds: scarlet, ox-blood, claret, in a variety of shapes and patterns.

'Wait,' she says, pushing me back gently, coolly. 'I just need to look under your arms.'

I lie back, damp with perspiration as she prods into my gross armpits. This time her face is right over me and I can't miss the eyes on mine, unblinking, intense.

'Okay?'

'Mmm.'

'You're nervous.'

'No.'

She slides her gaze down my body, slides her hand down over

it, too, gently towards my waistband. It feels like a caress.

'Any pains here?' she asks, slipping her fingers ever so slightly under the denim fabric.

'The usual. I'll be fine. I can feel those painkillers working already.'

'Great.' She sits back. 'Pop your things back on. Like I say, I'm not worried about anything.'

Isn't she? She's watching me stand and fumble with my bra, sitting on the bed and staring at the body her husband touches almost every day, watching my muffin-top flesh spill over the top of my jeans. Of course she's not worried. At least, not about the competition. She's thinking *why*? Or maybe she's sizing me up for a threesome? More than once it has occurred to me that they're playing some hugely complex game with me, and that if I watch closely enough, I might eventually learn the rules.

As I reach the door, she says from the bed, 'We need to get you some new clothes, don't we?' I turn, not sure whether this is an insult or a kindness. 'The weather's getting warmer. You can't go round in the same old jeans all the time.' She stares at me from the bed, assessing my clothes size, perhaps. 'I'll sort some stuff out – if you don't mind second-hand.'

'No. Um. I don't think your stuff would fit me.'

'Oh, I don't mean my stuff necessarily. There's a whole wardrobe of clothes in the barn that various girls have left.'

'Girls?'

'Vulnerable women – like Violeta. Over the years they've left heaps of clothes. Some of it's maternity wear, but you can sort through it. I'll give you a key. You can help yourself. The first big cupboard on the right as you go in.'

'Okay.' *Maternity wear.* 'Thanks.'

If only she wasn't so *good*. If only I wasn't such a *shit*. She follows me down the stairs. I somehow want to shake her off, and I can hear the girls playing with the lambs outside, so I head for the front door.

'You're mixed-race,' she says behind me, 'aren't you?' The way she says it, it's like something I haven't owned up to, some sort of misdeed on my part.

I turn to face her. 'Possibly,' I say, trying to contain my outrage at the look on her face. '*Probably*. Who knows?' I don't think I've ever considered it much, it being such a tenuous link. When I was little, relatives and friends would pat my springy hair as if I were an interesting breed of dog. I can't say it's ever played a significant part in my life. 'Does that matter?'

She narrows her eyes at me, troubled, like she disapproves, although whether at my attitude or my race it isn't clear.

'Of course not. Not at all. But didn't you say your family was Cornish on both sides?'

'My dad's adopted. His birth mum was Cornish, but we don't know anything about his bio-dad. Probably mixed-race.'

She lets out a slight sigh. 'You didn't say.'

She really does make it sound like something I should have confessed to earlier. Later, I will think of all sorts of smart things I should've said to her at this point, but now I just say, 'I didn't realise it mattered.'

'It doesn't.'

But there's another little sigh, which for all the world sounds tinged with disappointment.

Oh was it by a black man got or was it by a brown?
Or was it by a ploughing lad a-ploughing up and down
That gave to you the baby that you wear as your new gown
That you've rolled up all underneath your apron?

I head to the door again, wishing more than ever that I could speak to my sister. There's a lump in my throat the size of an apple. Then I remember.

'Could I have the full address of this place? I'd like to write a letter.'

'A letter? Of course. It's just Amberside, Ribley, Gloucestershire.'

'But what's the postcode?'

She goes into the kitchen. I follow her. She takes a piece of paper from a notepad and jots it down for me, her writing shapely but controlled – even at speed. I stuff it into the pocket of my jeans, and try to shake off the feeling that she was reluctant to give it to me.

Chapter Twenty-Three

I copy out the address carefully on some lined paper from Henna's school book. Then I write:

Dear Erin,

Bet you never thought I'd write an actual letter! This is going to be short, but it's just to tell you I'm fine. I'm actually really happy here. If it weren't for what's happening chez vous it would be idyllic. They're a bit hippy-dippy so I'm eating lots of quinoa and Quorn cutlets and the like (<u>I know!</u>). Oh, and they also have kombucha (a lump of slime they make tea out of that looks like someone's liver). They're very environmentally friendly (you'd approve) and old-fashioned. They don't even believe in the internet (!!!!!!!!!) and have no mobile phones, but there is a phone signal up on the ridge. The reason I'm writing is because I've lost my charger, and of course they don't have one, and we're in the middle of nowhere. The house landline number is above, but it's not very private. Everyone can hear what you say, so I can't talk about them on it. Also, I can't phone you easily as it's a payphone and it's hard to get the coins.

So please, please, please buy me an iPhone charger online and have it sent direct to the above address. And also, please write to me and let me know what's happening with Mum and Dad – and Dani, of course. I really want to know. And tell Mum I'm safe and everything's okay.

The girls here are really nice: Henna (13) and Daisy (5) –
she's a hoot. I'm sort of their governess, like Jane Eyre. Only
Mr Rochester's wife isn't in the attic – she's slim and clever and
beautiful. She should be in the attic. I'm working on it.

Really miss you,
Write soon and tell me your news,
Caitlin xxxxxxxxx!

I seal it, but I have no stamp. The stamps in my purse are Italian.

Outside, Violeta is holding one of the lambs. The girls are chatting and laughing, and it's the first time I've seen Henna looking really happy. Her face is alight with smiles, relaxed and showing teeth I've rarely seen. Violeta is very pregnant now, and although she's radiant, holding Henna's lamb, a few strands of her dark hair tumbling out of her hair clasp and surrounding her pretty face, she does seem tired. I've asked her a few times if I can help her with tasks, but she always says no, it's what she does.

'Look at Sausage, Caitlin,' calls Daisy. 'She's jumping all over the place. Isn't she stupid? Stupid Sausage!'

Luke made me feel stupid.

'Stupid's a bit harsh, isn't it? Silly or daft, maybe. That's a bit more affectionate.'

She frowns, considering this, then smiles. 'She's a daft Sausage. And I love her. Daft Sausage.'

I tell them I'm just off to stretch my legs in the woods, if anyone fancies coming.

'I'm good,' says Henna.

'Me, too.'

Daisy likes to do whatever Henna does, keen always to stay in her good books. But they're having fun, and it's a Saturday, and I'm quite pleased to be walking on my own, because I have a plan.

I climb up the path through the woods until I come to the little parking area. There's a grey letterbox on a pole, which I imagine serves Amberside. I must ask to get hold of a key for it. But this isn't why I've come here. I take a few steps further up the track so that I can see Joe's cottage. There are two cars in the far driveway, so I guess one is his and the other belongs to the mysterious Cal. I glance up at the bedroom windows, and see the same dark figure in the right-hand one, and I immediately look away, tempted to turn tail. What if Joe isn't in, has gone for a walk, and I am left to deal with Cal on my own?

Filkins is on the wall, grooming himself. I go to stroke him, thankful for something to do while I pluck up courage to enact my plan. I daren't look up again at the bedroom windows, but after a while I have the distinct sense of being watched.

The path I'm standing on overlooks the side of the house, but there is a little rusty gate in the garden wall, leading across a garden to the front door, which is on the left, next to two cars. After I've pampered Filkins all I can, scratching his head, rubbing under his chin and his cheeks, he stretches out along the top of the warm stone and flops on to his side, baring his tummy for me. I know if I attempt to stroke it, he'll bat my hands away, so I take a deep breath and open the gate. It sobs on its hinges, and I cringe, hoping the stranger's eyes won't be alerted by my approach.

The door is yellow and has clearly been painted over several times, with the edges of previous peeling layers standing out like countries on a map. I ring the bell, which possibly makes a distant sound somewhere in the house, although it's not certain. I wait, awkwardly, looking down at the mat on the doorstep which says 'Come Back With A Warrant'. Someone here has a sense of humour, anyway – presumably Joe.

I hear a door open inside as music – some sort of heavy metal – gets louder. Then the yellow door swings open and there is Joe in grey joggers, dishevelled, spliff in hand.

'Um. Hello. I—'

'Oh, hell-*o* . . .' He clearly can't remember my name. Not

surprising, considering the state he was in last time I saw him.

'Caitlin,' I supply.

'Sorry, Caitlin. Of course. I think I was out of my head when we met. You're at Marcus and Mimi's, right?'

'Yeah. Um . . . I'm sorry to bother you, only I was just passing and I wondered if you had a spare phone charger I could borrow? Or if I could leave my phone here to get it charged? Only I've lost my charger and I can't make any calls.'

He looks at me curiously. 'Right. I'm just charging mine in the kitchen, but it should be done by now . . .'

'Oh, I don't want to—'

There's a voice from upstairs: 'I have a phone charger! Joe? I have a—'

'Nah, I'm on it, mate!' He indicates behind him with his head. 'Cal. He'd need rubber gloves and a ten-foot pincer to touch anything of yours.' He laughs and puts his hand out for my phone. 'An iPhone. No probs. I'll charge it right away, Caitlin. Come back around . . . say . . . after lunch? It'll be all done. No later than 3.30, mind. My shift starts at four.'

'Thank you.'

'You should wear gloves,' says the voice behind Joe. 'Now she'll have been exposed to any virus you might be carrying.'

'God, Cal, what are you like?' Joe looks at me with mock horror. 'Such a big girl's blouse.' I open my mouth to defend the voice from the vile expression, but only see two bare feet on the stairs, and the door is already closing. 'See you later!'

I stand in a cloud of weed smoke, bemused and elated. Soon I can ring Erin and find out what on earth is going on at home.

Chapter Twenty-Four

When I get back to Amberside, the girls are no longer outdoors with the lambs. In the kitchen I find Marcus scavenging some bread and jam.

'You won't want your lunch,' I tell him.

He gives me a woeful look and reaches out to grab me. 'A man gets hungry.' He looks around for onlookers, then buries his face in my breasts, the ones Mimi examined less than an hour ago, the ones she wasn't worried about. 'Fancy a post-prandial three whistles? Say, around two o'clock?'

'Can we make it three? I've managed to get my phone on charge, and I really need to phone home as soon as I can.'

'*What?*' He seems taken aback. 'What do you mean?'

'There's stuff going on at home. I just need to check things are okay. Let them know I'm okay, and—'

'No, I mean, where did you find a charger?'

'Joe's.'

'What?'

'Don't look so surprised. I haven't *found* a charger. He's just charging it for me. And I have to pick it up after lunch, so three o'clock would be better for me. If that's okay?'

He looks devastated, almost angry. 'What have I told you about going up there?'

'Nothing.'

'You can't . . . you can't visit other people's houses. There's a pandemic on, you know. It's not safe to visit other people's houses. And Joe's a policeman. He comes into contact with all sorts of people. You could be putting the girls at risk, have you thought of that?'

'I didn't go in. I didn't touch him.'

He places his two hands down on the kitchen table quite heavily, as if he's about to spring into action, as if something must be done.

'Caitlin! Caitlin! We can get you a charger, for God's sake.'

'But you haven't. You keep saying that, but you haven't, and I need to make a call as soon as possible.'

'We'll get a charger this afternoon, okay? I've got to get some shopping in at some point anyway. Come and find me when you're done.' His voice softens slightly. 'We'll go on the hunt for one, you and me.'

Fucksake. Now he tells me.

'Okay. Great. But I have to make a call first.'

'What's so special about this call? Aren't you happy here?'

'Of *course* I'm happy. I love it here. I just need to hear their news.'

'Not checking up on lover boy, then?'

'No.' He can be quite childish sometimes, but the hint of jealousy is almost endearing. 'Nothing to do with Luke.'

Although, actually, that isn't strictly speaking true. It has a lot to do with Luke.

When Erin rang me that second time, she told me something else, something far worse, about our little sister. It was after we got to Avignon. Luke, Lotti and Tom were in the living room, discussing what to eat. I was sitting on the lid of the toilet, having taken the phone into the bathroom.

'Listen, Caitlin, I have to talk to you. When I rang you last time, I didn't tell you everything. I was going to spare you, but I think you need to know.' I looked at the overflowing bathroom bin and felt my stomach churn. 'Dani's been in a mess the last few days – I mean, a total mess. I had to wheedle that stuff about Dad and Lotti out of her – because obviously she was worried about Mum, and about Mum and Dad splitting up – but this, I mean, she just blurted it out in a kind of volley of tears when Mum was out shopping. I honestly . . . I don't really know . . .'

'Tell me.'

'Well, it was that time when Lotti was having teacakes with us. I don't know if you remember . . .? You know, last summer when . . .'

I did.

'Mum and her were having a laugh – we all were, and then Dani got up all poker-faced and walked out. Can you remember?'

I did remember. I remembered because it was so unlike Dani. She was never a moody teenager like me. She seemed to be grown-up before her time. It was as if hormones had passed her by: no acne, no mood swings, no drugs or alcohol to speak of. But I do remember that afternoon. And I asked her later what had got into her, and she said she was just tired of everyone being in the house. She couldn't wait for the 'visitors' to be gone, and have things back to normal. To be honest, I was almost relieved that she had shown us a little corner of her irritation. I could never stand her being perfect.

'You still there, Caitlin?'

'Yes.'

'Okay. Well, anyway, she went to the barn to see Dad, knowing Lotti wasn't with him. She said she wasn't sure what she was going to say to him, but she had a vague idea about challenging him, telling him she'd seen him with Lotti. Because, she said, it wasn't fair that the burden of telling Mum rested on her shoulders. This was all last summer, of course. Poor Dani. She's been through hell on her own for months before telling anyone.'

'And . . .?'

'Well, Dad wasn't in the barn when she got there, or at least he

132

wasn't in the main bit, but she thought she could hear someone. So she went to one of the rooms and pushed the door ajar, and she saw him, standing there.'

'So . . .?'

'He was standing there, with his back to her, gazing out of the window and moaning. And then she saw a hand clutching his hip, and realised that Luke was hidden from view, but on his knees in front of him.'

'*What?*' Even as she told me this, I could hear Luke laughing in the living room. I sat on the toilet lid and watched a cockroach crawl over the roll of toilet paper on the floor. My head swam. 'You can't mean . . .?'

'Oh, God, Caitlin, I wish I didn't have to tell you this, with no one there to support you. Just come home. Just get yourself back here while the trains are still running. Get a flight. I'll pay. Just get back.'

'But Luke isn't into men. I mean, he's not. I'd know, wouldn't I?'

'I don't know. But our *father*! I'd never have thought . . . not in a million years.'

'*Fucksake!* Dad!' I sank onto the floor, pushing my palm into my forehead, hard. 'This isn't true!'

'I know. I can't believe it.'

'No!' I was crying then. 'If it's true, I don't know who he is! Can he really be so fucking self-indulgent? Seems he never turns down a chance for a bit of pleasure.'

'Oh, Caitlin.'

'I feel sick.'

'Me too. That's how Dani felt as well. She's kept it in all these months. Buried it somewhere. I mean, her grades have been going down at school, and she's been more withdrawn and tetchy, but it's the first she's ever spoken of it.'

'Has she told anyone else? Anyone at all?'

'No. That's what worries me. I mean, I'm glad she hasn't, for Mum's sake. But for her—'

'Jesus, has he *no self-control*?'

'None, it would seem. Mum can't possibly stay married to him. What do you think?'

But I was too busy sobbing, hyperventilating, trying to order my thoughts. Within two days, I had learnt that my father was not only unfaithful to my mother, but that it was with two different people, of two different genders, within a couple of days. And one was my boyfriend. And it was one thing struggling to get a handle on Dad – but Luke? I already didn't care what his sexual tendencies were, because I knew, straight away, that he had betrayed me in the worst way possible. If he had been dishonest about his sexuality, he had been even more dishonest about his motives. They were clear: A literary agent for a blow job. *As if.* And having me as a girlfriend was just his way of staying in touch with the famous author. Poor, grovelling Luke – he had no idea it didn't work like that. Dad could take all the bribes you could heap on him – and enjoy them all – but he couldn't get your book published for you. He couldn't even get his own books published any more, and he had real talent, and all the connections.

'Caitie, I'm sorry. I'm so sorry. Just get yourself home . . . Okay?'

'Yeah.'

I wiped my tears and snot on the back of my hand, because I couldn't bear to touch the toilet paper. The cockroach scuttled along the skirting board and disappeared into the tiniest crack. Cunning little bastard.

Chapter Twenty-Five

When I find the girls, they have the television on and balls of wool and knitting needles all over the floor. They tell me they found this hoard of wool in a cupboard and Mimi told them they could have it: it belonged to various women in the house who have been and gone. Henna has a vague memory of knitting, but can't remember how to cast on, and Daisy has never been taught the stitches at all. I spend the rest of the morning showing them what to do, and we decide we'll all make useful rectangles. Daisy is embarking on a skinny pink scarf for Violeta's baby (I don't tell her this would be a health hazard) and Henna is going for a jumper in baby blue: a rectangle for the front, another for the back and two for the sleeves. While they settle into it, I spend the time before lunch pairing mismatched needles, rewinding wool from a tangled mess of five different colours, and wondering what Erin is going to tell me by letter about the state of our little sister, and of our parents' marriage.

God, I can't bear to think what Mum's going through right now, and how little I've thought about her this year; how I tried to avoid talking to her when I got back to England and she kept texting me. The thing that makes me feel really bad is that I know Mum would give her right arm for me. I mean, she really would. And she'd give another arm for Dani, and a leg for Erin. And another leg for Dad. In fact, she'd cheerfully become a stump for all of us. It sets such a high bar on selflessness, sometimes I think

I might as well give up now. Well, actually I probably never tried, being the selfish loser I am, but aren't you supposed to learn from your mother?

Erin reckons that's the whole problem. Silencing their own needs is something that women pass down the generations. She sees Granny Rostock as having passed on to Mum the importance of ironing handkerchiefs and darning socks and hand-turning shirt collars and embroidery and feeding every individual who crosses her path, even if it means not eating herself. I sort of get what Erin means. Mealtimes are all about mothers feeding themselves last, or not at all. And now I think of it, no matter how important Mum tells us a good education is, no matter how much she bangs on about the sisterhood and women's rights, she somehow demonstrates her own self-neglect every single day.

And we are left guessing at her real needs, the same way she was left guessing at her mother's needs, because they have never been voiced. They pass on their muteness and self-neglect to their daughters.

Well, I won't ever be like that. No fear. I don't even like children. (I guess Daisy and Henna are okay.) And you won't catch me giving some greedy little screamer my piece of the pie. Let alone an arm. Still, this image of Mum is a hard one to push out of my head now, and it bothers me.

Mum didn't want me to go to Italy. She didn't say that, of course, just kept coming up with things like, What do you really know about Luke and Lotti? Won't you feel a bit too dependent on them? Even Dad seemed to think I would be better applying to uni and not taking a year off travelling, even though he'd always recommended it. But Mum kept on and on, while all the time saying it was entirely my decision, of course. She never actually stops us from doing anything, just lays her concerns under our feet for us to trip over. Yeah, right. I told her to fuck off. Or to leave me the fuck alone, or something. There was a *fuck* involved somewhere. She seemed really hurt; and I thought, *Good*.

Henna is chuntering away about history. 'History books tend to just tell you about wars, like men's violence to each other, but do you realise it's mostly women who've driven the economy of every country? Women who have enabled everything to happen? With so-called simple domestic skills like this. Knitting. So, like the Viking sail? It was women who carded all the matted wool, made the thread, wove the fabric. It would take one woman *three years* or something just to weave the material, let alone all the processing of the wool and spinning it into yarn and everything. Imagine. And then there was all the stitching by hand. It really makes you think.'

'I wouldn't want to spend three years making a sail,' says Daisy. 'I'd be . . . *eight* when I finished it.'

I look at the stitches in my knitting. What an amazing skill knitting is. I've forgotten how to do many of the intricate patterns with stitches that my gran taught me, but even this simple plain-and-purl knitting is a marvel. I picture the favourite Fair-Isle jumper she knitted me: grey with a delicate pattern of dark green, white and black. It was a mathematical triumph. My gran, who left school at fourteen, held all those equations in her head. And I left it in Avignon! I took the jumper with me to Florence, packed it in my suitcase for France, and then left most of my stuff in a mad hurry to get away from Luke. It must be there somewhere, in that cockroach-infested flat. I hope Lotti remembered to pack it when they came home – if they made it home. It means I'll have to contact her again. But I can't bear to think of her wearing that jumper, each stitch a moment of my gran's precious life.

I miss Mum and my sisters, annoying though they can be. At least Mum tried to warn us about men. She tried, in her own dippy way, to make us strong women. She just hasn't got the role model thing worked out.

I remember one morning last summer when I started seeing Luke. Dad was out – or crashed out somewhere – and Erin swept into the kitchen in mock horror.

'Oh. My. God. Now I've seen it all!'

Mum barely raised an eyebrow, and I didn't even look up from my porridge.

Dani muttered, 'And what's that?'

'Caitlin's subjugation to the male sex.' She delivered this with irritating satisfaction.

'What the . . .?' She had my attention then.

'Just happened to be passing your room when you were preening in front of the mirror, and saw your new little landing strip.'

'Fuck off!'

'Yes, folks, Caitlin is shaving her pubes for a guy!'

'You can talk.'

'Yes, I can. I've gone for the full hearth rug, now. Matt prefers me *au naturel*.'

'Oh, good God,' said Mum, 'He *prefers* you . . .? How very liberated.'

She sighed and leaned her forehead melodramatically on the fridge door to show her exasperation with our mini-sisterhood, sending a pasty fridge magnet flying to the floor, along with a list for tomorrow's Tesco shop.

'Do you mind?' Dani frowned. 'Less muff-talk. I'm trying to eat my muesli here.'

'Where's Dad?' I could see Erin wanted to deflect from her now less-than-feminist pelt.

Mum: He's resting.

Erin: Says the super-feminist who's doing his shopping later.

Mum: At least I have always had a full forest. And I don't care whether he approves or not. But he always has.

Dani: Oh, my God.

Erin: But look what you put up with. He's such a self-indulgent Celt!

This was actually Mum's affectionate term for Dad, when she lost patience with him: 'You self-indulgent Celt!' Which always surprised me, because she herself was prouder of her Celtic roots than any of us. But now I think of it, perhaps it wasn't 'Celt' she said – or meant – after all.

In recent months, Luke used to make a list of my faults and fire them at me when he was fed up. He hadn't moved on from childhood, and like a child, he failed to see his own faults, only things that irritated him in other people. Things about me that irritated him most included my inability to read classical music, my lack of interest in 'real' literature, my love of English tea, cheap bangles, sandals and incense sticks, my propensity to giggle at pompous phrases, my propensity to giggle, my lopsided ears, my worn toothbrush (he had an electric one with replaceable heads), my slippers, my coloured hair-grips, my flaking toenail paint, my raspy singing, my hideous taste in clothes, my inability to reach a top C or to look good in shorts, my predilection for Marmite, my tendency to get bitten more than him by Florentine mosquitoes, my hairbrush. Especially my hairbrush, which had the cheek to contain hair. And don't get me started on medieval paintings. Jesus wept. Or would've done if he'd heard Luke rant on about what I didn't know about the Medicis or chiaroscuro or medieval iconography.

Mum would be appalled if she knew, and I really don't want to tell her. Luke had only chosen me because he wanted to get pally with my dad, and I may have known it, at some level, from the beginning. I think she did. And I probably guessed, too, that Dad thought he was a total dick, but I suppressed that inconvenient thought, too. It didn't stop me following Luke around and craving his approval, mortified if I didn't live up to his high but very reasonable standards. I cringe now to think I shaved my pubic hair for him. It wasn't worth the itch. Or, frankly, the sex. I might've had more fun with his toothbrush; (I might've reached a top C). At least I would've been able to turn it on.

Chapter Twenty-Six

When I reach the cottage again, it is just after two. The door opens before I get a chance to ring the doorbell. Joe beams at me.

'Hi! Caitlin! Hi!' Then he sweeps his hand through his hair and looks around, bewildered. 'The phone!'

'Yes.'

'Yeah. The phone. Thing is . . . thing is, it's gone.'

'What do you mean?'

He looks at me helplessly. 'I had it here – right here – charging in the hallway,' he points to a plug socket with a charger in it, like a mouse that's got stuck in the wall, its long white tail trailing limply on the hall carpet, 'and now it's disappeared.' He looks puzzled and exasperated.

'Well . . . has anyone been here?'

'No one.'

'Have you asked your housemate?'

'First thing I did when I saw it was missing.'

'Shit.'

'My thoughts exactly.'

'I don't understand. How can this have happened?'

He shrugs dramatically. 'Look, I don't know. We don't always lock the doors when we're in. It would be easy for someone to kinda walk in and take it.'

'Do you often have burglars out here? I mean, I've been here six weeks and I don't think I've ever seen a living soul.' And I don't say what I'm thinking, which is that I've never heard of a policeman who doesn't lock his doors.

Joe seems to take pity on my growing agitation.

'Listen,' he whispers, pulling the door to behind him and beckoning me away from the house. 'I hate to say this, Caitlin, but Cal can be a bit . . . I mean . . . he's a bit obsessive about data and stuff.'

'You think he's nicked it? Why on earth . . .?'

'I know, I know, man. It's weird. But trust me, if he's got it, I'll find it.' I hold my head in my hands, desperate now. He can't possibly understand how important this is. I'm irritated by how casual he's being about it, standing there now with his hands on his hips. 'Okay? Okay, Caitlin? Look, I'm gutted. But I'll do my best, okay?'

He goes back in the house and closes the door behind him, and I'm left staring at the mat which tells me to come back with a warrant. Maybe I will.

Chapter Twenty-Seven

Jesus! I rush back down through the woodland path, almost growling with rage. I don't trust Joe. He's about as bent as a copper can be. If he even is one. I make a plan in my fury to go back up there at 3.30, as soon as he's gone, and question this weird Cal. And I'm not going to leave without my phone.

I find Marcus in the kitchen with Mimi. They have their heads together over a sheet of paper.

'Ah, the very person. We've done the shopping list. Ready for our little jaunt into Cheltenham Waitrose?'

'I'm not coming.'

'Why ever not?'

I sigh. 'Because Joe doesn't have the phone. He's lost it.'

'That'll be Cal,' says Mimi.

'I'd say so,' Marcus agrees.

'*Fucksake!*' I'm so angry that I shout it.

'Caitlin, please,' says Mimi in her best mother-of-Bambi calm. 'The girls might hear.'

'What do you mean, "That'll be Cal"? What does that even mean? Is he some kind of monster or something? A kleptomaniac now, as well?'

They exchange looks. Marcus sighs. 'We think he's linked to GCHQ. He's got something to do with intelligence. We don't need any snooping. You know what goes on here.' I sigh, heavily. 'Seriously, Caitlin. You need to keep away from him.'

'Why would he be interested in *me*?'

'It's us.'

'Isn't that a bit paranoid? I mean, I'm sure he's got better things to worry about than your weed farm.'

Unless, of course, there's something they're not telling me. I see them exchange looks.

'Haven't you told her?'

'I'll explain,' says Mimi. Now I'm all ears. 'You're quite right – a dope farm is hardly a matter of national importance, but there are other things, and we can't afford to have anything tweak the interest of . . . the authorities. Whoever they may be.' She is very calm, as usual, and I am beginning to resent the tone she seems to take with me, as if she shouldn't have to be telling me to wear my tie on the way to school. 'What I do here is controversial. You see, Suze's partner, Arrow, is involved in business which brings him into contact with what you might call people traffickers.' I remember Suze as the gravelly voiced woman who was here on the night I arrived. 'He himself is not involved, but he does see many girls who come here from Eastern Europe and find themselves tricked by the promise of work and accommodation and forced into the sex trade. They're not paid. They have to give all their money to their "employers" and when they get pregnant, they're on the street with no money, no passport.'

'Why do they let them get pregnant, if they're working?'

'They don't. They give them contraceptives, but many of the girls don't believe in contraception. It's against their religion. Or else they think they're being drugged. Either way, some of them end up here. Suze and Arrow rescue them, and I take them in. They get free board, and when they want to go, I give them a lump sum of money in lieu of wages, which is big enough to start again, to get back home, to take a college course, whatever.'

I feel chastened, as she knew I would. It's a subtle tugging of the rug from under me. See how good I am, Caitlin. See how pointlessly angry you are, how selfish, how indulgent, how ignorant.

Fucksake. She's doing all this for the sisterhood, and I'm screwing her man. I hate myself.

'Violeta? Is she one of them?'

Mimi nods. Marcus puts a hand over Mimi's. 'This work means a lot to Mimi.'

God, it's like the two of them are ganging up on me. 'So why don't you just tell the police?'

'It's not that simple,' says Mimi. 'We often need to get them false passports, for one thing – that's Arrow's area of expertise. And if we bring the police attention anywhere near here, with the farm and so on, that's Marcus's business down the drain. And that's what finances all the help we can offer.'

Marcus's *illegal* business. She fails to mention Marcus would end up in prison for running this place, no doubt. She's managed to make it all sound like some sort of Red Nose Day charity. Sex slaves, false passports . . . What have I got myself into here? It's no wonder they're jittery about Cal. No wonder they foster their friendship with a bent policeman.

'So,' says Marcus, 'are you with us? Or against us?'

He gives me his best puppy-dog eyes, and a half-smile.

'With you, of course.'

'Shopping, then?'

I stand up. I'm still pissed off.

'Actually, no. Next time. I would like to go to a town, to a big store. But right now, there's no point unless they sell phones.'

He looks put out.

'You can use the phone here,' says Mimi. 'I've managed to get some more pound coins.' She produces a little coin bag from the drawer and offers it to me. I take them sulkily. I don't want to make a phone call in front of them, and she seems to sense this. 'We'll go and write our shopping list on the swing chair. Come on, Marcus. Let's give Caitlin some privacy.'

It's not ideal, but I'm prepared to take my chances. I'll ask Erin to send me a phone. I know Mum would fork out for it.

Deep breath, lift the receiver. The dialling tone I heard last time isn't there, but I dial anyway. Nothing. I replace the receiver and lift it up again, and again, and again. There's no dialling tone at all. I trace the wire down the wall, across the skirting board and towards the front door. It hasn't been unplugged. I unplug it and plug it back in again. There is still no sign of life in the phone.

I make my way out of the front door and go and stand in front of them as they drift back and forth in the swing chair.

'It's dead.'

'Surely not.'

'Dead as a dodo.' I try not to look accusing, but my nostrils flare and stiffen. The broken wicker sticks out of their chair in its hedgehoggy way and makes them look prickly.

'That's impossible,' says Marcus, getting up. He goes into the house and I follow him. I watch as he tries the phone, and I try to work out if he's pretending to be surprised. I just can't tell. He blows air up his face. 'Makes no sense. It was working yesterday. We got all those new coins for it.'

I sigh as heavily as I can. Mimi comes in and raises her eyebrows in expectation. He shakes his head.

'Look, I'm sorry. What can I do? Fancy coming shopping with me anyway?'

'No. You could post a letter for me, though.'

'Of course. Have you got a stamp?'

I haven't, and Mimi glides over to a dresser and opens a drawer to find me one. While her back is turned, Marcus raises his eyebrows at me.

'Later . . .?' he whispers. 'Whistles?'

I shake my head. There is something else I have to do.

Chapter Twenty-Eight

I climb back up the path through the woods. There's only one red car outside the cottage. Good. Filkins isn't on the wall. He's probably crashed out on my bed. I don't look up to the bedroom windows, but stride straight to the door and ring the doorbell, breathing heavily.

I hear footsteps on the stairs. Then the door is opening, and it's not Joe, but a different man. He has dark hair and eyes and is wearing faded jeans. He looks startled, and steps backwards into the hallway.

'Oh,' I say. 'Um . . .'

'Two metres.'

'Of course. I'm sorry. I forget.'

'It's okay,' he says, approaching the threshold again. He smiles. This takes me by surprise and undermines my resolve to be ruthless. Not that I was really expecting a monster, and his jittery backing away was hardly threatening, but the smile seems a genuine one, and makes his eyes half disappear. 'I forget, too, sometimes.' He displays a glorious set of very white teeth and his eyes disappear again. His voice is deep. 'I wasn't expecting you.'

'I was looking for Joe,' I say, disingenuously.

'Ah, he's just gone out on his shift.'

'Oh.'

I must look disappointed, because he says, 'Can I help? I'm

Kahlil, by the way, his housemate.' He holds out his hand and then quickly withdraws it. That smile again.

'*Kal*,' I say. Not Cal.

'Yeah, people call me Kal.'

'I'm Caitlin. I'm staying down at the house with Mimi and Marcus.'

'You're looking after the girls. Joe said there was a new . . .'

'Tutor – nanny. Sort of.' I shrug.

He leans against the door frame, relaxed now. 'I've seen you around – stroking my cat.'

'Filkins? Yes, I love him. He's gorgeous.'

As if in acknowledgement of my fandom, Filkins slips over the garden wall, saunters over and slinks around my shins.

'He likes you, too.' He smiles again.

'I'm afraid to tell you, but he spends a couple of hours every afternoon on my bed, lapping up all the affection he can get.'

'He's such a flirt. He seems to love that house. Joe says the girls make a fuss of him, but I think it's all the mice. And you, of course.'

He looks away shyly. The arm which is not against the door frame is holding his waist. It is a warm brown, veiled in velvety black hair, and his hand is lean, with a woven leather bracelet around the wrist. I bend down to stroke Filkins to stop myself gazing at Kal's flesh.

'He likes that,' he says.

There's an awkward silence, in which I can't help looking at Kal's naked feet, which are in my eyeline. Filkins gets bored and swaggers past his human into the house. I get to my feet, knowing I have to speak. I'm not going to be invited in to discuss things, not with this pandemic, so speak I must.

'I was just going to ask him – Joe – if he'd had any luck with my phone. Only I've lost my charger and I can't make any calls, so he said he'd charge it for me.'

'That's right, I was here when you came. I tried to offer a spare charger. You can have it if you like.' He turns slightly, as if he can go and get it if I want. His eyebrows are raised, waiting for me to accept.

'Thank you, but . . . there's no point now.'

He looks confused. 'I mean, you can keep it.'

'But I came back to pick up my phone and it had gone.'

'Yes. I was here. I heard the doorbell go.'

'Joe said it must've been stolen.' I look down at the path, my cheeks beginning to burn.

'*Stolen?* It wasn't stolen. There must be some mistake. He gave it to Marcus when he called by.'

A rush of blood and adrenaline makes me fizz all over. A penny drops, but I can't see where it drops or why. 'What? When?'

'Late morning? Half eleven, maybe?' He looks at me, confused, while I digest the information. 'I'm guessing Marcus hasn't seen you yet, to give it back.'

'Are you sure? Are you sure Joe gave it to Marcus?'

'Yeah. It was charging in the kitchen. And it annoyed me because he invited Marcus in. I mean, I don't like having to keep reminding him about the rules, but it pisses me off. It's bad enough sharing with a super-spreader like a policeman, without him being so slack with his friends. It's my home, too.' Filkins is pushing at his legs, and he bends down to pick him up. 'Sorry. I know Marcus is your employer but . . . he can be a bit . . . casual.'

'Don't apologise. You're right.' I watch him petting the cat and hugging him close to his neck, where his dark hair meets the skin. 'He had the nerve to tell me off for coming up here,' I say, 'exposing the girls to germs.'

'That's weird. He almost seems to me like a virus denier.' I feel sick. 'I'm surprised *he* didn't lend you his charger.'

'They don't have phones at the house.'

'They don't have phones? No way!' He looks incredulous, like I did when they first told me. 'Are they having you on? They're running a business, aren't they?'

'I know. I didn't believe it when they first said, but . . . no phones. No internet either.'

'No *internet*? I would feel like a prisoner. That's terrible.' He frowns, as though he really is worried about this, as though he can't work it out. 'I mean, I know they're a bit hippy and so on, but . . . I just don't know how they work like that.' He shakes his head in disbelief. 'I wouldn't be able to work from home without the internet. I'm on furlough, fortunately.'

'What do you do?' As if I didn't know.

'Web design. Well, actually, I'm an animator. I do the pictures and stuff.'

'You're an artist?'

'Loosely speaking. Joe calls me a computer geek.'

'But you draw and design?'

'Yeah.'

'You're not in intelligence, then?'

He laughs. That smile again. 'Let me guess where you heard that. Joe tells everyone I'm a spy. I'm drawing a bear at the moment.'

'A bear? I'd love to see it.' I'm not sure if I'm testing him out or not.

He looks coy. 'It's pretty crap.'

'I bet it's not. I'd really like to see it.'

'Wait there.' He plonks the cat down and, turning, he takes the stairs two at a time in his bare feet. When he returns, he's carrying a large sketch pad with loose papers in it. 'This is today's attempt.' He holds it up for me to see across the gap between us.

It takes my breath away. 'Oh crumbs. That's . . . You're . . . Wow.'

He laughs. 'I don't think I've got the nose right.' He flicks over the pages and I see other attempts, all equally good from where I'm standing. A page falls out and he picks it up. 'One of Filkins.'

It's wonderful.

'He's perfect. You've captured him exactly!'

'He does spend some of his time with me – when he's not lying on your bed.'

I'm struck by the thought that this cat is a link between our two beds. Perhaps it strikes him, too, because he looks awkward suddenly.

'At least I get him in the evenings. Cupboard love, of course, but he always sits on my lap every night when I'm watching TV.'

The cat looks up at him from his ankles and miaows. We both look at him. Filkins is like the child people interact with at parties because they don't know how to interact with each other. After a few long moments, I can't stay any longer without something interesting to say, and nothing springs to mind.

'Well, I'd best be off. Um . . . I'm sorry I bothered you.'

'Oh, no. You didn't. It was good to meet you. Wait!' He turns and runs up the stairs again. When he comes back, he holds something out in his hand. It has a long white tail. He steps forward and places it on the path between us. It's a charger. 'You can have it. It's a spare one.' He steps back onto the threshold. 'When you get your phone back.'

I'm about to say that I won't get it back, when an overwhelming gratitude to him makes me reach down and scoop up his gift. 'Thank you.'

'Goodbye then.'

'Bye.'

Then he calls after me: 'Ask Marcus for the phone. He's got it.'

Chapter Twenty-Nine

I try hard not to look at Marcus over tea. Fortunately, the radio is on and Boris is telling us that we are on target for mass testing by the end of May. There's a general warning that we are not out of the woods yet, and the prime minister's own near-death experience should remind us that we need to take social distancing seriously.

At this, Marcus says, 'It's unbelievable how slack some people are being about this pandemic. You just can't be too careful,' and he gives me a slightly righteous glance.

I have to look down at my chickpea and spinach cutlets and clamp my jaw shut. This is the man who was in Joe's kitchen earlier – Joe and Kal's kitchen – against all lockdown rules. I keep imagining what I'm going to say to him when we're next alone. I'll almost certainly shout at him. I'm fuming. Whatever else I know about him, I know he's lying. But perhaps I shouldn't say anything.

I remember some advice from my dad once, when I was eight or nine. He used to take me walking with him sometimes, and we'd sit by the stream and just look at the dragonflies and the coots and let the smell of damp earth and the songs of local birds fill our heads. He said he couldn't do that with Erin or Dani, because Erin kept talking and Dani couldn't sit still. It was a strange compliment, but I was glad of it. Anyway, I remember this one time: I had been upset because a kid at school (my so-called best friend, actually) had been bullying me and just generally being mean.

'So,' he said suddenly, into the discreet calm of the stream-side, 'what do you know about your friend that she doesn't know you know?'

It seemed a strange question, and I had to think about it for a while.

'She stole my new furry tiger pencil case.'

'And how do you know she stole it?'

'Because I saw it under her bed when I went round to play. And I know it was mine because it had my broken pencil sharpener in it.'

'Did you take it back?'

'No.'

'Why was that?'

'I don't know. I told her the next day that I really missed my tiger pencil case, and I thought she'd give it back then. Or maybe pretend she'd found it so I'd be all grateful to her. I thought she would. But she never has. And anyway, I have a new one now.'

'Hmm,' said Dad. 'So now you know something about her that she doesn't know you know, and that gives you a certain power.'

'What power? She's still got it.'

'Yes. But now you know she can't be trusted. And because she doesn't know you know that, you are in a stronger position.'

'But she thinks I'm stupid.'

'Even better, because you aren't. And one day, when she wants you to believe something that isn't true, you'll outwit her.'

I didn't really know what he meant at the time, but I think I do now. I think how I'll say nothing to Marcus about what I know. If he doesn't know I know he has my phone, then I have a better chance of finding it, because he'll be off guard. So when he grabs my elbow after tea and whispers, 'Three whistles at three tomorrow,' I nod, and try to look like my usual keen-as-mustard self.

I want to think there's an excuse for what he's done. It is, after all, quite possible that Marcus has stolen my phone because he's a bit obsessed with me, and wants to get someone to examine all my calls on it, to find out what I used to say to Luke, to find out all about our love life. That would make sense. He keeps on and on asking about it. Maybe big, buoyant Marcus is insecure. Maybe I've been in denial all this time because I don't think I'm worthy of anyone's adoration, but perhaps he really is totally smitten.

I keep trying this out for size, desperately attempting to make it fit. Because the other option is too uncomfortable. If he hasn't taken it because he wants to find out about me, he's taken it to stop me communicating with the outside world. To keep me here. Or to trap me. Either way, I'm going to find out.

Daisy is sprawled on the floor, designing a space helmet to stop people getting the virus. She has already finished eight careful pictures of Mimi with her recipes, and I'm stapling them together to make a book. Henna is knitting.

'Tell me about your mum,' I say to Henna.

'She was beautiful – and very gentle.'

'Like Mimi?' I don't know why I said that – it's not very sensitive.

'Nothing like Mimi.' Henna speaks to her knitting.

Daisy doesn't look up, but starts to look even more interested in her design. I remember that trick from my own childhood. But Henna doesn't seem to care about dissing Mimi in front of Daisy.

'She wasn't a bit like Mimi. Mum was a real mum. She hugged people, she did kind things for people, and she always put us first. She was a *true* eco-warrior, too. Not like Mimi and Marcus, who just pretend to care about the environment.'

'There are photos of Henna's mummy if you want to see her,' says Daisy, putting her crayon down and going over to a cupboard in a wooden dresser. Henna puts her knitting down and gets up to take control.

'It's this album.' She sits back down on the sofa and flicks through the pages. I sit next to her, and she points to a line of people in front of the house, which is decked in bright green Virginia creeper and red roses. 'Guess which one is Mum.'

There is a very obvious Marcus, looking sun-browned and really no different. There is Cliff, with a few dark hairs still in his beard; there are a couple of guys with guitars and another guy with a beard, smiling and friendly, with a carpenter's apron on; there is Mimi, looking stunning in her casual way, and there are three other young women and two children.

'That's you,' I say, pointing to a sweet little girl in a flowery dress. Henna nods, pleased that I've got her, looking so unlike herself now. 'You look so sweet.' She makes a noise that's not bitter enough to be a scoff, and which melts into a pleased chuckle. 'So this must be Bryony?'

A girl of about ten or eleven stands awkwardly next to Henna, a baseball cap on her head, and holding one arm across her waist. It's hard to see her face under the cap. Of the three other women, one of them stands out. Two of them wear jeans and T-shirts and could be Mimi's rescued sex slaves, but one has flowers in her hair and a long, floaty dress, gathered under the bosom. She has various leather thongs about her neck and bracelets on her arm, and one arm is resting around Henna's shoulder. She is smiling with all her face at the person taking the picture. I see straight away the warmth that Henna spoke of. It's clear, too, that she's very pregnant.

I point. 'That's Thea. That's your mum.'

She beams. 'Yes! That's Mum.'

'She's pretty, isn't she?' says Daisy, who has squashed herself onto my lap to lean across the photo album. 'Is that a baby in her like Violeta?'

'Yes.'

'Your other sister? Kitty?'

'Yes.'

Henna turns the pages back, and there are other pictures, closer

154

ones, of Thea less pregnant making bread, Thea feeding chickens with her girls, Thea standing between Marcus and Mimi, their arms slung over one another's shoulders. They all look so happy.

'She always wore those floaty dresses. I don't know what happened to them.'

'Would you like to find them?' I ask. 'I might have the key to a few of them. No promises, though.'

The key Mimi has given me opens a tall, wide cupboard in the barn. There's a long rail of hanging clothes, and several shelves stuffed with tops and trousers. It's a treasure trove. One of the doors has a long mirror in it, and I prop it open with a spare spinning wheel. We whoop with pleasure and horror and amazement as we take out the hangers and try clothes up against ourselves in the mirror. There are dungarees, cheesecloth shirts, bright kaftans and long, flowery summer dresses. There are stone-washed jeans, leggings, harem trousers and skinny jeans. There are woolly hats, berets, cardigans and long baggy jumpers. These clothes have belonged to women short and tall, slim, plump and pregnant.

Daisy stands in front of the mirror in a massive chunky-knit purple jumper, swinging the part-empty arms back and forth. 'Look, Caitlin! Look! How do I look?'

'Gorgeous!' I say, winking at her. 'That colour is really you!'

I try on some clothes, because that's what I'm here for, and eventually find some dungarees that fit. Probably maternity, dammit. I also find a couple of nice lumberjack shirts and a couple of long-sleeved T-shirts. I see Henna trying on clothes and almost smiling at herself in the mirror.

'That looks great on you,' I say when she turns about in a floral dress. 'Is that one of your mum's?'

'Yes. I think it is. I think I remember it.'

I rummage through the rack and pull out another one. 'Here. I think she's wearing this in one of the photos.' It's another floral dress, less voluminous, and she was wearing it feeding the chickens. 'Try it on.'

As she takes the dress she's wearing over her head, her bony shoulder blades look like wings about to open on a tiny bird, and a surge of affection for her, a desire to protect, makes me reel. I'm back in a rural restaurant in Italy, where we were served songbirds. I thought they were illegal. *Pettirossi*, I heard the waiter say. Robins.

Luke ate his in front of me, telling me, like a connoisseur, how serving *ortolan* in France was now banned, how the little buntings were fattened up, then plunged, alive, into vats of Armagnac brandy, cooked and plucked and eaten whole – feet, bones and all – as a delicacy. He told me this in his usual informative way, feeling the need to educate me. He went on to tell me how they still caught some songbirds with glue, which stuck the unsuspecting creatures when they perched, helpless, unable to fly away. I went to the toilets and threw up. Then I went back and watched him eat his robin in front of me, leaving the spindly bones in a little heap, dabbing his mouth with a white napkin. I could barely look at mine, its helpless angled wings jutting out like two miniature boomerangs. And since I wasn't eating it, Luke ate mine, too, with swagger, lording it over my plodding, unsophisticated tastes.

Henna's thin arms, now jutting out at an angle, remind me so much of that little robin served up on a dish. I don't want to stare at her undressing, but I resolve to catch a glimpse of her naked arms when she takes the next dress off, in case there are any cuts. Mum always says it's the gym teachers who spot the cutters first, in the changing rooms. It's the one place they can't hide. And now the idea's in my head, I can't chase it away.

'You look stunning,' I say, when the dress is on. 'Really. Doesn't she, Daisy?'

'You look like a princess.'

Henna goes for a mock-vomit look, but checks herself. She

stands sideways-on in front of the mirror, taking furtive, surprised glances at her reflection.

We all take some clothes away with us. I'm assuming Mimi won't mind me sharing the treasure. As Henna pulls the dress off over her head, it gets momentarily stuck, and I have a chance, helping her, to look again at her grub-pale skin. It's hard to see the insides of her arms , but there don't appear to be any cuts. What I do see, though, makes me catch my breath, and will haunt me for weeks.

Chapter Thirty

'You took your time,' he says, standing by the door to his lair.

I say nothing, still struggling not to show my fury, but I shrug instead. He follows me up the steps and starts undressing me as soon as we're in the room. I have to make an effort to respond to his whispers and enticements. Thoughts dart to the surface and dive again, just out of reach. I catch the tail of one – self-loathing, perhaps – but before I can examine it, it wriggles out of my grasp and is gone.

He smells of betrayal, and it's bitter. When we lie down together, the scent of his skin is literally more acrid than usual. Perhaps there is fear in his sweat.

'You shouldn't be angry with *me*,' he says.

I breathe slowly, containing myself. 'I'm just upset about my phone.'

From where we are lying on the bed, I can see the door to his secret 'office'. It's closed, as usual, but now there is an old-fashioned iron key in the lock and a bunch of keys hanging from it. I recognise them as his car keys from the key ring in the shape of an acorn. If I can just steal his keys some time . . . Or maybe if he falls asleep after sex I could creep over in a moment, unlock the door and find my phone. I'm certain it's in there. This is his secret place; it's bound to be here. He has no artifice. Or so I always thought.

'*You* would be upset if you'd lost a phone – if you hadn't seen your family in nine months.'

'I've told you who's taken it. You only have yourself to blame.'

'Kal?' I fix him with a stare, but I let him stroke my hair. 'Hard to believe he's such a monster.'

'He can't be trusted. He looks sly, don't you think?'

'I wouldn't know.'

He gets up suddenly on one elbow and grips the top of my arm, hard.

'Don't lie to me! You've been up there again, and you've met him!' As he says this, he raises his hand and brings it down as if to strike me, but before he does, he tips me towards him and it lands on the ample flesh of my backside. 'I told you not to go up there! I told you it was dangerous!' Then he rolls me over completely and slaps it again, and again and again. He slaps me, talking through gritted teeth; he slaps me over and over until I cry out, until I scream out too loudly for his liking. And all this time, I run through what this means: Marcus has been in touch with Joe. Kal has told Joe I was up there, but what I don't know is whether Kal told Joe he'd told *me* that Marcus had the phone. Maybe Kal just asked Joe why he'd lied to me. Maybe Marcus still doesn't know I know.

The trouble is, the distance between trust and distrust seems too vast to cover in one leap. I can't help that feeling I had about Dad – that there should be a few stepping stones in between them, to help me get there, to help me accept that Marcus isn't who I want him to be.

When he's done, he rolls me back over and softens his voice: 'You've been a very naughty girl,' like he's turning it into some sex game or something. Fucksake. I'm smarting from the blows, furious and shaking, and he starts stroking me, feeling inside me. 'Oh, I think you liked that, didn't you?' He has somehow managed to arouse my body despite my better judgement. I'm ashamed and shocked by my disconnection from it. He caresses my skin, probes me in my most secret places, whispers gently now, 'That's it. You just need to be a bit more obedient, Caitlin. You need to be shown who's boss.'

He doesn't stop until I'm groaning in a different voice.

Afterwards, I am lost. Or perhaps I've just lost some more respect for myself. I'm not a good person. I'm the rotten apple in our family, and I've known this for a very long time, ever since I started concealing the truth from my parents.

They used to go out sometimes, Mum and Dad, when we were younger. They paid Erin like a proper babysitter, even though she was only three years older than me. Okay, eight years older than Danielle, but still. But then Erin started going out with her teenage friends, and Mum seemed to wilt a bit in her social life. If Uncle Aaron was about, she and Dad took advantage of it to go somewhere, and he'd stay over, then have a drinking binge with Dad the next day, and have to stay over Saturday as well.

Everyone liked Uncle Aaron because he was jolly. He was Dad's brother – 'the real son,' Dad used to say, because his parents had Aaron after they'd adopted him. He made people laugh, he told Mum she was beautiful, he praised her cooking. 'You're one lucky bastard,' he used to say to Dad, and then let Mum tick him off – enjoyed her ticking him off, coy as a little boy. I thought he was the funniest man I'd ever met, when I was eleven. He would read Dani a bedtime story, then let me stay up later than I was supposed to, watching videos. He bought me exotic snacks like Doritos and chilli flavoured crisps, and I'd munch them leaning into his chest.

I haggled with him at bedtime. Only if I got a story like Dani had. I was too old for stories. OK, then, no can do. I'm not going to bed. And then he'd read me something in such a ridiculous voice I was in hysterics, or he'd tickle me until I begged him to stop. And then one time he didn't stop, just kept going slowly. Very slowly. And told me, 'You're the sort of girl who likes that, aren't you?'

I can't remember how often it happened, but I know when it didn't happen any more. I locked myself in the bathroom and stayed there until Mum and Dad came home. I told them I felt sick. I didn't say how long I'd been there, and neither did he. I should've said something, but he didn't bother me after that, and I never told, because he'd made me complicit in the confusing set of sensations that went with what he did. *You're the sort of girl who likes that, aren't you?* Cunning.

I lie staring at the ceiling beams of Marcus's lair. I can't imagine being affectionate towards him now, after his aggression, or making small talk. He must sense something has changed, because he pulls my head around to face him and cups the side of my face gently. He stares, watching my eyes like a frightened child.

'Caitlin!' Like there's a question in that whisper. My thoughts are bobbing around, not secured to anything. He's holding my eyes with his, like a jeweller gauging their worth. I don't even see his lips when they breathe an urgent, 'Don't leave me!'

Here he is, loving me.

'I won't.'

'Swear you won't.'

'I swear. I won't leave you, Marcus.'

For a reply without hesitation, it's the best I can come up with. And anyway, this changes things.

He needs me. I soar.

He rests his forehead on mine, and we stay like that, pressing into each other's sweat, like a blood oath with different bodily fluid.

I may have dreamed of him loving me so passionately, but to indulge in this moment of rocketing self-esteem seems risky. I instinctively try to defuse the situation. I quiz him on what I want to know, attempting to sound casually post-coital. 'Tell me something: why is Mimi so anti-abortion?'

'Ah!' he says, folding his arms behind his head, as if settling himself for a return to less hostile times between us. 'That's easy. Ever since she had Daisy, she can't have children of her own.'

This is not good. Now what can I say that isn't mean? My attempt is pathetic. 'I know people who can't have children, and it doesn't make them pro-lifers.'

He sighs. 'Well, you know, she just can't bear to see other people trying to get rid of children when she can't have one.'

Poor Mimi. I'm a monster.

'But Daisy's so lovely.'

'Yep. Great kid. I guess Mimi just . . . you know . . . loves kids.'

Really? Not so's you'd notice.

'Is she homophobic?'

'Good grief? What makes you ask that?'

'Something she said about not wanting the children to learn about gender education and stuff.'

'Oh, well, that's nothing. She's a bit old-fashioned, that's all.'

'Old-fashioned? Is that what you call it? Is she a bit "old-fashioned" about race, too?'

'Hey, what's got into you?'

'She seemed bothered that I might be mixed-race.'

I've never *identified* as mixed-race, because no one has ever attached that label to me before. I've just been trying to work out what it is to be me. I do have springy hair, shapely lips, good teeth and tan easily, but then I have grey eyes and otherwise look like my mum. I did overhear a friend's grandmother ask once who the 'half-caste' girl was when we were playing round her house. I didn't know about castes, and understood being only 'half-cast' to mean something not quite ready, like an unfinished plaster cast or a blancmange that wasn't fully set. A bit shapeless. That made sense because I've always known I was the unremarkable one in our family, the bland one. Although, of course, they think I made up for it all by 'going off the rails a bit' as a teenager. What do they know? I'm aware that as the middle daughter I am contractually obliged to be challenging and attention-seeking, but it's an obligation I've barely scraped the surface of, despite my best efforts.

I remember sleeping in our barn once because I'd come home

so early from a party (9.30 p.m.) that I didn't want them to know. I couldn't bear the way my older sister, Erin, would laugh at me. I let them worry their socks off that I hadn't come home, then rocked up in the kitchen at 6.30 a.m., letting them think I'd been out all night being reckless. I did it to Erin, really. I was so pissed off with her getting all the attention. Not that it did a lot of good. My parents just thought I was selfish and not to be trusted to go out late again, etc. So, yeah, I got myself a nice little reputation without the fun. Still, it was better than bland.

'That's just her interest in genes,' says Marcus. 'She's fascinated by inheritance – eye colour, hair colour. It's the scientist in her. She loves the way you look. She does.'

I stretch my arm up the wall by his bed, enjoying the coolness against my skin. 'Did she tell you she had a good look at my body yesterday? Breast inspection, the works.'

'No way! Now *that* I would like to have seen.' He takes an arm from behind his head and strokes my shoulder. 'What brought that on?'

'You'll have to ask her.' I try to sound enigmatic.

'Well, Mimi definitely likes you. And you're really good with kids, aren't you? You seem to be settling in well. They all like you. I knew they would.'

I'm excited by this new version of us, him being needy and me popular and lapping it all up; until suddenly it scares me a little, and makes me feel unsafe. Less than half an hour ago, he was someone else. I've seen the set of his jaw now, and I can't unsee it.

Chapter Thirty-One

The days pass, the grass grows lush and long, and the buttercups scatter themselves among its new green blades. Forget-me-nots nod in tender blue clouds along the paths, and when the girls and I go walking as far as the stream, great mounds of willow-down have become caught in heaps along the undergrowth, in clumps of nettles, on the verges of paths, in the roots of trees. It's like snow. May puffs out the world in a glory of green and steeps everything in warmth. The earth begins to crack in its heat; not a single aeroplane scratches the flawless blue-domed surface of the sky. No one is travelling. The last days of May, and no letter arrives.

I imagine a slow postal pick-up, and a slower delivery than usual. I picture my letter dropping on the mat in our Cornish home. I see Dani or Erin or my mother pick it up. Then I imagine the steady days tumbling gently one after the other as Erin finds time to reply, and then her letter waiting patiently at the bottom of a red letterbox set in the stone wall of our nearest pub, where a plaque announces collections at 4.00 pm on each day. Probably it has all slackened off in the pandemic.

May slides into June, and the house feels more familiar and more oppressive. Sometimes I imagine observing myself from the woods, or looking down from the ridge, and seeing a small ant-like creature scurrying up the slope, carrying its hopes and dreams on its back, ready to deliver to Marcus's nest.

Mimi always asks how I've slept when I come downstairs in the mornings, or how the tutoring is going, but I don't think she ever listens to my answer. Instead, she has her back to me and continues with whatever it is she's doing: chopping, measuring, making coffee. Sometimes I see her use a lethally sharp knife, which is curled and serrated, to scoop out the soft flesh of a grapefruit. When she does eventually turn to look at me, she bores right into me with her seagull-sharp eyes, as if asking something more urgent than how I slept. *How was sex with my 'husband'?* perhaps.

Another crushing image is Violeta hauling the vacuum cleaner upstairs, wheeling the waste bins out on to the track. One morning I'm shocked to see that she has washed and ironed my 'new' dungarees. She's laid them out on a chair in my bedroom, just like my mother used to do with my school uniform. This is terrible. I gather the sheets and duvet cover from my bed along with my personal laundry, and I take it down to the utility room by the back door. Ashamed, I bundle it all into the washing machine and wonder why it hasn't occurred to me to do this for myself.

And I can't help thinking of all the washing and ironing that goes unnoticed in people's lives. Mum used to say that Gran's washing load was worse than hers, and her mother before her did even more. Gran would boil up used handkerchiefs, for example, in an old saucepan. Then she would pour off the viscid liquid and wash them again. Then she would iron them into neat squares or triangles, ready for members of her family to blow their noses into. Then they would sit, glued into scrunched balls, hard and crusty, up sleeves and in pockets, until the next washday when their intricate care process began again.

Gran was eighty-one when she died. Her decline seemed to go on for ever, but it all happened quite quickly, really. I remember the first time I accepted that it wasn't just a kooky bit of forgetfulness. I was heading round to her house after school to wait for Mum to pick me up or something. And I saw this old lady on the pavement, leaning on her Zimmer frame. She was naked from the waist down, apart from her knickers, which were round her knees, and she had wet herself – and worse. And I'd like to think I wasn't embarrassed, but I was. And this is the worst thing: her little legs were shaking. They were really trembling, as if she couldn't support herself much longer. This was my gran, who could fix anything, who had pushed me on the swings and yanked me off high rocks with her sturdy arms. To see her skinny, quivering bones was heartbreaking. She was all bent forward on the frame, with tears running down her cheeks, saying she couldn't find the toilet, and she had to get to Snozzle (that's how she always pronounced St Austell) to see her mum and dad, and they had a toilet. And what did I do? I phoned Mum. I put my coat around her nakedness and told her that her parents didn't live there any more because they were dead, and I tried to reason with her, to steer her towards her house, mortified in case anyone saw me. She just became more and more upset, and then Mum turned up and spoke to her cheerfully, as if nothing was wrong. She said she knew where there was a toilet, and then she could take her to St Austell to see her parents. And she helped Gran back to her house, where she cleaned her up and made her a pot of tea. Gran didn't mention Snozzle again, but was happy to watch a soap opera on the sofa with me.

'What you doing here, me 'an'some?' she said after her second cuppa. 'I expect you got homework, avee? You'd better be heading back and get on with it.'

She couldn't remember my name in the end, but she died with hundreds of songs still in her head.

'Please,' I say to Violeta, when I find her on her knees cleaning our upstairs bath. 'The girls and I can do this. You shouldn't be doing this with the baby so close.'

She sits back on her heels and I see the dark wisps of hair sticking to her sweaty forehead. Her pretty face is heavily flushed and blotchy. 'It's okay. I clean. No you.'

'But you're exhausted. It's no problem for me to do it.'

'*I* do.'

I sit down on the bathroom floor beside her. 'Do they look after you? Do they pay you?'

'Yes. I have food. I have house here. No more bad mans.'

'What will you do . . . when the baby comes?'

'I go back home. They give me money here. Big money. I go back home. I have boyfriend.'

So it's true, then.

'Does he know . . .?' I venture, stupidly, but I want to find out more about this slave trade Mimi claims to be scuppering with her good works. I want to know if it's really true. 'Does he know what happened?'

'No . . .' She throws her bath-cleaning sponge into a bucket and looks at me. 'You know . . .' She lowers her voice. 'What happened?'

'What?'

Her voice is deep and sexy. 'What . . . happened?' Then she laughs and makes emphatic kissing noises. 'What happened? *What happened?* So simple.'

I smile, out of my comfort zone.

*

One day when we've been shopping in Ribley, I see a corner of a letter poking out of the letterbox on a pole in the wooded parking area. I leap out of the Land Rover and retrieve it, and read the typed front with beating heart: '*Mr Stallard, Willerby, Greenoaks . . .*'

Marcus grabs it from me and scowls. 'Bloody new postman! We keep getting the wrong mail.' He sighs and slings it in the paper waste when we get to the house.

When nothing comes after ten days, I think perhaps Erin has gone to live with her boyfriend, and Mum dare not open the letter, as I addressed it to Erin. Perhaps they're trying to get their hands on a charger first. But I know Erin would order one online, and it would be here by now. I know she would. I know something I don't want to know: I know Marcus didn't post my letter.

I cringe when I think of him opening it and reading it. But I write another one, this time pleading for a phone as well as a charger, and I make sure I go with Marcus the next time he goes shopping, and I put it in the Ribley postbox myself.

Chapter Thirty-Two

The girls are poring over the photo album again, trying to work out if the dress Henna is wearing is the same one her mother wore in the last picture of her.

'It definitely is,' I say, pointing to the buttons going down the front. 'It's just a wee bit longer on you, that's all. And don't forget, she had a bump – that shortens things a lot.' Henna smiles and nods, pleased with my certainty. 'Right, let's nail the last module of history before our walk. Books out – and you, Daisy. You're going to write me a story.'

I think about what Henna said earlier about history books not telling the full story. I may not be the brightest tool in the box, but I know that the things we choose to record and collect, the photographs we choose to keep, don't always tell the truth either. This thought circles overhead like a buzzard.

After half an hour or so, once I've got them settled and engaged with a task, I go back to the album to put it away, and I look again at the photos. Not, this time, at Thea, but at Mimi. She stands there, looking back at me, and something strikes me about her. There are no more photographs in the album until Henna's birthday at the beginning of October, three months after Thea died.

The aroma of baking and cinnamon percolates throughout the house, and I pop out to the kitchen on the pretext of looking for some of Mimi's home-made biscuits, but I have another purpose.

There she is, with oven gloves draped over her shoulder, twisting the biscuits carefully off the baking tray.

'Mm . . . those smell good,' I say.

She barely looks round, but smiles a little, and I watch her graceful, practised movements, her glossy hair pinned up casually, exposing a neck so perfect I cannot believe that Marcus could possibly prefer mine.

'I'm glad I caught you, actually,' I say. 'I . . um . . . I wanted to apologise.'

'Apologise? Whatever for?'

'For being insensitive . . . before . . . about the abortion thing.'

She looks briefly at me, inquisitive perhaps, but continues to gather the biscuits and place them on cold plates to cool. 'That was a while back, wasn't it?'

'I know, but Marcus told me . . . about you not being able to have children.' Her delicate hands fumble over the opening of a plastic food container. I have her attention now. She drops the lid on the floor. 'Since Daisy.'

'Yes, since Daisy. That's right.'

'I'm sorry about that.'

She recovers the lid and fixes it firmly on the box. 'That's okay.'

'I can see how hard it must be watching other people decide to terminate a pregnancy that you long for yourself.'

She turns round to face me, a little flushed, opening her mouth to speak and then closing it. I half expect her to say I have no idea what she does or doesn't long for. She takes a deep breath. 'Well, thank you.'

'You must've been pregnant pretty much at the same time as Thea.'

She wheels back to the biscuits, but there is nothing to do with them now: they are all cooling on the plates. 'Yes. Yes, I was.'

Unreal. I'm spinning with the dubious thrill of knowing that Mimi, perfect Mimi, is lying to my face. She is lying, and she doesn't know I know.

'That's weird.'

'Why? Why is it weird?' She turns back to look at me, this time boring into me with her ice-blue eyes. It's so intimidating that I almost don't say it.

'Because . . . it's just that . . . in the photograph of her in front of the house, when she's very pregnant, you look . . . really slim.'

She swallows hard, grabs a plate of biscuits and holds them out. 'Would you like one?'

'Thanks.'

She hesitates, puts the plate on the table and sits down. 'Okay, look. The thing is . . . the truth is, Daisy is adopted. We didn't tell you before because we haven't told Daisy herself yet.'

'But Henna must know.'

'Yes, Henna knows. In fact, we sort of did it for her, really. For her and Bryony. In a way.'

Now I'm interested. 'How do you mean? Because they lost Kitty?'

She frowns slightly, as if I have no right to talk about Kitty or Thea, since I didn't know them. 'Yes, because of Thea and Kitty. It was a terrible thing to lose their mother like that, but to lose a sister, too . . . And Henna in particular had been really looking forward to having a little brother or sister, so we thought – now's the time.'

'You must've had to wait a while.'

I know for a fact that it takes ages to adopt, because one of Mum's friends did it. And it's very hard to find a new baby these days.

'Yes, obviously we waited a few months. It would've been in-sensitive to wheel a new baby in to replace the lost one straight away. No, we waited for a newborn baby to become available, and we found one a few months later.'

'That easy? I thought it was really hard to adopt newborns.'

She looks flummoxed. 'Yes, you're right. It is.' I wait, munching on my biscuit, trying not to make crumbs. 'The truth is – and this must go no further, okay?'

I nod.

'The truth is, Suze found her for us in the autumn. One of the Eastern European girls – lovely girl – she was going back home and didn't want the shame of it – didn't want the baby. And I know what would've happened if we'd gone through all the usual processes. It would've taken years, and because it was all a bit below the radar, Daisy might've ended up in care for a while first and . . . you know. We just wanted one quickly, and it made sense. And she was able to come straight home with us just in time for Henna's birthday.'

I'm not sure whether to be relieved or disappointed about Mimi's revelation. I know she's capable of lying, which doesn't, after all, feel like any sort of triumph, as I might have expected it to. If anything, it makes me a little wobbly. I want something firm and reliable to hold fast to in this new place. Instead, everything seems unmoored.

'Mummy, look!' Daisy has bolted into the kitchen and is holding out her gift. 'I made you a book!'

Mimi takes it and flicks through the pages, as Daisy watches her, holding her breath.

'Oh, darling, that's lovely! Aren't you clever!'

Daisy nods.

'She did it all by herself,' I say. 'There's so much detail in it.'

Mimi smiles at me, and then at Daisy again.

'It's amazing for a five-year-old,' I add, sensing that Daisy needs more from her mother.

'Yes,' says Mimi, looking at it again and then putting it on the counter.

Daisy smiles and swallows, pulling her sleeves over her hands.

When I get back to the girls after that conversation, I give them biscuits, and go straight to the photograph album again. I turn the pages. There is Henna on her birthday: *An unexpected birthday present!* And there is Daisy. It's a cute picture of her; you can tell immediately it's her. Something in the eyes. And Henna is holding her chubby little form.

'When's your birthday, Daisy?' I ask.

'I will be six on September the . . . twenty-eighth.'

'And when's yours, Henna?'

She looks up and sees me with the album. 'October fifteenth. That's me with Daisy.'

I smile at her and at the photo. I'm no expert on babies, but I remember my disappointment, aged five, when Dani was born, because I'd been expecting a sister I could play with, and what arrived was a blob I couldn't even have on my knee for months. There is no way this beautiful bouncing baby is seventeen days old. This baby is at least three months. This baby is Kitty.

Chapter Thirty-Three

At eleven o'clock the next morning I make the girls a drink and give them a biscuit. We sit at the kitchen table, chatting, and Violeta sits with us, pretending to be put out that we have made her put her feet up on a chair. Henna loves fussing over her, and is standing behind her, massaging her shoulders, when Mimi comes in from outside.

'Okay, listen. I've got a couple arriving this morning to take a look at this place for their baby. They're travelling with work for a few nights soon, and they're desperate for somewhere safe for their child, so I want to impress them.'

'They're not allowed to travel, though, are they?' says Henna.

My thoughts exactly.

'Yes, they are.'

'But that political advisor guy was in the shit for travelling in lockdown—'

'Language.' She looks at me with exasperation, as if I am clearly responsible. 'They are key workers. Both doctors of some sort. Anyway, I'm not going to be grilling them on the whys and wherefores. They are paying well and that's what matters.'

Henna looks like she might have something to say about this, when the sound of a distant car coming along the track makes Mimi bolt to the door. She comes back into the kitchen, almost breathless.

'They're here. Violeta, when I tell you, make them some coffee or tea and biscuits and bring it to the living room.' She looks her up and down with a frown. 'And try to look smart.'

'We'll make the coffee for Violeta,' says Henna.

'Yes,' I say, 'we'll do it.'

'You,' says Mimi firmly, pointing at me, 'take these girls outside on a walk somewhere and make yourselves scarce. Okay?'

'But Violeta's tired. She needs to rest.'

'*Now*, please!'

A bit shaken, I take the girls out of the front door and turn left so that we pass the couple coming up the flat track to the house. They are both impeccably dressed, and they smile with real warmth when they see us. We all say hello and carry on walking, making ourselves scarce, as instructed. Behind us, we hear Mimi's unusually effusive greeting.

'*She's* had a personality change,' mutters Henna.

Daisy is straining to look back and I take her hand.

'Why was Mummy so mean to Violeta?' she says. 'Why couldn't we make the tea? It's not fair.'

'I don't get it either,' says Henna. 'Violeta's ready to drop.'

It's a mystery to me, too, but I can't risk joining in. '*I* know. Why don't we do something else to help Violeta. Like vacuuming or washing?'

'That'll make too much noise.'

'Right. What about putting out the bins and the recycling?'

'We'll have to go back to the house.'

It's Thursday. Friday is bin day, and the recycling bins will be already outside with the rubbish bins. It involves taking everything to the very end of the track, which is a long haul for anyone. 'We'll go round the back of the house, so they don't see us. It's all outside the side porch.'

One of the boxes, for paper, is too full for the lid to stay clipped down. I open it and take off a couple of magazines and brochures so that I can scrunch down some looser paper underneath. I don't notice it straight away, until Henna gasps and grabs the lid off the ground to slam it back on the box, so violently she would have clamped my fingers if they'd been in the way. But still I catch a glimpse of it. The question is whether Daisy has seen it too: a stapled-together book, 'Mummys Ressippys', and the unmistakable drawing of Mimi holding her vanilla log with chocolate soil on the front.

I look round, but Daisy is ambling away, towards the lamb enclosure. Henna's eyes meet mine. She drops the cardboard recycling bag and goes after her. I follow.

Daisy has buried her nose into her lamb's neck. 'Daddy said we had to give the lambs back soon,' she mumbles. It's still not certain that she saw her rejected gift. 'Do we have to?'

I don't want to give her false hope, so I take in a deep breath. 'Well, they're Geoff's lambs, and they'll be happier back in their flock – eventually. They're herd animals.'

She looks panicked, as if she was banking on me giving an entirely different answer. 'But what if they get bullied again?'

'What? Sausage and Freedom? Not a chance. They're tough little lambs now.'

Daisy frowns and chews her lip. 'But what if they do? What if the other lambs kick them again?' She lifts her face from the lamb, gasping, her face crumpled. 'I don't want them . . . to go. Please!'

I kneel down and put my arms around her, and wonder if she has fed herself this new grief in order to let the tears come for the worse horror she's feeling, the one she has no words for. Did she see it? I feel her body rigid and immobile against mine, and then a sudden heave in: this is it. I let her cry it out, feeling the wet of her cheeks on my neck. She's inconsolable. Henna has come over, too, and stands there, chewing the side of her finger. Then she reaches out and strokes Daisy's hair. We wait like that, in the hot sun.

'It'll be okay, Daisy,' she says, with unusual affection. 'It's the best thing for them. We've saved them from harm, and now we have to be brave.'

After a while Daisy whispers, 'Okay,' and we make our way

back to the recycling. I carry the two boxes of paper and plastics, Daisy takes food waste, and Henna carts the big blue cardboard waste bag.

There are some thyme bushes along the side of the path, and I start to sing, in a weak attempt to lift our spirits.

> *'Come all you fair and tender maids*
> *That flourish in your prime, prime,*
> *Beware, beware, keep your gardens fair,*
> *And let no man steal your thyme, thyme,*
> *Let no man steal your thyme.'*

Daisy keeps her eyes fixed on the stony, sun-beaten path, and the smallness of her feet makes my throat ache.

'What rhymes with farm?' I ask.

'Arm.'

'Harm.'

I sing:

> *'Come all you small and playful lambs*
> *That frisk at Big Geoff's farm, farm.*
> *Don't mess, don't mess with our lambs unless*
> *You want to come to harm, harm,*
> *You want to come to harm.*
>
> *'For each one of our two brave lambs*
> *Will one day be a ewe, ewe,*
> *And every place where you like to chase . . .*
> *Will be their playground too, too,*
> *Will be their playground too.'*

I try not to think of my stolen thyme. In any case, it wasn't stolen. I handed it over freely.

'What comes next?' says Henna. 'In the real song.'

'That is the real song.'

'No – really.'

> *'For when your thyme is past and gone*
> *He'll care no more for you, you.*
> *And every place that your thyme would waste*
> *Will all run o'er with rue, rue,*
> *Will all run o'er with rue.'*

It takes us twenty minutes to get the recycling waste down to the end of the track across the field, turn right and onto a lane. I've never come out this way before. I look up and down the lane, bordered in thick green hedgerows, bursting with wild flowers. Even here there is no sign of a proper road, but here at least I can picture – should I ever need it – a way of escape.

We plonk the bags and boxes down on the verge, and Henna fiddles to fasten the Velcro on the cardboard waste bag, which doesn't quite reach across the top. She takes out some scrunched-up cardboard boxes in order to flatten them properly and make them fit better. I love how meticulous she is about things that matter to her.

'You could make your space helmet out of that,' she says, taking the last box out of the bag and handing it to Daisy.

'A *virus* helmet,' says Daisy. 'Not a space helmet.'

Henna smiles, with a tenderness I haven't seen before. Daisy still looks hangdog. Something has torn apart inside her, and I have to put her back together before it's too late. I have to come up with something.

'Oh, look at that!' I say, rejigging items in my box of paper, as if I need to get the contents to settle more again. 'Violeta has accidentally got your lovely cookbook caught up in a stack of papers to go out.' I retrieve it. 'Mummy'll be devastated if she finds out.'

Henna is quick off the mark. 'Poor Violeta! Let's not tell on her – she might get into trouble. She's finding everything so hard lately.'

'Yes, poor Violeta,' I say, eyeing Henna with gratitude. 'She's so exhausted.'

'Hang on a minute.' Henna looks at me, then back at the box Daisy is holding up to her head. 'Isn't that . . .?'

We both stand there looking at each other, squinting in the hot sun and in the heat of shock, the realisation so sudden that I don't know who is struck the hardest by the blow. The distinctive black arrow of the Amazon logo can only mean online shopping.

I nod. But I am way ahead of her. It's not hard to see how this could play out – how it almost certainly will play out unless we're careful.

'I tell you what, Daisy!' I say. 'Let's find you a better box. We can find a better box than that one for your helmet.'

I start to rifle in the bag, and so does Henna. There are a few flattened Amazon boxes, but other boxes, too: posh clothes companies, cereal packets, rice packets. I select a box that seems innocuous – floor cleaner or something – and make it up from flat. I offer it to Daisy and she gives me back the Amazon box, which she has made into a floppy parallelogram. It even has some black tape on it marked Prime. You tender maids, who flourish in your prime, prime. Beware, beware . . . I flatten it and shove it back in the bag.

'Let's keep this to ourselves,' I say under my breath to Henna. 'For now.'

She frowns at me, a snorting rage against Mimi and Marcus clearly building up swiftly.

'Knowledge is power,' I add.

Sleep won't come. The thought that Amberside really might have the internet, and that Marcus and Mimi are keeping it from me and from both of the girls, keeps buzzing in my head. What on earth could be the motive? And although I fail to think of one, the idea that he wants to stop me leaving does have a ring of truth about it. But if Marcus wanted to keep me here, there's no reason why Mimi would collude with him. And then again, it's hard to imagine how he could operate an underground business like his *without* the internet. Or for that matter, how she could find people for her nursery business. Maybe they're both hiding it because they're both doing something illegal, and no one can find what they have on their laptops if they don't suspect they have any devices. But surely it wouldn't hurt for me to have a phone? I drift off to sleep and dream of being trapped. I am trapped in a backstreet of Avignon, and Marcus is there and lends me his car. But when I try to start it, the engine has been completely removed, and he laughs.

I am up early and challenge Mimi as soon as I have her alone after breakfast.

'I hope the couple liked your nursery.'

'Yes, thank you.' She has her back to me, planting basil seeds in a tray. 'And thank you for keeping your distance.'

'Actually, we took the recycling up the track, and Daisy was looking for a cardboard box for a helmet she's making . . .' – My skin prickles with fear – '. . . and she found an Amazon box.'

'And . . .?'

Fucksake. She is *so* cool.

'And . . . that means someone here is ordering stuff on the internet.'

She wheels round, those gannet-blue eyes on mine again, as I knew they would be. I brace myself. She can't possibly have an explanation. But even though I know she can't win here, I'm terrified of her.

'Well . . .' She folds her arms (defensive, I think, but somehow she makes it look aggressive) and leans against the counter. For all the world I could be in the deputy head's office back at school, with Miss Heron about to give me a good ticking off for my lip piercing. 'I do indeed buy some things off the internet, Caitlin, but if you had bothered to look at the address on any Amazon boxes you found, you would have known they weren't sent to this address.'

My cheeks burn. The use of my first name stings; it's like a politician clipping an interviewer. Such a subtle put-down it's almost invisible, but cutting. It's true, I had only glanced at the address, and it didn't say Amberside. Anyway, that wasn't the point; parcels were coming here from Amazon. So much for being self-sufficient.

What I actually say is, 'So . . . you're not entirely self-sufficient.'

She looks almost relieved and smiles. 'Not entirely, no. When I visit Suze, she lets me use her laptop to make orders for the odd thing – clothes and so on. It's pretty hard to get anything decent out here. And now with lockdown . . .' She picks at the corner of her nail, ready to look away from me at last. 'I go and pick them up from her house when I visit. Or sometimes she brings them down.' She heaves a great sigh. 'Okay?'

I nod, sharing her relief, because it seems that some great storm has passed by without breaking. But I can't help the feeling that I have let go of something I should have held on to.

Chapter Thirty-Four

Some days later, something in the kitchen stops me in my tracks. The floor is covered in bright splashes of blood. I follow the red trail out into the utility room. There are patches of it everywhere here, and what look like partial footprints. They go to the side door and porch. A man's voice is making angry sounds, so I follow the blood marks on tiptoe.

Outside, Cliff is leaning against the wall, propped on one leg and inspecting the upturned foot of the other one. He has cut himself badly by the look of it.

'Let me see.' I go towards him and he flinches.

'I stood on a broken bottle. Thought I'd find a bandage or something.' He has a wodge of kitchen towel in his hand, but it looks serious.

I go and fetch him a kitchen chair to sit on, and place it on the grass by the outside tap. 'You need to wash the wound – get any bits of glass out – before you cover it.'

He hops over to the chair and sits down heavily.

I hold his gnarled foot under the tap for a minute and then place it on his other knee. 'Wait here a second – I'll get something to dress it.'

I did first aid at school once, but I can't remember anything, and I don't even know where the sticking plasters are. I call out to Mimi, but she doesn't come, so I open and close cupboards in the utility room. There are no end of boxes of rice and jars and bottles and small packets of things that look like they could be lint but aren't. At last, I find a box with 'First Aid' on it, and inside are a few plasters, so old they feel like dead leaves, and an ancient roll of yellowed bandage. I grab them, together with some kitchen roll and a bottle of lavender oil from Mimi's essential oil shelf, and I go back out to him. He's sitting in the hot sun, looking exhausted and forlorn. Ever since his little outburst on my first weekend here, I've been anxious to avoid Cliff, so now I'm going to make as good an impression as possible.

On my knees before him, I take his great old foot, wet the kitchen towel, and swab the wound, which is still bleeding profusely. I pick out the glass, then I wipe it with lavender oil. 'This'll help to prevent infection. Tea tree oil might be better, but I'm afraid it would sting. I think this'll promote healing.'

'Good.'

The wound is about two inches long and quite deep. I patch it together with the brittle plasters, but it looks like it could do with some stitches in it. I start to wrap the bandage round his foot. 'You should probably go to A&E with this.'

'No fear! Not with this virus around. You're doing a grand job.'

I try not to glow too much, but I'm pleased. 'If Mimi was here, at least you'd have a proper doctor to look at it, but I can't find her.'

'What doctor's that?'

'Mimi.'

'*Mimi?*'

I look up at him. 'Yes. She used to be a doctor. Didn't you know?'

'Doctor, my arse! That what she told you?' He shakes his head and sighs.

I tuck the end of the bandage in and swallow hard. 'There you go, soldier.'

He rests his heel down gingerly. 'Grand job there.'

I need to know more. Emboldened by the compliment, I ask, 'Have you been here long?'

'Here? Most of my life, now. I came here as a teenager back in sixty-five, and I've stayed here ever since.'

'Wow! What was it like then?'

'Mark's grandfather had it then, and I was just doing gardening work – friend of his son. Proper old house it was then, but flagging a bit. You know. Then when the old man pegged it, my friend Pete took it over – Mark's father – and he and I turned it into a commune. He was a good mate, Pete. Those were the days . . . we had musicians, a carpenter, lots of children running around, and my good woman, Karen. And his good woman, of course – before she left.'

'Marcus's mother?'

'Yes. Sally.'

'She died, didn't she?'

'No, she went off with a carpenter. Broke his heart. Pete might've told him she died later on, to stop him going to find her, in case he got hurt. Let's face it, if she'd wanted to see him, she had plenty of time to come looking. What sort of woman just ups and leaves a four-year-old, I don't know.' He shakes his head, and although I get where he's coming from, I wonder if he would've been at all damning if it had been Marcus's father who had left. 'But we were one big family, see. My Karen was like a mum to him. He didn't miss out. They were good times. Loads of music. Lots of animals and vegetables – totally self-sufficient, we were. Bit of weed for our own use, that's all. Yeah, they were good days.'

'You think it's changed a lot, then?'

'Oh, blimey, it all changed when *she* came. When Mark grew up and started bringing girls back . . . well, it was all fine until his dad died. Until Pete died. Then he brought *her* home. And then he started calling himself Marcus.'

'Mimi?'

'Mandy, Mimi, whatever she wants to call herself.' He looks around, as if checking to see if anyone is near. 'You should've got out while you could, that first weekend.'

A chill runs through my bones. 'How do you mean?'

'This pandemic. You're a bit stuck now.'

I gaze at him. His rheumy eyes don't look threatening any more, they seem anxious, wary. He looks about again and lowers his voice.

'Listen, if you get a chance – any chance – you get the hell out of here as soon as you can.'

Chapter Thirty-Five

The girls are keen to go to a big supermarket. They haven't had any contact with the outside world in ages, but standing outside in the hot sun in a queue that snakes right the way around the supermarket car park is not anyone's idea of excitement. Marcus insisted we didn't need masks as they're not compulsory, but now, looking back at the queue forming rapidly behind us, everyone else seems to be wearing them. I've let the girls down. We could so easily have made masks; it would've been a good activity.

'Why can't we wear masks?' says Daisy.

'Because it's a load of nonsense,' says Marcus. 'Good God, look at everyone. People are taking this far too seriously. It's hideous.'

'*Marcus . . .*' Henna frowns miserably, and I think I'll leave the counter-argument to her, as she'll have loads to say about this, but instead she just looks mortified and says she's going to find us a trolley. Everyone else seems to have a trolley already. Marcus looks about. She has made her way to the very edge of the car park and is disappearing behind a trolley collection shelter. I don't know why he's so hostile to masks. I'm beginning to think he wears a mask of his own all the time. I'm sure he told me his mum died. Why would he – or his father – say that? Why would you lie about a thing like that?

'Go with her, will you?' he says, with unusual concern.

I make my way swiftly in the direction I saw her go. She's not near the trolleys. I corner the trolley shelter: not here either. I begin to quicken my pace towards a little alley by the side of the supermarket, with a small arrowed sign saying 'Town Centre'. I hear loud voices just at the moment I spot her.

'D'you wanna sit on my face?'

Three lads have formed a barrier across Henna's path. Facing them, her back looks narrow and her chicken-bone limbs seem helpless. This girl, who could run circles around any of them in a debate, is no match for them in this dark supermarket alley.

I run up behind her. 'Fuck off, you morons! Leave her alone.' I grab her shoulder as she turns round, and walk her swiftly away from their leering, animal faces, back towards the trolleys.

'Suck my dick, bitch!' When I don't respond: 'Looks like you've sucked a few in your time, stupid cunt!'

At this point Daisy appears, with Marcus close on her tail.

'What are you playing at?' His face is fraught. 'What the hell were you doing over there? The trolleys are here!'

'She was chased by some boys,' I answer quickly. It's the first thing I can think of, although I don't think it's true. Perhaps she was making a run for it.

By the time we've queued up again and reached the yellow-jacketed man at the entrance, who waves a few people in at a time and makes sure we use the hand sanitiser provided, no one is expecting to enjoy the outing. But the vast array of food seems so unworldly after our isolation at Amberside, that the mood picks up quickly.

Gone are the arrows on the floor. This supermarket is spacious and people mill around like people normally do, only keeping a wider berth. Daisy exclaims in wonder at everything, and I put some colouring pens in the trolley for her, and a notebook for Henna. The environmentally friendly options to refill plastic bottles and cartons are pretty impressive, and it's a bit shocking how Marcus completely ignores them. Given how environmentally friendly he is. Not. The trolley fills up and becomes a mountain, topped by kitchen towels.

I can't help picturing Luke here in ten years' time. He's pushing a toddler (whose first word is 'subtext') around Waitrose in a trolley, and doing that *loud* kiddie-talk thing that weekend fathers do to show off their fathering skills to people who are simply looking for vegetables. 'Well *done*, Calpurnia! That *is* yuk. Shall we find the organic apples instead?' I picture him artfully sporting a flat cap and braces, resenting this demeaning weekly chore, because his marriage to the hideously wealthy daughter of a businessman has disintegrated in sad little increments after he discovered (and fastidiously outlined) her many faults. Not the least being the fact that her father doesn't believe in handouts, or share Luke's belief that certain future celebrity equals certain future security for his daughter, nor will it pay for his granddaughter's prep school or her pony, cello, nanny, etc. It's pathetic, I know, to think of Luke like this, but it gives me some solace. And if his adored daughter ever exists, I hope, above all else, that she develops a ferocious addiction to cheap bangles, Marmite and Newcastle Brown Ale.

The queue at the checkout spools down the full length of an aisle, and I tell Marcus that I'm just popping off to get something I forgot.

'Oh, don't you go disappearing, too. We're almost there.'

'I'll go with her,' says Henna.

Daisy is all set to come as well, but he puts his arm out to bar her way. 'You're all staying here. I don't want us to get split up again.'

'I just need something at the pharmacy,' I say, quite firmly. 'I'll be two minutes.'

I don't wait for a reply. I head straight for the pharmacy that I clocked on the way in. I have Gran's twenty-pound note in the inside pocket of my shoulder bag.

*

I sit on the lid of the supermarket loo with my eyes closed, listening to the thudding of blood in my temples. If I wait long enough, that second blue line that has appeared so swiftly might just disappear. I try to distract myself. I could just walk out now. I could wander into the centre of town and catch a bus or a train out of here. Except I have no money. So many times I've lain in bed and tried to calculate it. There must be an ATM here. I could find out. I'll do that. Then at least I'll know. And then next time – next time, when he knows he can trust me to come back – I'll run. Shit. What am I saying? Why should I have to answer to anyone? No wonder Bryony tried to leave. No wonder Henna wants to join her. I won't tell Marcus I'm pregnant. I don't think he'll want me to have it, but I don't want to risk it. If Mimi doesn't believe in abortion, then maybe he doesn't either. Maybe I can buy the morning-after pill here, without a prescription. My friend Hannah did something like that when we were at school. I remember we went to Superdrug, and it was way later than the day after. I'll go back to the pharmacy now.

It's still two blue lines, dammit. I shove it in my bag, in case I have to prove I'm pregnant at the pharmacy, and I stuff the packaging in the waste bin. There's a queue for the loo, trailing out through the door, which someone has wedged open with their foot. I try not to look in the mirror as I wash my hands, because I don't want to see a pregnant version of my stupid, stunned self, looking back at me.

In the atrium of the store, Marcus, Daisy and Henna are waiting for me, watching my approach now they've spotted me, so we have to go straight back to the car. Marcus looks pretty rattled that I hadn't mentioned going to the loo, so there's no point in asking if I can go back to the pharmacy for something else. Next time. And if the pharmacy says that no, the morning-after pill is not available, then what?

Shit shit shit.

*

On the drive home, everyone perks up a little with the air conditioner on. I try to catch Henna's mood, but she is inscrutable in her headphones. As we turn into the flat track up to the house, I'm cross with myself: I was determined to pay attention to this last bit of the route home, determined to see exactly how the road led into which lanes, and which twists and turns led all the way across the field, using the alternative route to the front door of Amberside, so that one day soon, when I have a plan, I will know exactly how to get out.

Chapter Thirty-Six

As soon as we've unloaded all the bags of shopping, I go upstairs to my room. Lying on the bed, my hand runs over my belly. In here is a small blob, the size of a kidney bean. But it's growing, day by day, multiplying its cells even as I think. I've already filled out a bit, and my breasts ache from time to time. For a while, I allow myself to imagine having Marcus's child. Amberside becomes my home and the girls are happy. Mimi drifts off somewhere into the ether. But the effort to stem my wonder at this growing thing is surprisingly easy, is overtaken by a realisation of my lack of choice here. If I decide not to have it – which is almost certain – my options are limited. They may not even exist. A rising panic pummels my chest.

There's a gentle tap on the door.

'Come in!'

Marcus stands in the doorway. 'The girls are putting the food away. Come with me. I need to take the car back up to the woods.'

'Why? It's much handier here. Why can't you leave it here?'

'It's closer to the main road up in the woods. This is only good for dropping off heavy stuff. It takes forever down those twisty lanes – a nightmare if you meet anyone coming the other way.' He comes over and pulls me up, his voice hushed and urgent. 'Come on. I want to talk to you – in private.'

Outside, he starts the engine, and we rumble down the uneven path to the lane. After a few turnings, he pulls the Land Rover to a stop at a small clearing by some beech trees.

'Have you got any lipsalve?' he asks. 'My lips are parched.' He reaches over and his hand is in my bag before I can stop him. He pulls out the pregnancy test like someone who knew exactly what he was looking for. 'I knew it!'

All I can do is sit, aghast, and stare at my knees. 'It's okay, I'll sort it out.'

'Get out!'

He's out of the car himself and my stomach pitches. What will he do now? Mimi's bound to find out eventually and he'll have to get rid of me. Maybe this is it. He's going to finish me off. I feel sick. I haven't had any morning sickness, but now I could throw up easily.

My car door is flung open. He has made his way round the car and is standing outside. He's going to tell me I got pregnant deliberately, that I manipulated the situation. 'Come on!' He waits for me to get out, then slams the car door, grabs my hand and walks me into the trees.

'Marcus—'

'Wait!'

He pulls me over to a giant tree trunk and pins me to it. 'What do you mean, you'll sort it out?'

'It's okay. I won't have it. I'll go away. I won't break up your marriage – your whatever – with Mimi. I know you say—'

He grabs my chin. 'Caitlin. You are not getting rid of this baby. This is *our* baby. Don't you see? It's *ours*, yours and mine.'

'But . . . I . . . We can have a baby if that's what you want,' I lie, utterly cornered. 'Just maybe not now. Not yet.'

'But I want this baby. I *love* you, Caitlin, can't you see?' He shakes his head, as if in disbelief that I could be so thick. He's laughing. 'Can't you *see*?'

'But what about Mimi?'

'Mimi? I've told you. We're not . . . she doesn't *love* me. I don't *love* her.'

'Marcus, I know you might think it'll be fine having two adoring women around you, but I don't want that. If I ever have a baby, it will be with one partner, and I intend it to be exclusive – and for life.'

'I know, I know. Look, wait! Don't move!' He runs back to the car and fiddles around inside, then bounds back towards me. 'That's why . . . listen.' He gets down on one knee. 'Caitlin Polglaze, will you marry me?'

Fucksake. This is like some kind of warped joke, but he's looking up at me with the beseeching eyes of a child. In his hand is an open blue box with a diamond ring nestled in velvet.

'It was my grandmother's. It's antique. I've never given anything like this to Mimi.'

I can't think straight. Moments ago it crossed my mind that he might be going to top me and leave my body in these woods to be eaten by crows. He can't mean this. He can't.

'But you don't believe in marriage. You said so.'

'Caitlin, listen to me. I'm deadly serious. You are having my child, and I love you, and we can be together – properly together, like you want. Mimi doesn't have to live at Amberside.'

Oh, God. He has read the letter I wrote to Erin with all that bullshit about Mr Rochester and the wife in the attic.

'How can she not? Daisy and Henna are there.'

'They don't have to be. It can be just you and me.'

'But I don't want the girls to go.'

There it is again – that feeling of too great a distance to span in one go. I had made the leap from trust to distrust, painfully, clumsily, and now I'm expected to reverse my steps, with no helpful stepping stones, just a wide stretch of water to bridge.

Suddenly he's on his feet, his face up against mine, his breath smelling strongly of the chorizo he had at lunchtime. He's too close, this man I have fantasised about for weeks, this man whose partner I have even imagined being crushed by a tractor so that the fantasy could have all the glitches ironed out. Suddenly I want him out of my face, out of my space, but his lips land on mine and his hands slide under the bib of my dungarees.

'No. Listen. I think . . .' I push him away. 'Listen, Marcus. You know how I feel about you . . .' (I don't know how he can, because I don't have a clue myself right now.) 'It's just that I'm not ready to have a baby. Not yet. Really and truly, I'm not. It's not that I don't want your baby – I do – it's just that I want it all to be perfect. You and me, and our family. Can't we just wait a year or two, while you sort things out with Mimi?'

I don't really hear what he says next, because I'm busy analysing my lie. I have no intention of having a baby for at least ten years and – I'm quite suddenly certain – never with him. But I see now that my readiness to say I do suggests a diplomacy that I'm not known for when wriggling out of a spot. Truth comes at me like a wave from behind: I am absolutely shit-scared.

Chapter Thirty-Seven

The evening meal is horrendous. I'm too churned up to eat anything, and Marcus keeps pressing me to eat, as if I need feeding up. Mimi looks between us, intrigued, and asks how the shopping went. Henna is quiet. Daisy looks desperate to fill the silence.

She says quietly, 'A man shouted at Caitlin in the car park and called her a stupid cunt.'

Silence. Mimi looks at me; I look at my barely touched plate of sweet potato and spinach polenta. I want to say I have never used that word in front of Daisy, because it's true, but I know there would be no point. Her silent rage seems to poison the air so that breathing becomes tricky.

'Well, that was very rude of him. I hope you *never* use words like that, Daisy. Do you hear me?'

'Yes. Don't worry, Mummy, I know. "Stupid" is a very rude word, isn't it, Caitlin?'

'That's right,' I say. 'It's not a kind word.'

'You should say "daft" instead, shouldn't you?'

'Yes.' I could fling my arms around Daisy. What a gem.

I can't face spending any intimate time with Marcus after the pregnancy result. He'll just renew his pressure on me to have the baby, and I want to make a phone call to the doctors' surgery first. I'll have to ask Kal. I don't think he'll want me to use his phone, given how safety-conscious he is, but I might ask if he'll dial the number for me. I could hold it with a pair of kitchen gloves or something. It's worth a try. So long as Joe's out.

I sit in my bedroom later and wish I could speak to Mum. I miss her. I don't even have a photo of her: they're all on my missing phone. I didn't even come back to England for her mum's funeral. I look at my bedside table and think of my gran. I have only three things belonging to Granny Rostock – Mum's mother – apart from all the songs she taught me. They are the locket, the travel alarm and an embroidered handkerchief. Granny Rostock tucked the handkerchief in my pocket when I went on the school trip to the Lake District, and it stayed in my pocket all the way to Florence. I spread it out flat on my bedside table now, and look at it. All the songs she sang had the same message: men make things happen; women are powerless – things happen to them. And I think of all the things she did, and all the generations of women before her, so invisible, so silent. The hours of singing softly to sleep, the night feeding and calming of children, the beautifully ironed clothes all spattered again with food or mud the next day, the lovingly prepared meals, eaten and leaving no trace. Not for them the dappled grey horse or the company car, the war memorial or the plaque on the office door, the gold watch or the retirement clock. Just more eggshells, vegetable peelings and dirty laundry. None of her work leaves a mark. Her songs speak of times when women had no voice: the only choice they had, the only power they wielded over their future, was the timely dropping of a handkerchief.

And this is the one thing that leaves a true trace of her. In one corner is a letter *C* for Caitlin and a posy of roses. Each embroidered leaf has two halves: one a darker green than the other, giving a sense of shape, of light striking it on one side. The rose petals are a darker pink at their base, as they disappear deep into the centre of the flower. Each stitch has been carefully thought through. This is my grandmother's work: careful, assiduous, quiet, skilful. It's so hard to believe that this wonderful artefact, this priceless treasure, was designed for me to blow my snot into.

I think about Marcus and his declaration of love. I can't quite take it in. Not so long ago I would've been punching the air at the thought of his words; but I feel like I did in reception class when I was awarded a gold star for bravery after hurting my knee. I'd longed for a gold star, but I didn't want the bloodied knee it seemed to have entailed. I lie in bed at night and try to imagine living here with Marcus and a child of ours, but I can't hold on to the picture. Just like the earlier fantasy, there are too many problems to iron out: Mimi would not slink off to another life, and even if she did, the thought of Daisy being separated from one of her parents would spoil things. And there's something else – something I'm missing. I need to look closer, or around the edges, or underneath a surface I haven't spotted yet. I can't make things add up. And way above all of this, the thing that fills my head at the moment is the thought that something is beginning to grow inside me, and I don't want it to. That is my choice: it has to be. There are so few choices open to me in this closed-off paradise, and I am not letting anyone else make this one for me.

> *I wish, I wish, I wish in vain,*
> *I wish I were a maid again,*
> *But a maid again I never shall be,*
> *Till apples grow on an orange tree.*
>
> *I wish my baby it was born,*
> *And smiling on its father's knee,*
> *And I were lain in yon graveyard,*
> *With the long grass growing over me.*

Chapter Thirty-Eight

We're coming back from our morning walk down through the woods when we spot something unusual. We see it before we hear anything. Marcus is standing in front of the house with his hands on his hips, facing away from us towards the track, where a car has been parked. It's a small, homely car, and not one you would choose to drive over rough terrain. A woman carrying a folder and wearing a long pink cardigan has made her way towards him and looks anxiously at him, head on one side. The body language is aggressive (Marcus) and defensive (pink cardigan). As we approach, we hear him raise his voice.

'I do *not* have to ask anyone's permission to home-school my children!'

'You're quite right, absolutely right, but Bryony and Henna have both missed a term now, and you do have to inform the headteacher – in writing.'

'Okay, well, I'll write to her headmaster by the end of the week.'

'Headteacher. It's a woman – Mrs Gregory.'

'Fine.'

'And you might like some free resources from the home-schooling representative of the local education authority.'

'No, thank you. We have our own tutor and *I* decide what they learn, thank you very much.'

'But Bryony – she'll be wanting to sit her GCSEs, and the

thing is, they're going to be done on teacher assessment now, so if she hasn't been taught—'

'Bryony's not doing GCSEs. She doesn't want to. Nor Henna.'

At this point she spots us nearing the front door. Her face brightens. 'Oh, you must be . . . Bryony? Henna?'

'Henna. Yes—'

Marcus has already swivelled round. 'Get into the house, please!'

He gives me a firm stare, and I usher them in, but Henna pulls back.

'I'd like to go to school,' she says from the doorway.

'Oh, well—'

'Don't talk to my children,' he says abruptly. 'I've said all I'm going to say. They're *my* children, and *I'll* decide what they learn!'

I pull Henna by the elbow and she jerks me away, but still joins Daisy inside. The three of us watch from the front window as the woman hugs her file to her bosom and makes a hasty retreat back up the track. Marcus watches her go, then returns to his polytunnels behind the house, and his illegal harvest. It's hard to imagine this is the same man who gave me such a tender kiss in the pub porch in Ribley.

Three times I make tentative trips up to the cottage, and on the third day I see what I was hoping for: one red car. Only Kal is in.

When he comes to the door, he doesn't conceal his pleasure at seeing me. 'I was hoping you'd come again. Did you get your phone?'

'No. Marcus said he didn't have it.'

'But I saw him take it.'

'I know. I believe you. But I think . . . I think he's hidden it, or something.'

'He's lying?' Kal frowns, or perhaps he's squinting at the sun, which hits him full in the face. 'I don't understand. That's a bit worrying.'

'Actually, Kal, I am a bit worried.'

'Wait here!' He comes out, crosses in front of me and walks to a little shed at the side of the garden. He rummages around, and then he emerges with two folded chairs. 'They're covered in cobwebs, I'm afraid, but we can sit in the shade – two metres apart, all legal.'

We sit, hidden from view by the shed, in the shade of an apple tree, its pink and white blossoms wilting now to reveal the tiny green orbs that will swell and ripen into apples. In the flower bed, I'm struck by the bold pink flowers of honesty. The chairs we sit on have rotting green canvas seats, and mine creaks under my weight when I move. I wonder if I'm starting to look heavier.

'Tell me,' he says, leaning forward. 'What is it you're worried about?'

I'm not sure how much to tell him. 'I need to make a phone call – urgently.'

'That's tricky. I've got an old phone, but I'd have to unlock it and wipe it and reset it, which takes a while, and you'd have to get a new SIM card. If you like, I could buy you a SIM card online.' He's trying to find solutions, and his teeth are pearly white as he sucks on his lower lip, thinking. '*Or* we could get you a burner phone for under twenty pounds, probably. You could keep the battery here.'

I can't tell him I think I have no money, because then he'll feel awkward and maybe offer to pay.

'That's really kind. I don't think I have time for any of that. I need to phone my family urgently.'

'Ah.' He rests his chin on his hand, thinking. His nails are beautiful, his fingertips spatulate. I could watch him thinking all day. Then he sits back in his chair and looks at me, excited. 'I tell you what! Sod it! You can borrow my phone. I'm taking enough risks living with Joe. Every time I turn on a tap or use the kettle I'm exposed to his viruses, and he even has people in sometimes.' I can believe this of Joe. 'So, if *you're* willing to take the risk . . .' He takes his phone from his back pocket, presses it with his thumb, and holds it out to me. 'Here.'

Phew. It's hard to believe what I'm holding. 'Thank you. Thank you, Kal. I really appreciate this.'

He smiles, pleased. I'll ring Mum – no, Erin. I want my mum. I want to feel Mum's arms around me and tell me it's all okay. But she'll worry and start giving me advice, which may be no bad thing right now. I thought I had all this planned out in my head, but having the phone in my hand is like being granted one fairy wish. I could tell Erin my predicament and she could find out online what my options are, and I could ask her to give me our local surgery number. And Mum's got enough on her plate without hearing I'm up the duff. Right . . .

Only . . .

I look at the keyboard. 07 . . . I don't know Erin's number. I always just click on her name. I haven't a clue how to ring her without my own phone. Kal has stood up, diplomatically, to inspect some honeysuckle and other weeds. I'll ring Mum. I know her number: 07750 100432 . . . or 234 . . . or 243. I make several attempts and get a number-not-recognised. Maybe it's not 07750 . . . I keep trying, watching Kal inspecting some stinging nettles like the judge in a horticultural show.

It's no good. I put my head in my hands and let out an involuntary whimper.

'What's the matter?' He comes over swiftly. 'Caitlin?'

The sound of my name spoken kindly sounds like home. I try to hold my face together. 'I can't remember their numbers.'

'Do you know the landline?'

'Yes. Good idea.'

I do remember this because Dad always said the number when he picked it up, like someone from the 1960s. And I know the area code. And Erin picked up the last time I rang it, from the house payphone, so I could be in luck.

It rings. Please let it be Erin. It keeps ringing, and I keep hoping. Now I don't care who answers it – just let it be someone. How can they be out? It's lockdown. Even if Erin has gone to live with her boyfriend, that still leaves Dani, Mum and Dad. Unless Mum's kicked him out. Unless Dani's gone to live with Erin and her boyfriend. Oh God. What if they're all dead?

'No luck?' He looks at me anxiously.

I hand him back the phone.

'No. I have to ring my doctor,' I blurt out. 'But I don't know that number either.'

'What's the name of the surgery?'

'I don't know. It's in Clemo Road, Tremellick.' I want to tell him everything, but I'm not sure what his reaction would be. He might be shocked and not want to befriend me; he could be from a culture that doesn't believe in abortion and refuse to help me. I plunge in, clumsily. 'Where are you from?'

'Bristol.'

'Do you . . . are you . . . do you have any particular religion?'

He smiles. 'You mean where am I *really* from?'

I cringe. I sound just like Mimi. 'I'm sorry. I'm just curious.'

'That's okay. My father's Muslim, my mother used to be Church of England, and I have no religious bones in my body. And I'm *really* from Bristol.'

I smile, apologetically. 'And I'm from Cornwall.'

'I love Cornwall. Which part?'

'Tremellick? Just down from Bodmin Moor.'

'Sounds great. I tell you what . . .' He starts typing at lightning speed with his thumbs. 'If you promise to invite me down to Cornwall one day, I'll give you your doctor's surgery number, okay?'

He holds up the phone with a picture of the outside of the surgery, and the phone number.

Thankyouthankyouthankyou.

I dial the number. He does another lap of the garden and then goes inside, leaving me with the message: *If you think you have*

Covid 19, or have a fever, please dial 111. To make an appointment, we encourage you to use our online appointment service. If you need to speak to a doctor, or for all other enquiries, please hold. The Cornish accent makes me homesick. There is a pause, then some music, and eventually: *Your call is number . . . nine . . . in the queue.* Music again.

After twenty minutes, Kal puts his head out of the door. He must have started to wonder if I'd walked off with his phone. He raises his eyebrows, hopefully, and I shake my head. After the next round of music, I am still number nine. I can't do this to him. But as I'm thinking about giving up, he comes out with two cups of tea and a little footstool. He places them between us.

'If you feel you can drink out of one of our dodgy mugs . . . do you take sugar?'

I shake my head. 'That's really kind. I should probably give up. This isn't fair on you.'

'No, keep going. Put it on speaker and have a cup of tea.'

There is something about the cup of tea that makes me even more homesick. Whenever I used to get sad or worried or wound up, Mum would always say, *I'll put the kettle on.*

'Thank you.'

We chat about our families for a while, and our plans for the future. I explain that I don't want to stay here much longer, that I'm starting to feel a bit trapped. I'm struck by how comfortable it is to be in his company, talking about normal things. I haven't felt this relaxed for a long time.

'You know, you could just write a letter to your family.'

'I've tried that. I don't think they posted the first one, and I posted another one myself, but I think somehow Marcus or Mimi are getting to the letterbox before me. I haven't heard anything.'

'Next time, give my address. I'll write it down for you. And if things get really bad, ask your family to come and pick you up. You can officially travel next month – from the fourth of July, I think.'

God, it's June already. When did that happen?

He sits back in his chair, framed in honesty.

'I don't think I can wait that long.'

Some petals of apple blossom float down and land on the phone, which pauses its music and says, *You are number . . . nine . . . in the queue.*

'I'm sorry,' I say. 'I'm wasting your time. I'd better get back, or they'll be wondering where I am.'

'There's no need to rush off. But look, come again tomorrow afternoon. We can keep trying with the phone. It's no problem.'

'Thank you! But what about Joe? I don't want him to see me.'

'Joe is out tomorrow, and the next day, then on nights for two days.'

'Tomorrow afternoon, then. Thank you, Kal.'

A weight is lifting. But as we sip our tea in the sunshine, I have no idea that something very different will happen the following afternoon, something terrifying that will turn everything on its head.

Chapter Thirty-Nine

Mimi says that Violeta is feeling a bit tired and is 'putting her feet up', which is why a new girl, Drita, makes our evening meal. I'm sure this isn't following the lockdown rules. Working in the polytunnels hardly counts as being a member of the household. I've clocked that Violeta doesn't have much time for Drita, and the couple of times I've seen them together, she's snapped at her. It's hard not to notice the way Drita avoids Marcus's gaze. Exactly like me after that first kiss with him in Ribley. She smiles at everyone except him, a sure sign that he's giving her one, if you ask me. Or about to, and she knows it. I catch him stealing brief glances at her, and I have a bad feeling about it. Not that I care or anything, it's just that I'd like to think . . . I'd like to think it meant something to Marcus, what we had. I don't think I could bear it if I was just one in a long line of convenient shags. I can't quite bring myself to hate him yet, because that would mean hating myself. I need to keep a sliver of myself loved and intact. Anyway, perhaps it's because I'm on high alert that I hear something unusual the following afternoon.

I'm lying on the bed in my room with Filkins at my feet. I've been trying hard to get my head around probability and statistics for Henna's lessons this week; how on earth could I do this at school just a few years back?

It baffles me to start with, the sound: so familiar, and yet so different. Two whistles, long and drawn-out. *Two*, not three. These are for someone else. This is a new code for Drita. I clamber up from the bed and look out of the window at the grassy slope up to the barn. There are the gorse bushes, doused in yellow flowers; there are the bramble bushes, the beech trees around the barn, their leaves so still they might be playing grandmother's footsteps. No sign of the Albanian girl climbing the bank. I gaze out of the window, waiting. I'm sure it was two whistles. Just two. Soon there'll be a second set of whistles. There's always a second round. I see now this is to confirm the number of whistles the first time round. *Three whistles, okay?* Not four, not two. Three. Then he'll repeat it.

If I go quickly, I can get to the barn before the second set of whistles. I can get there before she does.

I don't know what I'm thinking when I hurry up the slope. I don't think I have a clue what I'll say when I catch Marcus at his side door, doing his second volley for a new lover. My cheeks are heating up, but with what emotion I couldn't say. There's something driving me up there, and I can't stop it.

I look back down at the house: there's no one following me, not yet. I pass the back of the barn and duck behind a giant clump of brambles, from where I have a good view of the side of the building not seen from the house. The thorns catch at my jumper. I carefully un-snag it, crouching uncomfortably. I listen. There's moaning from inside the barn. It's a woman. I stand up and start walking towards his side door, heart pumping. Behind all the rusty equipment, the door is padlocked still. How can that be? Then it comes: two whistles again, long and clear. I go around to the main doors of the barn, and one is open. The moaning from inside is louder now. And what I see, as the great barn door closes, is not Marcus at all. It is Mimi. Mimi who has whistled twice, Mimi who looks as if I've caught her out. She is startled.

Chapter Forty

'Oh. You should go back down to the house.' I must look so completely baffled, so pathetic, because she says, 'It's not Marcus. It's me. He's back at the house. You should go and find him.'

But I've already caught a glimpse of the scene she's trying to close off from me, I'm already sidling past her into the barn. At the far end, on the double mattress, a woman lies panting and naked. Her chin is pointed upwards, her knees are bent.

'You need to go,' says Mimi, catching my arm, but I push past her, heading towards the mattress bed. Mimi hurries behind me. 'Caitlin, listen to me – you have to go!'

I crouch beside Violeta, and see her hair plastered to her face, her limbs shiny with sweat. She gives a slow-building moan, which keeps going, growling to a scream. I know this is all normal in childbirth, and I steel myself not to be shocked, but still I'm in a helpless panic. I try to reassure Violeta, but she barely notices me. Her eyes rock back and she heaves a great sigh, long and low, which climbs into another moan.

'How long? How long has it been?'

'Since yesterday afternoon,' says Mimi. 'I helped her up here then, but she didn't really start dilating until after tea.'

'What – *yesterday*? Surely she should have given birth by now?'

I know very little, of course, and all of it from my mother's comments over the top of *Call the Midwife* episodes, as she used to explain what was realistic and what wasn't. I also once 'helped' her deliver a baby in a car which had stopped in a lane somewhere between Bodmin and Lostwithiel, when a man waved us down because his girlfriend's baby had started crowning on their way home from Tesco. But all I really saw was the placenta coming out. Before that it was all my mum's backside, leaning into the car across the driver's seat.

'She's fine.'

'We have to get her to hospital,' I say.

'No! She wants a home birth. She's illegal, remember. I know what I'm doing.'

I try to reassure Violeta again, hearing my own mother's voice: *It's all right, love, you're doing really well. You're doing just beautifully.* I try to emulate her, hoping the panic doesn't show in my voice. Her eyelids are closing now, fluttering, and she's murmuring something in Romanian.

'It's okay, Violeta. It's Caitlin. You're doing okay.' I take her hand, but it feels limp and damp. My words are like small pebbles in my mouth. 'You're doing really well.'

'Help,' she whispers. 'Help.'

I turn and see Mimi at the sink in the corner, wringing out a towel. 'Let me call an ambulance.'

'No! There's no need.' Her look is almost fierce. 'You can't phone, anyway.'

I get to my feet and make for the door. 'I'll ask Joe. It'll only take me ten minutes.'

'He's working. He won't be there.'

'Then I'll ask Kal. He'll let me use his phone.'

'No!' She has followed me and grabs my arm quite roughly now. 'They won't know where to come.'

'Of course they will.'

'They won't be able to carry her up through the woods. Don't be ridiculous.'

She has a point.

'What about the track? The ambulance can come the long way

round. Then they only have to get her down to the house.'

'They won't know where to come.'

'I'll tell them exactly. Marcus can tell them.'

'No! I've told you – I know what I'm doing. I've done it before. The baby's almost here. Come and see.' Then, trying out a friendlier tone, 'You can help me.'

A loud moan seems to make the rafters vibrate, and takes us both back to the bed. Mimi beckons me to the bottom end of it and draws one of Violeta's knees gently aside. An apple-smooth oval of skin is showing behind the stretched opening. She is pushing now, and it grows in size, then seems to recede a little. With each push now, it grows a little more. I hold her hand and talk to her, through her apparent oblivion, telling her she is having a beautiful baby, telling her how clever she is, telling her to hold on in there; and all the while the giant lizard's eye between her legs grows and bulges.

But still the baby doesn't come. It must have been twenty-four hours by now. I do know this is dangerous. If she was in hospital, they'd be speeding up labour with drugs or a C-section. This doesn't seem right at all. I feel her pulse. It's very weak. I wish I could speak her language; I wish I knew what she was murmuring. If I had a phone, I'd ring Mum. She'd talk me through what to do.

'Maybe we should get her upright,' I say to Mimi. 'Get gravity on her side.'

'She can't support herself.'

'I could kneel behind her. I've seen it done.'

This isn't, strictly speaking, true. She smiles sardonically. Mimi doesn't like me knowing anything. She is the expert here. And anyway, I haven't seen it done, I've only seen it on telly, but it sounds logical to me. This baby has to come out soon, or I'm afraid Violeta will die. I think of the grave in among the gorse bushes. It's all very well Mimi saying she knows what she's doing, but she's got form.

'Help,' Violeta whispers, and then she's building up to another moan, but seems to have so little strength.

I climb behind her and lift her torso onto my lap. It's not much. I can't seem to lift her any more than that, and a great bellow comes out of her and I feel it in her ribs, like a monster determined to be heard. I've never heard or felt anything like it. I want to scream with her.

'Yes!' I say, instead. 'Yes.'

But I think, *No, no*; she's fading. Mimi is kneeling between her legs and telling her to push. She won't push, I think. She can't. She's exhausted; her limbs are limp in my arms.

Then there is a sudden tension; she becomes solid in my arms, damp and solid and howling. A rushing sound, a powerful earthy, bleachy smell, and Mimi fiddles with something, holds up a bloodied bundle, then smiles. Violeta slumps back on me heavily, done in. I raise my eyebrows hopefully.

'A girl,' says Mimi. She looks pleased, at last.

As she wipes the baby, I ease myself out from behind Violeta and make my way round to Mimi, who has placed some clamps on the umbilical cord. She asks me to cut it, and I take the scissors from her, hoping they're sterile, but not daring to ask. And then I cut this surprising thing, which is translucent and tough and spiralled like a stick of candy. Blood spills out onto a towel, and Mimi tells me to fill a bowl she has put by the sink with warm water from the pre-boiled kettle, and to tell her when it's cool enough to touch.

Soon, she is washing the baby with swabs of linty stuff and wrapping it in a towel. I turn to Violeta and start to congratulate her. She barely surfaces, and makes no sign of interest.

'Shouldn't there be a placenta?' I ask, turning to Mimi.

'Soon enough. She'll be okay.' She holds the baby close and shakes her head. 'Not sure about this one.' Seeing my startled look, she says, 'There are more towels here.'

I start to clear away the bloodstained towels around Violeta and replace them with fresh ones, and Mimi starts towards the door.

'Keep an eye on her, will you? I'll be back in a bit.'

I feel suddenly very alone. Violeta shows no sign of wanting to speak. She's clearly exhausted. I whisper platitudes to her and sit down on the mattress to wait for the placenta. I remember this bit from the roadside near Bodmin. I remember it slithering out like raw liver. I'm glad I know what to expect.

But the placenta doesn't come. And neither does Mimi. I wait some more: twenty minutes? Thirty? It's impossible to know without a phone. And I don't know how long it should take. When is too long? Violeta is still bleeding. I replace another towel. And then another.

'Violeta? Hey, Violeta, can you hear me?'

She's breathing okay. I find her pulse, but it's weak, or perhaps I don't know how to find a pulse properly. I've got no stopwatch to test it by. The breathtaking smell of birth is beginning to be blotted out by the metallic reek of blood. There's so much of it. I expect it's normal, but I don't know. Damn Mimi. She's probably showing everyone the baby. I go to the barn door and walk until I can look down at the house. She's making her way back up now, and I dare to hurry her along with arm movements.

'How's the baby?' I ask, by the barn door.

Mimi shakes her head and murmurs, 'I'm afraid she didn't make it.'

'What . . .?'

She pushes past me, then turns to mouth 'Dead', in case Violeta overhears. But Violeta is still barely with it. I climb behind her and prop her up again, whispering encouragement to her. I cling on close to the dead weight of her, glad she can't see my face, because it is helplessly distorted and running with tears.

Mimi tugs gently on the umbilical cord, and the placenta arrives. Violeta bleeds even more. I get up and keep changing the towels. She is quiet and damp and done in. Her face is sallow and bloodless. At about four o'clock – although it could be any time, as time is oozing stealthily away – Violeta stops breathing.

Chapter Forty-One

I feel horribly cheated. All that effort was meant to bring new life into the world, not lose two people. I've never seen anyone die before, never been so close to life's slipping away. It *sneaked* off. It's not fair. The filthy rotten cheat of it all. The worst of it is that someone will have to tell Henna – poor Henna – and Daisy, and it isn't fair.

Mimi tells me to go down to the house and ask Drita to delay tea by an hour. 'I'll sort things out up here.'

I can't wait to get out in the fresh air. The sun is shining treacherously as I make my way down, catching the grass at a gloriously low angle, making it the greenest of greens. But I'm queasy and my face is aching and sore with tears. 'Mum,' I whisper. I want my mum. More than ever, I want to speak to her, to feel her warm, living, sheltering arms around me.

I'm shaking when I reach the open front door, shaking when I rush up the stairs, and when I sink against my bedroom door and let rip with some unfettered sobbing.

In an effort to be composed again, I go to the bathroom, wash the blood off my hands and splash my face in cold water. When I go downstairs, incredibly, the girls are still working on their knitted garments. Daisy's scarf has become a pink worm long enough to lower Rapunzel, and Henna is trying to sew up her rectangles for Violeta's jumper.

'I can't get it neat,' she says. 'Will you show me how to do it?'

I put my hand over my mouth to stopper more tears.

'Are you okay? Caitlin?'

'Yes.' It comes to me suddenly that every second I don't tell them is a betrayal, and yet how can I tell them there is nothing left? Nothing left of Violeta but a bloodied heap. I imagine Violeta filling Henna's dreams, and I can't deliver this news without something to give her. I must retrieve something of Violeta's – a ring, a bracelet, a dress – anything, that Henna can treasure, that she can hold while she grieves. 'I'll be back in a minute!'

I'm running back up the bank, finding energy from thin air as I pump my legs beneath me. There's a crackling sound and a faint smell of bonfire smoke, and I know Mimi will be burning all the towels. The doors to the barn are ajar. I rush in and see Mimi bundling stained towels into a wicker basket. The body is on the floor, covered in a grubby-looking sheet. Not even completely covered, but rolled up like a pastry.

Mimi looks up, a trace of fear on her face. 'Get out!'

I'm too angry to obey her. I glance about. There is nothing obvious belonging to Violeta. Some shoes, perhaps, some joggers. Then I spot the scissors with which I cut the cord. They are on the sink. Before Mimi can stop me, I grab them and bend down beside the body. I clutch at the dark, damp hair, poking out of the sheet and still smelling strongly of her musky sweat, and lop off a giant handful.

'Caitlin! I'm warning you, get out now!'

She has her hands on me, and I shove her aside as I stand up, and march out of the barn. I turn the opposite way to the house and lean against the stone of the barn around the corner. Taking a scrunchy out of my hair to tie around the lock of hair in my hand, I lift it to my nose. As I round the corner to go back, I almost bump into Marcus. He looks horrified, and so must I. Behind him is Arrow. Both of them are smoking a spliff, but against the wall next to them, two spades are propped. They smell of freshly turned earth.

214

I make my way hurriedly to where they must have come from. It's such a maze of brambles and gorse that I don't find it straight away. I stop abruptly, and stare.

Barely a minute later, his voice is behind me, shouting, 'Get the hell back to the house – *now!*'

And as I stand and gawp at the open grave among the gorse bushes, breathe in the fresh mound of earth, I don't realise it's not even me he's shouting at. The girls have followed me up there, and stand just behind me, gaping at the shallow grave, white as winding sheets.

Then suddenly Marcus comes around a bramble bush with Arrow, and between them they are carrying the long bundle, wrapped in a striped sheet.

'Get them AWAY!' Marcus hollers at me now. And as he does, he must slightly lower his end of the cargo, for Violeta's head lolls out of the sheeting. Her eyes are half-closed and her mouth is open, as if she might be about to snore in her sleep.

'Is she dead?' asks Daisy, with the directness of her five and three quarter years. My crumpled face gives it away, but I nod anyway.

Henna squeezes her eyes tight shut and a wail goes up, loud enough and shrill enough to be heard from Joe and Kal's cottage, from Geoff's sheep farm at Foxes Haye, and certainly from the house, where Drita, unaware of things to come, busies herself with mushroom couscous. I open my arms and draw Henna towards me. She sinks into them, so different from the wilting body of Violeta I held earlier, so hot and pulsing and alive.

> Cold blows the wind over my true love,
> And a few small drops of rain.
> I never did have but one true love,
> And in the cold clay she is lain.

Her back is towards Marcus as I hold her, while I am facing him.

That clenched jaw again, that fury. He is not finished with me.

'I said get them the fuck away!' I gaze back at him. '*Now*, you stupid bitch!'

The last word makes everything around me fall silent. I feel I've been shot. Then I hear my pulse boom, and I steer the girls away and we weave through the bushes. As we make our tremulous way down the slope, I remember, and I slip the lock of hair into Henna's hand. She stops, and like me, the first thing she does is raise it to her nose. We are animals, all of us, I think then. Longing for touch and smell, needing our primal compass in grief. I usher the girls back home, turning my back on Marcus and his filthy spade. But all the way down I can't help thinking of that soft earth grave, and I know it is where I will go, too. And Marcus will dig it.

Chapter Forty-Two

Daisy can't sleep, and I bring her in with me. She is literally shaking, clutching Donkey tight against her neck. I've never seen anyone shake like that. I hold her close and remember when my rabbit died. I was ten, but had nightmares about him for days. This was the corpse of a *woman* she knew, and Daisy is *five*. Fucksake. It's like something experienced in wartime. And where's her 'mum' in all this? Mimi ate a late tea with us as if nothing had happened. She ate, as her children sat white-faced and traumatised in front of her, unable to lift a fork to their mouths. At least Marcus had the tact – if you could call it that – to stay away. Sometimes I think Mimi is a mother simply because she has a tag round her neck saying that she is one. She could just as easily be a Barbie doll. I hurried the girls off to the playroom as quickly as possible, and we tried to watch a nature programme on television. A bird of prey near some baby birds in a nest made Daisy burst into tears, and she couldn't stop. She put her arms over her head to cover it.

'Keep it out, keep it away!' She howled and shuddered, and Henna joined in.

'I'm going to run away!' she sobbed. 'I can't stay here.'

So here we are, Daisy and me, at only nine o'clock, curled up together in my bed in my darkening room.

> *'Dark is the evening, silent the hour,*
> *Oh, who is the minstrel by yonder high bower,*
> *Whose harp is so tenderly touching with skill?*
> *Oh, who can it be but young Ned of the Hill . . .?'*

There's a knock at the door, and Henna appears in the doorway, pale and limp.

'Can I join you?'

She lies on the floor and pulls out a yoga mat that used to belong to Bryony.

'Can I get my duvet and bring it in here?'

The three of us lie there, listening to the silence of the house.

'Everyone I love leaves me,' says Henna.

I think it is one of the saddest things I have ever heard. There must be something I could say to console her, but nothing wise springs to mind.

Then she whispers, 'I can't bear to think of her covered in earth.'

Daisy raises her head. 'What if she's not dead?'

'She is,' I say. 'I was there when she died.'

'How did it happen – exactly?'

I tell them as much as I can, minimising her suffering.

'But what did she say, at the end?'

'She just sort of . . . wilted. She was exhausted.'

'I don't ever want a baby,' says Daisy.

'It's not often like that,' I say.

'Well, it happened to my mum, too,' says Henna.

'Neither of them had a proper midwife. In fact, I'm not even sure—' I stop myself, thinking of Daisy. 'Well, her troubles are over now. Let's try and think of that. She's not suffering now.'

We gaze at the ceiling. Daisy has asked me so many times where Violeta is now, and I'm totally inadequate. I'm not prepared for bereavement in small children. Just like the National Curriculum, I'm learning as I go. We cling on to each other. Henna reaches a hand up to the bed and I take it. I find myself welling up again, although with a different set of emotions. Henna is reaching out to me, and I know I must help her. I'm tempted to give her hand the gentlest of squeezes, but I'm afraid it would be too much. Then I do anyway, and there's a slight return pressure.

'What's this?' Daisy has taken a neat triangle of cotton from under the pillow, and she's unfolding it.

'It's a handkerchief. My gran embroidered it.'

She holds up the delicate square of cloth by the corners. 'It's pretty. What's it for?'

'It's for blowing your nose in – or wiping away your tears.'

She lays it on the pillow and strokes the roses. 'But it's too pretty to throw away.'

'They didn't throw them away in those days. They boiled them up and washed them.'

Henna props herself up on her elbow. 'You see, that's proper recycling.'

Daisy folds it again, reverently, and puts it back under the pillow. 'Will you keep singing that song, Caitlin?'

> *'It is hard to escape from this young lady's bower,*
> *For high is the castle and guarded is the tower.*
> *But the mind knows the way where the heart holds the will,*
> *And young Eileen is gone with sweet Ned of the Hill.'*

We lie and listen to Daisy's first gentle snores.

'There's certainly a will,' whispers Henna, letting go of my hand. 'If only there was a way.'

Morning breaks like a reproach. So much sunshine bursting in through the cracks in the curtains, so much June brightness. Such indiscreet behaviour of the weather.

After breakfast, I suggest we pick some flowers to lay on Violeta's grave. Marcus seems to have been up and out before we come down, but Mimi now says we should stay close to the house.

Henna is tight-lipped, and Daisy says, 'What about some roses from round the front door?'

'That's a good idea,' says Mimi, smiling, all Mummy Bambi. I glance at Henna; if she were a cartoon, Henna would have a bubble coming out of her head saying 'Grrrr!', but actually she says nothing.

It does seem a shame not to get further away from the house, but we gather the necessary equipment and set to work. In any case, it's not long before Mimi glides off to her office, and so we're left alone outside the front door, with just the faint bumps and rustlings of Drita cleaning inside the house. Henna and I have secateurs, and Daisy is filling some jam jars with water at the tap by the side porch.

'All we need are prison uniforms,' mutters Henna. 'This is a prison.'

I don't know how to respond, but she needs me to say something. 'Not forever,' I say.

'Not for you, maybe. You can go any time.' Then she stops her cutting abruptly and looks at me as I fold my lips together, hoping to pass the gesture off as concentration on the task of snipping. 'You won't, will you?'

I'm struck by the urgency of her question, and my mouth is full of fluff as I try to speak words of reassurance: 'I haven't any plans to . . .'

Daisy comes round the corner of the house with two jam jars full of water. She's watching them intently as the surfaces rock back and forth in her hands.

'I've got six jam jars and I'm going to fill them all.'

Henna starts to remove the lower leaves from the bottom of the stems, so that Daisy can put them in the jars. The leaves are shiny and sticky with aphids. I fetch a chair from inside the house so that I can reach the copious red blooms above the front door-way. None of us says what we all three must surely think: that they are blood-red. Each one in my hand is an hour of Violeta's bloody suffering turned to petals. Some of the older flowers spill their petals in a red confetti onto the ground. Daisy picks them up and puts them in a bowl.

'I'm going to sprinkle these on top of Violeta,' she says.

I try to find some roses past their best to shake into her collection. There's something engraved in the mottled stone underneath the stems. It is an *E* and an *R*. The name of the house. These roses haven't been pruned for a couple of years; the stems are congested and some have clearly burst free from bits of ancient string. I snip one thick stem out and wriggle it free from the others: *B*. Out it comes, thorns piercing my one gardening glove and scratching my arm. I stare at the stone, my pulse like someone running on snow.

Chapter Forty-Three

I don't want to leave the girls alone, but I must give Kahlil my new letter to post. In it, I've told my mum to write to his address, and to remind me of her mobile number and Erin's. I tell the girls I'll be half an hour, and I leave them at the grave, arranging the rose jars and sprinkling petals. I wasn't sure Daisy was ready to revisit this scene of her horrors, but she seems content to kneel by the mound and talk to Violeta, making her epitaph out of small stones pressed into the soft earth.

> *Come dig me a grave that is long, wide and deep*
> *And cover it over with flowers so sweet.*

Kal sees me from his bedroom window and rushes down to greet me. But before he opens the front door, a delivery man comes round the side of the house and heads for the shed. He nods at me.

'In the shed,' he says, just as Kal answers the door. Then he's gone.

Kal sighs, exasperated, then sees me and smiles. 'Deckchairs? Tea?'

'I can't be long, but . . . yes, please.'

'Actually, we're lucky. Joe is on nights for two days, and he would normally be around, but he's out seeing Stella – against the rules, obviously.'

When he goes back into the house to put the kettle on, I go to the shed for the deckchairs. There, in a small pile just inside the shed door, are two large packages and a box.

When I go back to close the shed door, I can't help being curious, because I don't even know Kahlil's surname – or Joe's, for that matter. The parcel on the top is addressed to 'M. Stallard, Willerby, Greenoaks, GLOS' with a GL54 postcode. All three packages are the same, except the box, which is from a cashmere company, and addressed to 'Mrs Stallard'.

I must look stunned, because when Kal comes out with the mugs of tea he says, 'Everything okay? You didn't come yesterday. And now you look like you've seen a ghost.'

'Kal . . . Where's "Willerby"?'

He points in the direction of the house and laughs. 'That's where you're living.'

'And Greenoaks?'

'Well, that's the village. Haven't you been there? To the Co-op?'

'Where's Ribley, then?'

He shrugs, and my skin prickles all over.

'Ribley? I don't know. Never heard of it. Is it in Gloucestershire?'

'No . . .' I put my head in my hands, then look up at him. 'I don't think it is. I don't think it's anywhere. Or Amberside.'

He's frowning at me.

'Marcus's surname,' I say. 'It isn't "Archer", I suppose?'

'No. It's Stallard. And don't I know it! They're always getting their post dropped off here because it's easier. Joe gives it to them when they come and get it, but if Joe's not in, it has to be me.'

I tell him the address they gave me, and it takes a while to sink in, as it has for me.

'What? What the . . .? Why would they lie to you?'

'Because they don't want me to know they have the internet. These have to have been ordered on the internet, don't they?'

'And he lied about your phone. I know he took it.' He picks up his mug of tea and puts it back down again. 'Are they trying to trap you there? Why would they do that?'

I'm shaking my head, trying to order my thoughts. Do I tell him about the pregnancy? I don't want to. The story of how it came about seems so ugly now, and Kahlil is everything that isn't ugly. I want one thing unbesmirched and lovely, or I think I'll lose my mind.

'I think we should call the police, don't you?' he says.

'Not yet.'

He sighs deeply.

I try to get my thoughts straight. 'I just feel . . . I don't think that's the right thing just yet. I need to sort out what exactly's going on. I need something concrete. I think I need to get right away from here first.'

'What about your parents? You didn't take down my address.'

'Oh, I've brought the letter. Let me fill in your address now. I left a gap.'

He brings me a pen, and I write it on the letter for my mother. It occurs to me that she probably has written to me, to the fictitious Amberside at Ribley near Nettleford, with a non-existent postcode. Knowing Mum, she has probably sent me a dozen letters by now.

He takes the letter from me and waggles it. 'They'll get this one. I'll put a first-class stamp on it and take it to the post office myself.' I try to relax, and take a sip of tea. 'Don't worry, Caitlin. I'm on it.'

He makes me smile, then, with his own broad smile. We sit and sip for a while, wondering about Marcus and Mimi, and what they're up to. I tell him about the woman from the local council who came to ask about schooling, and he seems very concerned about Marcus's reaction. Nervous, I'm about to tell him about Violeta's death when he says:

'I assume your au pair had her baby?'

'Violeta? Yes. How did you know?'

'It's a guess. I saw Mimi with a baby, and it looked pretty newborn.'

I nurse my mug of tea on my lap and the heat burns through the denim of my dungarees.

'You saw her? When?'

'She was up here yesterday. I was out on the ridge path, coming back from my walk, and I saw her hurrying up the path to the woods, and she was carrying a bundle. It looked like a baby, so I assumed your . . . Violeta had just had her baby.'

'She had. She did.' I look at him aghast. 'She died. She died.'

'Violeta?'

My voice starts to wobble. 'Violeta and the baby. Both of them.'

'Oh, God. I'm so sorry. But . . . oh, I'm sorry.' He reaches out a hand, then withdraws it, remembering the rules.

I tell him what happened, from when I discovered Violeta giving birth in the barn, to the girls seeing Marcus and Arrow arrive with the body by the shallow grave.

'Oh, my God. Oh, those poor girls. This is terrible. That can't be legal either.'

'What time was it, when you saw her?'

'About four o'clock.'

'Yes. That was Violeta's baby.'

'But I should tell you something. I made my way back via the other side of the woods to the front of the house, to avoid her. I don't know – I didn't want to bump into her. I don't think she likes me much, and I wasn't in the mood for polite greetings. So I went up to my room, and I saw Suze had parked up, by the Land Rover, and she was sort of . . . pacing about, and then Mimi came and handed over the baby. And it was definitely a baby, because it started crying when they put it in the car seat.'

I stare at the house in front of me, at the thick yellow paint on the door, at the gentle pale stone, across at the prize-winning nettles, into Kal's anxious face.

'She told me the baby was dead.'

'Well, it was alive when Suze drove off with it.'

Chapter Forty-Four

Okay, I have to have a plan. I lie in bed and work on it. This is my new plan, and I'm pleased with it. My biggest obstacle to escape is lack of money. I don't know what the transport situation is – if there are any trains running at all – but even if I steal Marcus's car, I need money for petrol. All I have is a ten-pound note which was change from the pregnancy test. I need to get some money in my account, then I can just use my card. And if Kal was happy to brave the virus by letting me use his phone, he surely won't mind me sending an email. Simple. I can remember Dad's email address. I haven't wanted to contact my dad – especially not for money, but he's the one to ask. After all, he'll be feeling pretty guilty right now. It's the least he could do. That's all I have to do. And I make sure I have my card on me at all times, so that whenever there's an opportunity for escape, I can just slip away.

Instinctively, I put my hand out to the little bedside table. My card. It's not there, it's in my . . . Shit. It's in my phone. My phone, which has disappeared.

Crap.

Okay. So, I ask Dad for cash. He can't send it here obviously. *Hi Dad, I need to come home urgently, but there's no money left on my . . .* No. . . . *but I've lost my card. Can you send some cash? £200 if poss, and I'll pay you back* . . . No, I won't . . . *£200 if poss, and addressed to 'Kahlil . . . Someone, Something Cottage . . .'* Oh, God. How does that look? *I'm your daughter, honest, please send cash to an unknown person at an unknown address?* That's a common scam, isn't it? Oh, shit, shit, shit.

With my heavy bedroom curtains shut, the darkness obliterates everything. If someone was there, I wouldn't know if they were five feet away from me or five inches, unless I smelled their skin or felt their breath. But tonight, something is different. Something is stirring in the blackness of the room. There's a barely perceptible flickering. No . . . Yes . . . There it is again. I lie and watch it as the wall opposite slowly becomes its backdrop. It's coming from outside, not inside. And there is something else: an insistent pulse.

Maybe I'm not entirely well. I throw back the duvet and swing my feet to the ground. I'm not dizzy, just dopily tired. I open the curtain a little and look out. There it is: the flickering. Again . . . and again. And the pulse is alive in the air, beyond the distant horizon.

I lean on the windowsill. It's coming from the left, from the exact opposite direction to Joe and Kal's place in the woods. However much I crane my head, I can't see the source of it. As quietly as I can, I open the window as far as it will go and stretch my head out. The sky is intermittently lit up over the horizon, and the pulsing is a deep repetitive bass. Someone is having an illegal party. A party means people. This could be my lucky break.

I try not to creak any floorboards as I put on my dungarees, T-shirt and socks, pulling a thick jumper over the top of all of it. I don't expect to get past Marcus and Mimi's bedroom without them waking, but I do. Not quite believing my luck, I take the back door – at the side of the house – through the kitchen and utility room, so that I won't make a noise opening the front door, and so that I can take one of the torches hanging up on the wall in the side porch. I shove on my Doc Martens, which are by the door, and instead of crossing in front of the house, I go around the back, emerging onto the track without a single light coming on in the house behind me. I've made it.

There is a moon, slipping in and out of a couple of thin clouds, so I resist using the torch to light my way until the house has disappeared behind me. The track is long and winding across the fields, and at the end of it there's a junction with a narrow lane. This is where we brought the recycling. The flickering glow in the sky is coming from straight ahead of me now, so I take the right-hand option, which looks slightly less narrow than the left-hand one, knowing I must bear left at the earliest opportunity.

The lane becomes a little wider, bordered on either side by tall hedgerows which block out the moonlight. I cast my torch beam around for another path or lane, but there is nothing. I'm nervous now, propelled forward only by adrenaline. I try not to think what Marcus will do when he finds me gone, or if he has already been woken by the sound of the back door closing with its usual rattle. I have no money, no phone, nothing. I am relying on people. People who are perhaps so drunk or high they will lend me a phone without worrying about social distancing. The plan is filling out in my head with each step I take further away from the house. I'm on my way home.

Eventually there's a signpost, but it's just a little green post with the shape of a walker on it. It points off to the left. There's a stile. I loop the strap of the torch over my hand and climb over it. Then I turn the torch off and wait. There are voices. I freeze like a rabbit waiting for its predator to pass. But the voices are not coming from the way I've come; they are up ahead, across a field. There are dark shapes moving towards the light, other people making their way towards the music.

I must have been walking for half an hour across fields and paths and stiles before I see it. Standing on the edge of a small valley, I find myself looking down on a remote barn of some kind, and around it spill young people in hoodies, jigging up and down to the relentless thump of the bass. There are two lorries, which must be providing the lights and the speakers, and several small pop-up tents that look like molehills on the slopes. I make my way down towards them, confused and relieved.

There must be a couple of hundred people, but more keep coming, down the hillsides and out of the tents. The closer I get, the warmer it becomes, and the louder the music. The sweat is coming off some of the liveliest dancers as they bounce up and down with unimaginable energy. Some of the girls even wear knitted triangles on almost-bare torsos, but most are hoodied up, with big boots and clothes fit for camping in the chill night air.

'PLUR!' shouts one man in my face, and his breath stinks of weed and alcohol.

'Peace, Love, Unity, Rebellion!' shout some others, coming out from behind one of the lorries, waving bottles of water, the telltale sign of ecstasy doing the rounds. Sure enough, a man approaches me with a flirtatious look and puts an arm around me, encouraging me to dance, before offering me a molly.

'Sorry, mate,' I say. 'No money.'

He looks woefully at me for a minute, and then says it's on the house for a girl like me, 'if you know what I mean.'

I do. I move on through the crowd, looking for someone who might let me use their phone. The music is so loud, and the beat so enticing, that I just let myself go with it. I look up at the sky, and it's full of stars. I am free. I am nineteen years old and I'm dancing in the moonlight. I may be pregnant, but I get to choose now. I can make my own decisions. So I put my arms in the air and rock my head back to the sky and I dance and dance and dance.

At some point I become overwhelmed with thirst and go in search of water. A guy standing by one of the lorries offers me a swig from his bottle.

'Dance with me?' he says.

'Yeah, in a bit. Just get my breath back.'

'You on your own?'

I think fast. 'No, but my mates said they'd meet me here, and I think they've got lost. What's the address?'

He shrugs, and says something but the noise is too loud.

'What?'

'Ottersdene. Otters-dene . . . Barn or Farm.'

'Cool.' I make to get my phone from my pocket. 'Shit! My phone's in my jeans. Shit!' I pat my dungarees. 'I couldn't borrow your phone, could I?'

I look at him as winsomely as I can manage, and hope it's appealing enough for him to take pity on me. He pulls out a phone from his back pocket and presses his thumb onto it.

'Cheers,' I say. 'Okay if I just move away from the noise a bit?'

'Sure.'

But he follows me as I move to the outer edges of the crowd, and stands a little apart, his eyes on his phone the whole time.

I haven't a clue who I can phone, and not knowing a single number off by heart, I do what I've pictured myself doing a thousand times: I press 999.

Hello, emergency. Which service do you require?

'Oh . . . um . . . I'm at the rave in Ottersdene Barn. Just follow the music.'

I'm sorry. Did you say 'rave'?

'Yes. There's about two hundred, three hundred people here. You can't miss it.'

Are you calling for the police?

I look across at my companion and hope he can't hear. Of course he can't. I can hardly hear myself.

'Yes. Yes, that's right. As soon as possible. As soon as you can.'

Anyone hurt?

'Um . . . not sure. Don't think so.'

Ottersdene. How are you spelling that?

'Um . . . Like "otter" as in the animal, I think.'

In Gloucestershire? Okay, I've got it. Right, someone will be there right away.

I ring off and hand the phone back to him.

'Let's dance, then.'

All the time I'm dancing, I have my eyes on the horizons. The lorries have come on a track across this field, from a different direction to the path I came in on, and it's a proper tractor path, which leads to the barn. This is the track I keep scanning for the arrival of police cars. It's quite hard to see anything outside the straggly clump of bodies in perpetual motion. After ten minutes or so of dancing, I slip away and stand on a rise near the track. I want to be able to rush up to the police car and get myself taken to the station. I think about doing something outrageous, like taking a swipe at a police officer, or undressing in front of them, or smashing their windscreen, but all I really want to do is ask for help. I know if I can just get to the safety of a police station, I can get home.

There's a van arriving along the track. It looks like a camper van. There are no sirens going off, no flashing police lights. For a moment, I think it might be Marcus come to get me in his Land Rover, but that would be ridiculous, because this is a van. And then suddenly blue lights are flashing, and its siren is going like mad, breaking the surface of the rave music. People run in all directions, but a solid core of dancers keep going. The doors of the van open, and out get two police officers. They stand watching a second police car approach, also with flashing lights. I walk down towards them as fast as I can. I must get to them before any real trouble starts. I must put my case before they get lost in the crowd. There must be a space in their vehicles left for me.

'Peace, Love, Unity, Rebellion!' chant a bunch of the revellers, standing in a defiant row. I am feet away from the police van, standing in the dark.

Please, please help me.

I open my mouth to shout out and fling myself at them, when the officers get out of the second car. One of them has a loud-speaker, and as he turns a fraction to look at his colleagues, I see that it's Joe.

I look back up the way I came, and I run.

Chapter Forty-Five

Something wakes me. It's chilly. A dim light. A blackbird. I open my eyes. For a few moments I'm totally lost, then I feel the grass beneath me, and I know that I've fallen asleep. Last night, the rave, the escape, Joe. I sit up. The sky is a vast dome packed with stars still, but a band of amber is growing along one edge, like something promising happening in the distance. It reminds me of last night: the light in the sky, the pulsing of the bass, making my way towards it.

I appear to be sitting on a mound. I stand up and turn a full circle: it's long, and steeper at one end than the other. I scramble down its nearest slope and see a shadowy inlet in the side of it. I approach, wary. The little cave looks man-made. I consider exploring inside. Instead, I walk around the base of the mound and see another inlet, and then, on the far side, another. And on this side, there is just enough light to make out stones. This is a square stone inlet set into the side of the mound. It's a burial chamber. I have spent the night on a long barrow.

I'm so weary. I walk back up the shallowest slope to the top of the barrow and sit down again, surveying the view. The grass is cool now, but last night when I lay down, it was warmer. I have to make a plan. I could keep walking, find a house, ask for help. But every day on the radio we're reminded of the lockdown, the importance of staying away from other people. The rave last night was illegal. There will be fines – up to ten thousand pounds was threatened on the news. Who will let me in to their home?

I have to chance it. I lie back down on the grass and sigh, imagining what will happen back at the house when Marcus and Mimi realise I've gone. Marcus will be out looking for me in his Land Rover, so there's no point me taking the roads. I have no money. Not enough for more than a few sandwiches, I should think. If I could make my way to a police station in the next county – not Gloucestershire, not a police force with Joe in it – then I would be fine. But where do I start? Which is the nearest next county? I imagine making my way on foot to Cornwall. It could be done. I know which way is south-west, and if this warm weather continues, I could sleep out, somewhere sheltered. I can't even begin to think how I'll face Mum and Dad, though, or what I'll find when I get there.

The thing we never got about Mum was why she did everything she did for Dad. (We took it as understood that she would do everything and anything for us.) It was like she was asking to be a doormat. But she used to say that Dad had been so kind to her when they first met. It was on Plymouth station, and she'd had her bag stolen and missed her train home. He had paid for a new ticket (even though she found out later he was as poor as a church mouse) and bought her a cup of tea and a bun in the station café. He never asked for her number or wanted anything in return, and they only met again years later because he spotted her at a book festival when she was queuing to see someone else: a gardening expert. And he was kind all through their early marriage, until he started getting depressed, and drinking. You never forget someone who's been kind to you, she said. And then she seemed to keep on asking for trouble. Going into counselling, and dealing with everyone else's problems: angry adolescent girls with self-harm issues, distraught boys with angry acne and hidden knives. What was in it for her? we asked. She would speak slowly to us then, as if to foreigners who didn't understand her language: *There are rewards.* Our imaginations could only stretch as far as the occasional box of chocolates or unwanted Christmas soap she received from someone's grateful parent.

I suppose that's the thing about Dad. I remember when I was about eight, going on a day trip to some relatives not far from Penzance: we spent the day on a beach and Dani took her teddy with a newly knitted swimming costume, so I took my panda because I was always competing with her. I couldn't bear her getting all the attention – even though she was three and I was already eight and should've grown out of fluffy toys. I hadn't grown out of Panda, though, and even imagined he might be hurt not having a swimming costume, so Mum made him one hastily out of an old sock. Panda and Teddy sat on a rock and sunbathed while we played in warm rock pools or ran at the crashing waves. When we drove home, salty and tired, I didn't realise until we were minutes from the house that Panda wasn't with me. He was an hour and a half away, somewhere on a rock. There were hopeless promises to buy me a new one, but I wailed like a baby. I ruined the glorious day, frantic and inconsolable. I remember as if it were yesterday, lying in bed and watching the sun's glow dimming in the square of orange curtain, nervy with the fear that he had been washed away in the tide.

In the morning, Panda was sitting in my cereal bowl. Dad had driven a three-hour round trip to search for him on the beach straight after tea. Mercifully, it had been low tide. And although I know I was grateful and ridiculously happy, I don't think I thought it was any more than I could expect from a father. But it mattered, because it made me feel I mattered, and I see now how precious that was.

I try not to remember his kindness, because it just doesn't square up with how I'm feeling about him right now, and I'm not going to be deflected from this almighty hurt, thank you very much. What happened to him? What happened to that dad? Fluttering in the back of my head is a comment of Lotti's about my father's lowest ebb: 'It was shit anyway, with your dad. Just so you know, he couldn't even get it up.' That's information that Mum and my sisters don't have. I should get back and tell them. Although perhaps Mum can guess. I know why I don't want to think about it. I mean, *yuk, yuk, yuk*, obviously, but there's something else. It's the drink. He would've been out of his head with drink. A snifter here, an authorly bottle of wine or four there, a whisky nightcap, a morning hair of the dog. And I know why he drank. Why he *really* drank to oblivion. I had a hand in that.

But then there are the girls. How could I even think about leaving the girls? I try to tell myself it's by far the best thing to do. I can get them help. If I can get back to Cornwall, Mum will know exactly what to do. But what if I don't make it back? What if Marcus finds me? And I remember that woman in the cardigan saying he had every right to home-school his children. He's not accountable to anyone. Why would anyone believe *me* – pregnant, embittered ex-lover? And if they did believe me, Henna could end up in care or something. I remember the set of his jaw when Marcus thought I'd seen Kal, when he raised his arm. I remember his face when he saw us at the grave. *You stupid bitch.* Three words which undid everything. One dropped stitch and it all unravelled. And I remember Henna, howling in my arms, and Daisy, shaking all over, sobbing at the television, her arms protecting her from the bird of prey: *No, don't let him! No, keep it away, keep it away!* I remember waiting for her little snores as she curled inside my arms, and Henna's outstretched hand. Her skinny arm, how pale and frail it was when she tried on the dresses. And I see it, of course I do. The bruise, dark grey and green around the top of her arm. *There's certainly a will . . .*

It occurs to me that I am lying on top of a mass grave. Hundreds of bones lie beneath me, although what is left now? Layer upon layer of bones and earth, bones and earth: a sherry trifle of human remains, and me the cherry on the top. Erin says that you can tell the identity of a person from even a milligram of powdered bone, and from the tiniest trace of organic material you can build a story of how someone lived, and how they died. All these people beneath me . . . did they die of atrocities, or were they revered? Each of them would have been loved by someone; that was always so. But then, who is there to love Henna? And even Daisy – who really loves Daisy?

Then it's obvious: I do.

Maybe all acts of kindness are, in a sense, a rescue. It's time for me to be kind. I can't leave those girls behind. I have to find a way. Kal has sent my letter, so Mum will reply with the phone numbers. Or she'll ring Kal. Or I'll email. It will all be okay soon; I just have to keep calm. I have to get back before it is day.

I make my way back down to the scene of the rave: just a lot of empty plastic bottles and a few tents speckling the landscape. Right. From here I can work it out: back the way I came.

I get back just before breakfast, and I tell Mimi quite convincingly that I just went for a walk to clear my head. She looks furtive, as if I've caught her out doing something, but I can't work out what it is.

I need to stay close to the girls, as they're still in shock. I came to a firm decision on the walk home. I'm going to get these girls out of here with me, whatever it takes. I might even accept Marcus's offer of marriage – if it's still on the table – to lull him into trusting me while I plot to leave. I'm going to play the long game.

But what happens that night changes everything. Escape becomes urgent.

I go to bed early because I've been barely awake all day. I sink quickly into oblivion, the sort your body lets you indulge in as respite after a prolonged period of tension.

So when I wake suddenly, opening my eyes uselessly in the blackness, I have no idea what has woken me. I wait, alert as a fox. Somewhere in the house a door gently closes.

I roll on to my back, listening more intently. When nothing

further comes, my eyes start closing, heavy still with the weight of dreams. I turn. A muffled sound. Was that me turning? I wait, stone-still, hearing the conch shell sounds in my head. Again. A muffle, a creak, and now low voices. They're coming from nearby.

I'm awake now, properly awake. I swing my legs ever so gently over the side of the bed and tiptoe across the mat to the opposite wall and press my ear to it. Again: a muffled sound, a creaking, and now a whimper. Is Henna crying? I'm about to go to see her when I hear another voice. It's low and male, and Henna's is high and pleading, then urgent: 'I'll scream!'

Now there is whispering, hissing and silence. I stand on the cold bare floorboards by the wall and know I have let her down. I dare not move. Should I go in, or should I bide my time? Knowledge is power, I tell myself, or maybe I'm just a coward.

In any case, I'm too late. The door softly opens and closes. There are footsteps on the stairs. I go to my own door and open it gently. Crossing the narrow landing, lit up by the moonlight coming through the undrawn curtains of the landing window, I tip my head over the stairwell. Just in time to see the top of an unmistakable head receding into the darkness.

And I make a pledge to myself, there and then, that this will never happen to Henna again.

Chapter Forty-Six

'Thank goodness you didn't come ten minutes ago,' says Kal, standing barefoot at the door the next day. 'Marcus was here with Joe, and they've gone off to get some beer.'

I touch my chest with the flat of my hand. 'Phew! Close shave, then.'

'I have a confession to make. I haven't been able to post your letter yet because my battery's flat. I tried to start up the car this morning and it won't even turn over. But I will get it fixed, don't worry. And if I have to walk to the post office myself, I will.'

I'm disappointed, but try not to show it. 'Aren't you in the AA?'

'Yes, but I don't have Homestart. I can get it, though.'

'Could you? I promise I'll pay you back for whatever it costs – and soon.'

'I will – I'll sort it out straight away. Actually, if you want to avoid Marcus, I don't think it's safe for us to stay here, talking.'

I'm looking over his shoulder into the hall, and what I see gives me a real jolt.

'You okay? Caitlin?'

'That's Marcus's jacket.'

He turns, looks at a tan suede jacket slung over the bottom of the banisters.

'Yes. That's what I mean. He's coming back here. When he comes over to pick up his mail he always stays for a few beers, and we didn't have any in. So they've just gone off in Joe's car to the

Co-op. They'll be back in thirty minutes. They'll either stink the kitchen out with weed or they'll go in the garden.'

I close my eyes, trying to focus on what needs doing. 'Are his keys in the pocket?'

He shrugs. 'Want me to look?'

He takes a disposable glove from a packet by the door and slips it on his right hand. He approaches the jacket, which looks almost like Marcus himself, but with narrower, slumped shoulders. He reaches into one pocket of the jacket and shakes his head. Then he goes into the other outside pocket and pulls out a set of keys. There are lots of them, not just car keys, but a great jailer's bunch of door keys and shed keys.

'Yes!' I'm almost breathless. 'Brilliant. Bring it here, quick.'

He looks over at me, frowning a little. 'I can't steal them.'

'Oh, you can – you must!'

He plops them back into the pocket with a metallic crunch. I must look aghast, because he shakes his head and comes outside, closing the door behind him. 'Come on, let's talk somewhere else. We can't stay here.'

He leads me out of the gate I came in, and up a woodland footpath beside the house. I'm beginning to wonder if I can trust him. Why wouldn't he take the keys? I have to make him see why this is so important – so urgent – but there is very little time.

'Listen, Kahlil, this is important. I have to tell you something.'

Where do I start? What do I leave out? I steer him off the path into some trees. Mimi doesn't seem to walk through these woods except to go up to the car, but we can't risk being seen. The roots of an oak provide a clumpy bench to perch on, and I sit on it, leaning my back against the trunk. He doesn't join me, of course, but sits a judicious two metres away on some undergrowth.

'Listen, I told you about them burying Violeta, and lying about the baby, and I'm guessing Mimi is involved in sex-trafficking in some way and I know Violeta was pregnant with Marcus's baby and I know Henna's sister left because she was pregnant and—'

'Wait, wait. You think it was his?'

'Yes. I don't know for certain, but last night – here's the thing . . . last night I was woken by the noise of Marcus in Henna's bedroom next door, and he was . . . he was definitely planning to . . . I think . . .'

'Oh, my God!' He gapes at me. 'How old is she?'

'Thirteen. And the thing is, Kal, I can't just escape on my own now, I have to get those girls out of there. And I can't hang about. If I have his car keys, I can escape with them tonight!'

'You can drive?'

'Yes.'

This isn't, strictly speaking, true. I've had three lessons – with Erin in a car park. But how hard can it be?

'Hang on . . .' He has his hands on the sides of his head, as if working this out. 'Why don't we just ring the police? That's much safer. Imagine what he'll do to you if he catches you escaping.'

'I've thought of that. I tried to escape two nights ago. I heard music and saw a light in the sky and I followed it.'

'Oh, yes, it woke me up. Wasn't that the rave that was on the news?'

'Yes. Only I didn't know, but that's not the point. The point is, I was there, and I got someone to lend me their phone and I dialled 999 and everything, but guess who turned up? Guess who came in the police car?'

He closes his eyes and sighs, 'Joe!'

'Yes!'

'He did say he'd been called out to a rave nearby.' He scratches his head. 'But that doesn't mean you'll get him again. Won't the police put you in touch with child services or something, if you tell them about Henna?'

'Yes, I'm sure they would. I'm sure they'd come and seize his laptop. That's if he doesn't manage to convince them he hasn't got one – he has all sorts of safety mechanisms in place for the weed farm – but I can't risk it. Henna and Daisy might be shipped off into care, and what if they denied everything? Or what if I ended up like Violeta?' There's an implication I hadn't intended there. I don't want to tell him about my pregnancy – not yet. 'Buried, I mean. Never heard of again.'

'Okay. But you could ring up and just talk to someone at the police station.'

'I can't risk it. Joe has *access* to police stuff. I have to assume that. It's too risky.'

He doesn't look convinced.

'Kahlil, I'm scared. I'm really scared.'

He reaches out an arm, and then drops it, exasperated with the distancing situation, or himself. Slowly, he starts to nod.

'Okay . . . okay. If you take his keys, he's going to get suspicious. He's going to search your room – everywhere you could possibly hide them.'

'That's a risk I have to take – don't you see? I have to!'

He scrambles to his feet. 'Well, you'd better go and get them before he gets back.'

'God, yes.'

'Make it tonight, then – for the escape – if you don't want to get caught. Joe will be out then. If Marcus does come looking, I can say I saw you and the girls walking out towards Foxes Haye earlier or something. *Oh, shit!*'

I follow his gaze between the trees. Joe's car is back beside the house. He shoots out an arm to stop me proceeding.

'Quickly!' he hisses. 'Back through the woods, go back the long way round.'

Later, the police would question Kal repeatedly about why he hadn't rung them, given what I'd told him. I guess that was my fault.

Chapter Forty-Seven

I know Marcus is lying to me, but I don't know it enough to convince myself. There's a whole layer of wanting to believe, of longing for what he says to be true, and that's on top of layers of desire. It's a protective skin of willingness to be wrong about him.

I know he's out with Joe. Mimi's in her study, and the girls are both busy with the lambs. I have a small window of time when it's safe to go up to the barn alone and shake some sense into myself. And a few days ago, out walking, I saw what I needed to help me.

I make my way up through the damp and crafty woods, along the paths narrowed by bracken and nettles, until I am out into the grass-scented air of the afternoon. I tread stealthily along the ridge, just low enough on its far side not to be seen by Mimi's office window, and I come up behind the beeches and descend to the barn under cover of trees and bramble. My heart is thumping as I skirt the stone walls. On one side, the door to Marcus's 'study' is padlocked. I wander around to the other side, and look up at the window. It's about an inch open on an old iron catch. I sigh. Now that I'm standing right beneath it, the little window is higher off the ground than I remembered it. I walk back round to the rusty farm machinery outside the padlocked door, in search of what I saw the other day. Still there, on its side, but it needs pulling out. The wooden stepladder is so covered in cobwebs and spider eggs that it seems almost sewn into the fabric of the shadows. I try to pull gently, but it requires all my strength, and there's a clatter as an old plough head falls over and topples a rake leaning against the wall. I look around. I'm not visible to the house. I breathe. A friendly wood pigeon sets up a deep fluting to help cover the noise.

I drag the ladder around to the little window, making sure there's enough foliage around me to shield me from Mimi's study window back down at the house. Okay. I search for a stick, one that is straight and solid, which takes longer than I hoped. Gently, I open the stepladder and stand it up sideways against the wall. I need to get as close in as I can. The window is still higher than I would like, but standing on the top, I can poke the stick into the gap and try to lift the catch. That's the idea, anyway, but it doesn't work. I go up and down the ladder several times to find a stick with the right heft to lift a catch, but slender enough to go through the gap. Eventually I find a rusty old tent peg, which seems perfect. It lifts the latch straight away, but it takes a few attempts to work out how to hold the latch up long enough to ease the window open, using the peg as a lever.

At last I have it open. It's wide enough for me to squeeze through, but now that I survey my success, it really is too high for me to pull myself up, even from the top of the ladder. It wouldn't be too much for someone fitter than me, but it requires some serious arm muscles to raise myself high enough to get a leg over that window ledge. I stand and gauge it for a moment. Giving up can't be an option, because just inside that window, just out of sight, waits all the evidence I need. I go back round to the rusty equipment. Nothing. I lift the latch on the big doors at the back of the barn and look inside. I'm nervous now. Anything I borrow must be put back, and I don't know how long I've got. This has already taken longer than I intended.

As I remembered, there are a series of clear plastic storage boxes beside the wardrobes. I test them out for weight, not wanting to take everything out, and settle on a box of pullovers. I take it out to the stepladder and try to position it in such a way that I can stand on it, but it's too unwieldy: I need something smaller. More nervous now than ever, I go back and seek out a box half the size, but there is nothing. Eventually I spot a cardboard box of magazines, and I carry it round the side of the barn and lift it up on top of the ladder. It just about does it.

My inelegant entrance over the windowsill on my belly stops the wood pigeon in his song. He waits while I get to my feet and gather myself, and then starts cooing amiably again.

I look about me. It's cramped. There's a large calendar on the wall with all sorts of markings on it, a cork board with photos of the girls climbing over him when they were smaller, and curling old photos of a boy with tousled hair – presumably Marcus – standing with a woman's hands on his shoulders. I imagine this is the mother who left him. I take a moment to examine her face for clues of betrayal, but there is nothing. Just a woman smiling at the camera. Marcus is smiling, too, but with a hint of anxiety about the eyes. I want to put my arms around the little boy. Maybe his mother has already left and this is Cliff's wife. I straighten myself and look about. There's an old swivel chair, a tatty desk, a black box with a tiny blue light, and there, right in the centre of the desk, is a laptop.

Bastard. I knew it. I knew, didn't I? I knew it. Fucksake.

I open the laptop, but I know there isn't a chance of getting into it without a password. That might be easy in television dramas, but I don't rate my chances. The main thing is, I have to find my phone – it must be here somewhere. I open each of the three drawers in the desk, scrabbling through them: random wires, papers, pens, envelope files, packets of mints. I feel some strange cubes at the back of one drawer. No phone. He must have a phone himself, but wherever it is, it's not here. In any case, I've found something important: the fact of his lying. This man has internet.

I breathe out heavily. Next to the laptop is a desk diary with sheets of card in it. I take a peek. The cards are in Mimi's un-mistakable neat hand: *Sunday 5th April, Monday 6th April, Tue 7th*

April, Wed 8th April. The next card has more dates, in June. Each card has a capital letter on it. I stuff them in the bib pocket of my dungarees. I am about to look and see how he has transferred this information to his diary, and what it turns into, when I'm pulled up short by a voice nearby. I freeze.

Outside, a female voice gives a short giggle. I stand back from the window, tiptoeing over to the door for safety, and strain to hear. It's coming from the other side of the barn, where the padlocked door is. There's a low voice now, followed by a rattle and click. Jesus! It's Marcus at the padlock. He's coming up the steps to his lair. Footsteps on stone.

'Voilà! My secret hideaway!'

'It is nice. Why you have?'

'Sometimes I like to get away from it all.'

There is a pause. 'What is that door?'

Shit! Shit, shit, shit. He won't open it for her. He won't.

'That's just my private office. All my paperwork.'

Another silence, longer this time. I try to get my ear as close to the door as possible, but I don't want to make even the slightest noise. I wait. I breathe. I listen. Then his deep, liquidy voice:

'What just happened?'

Fucksake!

Muffled words. He'll be kissing her now. How will she fare? More silence, threaded through with little rustles and moans. God, this is . . . This is . . . *shit.*

'What about your wife? What about Mimi?'

A light laugh. 'Drita, sweetheart, I'm not married. What made you think I was married?'

'Well, you . . . you are not?'

'Nope.' More weird silence. 'What are you afraid of? Let me touch you.'

This is unbearable. I don't want to hear any more. Except I do. He won't do it – not this time. He hasn't whistled for her. He'll just be reeling her in this time. This is just the grand tour. No, he'll

247

leave her hanging on a thread of longing, so that next time she'll be crawling up the walls for him. That's what he does.

More ominous quiet. Little sobs and gasps.

He'll tell her he's never felt like this before. Something's happened. Something's happened, my foot! Something's happened in his trousers, more like. The bastard. The little . . . I can't find the words. I have a sudden vision of Signor Tiraboschi in his hardware store, angry at an unknown aggressor on my behalf. *Cazzo! Che cazzo!* I remember how it took him almost a spit and a hiss to say – that's why it was so good – and I spit and hiss the word inside my head. The sobs and moans are getting more vocal. She's going for it. Marcus wasn't expecting that. My God, she's actually going for it, first time. She didn't take much persuading about his marital status. Huh. So much for *her* loyalty to the sisterhood.

If I wait until this is all over, there is a slim but horrible chance that he might let her go and then come into his study. There's also the chance that he might walk back with her around the other side of the barn and spot the ladder against the wall. I have to go now, while he's otherwise engaged, and while there's noise to cover me.

It's not so easy to get out. I straddle the windowsill and have to manoeuvre myself on to my front, from where I waggle my feet around in search of the elusive box on top of the stepladder. It seems a lot further down than I expected, and requires a lowering that my arms aren't strong enough for. But panic is beginning to rise now, and I'm making too much of a rustling in my scramble to escape. One false move and I'll kick the ladder to the ground. I'm almost sick with fear as I drop onto the side of the box; the ladder wobbles and I grasp the edge of the sill. I use the edge of the open window to balance as I slowly remove my remaining hand from the sill and lower myself down the ladder. I lift the box of magazines onto the grass and carry the ladder back round. I can't put it back exactly where it was without a scraping sound that will alert Marcus, so I just lay it gently on its side. Then I go to replace the box of magazines, telling myself that if Marcus spots me in the barn, I can legitimately say I was looking for some reading material; but as I pick them up, I see the open window above – wide open, and not the way I found it at all.

I'm tempted to run for it. I stand and listen. There's still some action going on in his lair, so I go back to the tools, where I find a rake. I know it will make a noise, but as carefully as possible, I push the rake handle against the open window: clack. As soon as it's almost closed, I drop the rake and run down the bank, back to the house and the comfort of my room, heart racing. *Cazzo, cazzo, cazzo!* I want to hide in a rabbit hole and never come out and I want to die I want to die and disappear and never be found I want to go back to Dover and when the Land Rover stops I say fuckoffMarcusandMimi! How could I have been so *stupid*. So pathetically *predictable*. How could he . . .? How could I . . .? Of all the foolish maids who ever walked out on a May morning, I really do take the fucking biscuit.

I take my time to fully experience the heady torture of betrayal. The whispered *What just happened?* What a shit. Suddenly I hear Violeta saying that in a sexy voice while cleaning the bath. She was imitating him. That's what happened. Of course that's what happened to her, too. I think of the impact it had on me – how special I felt, how easily duped. I try to calm down, to let the truth seep in slowly, but I'm drenched with it, can't hold it all in the loose weave of me. I think of our passionate encounters. They must have all been fake. How many others have there been, just like me? There were no photos of other women on his desk. Just that one of his possible mother. Maybe that's what it's all about. Maybe each time he seduces a woman he gets to feel the power of the man who lured his mum away from her four-year-old son. And each time, he gets to be a winner instead of a loser. It's no good, I can't excuse him. Whichever way I look at it, he is an almighty deceiver. What lies. What trickery. What a complete fool he's made of me. I imagine what would've happened if I'd flung that little study door open and confronted Marcus. Oh, yes! But I know the door would have been locked from the other side and I would've just made a rattle that alerted him to my humiliating eavesdropping. I keep replaying the event over and over to make it turn out differently, usually with me coming off better: more courageous, more virtuous, more kick-ass.

I can't bear to look at Marcus over tea. Looking at him is like staring at my own stupidity. It's as if Marcus is wondering how much longer he has to pretend to be attracted to me before he can dispense with the charade. Can he stop returning my smiles yet? Not touch my arm when I touch his? Can he stop smiling at my jokes yet? And always he has to embrace me at bedtime, to keep up the pretend values of the house for my replacement to believe in.

Instead of talking to him I play word games with the girls, and encourage little in-jokes to keep him out of our sphere. Tonight I will tell Henna my plan. We'll secretly pack a few favourite toys of Daisy's, then wake her up when we leave: she might let the cat out of the bag otherwise, and I don't want to ask her to keep a secret. Henna is another matter. She is longing to leave, and I know she'll be complicit in the plan.

Now I know that's where he keeps them, I'll steal the keys from his jacket. It's on the back of his chair right now, but later, when he's gone to bed, it will be hanging on the hooks by the front door. That's when I'll fish them out. And I may not remember very well how to drive, but I have had those lessons with Erin – last summer. How hard can it be? I imagine a Land Rover is pretty much like any other car. Where there's a will there's a way. I just need those car keys. Maybe I can even unhook the car keys and put the rest back, so he doesn't realise they're missing, so he hears the familiar jingle in his pocket until he next uses his car, which could be days away. By which time we'll be *o'er the border and away*, although not with Jock of Hazeldean. Very much without him, thank you. We'll be on our way, the three of us, to freedom.

Tonight. It has to be tonight.

Except that after tea, Henna vanishes. She just disappears into thin air.

Chapter Forty-Eight

Neither Marcus nor Mimi notice, of course. I do, because I want to talk to her. Daisy notices, but has no idea where she could be. She's not in her room, she's not out with the lambs, and she's not in any of the downstairs rooms. Daisy even goes into Marcus and Mimi's room. We search everywhere, but secretly. I tell Daisy we mustn't ask Marcus and Mimi where she is in case it gets her into trouble, but really, I want to give Henna a fighting chance. Once Marcus realises, he'll be out there scouring the fields with Arrow, and then with Joe, when Joe comes off his shift.

Daisy is still anxious when I put her to bed.

'Can I sleep with you?'

'If you clean your teeth and put your pyjamas on now, I'll check up in the barn.'

I'm hoping to find Henna lying on the mattress-bed in the barn, grieving for her mum and Violeta, but she's not there. I make my way through the gorse to the graves, but she's not at either one. She's gone, and I knew it straight away. She's gone to find her sister; she's gone to escape Marcus; she's run away to be free of the terrible memory of a dead Violeta hanging out of a sheet like a wrap filling. Perhaps, like her sister before her, she intends to come back for her younger sibling. But even as I hope she'll make it, I worry that she has no money, and worst of all, she is a girl alone with no money. She could be even more of a victim outside her prison than she is in it.

I am rooting for her. I had better not steal the keys tonight. Much as I can't stay here with Daisy now, there is a small chance she might turn up in the next day or two, like me when I cut my losses and came back from the rave, and I can't think of any fate worse for her than remaining alone in this place. This beautiful, grass-scented, godforsaken hell. We'll wait until Joe's round of night shifts next week. I already see myself creeping out of the house holding Daisy's hand; I fumble for the ignition in the Land Rover, hear it stutter into life. Kahlil's light will come on, and he'll wave us on our way. I go through it in my head, as Erin showed me a few times in a car park: gear in neutral, clutch in (left foot), accelerator down (right foot), ease up – no, wait: turn ignition on. Okay, *then* clutch . . . Maybe, before it happens, I'll even manage to go to the shops with Marcus and check out the petrol gauge. If it's low, I can tell him, so he'll fill it up. I just need enough to get us to Cornwall.

All these things go through my head as I embrace Mimi and Marcus, who by now are watching a television cop drama in the living room with Drita. Seated between her partner and his lover, Mimi looks like a woman I should feel sorry for. I embrace them all and say I'm heading up for an early night.

'Sleep in peace,' I say.

'Where's Henna?' asks Marcus.

'I think she's already gone up.'

'Huh. That's the second time this week she hasn't said goodnight.'

I imagine him going up to try and extract a kiss, or worse, so I say hastily, 'I think she means to. Just, she was feeling really sick and gripey. Bad period pains, I think.' *You knobhead pile of shit*, I fail to add.

'No,' says Mimi to the television. 'It's not her period yet.'

I'm in danger of panicking. I swallow hard. 'Oh, well, I'm off up.'

'Sleep in peace, Caitlin.' Mimi looks at me now, swinging her eyes from the screen to sweep me up and down with a look that manages to be both patronising and faintly sensuous.

"Night.'

Marcus doesn't look at me. I feel as if I've been erased.

Daisy is asleep when I join her in my bed. I wrap myself around her, relieved that I don't have to lie about not having found her sister. Shit. What is Mimi *like*? Fucksake. What was that look? She's a curious mix of obsessive interest and total indifference. I don't think Mum ever tracked my periods. I'm in such a muddle. So many things have freaked me out today. Marcus and Drita. Well, mostly Marcus. I squeeze my eyes tightly shut as if to block out the imagined sight of him kissing her. I can't block out the sound of him rehashing the exact same words he told me, though. Was there ever anyone more stupid than me? What an utter fool I've been. Pathetic. I see myself, as if from outside, frozen to the spot in that study. I see the laptop. *We don't have internet here.* Something is tugging at my memory, something waiting to make sense. The key to everything. The key – ah, the key. No, Cliff saying . . . what? Before *she* came. As if she changed everything. She is what it's all about.

With the first lemony light of sunrise on the ceiling, a door slams. Raised voices: Marcus and Mimi. I get up to check in Henna's room and she's still not there. When we go down for breakfast, Henna is sitting at the kitchen table like a ghost of herself. She is motionless apart from her mouth, which moves slowly, chewing some bread. She doesn't look up when we sit down. Marcus informs us that we are all 'grounded' from now on, including me.

'You, Caitlin, need to keep a better eye on these girls. They are in your care, and from now on, they don't leave the house.' I'm too stunned to speak. 'And neither do you. And just to make that easy for you, I'm going to be locking all the outside doors.'

*

254

He's cast her down in a cabin of stone
Where forty locks did hang thereto.
'Ha ha, bonny maid, will you weep now?'
'You heathenish dog, not yet for you.'

Chapter Forty-Nine

When Daisy asked to sleep in my bed that first time, there was a weird torment tilting my stomach, a dull sense of recognition. I ignored it because there was so much to deal with, so much urgency in everything. But now, when Henna unrolls the yoga mat on my bedroom floor, the feeling returns, a jolt so severe I could be standing on the deck of a roiling boat.

For a moment I'm disorientated. I see my mother in the kitchen, watch her profile as she stands near the sink peeling carrots, or potatoes, or whatever she used to do to prepare the mountains of food she had to make for us all. I can see the folding of her lips as she worked, the little line between her eyebrows and the wet tail of a tear on her cheek when she turned to wipe her hands. I see her, too, sitting at the kitchen table after a meal, twirling the pepper pot, eyes too concentrated on something else to be listening to our conversation.

But I know where she was; I know now, as if someone has just nudged me in the ribs.

She was taking stock of herself as a mother – how she could have missed the signs. Of course. I missed them, too. Because Danielle proved to be even more compliant than me, and I didn't see it because I wasn't watching out for her. But she did tell, eventually. When her school work went downhill and when she begged Mum and Dad not to go out; when her teacher asked if there was 'something wrong' at home. Over a year. And all that time I said nothing because Uncle Aaron had given up on me. But I remember now as the little phrase clutches my throat: 'Can I sleep with you tonight, Caitlin?'

And I said, No. Over and over, I said no to Dani. She must've been six. It was an abrupt end to her Hello Kitty life; there was no more safety in her fluffy animal-strewn bedroom. And it was all my fault. *Can I sleep with you tonight, Caitlin?* No! No, no, no.

I remember bundling into the kitchen from school with Erin and complaining that there were no snacks in the fridge. There were always snacks, put there by the magic snack fairy, the one who never failed. Did we even stop to look at Mum, exhausted and apologetic, on her knees under the sink trying to refit the U-bend? Or frantically trying to remove felt pen from the table-top, her hair sticking to her wet cheeks? I never asked myself why Uncle Aaron suddenly stopped coming round, why she retrained as a counsellor, why Dad called himself a waste of space once and started to drink more, and alone.

She got us visiting the elderly then, Mum did. She had me and Dani knit them blankets, square by wretched square, until we could've kept the whole of Cornwall warm. Made us deliver them all in person, and see the smiles, feel the squeezed hands. She bought us a rescue dog, too, and had us look after him. I didn't see how she was rescuing us.

We lie in my room again, a sad little trio, but the ceiling gleams with moonlight. I start to sing gently, '*And the moon it shone gently and clear-o . . .*'

'Don't stop,' says Daisy, from under my arm. 'Sing us the moon.'

> '*Well, it's of a sea captain who sailed the salt sea,*
> *And the moon it shone gentle and clear-o.*
> *"I'll die, I'll die," this captain did cry,*
> *"If I can't have that maid who walks on the shore,*
> *If I can't have that maid on the shore."*

'It's called "The Maid on the Shore".'
'Go on,' says Henna from her makeshift bed on the floor.

> *"Well, I have got silver and I have got gold*
> *And a-plenty of costly fine ware-o,*
> *Well, I'll give half to you, oh me gallant young crew,*
> *If you fetch me that girl who walks on the shore,*
> *If you fetch me that girl on the shore."*

> *'So the sailors they got them a very long boat*
> *And off for the shore they did steer-o,*
> *Saying, "Ma'am, if you please will you enter on board*
> *To view a fine cargo of most costly ware,*
> *For to view a fine cargo of ware."*

'I'm not sure it's very appropriate, actually.'
'Go on.'
Daisy is beginning to snore softly. I sing very quietly.

> *'Well, with much persuading they got her on board,*
> *And the moon it shone gentle and clear-o.*
> *She sat herself down in the stern of the boat,*
> *And back for the ship the young sailors did steer,*
> *And back for the ship they did steer.*

> *'And when they arrived alongside of the ship,*
> *The captain he spat out his chew-o,*
> *Saying, "First you will lie in my arms all this night,*
> *And then I'll give you to me jolly young crew,*
> *And then I'll give you to me crew."'*

'Oh, no. Does it end badly?' asks Henna. 'I can't bear it if it ends badly.'
'Don't worry. The moon is shining gently and clear-o, and fine

witchy things happen when the moon shines gently. It usually signals a bit of feminine guile.'

> *"Oh, thank you, oh, thank you," this young girl she cried,*
> *"It's just what I've been waiting for-o:*
> *For I've grown so weary of my maidenhead*
> *As I walked all alone on my rocky old shore*
> *As I walked all alone on the shore."*

> *And she's robbed 'em of silver, she's robbed 'em of gold,*
> *She's plundered that costly fine ware-o.*
> *The captain's bright sword she's took for an oar,*
> *And she's paddled right back to her rocky old shore,*
> *She's paddled right back to the shore.*

'Well, there's more, but that's the gist of it.'

'So, she was safe?'

'Yep. They rant and rave for a bit and sink deep in despair-o, but she says, Tough, me old chums, I got the better of you lot. She's back on her own territory, back on the shore.'

> *"Now your men they weren't drunk and your men they*
>   *weren't mad,*
> *And neither sunk deep in despair-o.*
> *But I deluded your crew and likewise yourself, too,*
> *Captain, now I'm a maid on my rocky old shore*
> *I'm a maiden once more on the shore."*

'I wish I was on a shore.' She puts her two arms straight up in the air, as if reaching out for the moon's glow on the ceiling.

'Well . . .' I keep my voice as low as possible, almost a whisper. 'You can be. I've got an escape plan.'

I let the sentence hang in the quiet air, innocent as a dove.

'Escape? What . . .? You as well?'

'All three of us. Daisy must come, too.'

'Are you sure? Won't she . . .? What plan?'

'Well, I haven't refined it yet. Basically, I'm going to get his keys, and on a night when Joe is working nights – so not at home in the cottage – we're going to go up and drive Marcus's car all the way to Cornwall – to my parents. And they'll know what to do.'

She props herself up on her elbow now. 'But won't they call the police? And then I'll be sent straight back here.'

'Don't worry. My mum's a counsellor. And anyway, the police can help you find Bryony. And you won't be sent back here after what's happened. If you tell my mum . . . you know – everything – they won't let you anywhere near this place again.'

'You don't know what's happened.'

I wait. Maybe if I wait long enough, she'll tell me. 'I think I might have some idea.'

We are so close and still now, that our breathing crashes through the silence and, slowly, begins to synchronise.

'Did he do it to you?' she asks the ceiling.

'Yes. No.' I have to be honest here, and it's hard. 'It wasn't . . . he did, but . . .' The truth is . . .' I'm so tired of all this deceit, so very tired. 'The truth is, I was all for it at the time.' I feel like I've just coughed up a fish bone. 'I gave consent.'

'You liked it?'

My instinct is to say *No*. Because I don't want to have liked it. I don't want to be the idiot girl who made a stupid decision. I take a deep and painful breath.

'Yes. I did. He made me fall in love with him actually, and—' *No. Stop this. Listen to yourself.* 'He didn't make me do anything. I just fell for him. I was flattered. I felt like I was walking on air. And now—'

'God.'

She may never trust me now. That might be the end of any escape plans.

'Henna . . . has Mimi given you any pills?'

'No.'

'If she does, don't take them.'

'Why? What pills?'

'Nothing.'

'Did you really like doing it with him?'

I feel grubby saying it now. But I have to own it. The feelings I've had have been wonderful. Lust isn't grubby.

'Look, there's nothing wrong with . . . lust is okay. But you have to *agree* to anything like that. You have to want it to happen. And I did. I wish I hadn't now, because I don't think he ever cared a hoot about me.' *Go on. Just say it.* 'And I'm pregnant.'

There's a silence.

'Are you going to have it?'

'No, not if I can get out of here.'

There's another long silence.

'Is that what happened to Violeta? Was it him?'

'I think so.'

'I hate him.'

Chapter Fifty

I don't sleep well, partly because there's no room with Daisy in the bed, and partly because I deliberately stay awake until around two. In the early hours of the morning, I creep downstairs and rifle through the pockets of Marcus's jacket, which hangs by the front door. There are no keys there. I go back to bed, defeated.

In the morning I'm woken by a curious sound. At first, I mistake it for the screech of a crow, but then it becomes the unmistakable sound of a baby crying. Daisy is already up, and has gone downstairs, and Henna is still curled up on her yoga mat on the floor.

By the time we are all down at breakfast, the noise has gone, but Mimi emerges into the kitchen patting a tiny baby on her shoulder, and jigging it round the room.

'When did the baby get here?' I ask.

'The couple brought her two days ago, actually,' says Mimi, 'but she's been as quiet as a mouse until now.' She takes a big breath and turns her head to the dark downy head on her shoulder, and smiles. 'Haven't you?' She looks around at her audience (me, Henna, Daisy, Marcus and Drita). She emanates goodness.

'Two days?' says Daisy, a little put out. 'What's its name?'

Mimi holds the baby away from her and looks it in the face. 'Molly.'

'Molly! Can I hold her? Please! Please?'

'I don't want her to get upset again.'

There is something discordant about Mimi holding a small

baby. Her figure-hugging jeans and clinging T-shirt would look more in place on a model in the fashion pages of a magazine. Even though she appears to wear no make-up and she goes for the effortless natural look, it's hard to imagine Mimi with an up-all-night face, leaking breasts and sick on her shoulder.

'Please, Mummy. I've never held a baby. I'll be very careful.'

Mimi sighs and brings the baby over to the table, holding her in the air while Daisy pushes back her chair and readies herself, excited.

'You need to support her head. That's it.'

She lowers the baby into Daisy's arms, and Daisy can barely control her joy.

'Hello, Molly . . . Hello!' She talks to her in much the way she talks to Sausage, and I'm slightly anxious that she will have to give this precious thing up soon, too. I see Henna's sullen face, gazing at the pair across the table, and I recall her comment once: *Everyone I love leaves me.* She doesn't know, as she looks at Daisy, that she's looking at her own sister. I have to keep them together.

'Now,' says Mimi, pouring herself a coffee, 'I want you girls in the playroom this morning, okay? Make sure you're with them, Caitlin. The couple are coming to pick her up, and I want them to know that it's totally virus-free here. And I want to convey an atmosphere of total calm and professionalism.'

'We always convey an atmosphere of total calm and professionalism,' Henna mutters dryly.

Mimi tightens her nostrils, but otherwise ignores her.

'Why are they picking her up so soon?' asks Daisy. 'She's only just got here.'

'They didn't want to leave her for very long. They only needed somewhere for two full days and nights. And they're paying well for it. You wouldn't want to leave a very young baby for too long.'

'How old is she?'

'Guess.'

Daisy has no idea. 'One?'

'Two months.'

This could be my opportunity. All the doors are locked. When Marcus goes out in a minute he will do so through the back door, and he'll do it when I'm not looking, so I won't have a chance to see where he gets the key from. But when this couple come, Mimi will have to unlock the front door. She wants to create an impression. She won't want them brushing past the hanging cheeses and cardboard mobiles and smelly boots that line the way from the back porch through the clutter of the utility room to the kitchen. She will want to show them in through the oak door into the hall and the living room, with its pretence at shabby chic. She will have to use a key, because the door has been Chubb-locked by Marcus, and I am going to watch where she gets that key from.

After breakfast I go upstairs to visit the bathroom, and I overhear Mimi say something in a low voice to Marcus. 'Not until they've turned up. Not before. Keep them locked in until then.' So I'm hopeful that we'll be set free after the visitors this morning, and the first thing I must do is go and see if I can speak to Kal.

I pass Marcus on my way down the stairs, and reach out and put a hand on his arm, mouthing, 'Can I have a word?'

He turns and looks behind him, and indicates the room next to Daisy's, the one that used to be Violeta's room. I follow him in and he closes the door behind us. The way he looks at me is both inquisitive and wary.

'What is it, Caitlin?'

'Couldn't you take us out on a shopping trip or something? I think the girls are quite scared. I mean, they've been really traumatised by Violeta's death.'

He squidges his mouth into a half-smile which seems to say 'No thanks to you,' but I might be imagining it.

'I'm sorry, but it's too dangerous. You do realise Henna ran away, don't you? I found her three miles away, hitching on a main road.'

Arsehole, bell-end, slimy fucking toad.

'But why would she want to run away?' I try to sound convincing.

'She's doing what Bryony did. And God knows what happened to Bryony. Henna's only *thirteen* – she's far too young to be roaming the countryside on her own at night.'

Knobhead.

'And anyway, what if the police had found her and brought her back, instead of us? She could've told them anything and then we'd be having the police sniffing around here.'

I try not to look hopeful.

'But we'd be with her,' I say. 'We wouldn't have to go to a supermarket. Just Ribley.' The word tastes sour in my mouth, but I don't flinch as I say it. 'Just Ribley. It'll be a little outing for them. They need something to take their minds off it all.'

He puts his hands on my shoulders then, and starts to massage my neck gently. His eyes fill with tenderness.

'You care about my children, don't you?'

'Of course.' And then I add, with as much conviction as I can muster, 'I'd like them to live with us, Marcus. That's if you still . . .'

'God, Caitlin!' His neck is warm on my cheek as he pulls me in, and I smell the shower gel on it. 'You didn't think . . .? Babes, you're still all I want. I'm sorry I called you . . . I was so stressed. I'm sorry if I've seemed to be neglecting you.'

He kisses me then, and it's hard to believe that it's not genuine. He melts into me, and, honest to God, if I weren't on my guard, I can see how a girl could be lost all over again. He takes my hand between his then, and says, 'You'll be able to wear that ring openly soon, and we can tell everyone.'

I look at his big brown hands and think how I used to love them moving down my body, or holding the steering wheel; how I loved the sinews of them, the firm *S* shape between wrist and thumb, the flatness of the nails. Now I see hands that carried Violeta's corpse carelessly, that shovelled earth on top of the woman he once made love to. He touches noses with me.

'I've just got to sort some stuff out before I tell Mimi.'

Yeah. Like he's ever going to tell her we're engaged to be married. I don't know what's going on here, but I'm pretty sure theirs isn't the sort of union that has glued itself together over the years just because he's stuck around long enough, because he's fixed enough grouting or because she's made him enough damson jam. There's a deeper bond between these two, and there's something weird about it.

'But where does it end? This . . . locking-up palaver? You can't keep her imprisoned forever.'

Or me. I give it another shot. 'She needs something to occupy her.'

He takes my face in his hands and I can't tell, looking as warmly into his eyes as I possibly can (mustering all the acting skills I employed as a member of the crowd in *Oliver!* in year 9), whether he is suspicious of me or trusting.

'Leave it with me. I'll see what I can do.'

Ten minutes later, he pokes his head around the door of the playroom and says he has a task for us all: we must empty Violeta's room of all her belongings, and tidy it up for Drita's use. We can do it after the visitors this morning. He chucks us a roll of thick biodegradable bags.

'Make sure you divide the rubbish up. Anything metal, hard plastic or electrical needs to go down the tip.'

I hardly dare look at Henna.

We hear the sound of tyres coming along the track, like bacon spitting in a pan. Car doors shutting; the front door opening; Mimi's most unrecognisable voice yet. You can hear the smile in it, all her gleaming teeth on display. Henna, Daisy and I fall silent together, as if we have agreed to listen.

New voices are a treat, a delicacy as fine as chamber music. But sadly, after the initial feminine notes of wonder at the house, the voices disappear into the long dining room on the other side of the hallway, and become too faint to enjoy. It feels as though the air from the outside has displaced the fug of the last few days and refilled it with new possibilities. Thinking of this, I go to open the windows. The sashes only shift up about four inches, but the breeze is sweet-scented and cool.

'When can we go out again?' asks Daisy.

'Soon,' I say, winking at her. 'We'll go out together, the three of us. We'll make a plan.'

Henna looks up from her book and Daisy, sprawled on the floor, hugs my ankle. I know they're relying on me. I can't let them down. I don't think I've ever had so much responsibility in my life. Not since when Dani was small – and then I blew it. This time I have to get it right. I will get them out of here. I just have to think of a way.

Filkins appears on the windowsill and slithers through the gap. He flops on the floor and presents his tummy for group admiration. We all comply, and he is in heaven. We spend twenty minutes or so pampering Filkins. He doesn't know what he's done to deserve such attention. It's his sudden movement that alerts us to the couple leaving.

'Well, I'm very glad to have been able to help you.' (Mimi.)

'We can't even begin to tell you. We can't even begin. We're so grateful.' This is a man's voice – a gentle, measured man.

The front door opens with its familiar woody clunk. The voices are now in stereo, waning from inside the house, growing through the window gap, wafting in with the sweet breeze.

'She's so beautiful,' says the mother. 'Just like her mother.'

Henna pulls a face at me. Daisy copies her.

'She certainly is,' says Mimi, slightly louder than the woman.

The space between the voices is growing now. The couple are moving towards their green car, which is parked a few metres further away from the house, just beyond our window. Daisy goes to kneel at the window and peeps out. We can see the backs of the couple as they approach the car with the baby in a carrier seat. The woman pauses and looks back at the house. She is wearing pastel blue and a dreamy smile.

'We're going to call her Grace!' she calls to Mimi.

'Lovely!' or something like that, from Mimi.

But no one is listening to Mimi now. Daisy turns her head and frowns.

'Why do they want to call the baby Grace if she's called Molly? Did they forget?'

The car doors slam, one after another. Henna gets up from the sofa and stares out of the window, her eyes fixed on the car as it winds its way up the track. She says nothing. She knows suddenly that the baby wasn't called Molly at all, because Violeta didn't have time to name her.

Chapter Fifty-One

We make the clearing out of Violeta's room stretch as long as we can. It's an elegant room at the front of the house, with a long sash window overlooking the field up to the ridge, yellow damask curtains and a walk-in wardrobe. All of which makes the scant possessions that Violeta amassed over a year seem unspeakably sad. Daisy disappears among the hanging clothes, and Henna paces around, pausing to examine things reverently. Then she picks up a baggy cardigan, sits on the bed and rocks herself over it. Her face screws into a tight red knot. She seems so small and helpless.

'I loved her,' she whimpers, gasping for breath as the tears come. 'I loved her so much!'

I sit down next to her and hold her, and she lets me, snorting and wailing while I bury my nose in her hair parting, waiting out the trembling of her tiny wings.

Later, when she's ready to explore the room, I make a start on the drawers of a tall oak chest, pulling out the clothes and placing them on the bed to be sorted. There are knobbly cardigans, T-shirts the colour of a winter sky, and bras with the elastic stretched to a frill. (I take a couple of these for myself, as my own bra no longer fits.) Henna holds each item in turn like a religious relic, and makes slow piles based on criteria she does not share with us. I work my way through the drawers, uncovering nothing but the modest essentials of Violeta's restricted life.

In her bedside table is a shoulder bag with a purse. There is nothing in the purse but a five-pound note, some loose change, a Co-op card and a creased photograph of a family outside by a tree. It must be her parents and sisters. One of the girls is clearly a young Violeta, wearing leggings and a T-shirt, a contented smirk on her face, as if someone has just promised them all a treat after the photo. Henna will treasure this photograph.

In the bedside drawer is a diary with entries in another language, a tube of corticosteroid cream, pencils, nail clippers, free-gift sachets of face creams, eyeliner, lipsalve, used-up lipsticks, knitting patterns. It is a humble haul. Inside the diary is a slip of paper with figures written on it: '10,000 pounds = 56,800 lei'. Big money. *They give me big money. Big. I go home.* Poor Violeta – she never got her big money, her passage home. I wonder what Mimi got for the baby. Big, big money.

Right at the back of the drawer, in the grime of dust that gets under my nails as I cast into the corners, is a small box. Daisy is swirling round in a pink pullover with sleeves way too long for her. Henna has her head down over the diary. I open the box.

I already knew what it was, I think, before I even saw the diamond, identical in every way to the one Marcus gave me. Unsure why, I slip it into my pocket. Poor Violeta, knowing when I arrived it had all been a sham. How dignified she was, refusing my help when she was crouched – at eight-and-a-half months pregnant – cleaning the scum off my bath, when she washed my sheets and put food in front of me. She had been promised marriage, too. Swift change of plan. As she rested her swollen ankles in their cheap plastic sandals, she knew she had been replaced, but had the self-preservation to wait it out for the ticket home.

Later I will examine the ring for a hallmark, and discover that, like mine, there is nothing engraved on the inside of the gold band. And I will remember what it was that had startled me when

I felt the shape and weight and texture of it as I pulled it out of the drawer. It reminded me of something: the little cubes in the desk of his secret office.

I lie on my bed with Daisy beside me. Henna is on her yoga mat, hugging her knees, bent over a photograph, with fat tears rolling down her cheeks. The sun is still sinking outside, but Daisy is asleep.

They must be laughing about me behind my back, Marcus and Mimi. How many times have they played this stunt together? How many more of his grandmother's unique antique rings were in those boxes? I imagine the two of them in that bedroom of theirs. Does he describe my naked flesh for her? I expect she gets off on it somehow. The way she looks at me sometimes, so suggestively, but with an edge of contempt, as if she's been there herself, inside my thighs. As if she's heard me cry out. Marcus said she was the money-maker; she drove the business. I remember what Cliff said: *It all changed when* she *came.* How ridiculous they must think I am, so totally fooled by their clever tactics. I thought I knew betrayal, but here I am again. Betrayal blindness. As if that's just what I'm destined to do forever: fill in the blanks with what I want to see.

In Italy, Lotti and Luke would have friends round, other teachers from their language school. There were two guys from Cambridge who used to play guitar. Me and Tom were often the only people in the room without a degree. They rated Tom because he played better than them, but I was just the girlfriend, the empty-headed numbskull who filled the glasses. How pathetically I used to lean into Luke, flattered to belong to him, barely included in his conversation and happy with the crumbs. How carefully I listened to their discussions, hungry for knowledge, focusing on what they found amusing, repeating their words in my head later as if I was swotting for an exam. (Yeah, I know: pity I hadn't done that for my A-levels.) I didn't dare contribute, because I knew he would find some subtle way to ridicule me. Or else he would wheel me out to confirm his friendship with Trevik Polglaze, the Booker Prize nominated author. '*What is it Trev always says, Caitlin? Oh yes . . .*' I see now how much I relied on him noticing me from time to time, because when he didn't, I didn't exist.

Here I am again.

And yet.

'Caitlin?'

'Yes?'

'You know Violeta's baby?'

'Yes . . .'

'It didn't die, did it? That couple took it away, didn't they?'

'I think so. Yes.'

'Mimi *lied*! I bet she got money for it! God!' I can hear the brittleness in her voice, about to break. 'Oh God, oh God! Caitlin!'

'What is it, Henna? You okay?'

She's gasping. 'D'you think Mum died like that – because Mimi didn't take her to hospital?'

'I think she did, yes. But she may have wanted a home birth. It sounds quite likely she chose that.'

'Yes, but . . . you don't think . . . you don't think my mum's baby survived, do you? Like Violeta's? And they *lied*?'

I miss a beat before I reply, and I can hear her catch her breath.

'Actually, I think she did survive, yes.'

There's a sudden rustling as Henna props herself up on one elbow. I see her silhouette in the remaining light.

'What? And they *sold* it?'

'No.'

'Where is she, then? D'you *know*? Where's Kitty?'

'I only just found out myself.' I want to tread delicately, but this is all too urgent, and she deserves to know.

'*Where?* Where is she?'

'I *think* she's here.'

'In the house?'

'Here. On the bed, asleep.'

Henna's breathing is like someone who's been running and has stopped for a rest. There are no words. Just breathing. Then: 'Daisy . . .? *Daisy?*'

'Yes, I'm pretty certain.'

'Daisy!'

'Yes.'

'Oh my God.' She breathes heavily. 'What . . .? Can I . . .? Can we swap places?'

And we do. Carefully, as if wrapping glassware, Henna curls up around her sister, and whispers apologies, whispers that she will take care of her, and strokes her, and whispers some more. Her breathing becomes wet and snotty in the silence that follows, and I know she's crying. Then she sleeps – deeply. It is probably the first time she has truly held someone she loves for a very long time.

I rest a hand on my belly and try to see if I can feel anything, but I can't. It aches from time to time, like a period pain, and my breasts are sore and swollen. I slide my hand up to my chest and feel something hard. It's the cards I stole from Marcus's drawer, still in the chest pocket of my dungarees. I take them out now and squint at them in the dim light from the window. Each card has dates on it, and sure enough, I recognise the dates Mimi mentioned as being when I would be most likely to conceive. I've worked them out myself: approximately two weeks after my last period. And in the top corner there is a capital letter *C* in felt-tip pen. For Caitlin? What a piece of work she is! She had me lined up for this, and Marcus was in league with her. I feel sick. Before I find somewhere to hide them, I glance again at the other cards. There is *V* – for Violeta, no doubt – and *D* . . . for Drita? This is horrible. But the next one sends a chill through me. In the top corner, in thick felt-tip, is the letter *H*.

Daisy is curled up in my bed in a too-big jumper, Henna wrapped around her. They need me. I do exist. And if it's the last thing I do, I'm going to get these girls out of here.

Chapter Fifty-Two

It's Wednesday already. The doors are still locked. If Joe has the same shift pattern this week as last week, we need to leave on Friday or Saturday night if we're to escape in the car. But getting hold of these keys is proving impossible. When Mimi opened the door to the visitors yesterday, we were shut in the playroom. And I don't know how Drita gets in and when she arrives for breakfast. If they were planning to set us free after the couple's visit, something has changed their mind. Daisy keeps asking about the lambs, and Marcus assures her that Drita is seeing to them. They're eating special lamb meal now, so don't need bottles any more.

'They'll need to be let out to proper pasture soon, anyway,' he says over breakfast.

'We can make a bigger field.' Daisy's face lights up as she says it. 'Sausage will love that!'

Marcus takes in a deep breath. 'Daisy, my princess, I think Geoff will want to put them back in with his sheep.'

Her face crumples.

'We talked about them needing to go back, didn't we,' I say, stroking her hand.

Marcus speaks with his mouth full of toast and Marmite: 'And I saw Geoff. He's taking them this week some time.'

'No!'

She puts down her milk, her top lip covered in it, and gazes desperately at me to deny it.

I look at him, as he burps internally, stuffs in another mouthful of toast and tilts back in his chair. He sticks one big socked foot up on a neighbouring chair and says in toast-muffled syllables, 'It's a learning curve. You knew you couldn't keep them. Get used to it.'

The playroom is at the end of the house and has two windows: one facing the front, and the other facing the side out towards the track. We keep each one ajar so that we can hear the birdsong and smell the scents of outside. Daisy wants the door open, too, but Marcus or Mimi or Drita come to close it whenever she opens it.

'Don't lock the door!' she shouts every time. 'Please, *please* don't lock it!'

But there is no key in the playroom door, it just feels so very locked, because the only times we venture out, someone – usually Drita – is there to watch us go up to the toilet and come down again. She might as well have a set of jailer's keys around her waist. Perhaps she has.

Something is different about the aloe vera plant pot on the windowsill. There are two orange lion-heads sticking up from the earth.

'What have Mummy and Daddy Lion done now?' I ask.

Daisy remains silent, and pushes the heads under the earth with her penguin pencil sharpener, until they're completely buried.

How sluggishly the time passes. We try to chart it in birdsong, lamb bleats and the familiar clinking of cups marking coffee breaks, tea breaks and food preparation. The shuttings and openings of doors are a torture. Gone are the opportunities to search through pockets and cupboards; there are always eyes on us. If I could just run out, run up and hide at Kal's, or hide in the woods until dark and then hitch along the road, or else I could walk to Geoff's farm and tell him everything. But then the police would be involved and I can't be certain the girls wouldn't end up in care. I have to get home to Mum. She'll know what to do. So, maybe I could just run out. Next time I hear a door open. Push past whoever opens it. The element of surprise could work. Who would stop me? Could Drita rugby-tackle me to the ground? I'm pretty solid. But if Marcus caught me, then he'd know. He'd know my intent, and the one golden chance would be over.

Henna is writing her own manual on the environment, based on Greta Thunberg's speeches. She reads out passages from time to time. It is angry, articulate and punchy. Daisy is now knitting a blanket for Sausage. It's a vibrant red acrylic mix. If we are locked in here for another few months she might finish it, and I admire her tenacity and the determination on her face as she whispers, 'In, over, under, off,' stopping every time she remarks on anything, which is often.

I finish casting off a little red and blue striped item I've been making, and dress Donkey in it quietly. When Daisy notices it, she stares, bewildered.

'For Donkey? You made Donkey a jumper?' I nod. She swallows. 'He's never had anything of his own before. He's so happy!'

'Well, it's high time he did. All the best-dressed donkeys are wearing them.'

'Thank you. This is the best present ever! *Ever*. Apart from my bracelet.'

'Bracelet?'

She shows me her wrist and the cheap nick-nack I gave her in the car on the day they first picked me up. Her expectations of pleasure are so limited. It makes me ache that she can be so delighted by a plait of purple nylon.

We all hear the vehicle coming along the track. Alert as squirrels, we rush to the window looking out from the side of the house.

'It's a car!'

'Sounds more like a truck.'

'Could be that education lady.'

There are glimpses of it in the far field before it disappears behind hawthorn and elder, then it winds into view as it approaches the house.

'It's Geoff!'

He slams the driver's door as he gets out, and we wave frantically to him, but the truck is further along now, past the front door and near to the lambs.

'Hello there!' we hear him shout.

The front door opens.

'Wait, please. I get Marcus.'

Drita must be going the other way around the back of the house to the polytunnels, because she doesn't pass our window. Daisy puts her face right up to the window and sticks out her hand.

'Hello! Hello! Hello, Geoff! We're in here!'

Geoff comes over to our window.

'Well, hello! I was hoping I'd see you young ladies! Are you going to come and show me how well you've been looking after those woolly girls of mine, then?'

'We *can't*. We're locked in.'

Jesus. Now! Run!

I dash out through the playroom door, run across the living room out into the hall, and slip through the front door. I'm out! I hardly have time to think. I don't know which way to run. Right – up to the woods? Then I'll meet Drita and Marcus coming around the house. Left – and run past Geoff? All the empty hours we've tried to condense, and here are a few seconds that are crammed full with possibilities and crucial arguments stacking up on both sides. Right or left. I leap towards Geoff, and before I reach him . . .

'Geoff! My good man!'

Fuckit.

I don't turn round to acknowledge Marcus. Instead, I reach out a hand to Geoff, as if I wasn't darting past him at all. 'Geoff! It's great to see you!'

He looks at me and smiles, but doesn't take my hand.

'Better not. Social distancing and all that. The wife's got me being careful.'

'Of course. Sorry, I forgot.'

Marcus, who comes right up next to me, all ready to slam Geoff on the back, retreats a little himself.

'Ah, yes. Can't be too careful.'

The girls have followed me out of the front door now and, hearing their feet crunch on the path, he swings round.

'Get back inside!'

'Oh,' says Geoff. 'They said they were locked in.' He chuckles. 'They been naughty or something?'

I watch Marcus. *Get out of that one, shithead.*

'They've got the virus. They're in quarantine.' He takes a deep breath in, like someone who has to make difficult decisions to do his duty for the community.

'Oh, that's a shame, that is,' says Geoff, his eyes following the girls back to the house. 'I was hoping you could say a proper good-bye to the lambs. I'm fetching them off home.'

'But we haven't got the virus,' says Daisy. They've retreated to the front door, but stand half-in, half-out.

'They're near the end of their quarantine,' squirms Marcus. 'They only had a mild temperature a week ago, but I'm playing safe.'

You slimy fucking bastard.

'Good man. Well, I don't suppose they'll give it to the lambs, if they want to give them a bit of a cuddle before I take them.'

Marcus gives a stiff smile to the girls and nods. I join them as they go over to the lamb enclosure and take out their treasures.

'I'm making Sausage a blanket but it isn't finished.' Daisy pushes her face into her lamb's neck to hide her trembling lip.

'Well, that's all right, my love. You can bring it up to the farm when you come to see them. They'll want you to come and visit when they've settled in.'

'Can we?' says Henna, glancing at Marcus.

''Course you can!' Geoff pulls down the back end of his truck, which has a cage in it. ''Course they can, can't they, Mark? You girls can come any time you like. I'll be disappointed if you don't.' He puts his hands on his hips and smiles at the girls with their lambs. 'I reckon those two lambs'll recognise you straight away, and all. Oh yes. They never forget a face, sheep don't. Not if you've been kind to them.'

Marcus scratches the back of his head, somewhat floored by this usurping of his authority. Drita has brought out the feeding bottles and some feed from the cupboard in the utility room. I offer to go and fetch the tubs of powdered milk-replacer, but Marcus stops me, standing behind me and placing his hands on my shoulders in what could pass as a friendly manner.

'Drita can do that.'

Bastard.

With the lambs safely in the truck, we wave goodbye, vowing to visit in a week or so, when they've settled in. Marcus eyes me as we turn towards the house with the steely glare of a teacher who's caught you smoking behind the bike shed. Only there's more at stake than after-school detention. He knows. I've blown it.

Chapter Fifty-Three

After lunch, Marcus tells us that we will all be sleeping back in our own beds from now on. He ignores Daisy's pleas and says we need to get back to some normality.

'We haven't got the virus, have we?' says Daisy quietly, when the three of us are back in the playroom.

'No, sweetheart.'

'So Daddy told a fib.'

There's a silence that needs someone to plunge into it, but I don't know what to say. Eventually she continues to knit, mouthing the actions slowly to herself: 'In, over, under, off.'

'Unbelievable, isn't it?' says Henna later, looking up from her environmental thesis. 'He lies about us without even flinching. He's a fucking liar!'

'Careful!' I whisper. 'The window's open.'

'I don't give a flying fuck! He lied about Bryony – he lied about Violeta. He's never done anything but fucking lie to us!'

This is so out of character that she looks as startled as we are. Daisy sucks her lip and keeps her head down. She knits. Daisy. I'm not fooled. I know the mute understanding of a small child, the deceptive alertness of the bowed head, seemingly focused on something else. A wordless language, full of emotion and buried deep. A depth charge biding its time.

Minutes later we hear scratching and tapping on the playroom door. We freeze. The sound of a drill. Silence. The door rattles in its frame, then creaks. Finally, the unmistakable sound of a bolt being drawn across. Daisy starts to tremble. She lies on the sofa next to me and rocks her head back and forth.

'No, no, no, no. Don't lock us in. No, no!'

Henna, stunned, says, 'It's what he used to do when Bryony left.' She looks down at her lap and plucks bits of lint off her leggings. 'Will you help us?'

'Yes. Don't worry, it's going to be okay.'

This has to be the age-old promise of adults to children, but this promise must be kept. Filkins slides across the windowsill and hops nimbly onto the sofa, where the three of us stroke him to calm ourselves. We sit like that, soothing Filkins, smoothing out the creases in our nerves, and thoughts of Kahlil doing this himself later make me smile.

'Daisy, do you have any ribbon in the bag of wool and stuff? Can we put a little ribbon on Filkins?'

As she's rummaging through the bag, I ask Henna for her finest pencil or pen. She goes through her pencil case and selects a pencil which she sharpens to a point.

'Any good?'

'Brilliant! And a notebook.' Then I lower my voice to a whisper. 'I have a plan. I'm going to say very little because the window's open, and we're going to need it open in a moment.' They both come and kneel beside the sofa. 'Daisy, I need you to take over the stroking of Filkins. Very gently. He mustn't get up.'

She does as she's told, like a vet carrying out an operation. Slowly, as small as I can, I write a tiny message on the notepaper.

'Do we have a scissors?' Henna hands me a pair, and I cut out the writing. It's about an inch square. I fold it up several times until it's as small as a currant. 'Right. Somehow, we need to fix this message on Filkins, then he can get help.'

'But Filkins is Kal's cat.'

'Yes, and Kal is my friend. He's kind. I think he'll help us.'

There is a lull while this sinks in, and while we think of ways to attach the message to the cat. We consider sticking it to the back of his name pendant with Sellotape, but it might come off, or the wrong person could read it.

'We could sew it into the end of his ribbon.' Henna tries wrapping the little seed of paper in the ribbon. 'It would hardly show at all.'

'That could be a problem. We need to not draw attention to it, but to find some way – like the ribbon, perhaps – to make Kal focus on his neck this evening, when Filkins is on his lap.'

'So just a small piece of ribbon, not a big fancy bow.'

'Exactly. And something subtle around his neck that no one else would even notice. Something small that is also a container.'

I think of a tiny plastic suitcase I saw Daisy playing with once, no bigger than a thumbnail. Henna starts to hunt for it in the bottom of a toy box, but keeps getting distracted by other toys: miniature cakes, plastic shoes, a tiny stethoscope. We tip the box up and the contents spill out onto the floor. The two of us, on our knees, scrabble through the small items, while Daisy continues stroking Filkins. There is no suitcase to be found, or any other appropriate container.

We shove everything back into the box, and as I lean over to sweep my hand under the sofa, Daisy grabs at what is dangling from my neck.

'What about your lock-it?'

My grandmother's silver locket.

'You. Are. A genius.'

She gives a coy smile.

I unthread the little oval locket and Henna presses the folded nub of paper into it.

'There!' she says. She takes off Filkins' collar and threads his new item of jewellery onto the metal ring from which his name tag dangles. Meanwhile, Filkins, astounded at this turn of events, is soothed by Daisy stroking his chin. He goes with the flow, lying

283

back and closing his eyes, totally chilled within seconds. I snip off a small piece of dusky pink ribbon and attach it to the back of his collar, hooking it into the buckle.

When we reattach the collar, Filkins is exasperated. He gets up and saunters over to the window to leave. Good. The ribbon is just noticeable enough for Kal to be curious about his collar. I only hope he sees the locket, and thinks to open it.

At teatime in the dining room I wait for Mimi to notice, and she does.

'What's that around your neck?' (Like she doesn't know.)

I take hold of the 'antique' engagement ring I have threaded on to the silver locket chain. 'This?' I try to look awkward, caught out. 'It was my grandmother's ring.'

Marcus looks at the ring he gave me, and pretends to appear mildly interested, as if he hasn't seen it before. 'Eat up your broccoli, Daisy, or you'll never grow big and strong.'

Daisy puts her fork down gently. 'I don't give a flying fuck,' she says, cool as you like.

Cliff, further up the bench, seems to cough up his tarragon-stuffed mushroom. I know if I catch Henna's eye, I risk bursting into giggles. The moment is compressed and could spring open either way, to fury or hilarity. Mimi's face has darkened. She looks at me and I shrug.

'Television,' I say. 'There's nothing else to do when you're locked in.'

She breathes heavily. 'Well, don't let me ever catch you saying that again, Daisy.'

I can see Daisy is about to ask for an explanation of the phrase, so I fondle the ring again at my neck, and Henna asks, 'Is it very old, the ring?'

'It's an antique,' I say, grateful to her.

'It must mean a lot to you,' says Mimi, a wooden smile on her face. The gentle doe deer has evaporated. She reminds me now

284

of a shop mannequin: the smile subtle and ambivalent, and no warmth behind the eyes.

'I treasure it.' I fumble with the ring and kiss it. Then I venture a shy glance at Marcus. 'It means everything to me.' My voice sounds ridiculous: pathetic and needy, like a sulky child. Unreplaced by anything else, the words contaminate the air, like words not rubbed off a whiteboard from the last lesson.

Eventually Mimi says, 'It's beautiful,' in that calm, authoritative way of hers. She has pronounced a piece of tat beautiful. But then she knows it to be tat. The tiny curl on one side of her mouth shows that she's enjoying this little game with Marcus. She's enjoying my ignorance and credulity; she's enjoying their pretence. But I know we are all pretending.

Chapter Fifty-Four

When Drita fetched the lamb feed, she went round the side of the house to the back door. There must be a key in the porch there somewhere. And there must be one inside the back door, too. That's why Marcus pressed down on my shoulders, why he didn't want me to fetch the milk-replacer from the cupboard by the back door.

There is no point begging Kahlil to help us escape if we can't tell him where the key is. I try to picture the porch, and where I would hide a key. It's cluttered with coats and scarves and boots. That seems the most likely place: a wellington boot or something. But I don't have access to the outside porch. If, at night, I creep downstairs, I might find where the key is hidden to open the back door from the inside. I've already tried all the cupboards. Maybe it was inside the milk-replacer tubs. That's why he wouldn't let me go there. Or in a plant pot on the windowsill. It must be easily accessible, because Drita came out pretty smartly with those bags of meal. I resolve to go looking tonight. I'll put my gran's alarm on for three o'clock and bury it under my pillow so that it won't wake anyone else. I read somewhere that this is 'the dead of the night', when most people are likely to be asleep.

I keep checking the luminous face of Granny Rostock's travel alarm, and I must eventually fall asleep because the drilling buzz of it comes through the pillow as a total, sleepy surprise. I turn it off and wait. There is a complete hush; just the sound of owls hooting back and forth to each other. Eventually I creep downstairs in my bare feet. I know where the creaks are off by heart, but even with the slowest, surest pace, the wood moans slightly, as if turning over in its sleep. If Marcus or Mimi catch me on the first landing, I'll say I thought I heard Daisy cry out. If I'm caught on the ground floor, I have no excuses.

The moon is plump and high in the sky. The only other light comes from an electrical switch by the hob, and then in the utility area from the dishwasher, where the red light stays on although the cycle has finished. I know there are torches hanging by the back door, and I unhook one. I stop and listen, hearing only the pounding of my own pulse. Tentatively I switch on the torch and shine it at the floor. The boots and shoes are beyond the door, and I know, even before I press down the handle, that it's locked. Okay, there is the lamb feed cupboard. Gently, I open it and root around. I remove the two empty tubs and open the lids. Nothing. On the floor, shoved under the worktop between the cupboard and the wall, are a few old pairs of shoes and socks. I scrabble around inside each one. Nothing. I uncouple the socks and feel inside. I put everything back where it was. On the wall is a clock, but there is no key behind it. A dried-up plant has neither a key underneath it nor inside its felty clump of earth. I feel all along the curtain hem at the window. But this is too complicated. It really can't be so well hidden. Drita comes in here and goes out with ease. There haven't been any key-shapes in her pocket, and this is a sturdy metal Chubb lock.

I bend down and try to look through the keyhole. The torchlight seems to go right through and light up the glass of the outside porch door. So there's no key in the door on the outside. *Dammit*. Kal could've opened it if there was. It's hopeless. I thought I would find this easily.

A sudden creaking makes me freeze. I turn off the torch. It's so quiet and distant; perhaps it's Henna getting up to use the loo. When my breathing is steady, I make my way swiftly back through the kitchen and peer at the bottom of the stairs. There's no one there, so I head up as quickly and noiselessly as I can.

Henna's door is closed, but there's a noise. Now what? It's so tempting to slide back into bed, but I know in my bones that it's him. I could go and flush the toilet in our second-floor bathroom, just metres from where I'm standing. But there are sounds now – ugly sounds – and I can't bear it. Come *on*. Open the door. But what if . . .? Uncle Aaron whispers slyly in my ear, *I know you're the sort of girl who likes this.* I can't protect Marcus any more. I can't pretend. Even if our entire escape plan is scuppered. Come *on*, Caitlin. Stop him.

I knock quickly. There's a rustle. I open the door in time to see the dark shape of a man compose himself.

'You okay, Henna? I thought I heard you talking in your sleep— Oh! Is that you, Marcus?'

'Yes. I thought I heard her cry out, so I came to check.' I don't know if he buys into my innocence or not.

'I'm fine,' says Henna. 'Really. It was just a bad dream.'

Marcus has stood up now, and I stand in the doorway, showing no signs of leaving until he has. It's so shadowy, he could *be* Uncle Aaron. I wait for him to reach the stairs and then I say, 'It's okay. It's normal, sleeping alone after all that's happened. I'll see to her.'

I can't make out his expression. He makes his way swiftly down to the next landing and the room he shares with Mimi, and it's hard to tell if my muffled alarm clock roused him in the first place, or if he was lying in wait for the dead of night as well.

I return to Henna's room and sit down on the bed beside her.

I wait; she waits. The house is bloated with silence. At last, the owl again; its partner's reply.

'We'll leave on Friday night,' I whisper. 'The three of us together. Are you in?'

'Of course I am.' She sounds as if she is about to say something else, but stops. Then: 'Why Friday?'

'Because that's when Joe is on nights. Friday and Saturday. He won't hear us start the Land Rover.'

'But we don't have the keys to the Land Rover. We can't even get out of the house.'

She can't see me rub my forehead in the darkness. I start to picture tying sheets together, breaking a window in Violeta's old room – which is the furthest from Marcus and Mimi's – and slipping out down the side of the house. Too much noise. Daisy would never be able to stay quiet if she'd been rudely awoken in the middle of the night to perform in an assault course.

'I'm working it out. Kal will help us. But we have to be ready. It's our big chance.'

'I don't get it, though. And where will we go? I don't want to end up in a home.'

'I told you. We'll go to Cornwall.' If I say it often enough it will come true. 'And we need to be ready. Take the bare minimum – one precious thing. Nothing heavy. Wear layers.'

'Photographs of Mum.'

'Yes. And we can't tell Daisy.'

'Wait – but she's coming, right?'

'Yes. But a secret may be too much of a burden for her, and if she lets something slip, she'll feel terrible. We'll tell her when she goes to bed. We'll explain how we'll wake her up and go on a secret trip to the seaside.'

Henna sighs. 'This *has* to work. I don't know what they'll do if they catch us.'

Chapter Fifty-Five

Thursday. If Kal replies, I can ask him to bring us a screwdriver. If he can put it through the gap in the window somehow tonight or tomorrow, I can unscrew one of the locks. This one. This window in the playroom that faces the tracks to the side of the house. I'll have a go now! But looking at it, there's no hope of finding anything in this room that resembles a small, cross-head screwdriver. And then there's stealing the Land Rover with no keys. I've already thought we could hire a car or something. Or we could get a taxi to the train station, although I have no money. Oh, but there are no trains. Are there even taxis? Worst-case scenario, Kal might let us borrow his car. If it's fixed.

A horrible feeling keeps trying to surface, a feeling that Kal may not be that committed to helping us after all. He did seem really shocked when I told him about Henna, but then he wouldn't take the keys for me. He wouldn't even let *me* take them when I could. He would probably call the police. They might turn up any time now, the police, and Henna and Daisy will be separated and put in care or – and I can't dwell on this – eventually returned to Marcus and Mimi. Or just Daisy might be returned to them, to grow up alone, ready for Marcus to impregnate her one day.

I mustn't get hysterical. I must keep looking for the keys, and focus on tomorrow night. The three of us need to stay as calm as possible, and that's my job. I'm the grown-up here.

Later, I will realise that these numbered days gave me more agency than the whole year I spent with Luke.

Thursday drags. Through the windows we feast our eyes on all the different greens of the grassy bank, which holds swathes of dandelions and daisies trembling in the breeze; then up higher, the gorse flowers are tumbling in clouds, a milky way of gold all over the bushes. To the right is the old wicker swing chair I saw on my first day, the Buddhas with grass growing out of their heads. Up by the barn, if you look long enough, house sparrows are nesting. A pair of wood pigeons coo to each other from the copper beech tree; sometimes you can catch the swooping forked tail of a swallow as it flies up to its new nest under the eaves near our bedroom windows. Places to live, to bring up their young. They woo, they warn, they sing for the hell of it. The world is loud with birdsong. Further out, along the paths, the sweet reek of May blossom and cow parsley thickens the air, and it creeps into the playroom like a promise.

Outside there is drama: the ongoing disputes and joys of creatures great and small; the growth spurts of flowers and trees and fungi and slow worms; insect empires expanding under stones. Inside, there is the same turgid soap opera of the house: the distant hum of the washing machine, the occasional excitement of its spin cycle; the hiss and clank of the old pipes in the walls and the sobbing and sighing of door hinges. The house breathes and wheezes like an elderly person. And I am beginning to feel that I could stay here long enough to become an elderly person, that I will wear a patch in the sofa arm with my bony elbow, that I'll be waiting for Filkins to show up with a sign until I develop swollen ankles, a passion for *Last of the Summer Wine* and an unhealthy attachment to the TV remote. A robin lands on the windowsill, contemplating all the insects on the climbing rose leaves. Then we watch him watching us. We must seem like strange sea creatures moving slowly in our dark aquarium. Just a thin sheet of glass separates out there from in here. Our iron bars are a Georgian window. Or so it would seem. But the three of us understand, in our different ways, that there is more than glass and wood keeping us locked in.

'Did your daddy ever lock you in?' asks Daisy, kneeling at the slightly open front window and appearing to put this question to the robin. Her bare arm is resting on the stone sill, and she picks listlessly at the loose paint on the frame.

'No,' I say. She turns briefly, wanting more. I'm not sure how to play this. 'If he had, my mum would have unlocked us.'

Perhaps I've gone too far, but then again, I'm not dissing Daisy's real mum.

She shifts her arm a little on the sill. 'What were your mummy and daddy like?'

My mummy and daddy. Let's see. Henna looks up from her thesis long enough for me to know that she's listening. When she looks down again her pen doesn't move.

'Well, they're still around. My dad writes books – stories – for people to read.'

'What sort of stories?'

'The same sort of stories you read, really – adventures and stuff, but for grown-ups. Although he hasn't written much lately.' Moving swiftly on. 'And my mum . . . she looks after people with worries.'

'What sort of worries?'

'Children at school who aren't happy about something – like they may be being bullied, say, or having trouble at home.'

Henna carefully pours some water from a small jug into the pot of the aloe vera plant on the windowsill. Just visible in the soil is the yellow pate of Mummy Lion. Daisy bites her lip and pushes the head hard into the earth until it disappears. Then she comes to sit next to me.

'What's she like, your mummy?'

'My mummy? She's kind. Um . . . She's a bit daft. I miss her.'

I feel such shame now when I think of my mother. Not just because I gave up on university for a little creep who betrayed her as well as me. Atrociously. She may even have known he was up to no good. And then Lotti, too. If I think Lotti betrayed me, it's as nothing to what she did to my mother. But more than any of that, I know that the uncomfortable feeling I have, the heartbreak in the pit of my stomach when I think of Mum, is because of the way *I* betrayed her.

I can picture Lotti, leaning against the counter in our sprawling kitchen the day she arrived, looking around.

'You could do so much with a place like this.' (Was she already imagining taking Mum's place?) 'I'd paint it all in a subtle sage grey.'

Luke, I remember was nodding. 'Smart.'

'This is the sort of colour my gran would like,' she continued, unaware that Mum had entered the room.

'Oh,' Mum said. 'Is she decorating? I can find the colour name for her if you like.'

Lotti turned round and, bold as brass, said, 'Actually, I think I know it. Isn't it Vanilla or something? A Heritage Paint?'

My mother, bless her, looked eager. 'Magnolia something-or-other, but no, it was from B&Q. Very reasonable. I'll go in the shed and find out before you go.'

'Thank you, Mrs Polglaze.'

Lotti and Luke were both smirking, and the horror of it is, so was I. But I cringed, too, because I knew Mum would offer them instant coffee and try too hard with paper napkins.

And then there was the awful time when Lotti, whose mother is Italian, asked Mum how she made her lasagne. We were all eating around the big table and Mum was flushed from cooking for seven people – something she pulled off every night they were there, with a different dish from her repertoire. And she had fallen into the trap, and told Lotti in great detail how she made lasagne. How you didn't need to be bothered with passata or red wine or mozzarella. A couple of cans of chopped tomato and cheddar would do the trick. 'That's what I always use. I'm glad you like it.' She'd write it down if Lotti was interested. Honestly, it was so easy to make.

I let them get away with sly stunts like that. I thought I was being so worldly and grown-up that I followed them around Europe and broke my promise to apply for a degree. And I probably broke my mother's heart in the process. And now it's been broken all over again. And what I want more than anything right now is to hug the squidgy softness of her and tell her I'm sorry. I need to get home and say sorry. Sorry.

'I wish I could meet your mummy.'

The lump in my throat feels right. I deserve to be strangled for the cruelty towards my hapless mum.

'Well, maybe you can. I'd like you to meet her, too.'

'Is it far away, where your house is?'

'It's in Cornwall, not too far from the sea. The house is a bit untidy, but I don't think you'd mind. There are too many books for the shelves and they're everywhere, in twisty piles all over the floor that grow like beanstalks. If my mum turns her back for one minute there's another pile, growing up in a corner or in the bathroom or on the windowsill.' Daisy giggles. 'And outside there are flowers everywhere in the spring, but lots of them are wild, because she loves wild flowers best. And just a short drive or a long walk away is the sea, and sometimes you see seals off the coast, lolling about in the inlets. And when the waves come, they bob up and down like little boats. Sometimes they disappear – just like that – and then you see a little black rock appear, and it's not a rock at all, but a seal's head, nowhere near where it was before.'

'And is there a beach you can play on?'

'Oh, yes. Lots of beaches.'

Suddenly I miss the sea air. Back in Cornwall you can smell the weather changing – a whiff of ozone like a temper brewing – and the gulls sense it, too, coming inland in tight, circular flocks days in advance. I long for that Cornwall now, of wet weekends full of stories and make-believe, when rock pools were full of rubies and emeralds and Dad was still a hero and summertime lasted forever.

'There are lots of people who come to the beaches in the summer, but I know a special secret one where hardly anybody else goes.'

'I can't wait to go!'

She says this with total confidence in the adult that I represent to her, utter certainty that I can make this magical thing happen, as if we aren't locked up by two people intent on making sure we never leave. I have tried picturing what fate they have in store for us – as if imagining the worst will ensure it never happens – but I still can't quite see how there are any good outcomes. I'm the only person who can get us out of this, and my power all depends on Filkins walking through that gap in the window and delivering us from evil.

But Filkins doesn't come. He doesn't come on Friday either, except briefly, with the scrap of ribbon still on his collar and the message unread.

He lands daintily on the top edge of the sofa, and its back cushion slumps forward in response. Even the furniture seems to have given up.

Chapter Fifty-Six

Saturday. We hear the clunking around up above the playroom for some minutes before Henna works out what's going on.

'They're moving Drita in. She's taking Violeta's room.'

We both know this is the last first-storey window that we had any chance of escaping from. Daisy's has a lock on it, and so does the bathroom, and the other one is Marcus and Mimi's, and I don't hold out any chance of shinning down from their room unnoticed in the dead of night. Perhaps Henna is more worked up about the replacement of Violeta, which seems to her like a gross moral wrong of global proportions. I should go and hug her, but I ask her to read us some of her 'thesis' instead. I would rather she was angry – as she usually is – about the effect that our unwillingness to reduce single-use plastic is having on the planet. It's good that she has somewhere to focus her anger that's not about this house. I'm relying on her to be angry about the planet. To avoid catastrophic climate breakdown, she tells us, we have to do the seemingly impossible. This is the only world we've got. We're standing at a crossroads in history, but we haven't completely failed yet. There is still time. We can still fix this.

This is what I need to hear, as every possibility of escape seems to close down one by one: *we haven't completely failed yet*. There is still time. We can still fix this. Thank you, Greta.

During lunch, I follow Mimi to the kitchen when she gets up from the table.

'Mimi? Can I have a word?'

She looks at me as if she has never seen me before, as if I'm a rambler who has got lost and just called in to ask for directions.

'Can I help you?'

'Yes, maybe.' I look over my shoulder. 'It's a bit delicate. I think I may be . . . pregnant. I wonder if you could look at me and tell.'

Her face lights up. She puts down the fig frangipane tart she has just taken from the oven and puts her hands on my elbows with something like delight.

'Pop up to my room after lunch. The girls can potter in the kitchen with Drita while she tidies things away.' She passes me a pot of stem ginger custard to carry. 'I knew it. I can tell from the way you've gone off coffee.'

I don't want her pawing me again, but it seems a small price to pay for another look inside their room – to be in any other room again – and maybe track down these elusive keys. At the very least, it gives me a chance to convince her to give us more freedom. What possible defence could she have for locking up Daisy?

I've come up to the room on my own, while she stays with the girls at the table until Marcus and Cliff have gone out of the house. The locking and unlocking remain a mystery. The bedroom looks familiar and yet not. There is the pervasive scent of weed and sandalwood, but so many things I failed to notice last time, or paid little attention to. I home in quickly on a jacket draped over the back of a chair and rifle through the pockets. No keys. I go to the dressing gowns on the back of the door and check their pockets, too. I open a bedside drawer, feel about inside. There's a vibrator and a handful of posh underclothes with labels still attached to their glossy string. I close it quickly, and I'm about to go to the other side of the bed when I hear the creak of the third stair. Quickly, I sit on the near side of the bed and examine my nails.

The door swings open.

'Okay.' She pulls up a little chair and looks at me like a concerned aunt. 'Tell me all about it. When was your last period?'

'A few days after I arrived. About ten weeks ago.'

'Are you still taking the pills?'

'Um . . . yes.'

This is not strictly true. I carried on taking them after the pregnancy test, in the hope that they would make it go away, but stopped the day after Drita died. The day I knew they were probably sweets or hay fever tablets or breath fresheners. Anything but contraceptives.

'I expect you were already pregnant when you arrived. Unless . . .' She looks at me innocently enough. 'Let's see. That would've been the twenty-first? So you would've ovulated somewhere around the seventh, eighth, ninth of April. If you *had* had sex with anyone around then, I'd say you were ten weeks now.'

My stomach lurches. I recognise those dates. They are written on the card, still in the breast pocket of my dungarees, on the floor by the bed. Written in her own hand.

'But I imagine it was your boyfriend in Italy—'

'He's not my boyfriend.'

'If it happened before you arrived, it would be fourteen weeks. Your bleed was probably not a proper period. But let's take a look at you. Pop your things off.'

'All of them?'

'That would be easier.' She stands up and turns away in mock modesty. 'Just pop the cover over you when you're ready.'

There's a lot of 'popping' required. I strip down and crawl into their bed, visions of Marcus – having been tipped off – coming up to join us. I can smell Mimi in the soft linen sheets. They are dark red. If I turn my head to the centre of the bed, I can smell Marcus, too. They do it in here. I wonder how often. I think of them doing it in here, between these sheets. This linen absorbs their sighs and moans and sweat. It holds the fluid with which he is so liberal to all the women who pass through this house. I feel the linen in the centre of the bed for a crusty patch, but Mimi is peeling down the thin duvet now. She palpates my breasts, nodding slightly.

'Yes. The nipples are dark, you see? And larger, too, aren't they? Have you noticed that? I expect your cup size needs changing, doesn't it?' She looks down at the floor to my pile of clothing and picks up the bra I rescued from Violeta's room, its grey elastic sprouting tendrils of fine rubber. 'I'll get you a pretty one. Just let me measure you.'

She leans down to fetch a soft coil of measuring tape from a bottom drawer by the bed and proceeds to measure my breasts. I have to raise myself slightly as she passes the tape underneath me, leaning in close as she does. She smells of something spicy and dangerous – the same scent in the sheets, but stronger, like neat alcohol. She seems pleased with her results.

'I'm just going to feel your tummy, okay?'

I make some sort of nod or grunt and let her run her hands over my belly and down towards my pubes. She'd better not go any further. She's making all sorts of little murmurs of satisfaction.

'What do you reckon? How many weeks?'

She sits back and sighs. 'Well, I may need to do a little internal to tell you for certain.'

I sit up abruptly. 'Oh, no need. Just as long as I know I'm pregnant.' *You're not even a fucking doctor*, I think.

She gives a half-laugh. 'You're very nervous, aren't you. What are you afraid of? I am a doctor, you know.' *Gobshite*. 'Now just pop on to your tummy for a moment, and then you can go. I think you're a little tense.'

I do as I'm told, wondering what on earth the girls are doing downstairs, then I remember my other reason for engineering this encounter. I must stay calm.

'Mimi, I've been thinking about what you said, about abortion and that.'

'Ah.' She starts to massage my shoulders and my back.

'Yes. Now that I'm having a baby myself, I can't imagine having

299

an abortion.' This is such a hefty lie. I'm counting the days until I can be rid of this spawn of Satan.

'There you are, you see. So you've decided to keep it.'

'Well, yes and no.' This is a tricky one. I mustn't put a foot wrong here. 'I really don't want to bring up a baby myself unless I'm married – or not married, I don't have to be married. Unless I have a partner to be a proper father to the child. Do you know what I mean?'

'I do. And that's very sensible.'

I know she knows I'm pregnant. I'm pretty sure Marcus has shared with her all the fun of his fake proposal. I absolutely must convince her I think it's real, but also that I'm not a threat if I go away.

'So my plan is to keep it, if the father wants it. But if he doesn't – if he changes his mind – I was wondering if you could help me?'

'Help you?' There's a note of surprise in her voice.

'Yes. I was wondering if you could give my baby up for adoption, the way you do with the rescue women?' I try to sound as needy as I can. It's not hard. I'm terrified. I'm not keeping this baby, but if I did, the last person on earth I'd give it to would be fucking Mimi. I wouldn't trust her with my hamster. The thing is, Mimi, I'm not ready to bring up a baby on my own, I'm really not. I'm nineteen and I want to go to uni or something. Maybe. I don't know. But I don't want to be a single mum. Not yet, anyway.'

Good, I expect she's thinking. *That's what we want most of all. Your baby and not you. That's perfect.*

'Well, I think you've got this wrong. I can't just give babies up for adoption, obviously, but of course I can help you. Of course. There are ways. You just look after yourself and see how you feel when the time comes.'

'*Thank you*. Oh, and that's the other thing I wanted to ask. It's really, really hard sitting around inside all the time. I'm sure a bit of fresh air would do me and the girls good. We'll get rickets or something without any sunlight. And they're so bored. Couldn't we let them out just once a day?' *Ha*. The 'we' there is quite deliberate. I'm siding with her. 'If you're worried Henna'll slip away from me, now I'm pregnant and everything, you can send Drita or someone with us – or you could come. We just need to give them some fresh air.'

'I'll see what I can do.' I've heard that before. 'I can see you do all need a bit of fun.'

She stands up, as if signalling that I can go now. I get up and dress quickly. She watches me closely. Then she holds the door open just enough for me to go out, and as I do, she puts her hand on my cheek and strokes it. Maybe she's feeling for lies. Maybe they erupt on my skin and she can see them.

'I'm glad you're staying, Caitlin.'

I think for a moment she's going to kiss me or something, but she just glues her eyes on mine so that I can't move away. It's like she's a giant magnet and I'm an iron filing. Then she looks away and I make off down the stairs, not quite sure who was in charge of that meeting.

The afternoon drags on, now with the increased heaviness of knowing there is no obvious means of escape. I even consider setting fire to the top of the house and shouting 'Fire!' so that Marcus and Mimi would have to open at least one door, and if me and the girls were standing conveniently between the two main doors . . .

'Gather your photographs,' I whisper to Henna, confident as you like. 'Make sure you have all the photos of your mum and Bryony that you want to take. Pack them with your clothes.'

She has just brought the photograph album onto the sofa when there's a sudden movement and something stops her sitting down. It's a mound of fur.

'Filkins!'

At least he's come today. At least he's here. The ribbon is still on his collar, but I bury my fingers into his neck and find the locket. The tiny folded note is still inside. I close my eyes. I think this has to be my lowest ebb so far. I turn my face away.

'What did you say, anyway?' says Daisy, taking it out and unfolding it. 'It's tiny.'

Henna takes it off her and starts to read it out.

'Sssh! Keep your voices down.'

'"I have the keys . . . took them last week. Will . . . unlock . . . back—"'

I snatch it from her: '"Will unlock back door at 2 a.m. Sat, front door if I can't find right key. Come 2.30 a.m. Knock on my door."' I wave my arms up in the air. 'Wait – there's more on the back – "Sorry for delay – will explain." *Yes!* Yes, yes, yes!'

'Is this good?' asks Daisy, looking happy anyway.

'Yes,' whispers Henna, smiling like I've never seen her smile before. 'This is very, very good.'

'But, Daisy, don't say anything to anyone yet, okay? Don't mention this at teatime.'

'Are we going to escape?'

'Yes!' hisses Henna. 'Yes, we *are!*'

'I'll tell you when we go to bed. We're going to have an adventure.'

Henna freezes. She puts a finger to her lips and we all listen. Someone clears their throat in the living room. Silence. Then footsteps across the threadbare carpet, the bolt rattling across. Mimi appears at the door.

'Come on, Daisy. Let's get you some fresh air!'

Daisy looks confused.

'Come for a walk – with me.'

Mimi holds out her hand, and Daisy looks at us for an explanation, as if the wrong person has come to pick her up from school. I catch the panic in Henna's eyes, but nod briefly at Daisy.

'Can Henna and Caitlin come, too?'

'No, not this time, poppet. Henna can't be trusted yet, so we'll leave Caitlin looking after her. Come on, let's you and me have a nice walk.'

Daisy grabs Donkey and bites her lip. We watch as they leave the room, then stare at each other in disbelief. This was not what I had in mind when I asked Mimi for some fresh air. The next half-hour is torture. Can she have overheard anything? How long was she out there in the living room? We were definitely whispering. Henna and I are convinced we heard the throat-clearing coming from nearer the hallway. Mimi didn't overhear our plans. What is more worrying is that she's alone with Daisy, who does know them.

'Don't worry,' says Henna. 'Daisy doesn't trust Mimi, even if she loves her.'

'But she's only five.'

'Yeah. So she can still remember.' Henna chews her stubby nails. 'Mimi used to lock her in her office when she needed to go somewhere, if there was no one handy to look after her.'

'Lock her in?'

'A lot. Like when she was little. Sometimes just half an hour or an hour, while she popped out. A few times she just forgot about her. I'd come home from school sometimes and hear her howling in that painted shed.'

When Daisy is finally returned to us, her shoes are covered with a fine dusting of yellow pollen. They have been walking through the buttercups.

'I wish you'd been with me,' she says. 'It's lovely out there, but it would've been nicer with you two.'

'What did she talk about?' asks Henna.

'Um . . . she asked me what we do all the time. I said we knit and watch television and work.'

'Good. Anything else?'

'She asked what we talked about.'

'And what did you say?'

Daisy plays with the hem of her dress.

'I don't know. I didn't tell her anything. I didn't tell her about the adventure. I can't wait to go to the seaside!'

Henna darts a look at me. 'What was she like?'

'She was nice. We picked some flowers.'

'Well, I'm glad you had a lovely walk,' I say. 'Perhaps we'll see your flowers at teatime.'

She was nice. That phrase makes me shudder, makes me uncertain whether this is the right thing to be doing. Mimi may not be worthy of being Daisy's mother, or have any legal right to keep her here, but to Daisy, she *is* her mother. I mull this over as we sit knitting quietly together. Daisy suddenly pushes the heel of one shoe with the toe of the other. She has forgotten to change into her slippers, which are where she left them by the back door. She tries to push them off while she's still knitting – 'In, under, over, off . . .' – and it is the sight of those shoes, covered in seed, that strengthens my resolve. Marcus must never touch her.

Teatime is an extraordinary act of self-discipline for all three of us. We have told one another not to look too happy, not to appear different. Henna does a good job of mock gloom, and Daisy does her best to copy her, but she keeps grinning at me, and I have to stop myself from giving a reassuring wink. I'm keeping everything crossed. This could still go wrong. And then something happens that I hadn't bargained for. When tea is over, Mimi stands up and announces: 'We thought we'd have a singalong session tonight, to cheer us all up. Like we used to. Everyone welcome in the living room. Eight till late!'

Chapter Fifty-Seven

We have talked it all through, planned it as carefully as only people incarcerated can plan anything. We will leave our doors a little ajar, so that there'll be no noise on leaving our rooms. Henna will go downstairs first, in bare feet and pyjamas, so that if she's discovered she can say she went to get a painkiller from the kitchen. If all is clear, she'll go to the utility room and take out her rucksack from the sheep-feed cupboard where she'll have left it (packed with her clothes and Daisy's) while we were all singing in the living room. I will give it five minutes, then follow, fully clothed but barefoot, down the stairs to Daisy's room, where I'll wake her.

I discuss all this with Daisy when I read her a bedtime story:

'Daisy, would you really like to come to Cornwall with me?'

'Yes! Can we go? Will Daddy and Mimi let us?'

'I don't think they will. But I'm going to go anyway, tonight, and Henna's going to come with me. Would you like to come with us on an adventure tonight?'

'Yes! Don't leave me behind! Promise you won't leave me behind.'

This is what I hoped she'd say. I know it's wrong to ask a child to keep a secret, but there's little chance she'll see either Marcus or Mimi before she falls asleep, so I chance it.

'Of course we'll take you with us. I was hoping you'd want to come. It wouldn't be the same without you.'

'Will we see the sea? How will we get there?'

'Okay, so here's the thing: it's top secret. You mustn't breathe a word of this to Daddy or Mummy or anyone, because right now they're trying to keep Henna from going anywhere, and we want Henna to be with us, don't we? We couldn't go without her, could we?'

'No. I want us all to go – you, me and Henna – and can Filkins come, too?'

'I don't think cats travel very well. Bring Donkey, though. He'll love Cornwall.'

'But how will we get there? How will we get out?'

'In the middle of the night, I'll tiptoe downstairs and wake you up as gently as I can. You have to remember not to make a noise *at all*. Do you think you can do that?' She nods solemnly. 'If you say anything, Mummy or Daddy might wake up and put a stop to our adventure.'

'Our *adventure*!'

'Then I'll pick you up and take you as quietly as I can downstairs, and Henna will be waiting for us with a bag of clothes. But we'll change in to the clothes later. If anyone sees us, we'll say you were feeling sick, okay? I heard you cry out and I'm taking you to the kitchen to find a sick bowl or something. Okay?'

'I'll feel sick. I'll make sick noises like this – *burrrgh*.'

I give her a squeeze. 'Best make no noise at all.' I don't know what we'd have done if she hadn't been keen. I suppose these days locked up have lessened her loyalty to Marcus and Mimi. I can't begin to imagine how I'd have felt, if my parents had happily locked me up, but then it's hard not to believe in your own parents' good intentions when you're small and you rely on them. 'Remember, though, you'll feel really tired when I wake you up, and it'll take a while to realise what we're doing. Try to stay as quiet as a mouse, okay?'

'Okay.' She gives a few squeaks.

I stand at the door and smile, and in this moment, I see the woman she'll become, and how her whole future pivots on this night; how one day she might tell someone that she was taken away from the only parents she knew and never saw them again; how she might be grateful, or angry, or utterly fucked up.

The hardest part of the evening was always going to be this bloody singalong, and all the possible things that could go wrong with the normal process of getting everyone to go to bed and to *sleep*. The living room is set up for a fun evening that isn't going to happen. There are echoes of the first weekend I arrived, with beer and cider and whisky on the coffee table, along with nibbles such as peanuts and kettle crisps (carbohydrates, Mimi! What are you thinking?) and, worryingly, chocolate cake. I try to look as if I haven't clocked the cake. I won't be eating it, no matter how drunk they try to get me first.

There is no Joe to get high in the corner. He'll be scanning the countryside for parties to dismantle. There is only Cliff, Drita, Henna and me to sit around and pretend to have a jolly evening with our hosts. Marcus rolls himself a spliff, takes a few puffs and hands it to Cliff. Mimi pours drinks, and Marcus picks up his guitar.

Looking over at Henna, he says, 'I think it's time we let Henna try some cider, don't you, Mimi?'

I try to catch Henna's eye, but she has already taken a glass from Mimi. So this is it. They are going to get her drunk. They know something's up tonight. How do they know? Perhaps they don't know, but they are up to something, I'm certain.

'Henna,' I say, helplessly, 'remember your headache earlier?' I try to give her wide eyes. 'Maybe alcohol isn't the best idea – if you want to keep a clear head.'

She shrugs, takes one sip and continues to nurse the glass, which may be a good move. Marcus starts to play the tune to 'Killing me Softly', and after a while he asks me to sing it. I protest that I don't know all the words, so Mimi starts off and we all join in. How ridiculous, I think. He is killing me softly. He'll kill Henna and Daisy, too, as surely as he killed Violeta. Mimi pushes a full pint of cider towards me, and I nod, smiling. More than anything right now I would love to down a pint of cider, but I mustn't. I know my resolve would weaken with each sip. And they have never brought out the chocolate cake so early – never while Henna was still up. I'll have to be on my guard. If things go as planned, I'll be driving in a few hours' time: the drive of a lifetime. I can't be over the limit. Jesus, it'll be tough enough stone-cold sober. Clutch, brake, accelerator. Neutral, clutch in, first gear, handbrake off . . .

We sing a few well-known songs together; Marcus plays a guitar solo and Drita sings an unbelievably sweet lullaby in her own language. Up until now I haven't been able to look at her without seeing her poleaxed on Marcus's dick, but with her pale stubby fingers gripping the armrest of the sofa, her soft lips moving around these strange sounds, she looks suddenly very innocent, so unaware that she will never sing this to the baby she doesn't yet know she will bear to Marcus.

The evening wears on, and Henna looks tired. I'm hoping she'll choose the right moment to go up to bed and set our plan in motion.

'Caitlin, let's have one of your lovely songs.' Mimi is stroking my arm, as if she loves me, as if she isn't trying to fatten me up and steal my baby. 'Pretty please?'

She makes a pleading face at me – for whose benefit, I'm not quite sure. *Let's pretend I give a fuck about you*, I hear her think. It's for Drita, I suppose. So that Drita thinks we're one big happy family.

Marcus, sitting on the floor opposite me, stretches out and hands me his guitar. There is nothing I feel less like doing, but I take it, and strum idly, waiting for something to come. I'm angry, jittery. I want to be driving home.

She's rode till she came to her own father's hall.

What's that from? I hum, I strum. I close my eyes. I'm off . . .

> *'An outlandish knight from the north lands came,*
> *And he came a-wooing me.*
> *He promised he'd take me unto the north lands,*
> *And there he'd marry me.'*

I open my eyes a slit and look at Marcus. I continue singing about how the knight lies to her, and intends to drown her as soon as he has her father's gold.

> *"'Light off, light off your milk-white steed,*
> *And deliver it unto me,*
> *For six pretty maidens I have drownèd here,*
> *And you the seventh shall be.'"*

Here I look at Mimi. All the pretty maidens, and the next one will be Drita. If I can get away, I might stop it. Drita wears a half-smile. I could be singing about potato crisps, for all she knows.

I carry on, through the verses, until she tricks him, drowning him instead:

> *'Well, he swam high and he swam low,*
> *Till he came unto the side.*
> *"Fetch hold of my hand, you pretty fair maid,*
> *And I will make you my bride.'"*

I open my eyes to give Marcus another look, but see that Mimi has taken advantage of my distracted state to offer chocolate cake around, and that Henna has taken some.

'No!' I say. 'That's dope cake, Henna. Don't eat it!'

She pulls it away from her lips and stares at it. Mimi affects an oh-silly-me look. Marcus tells her to give it a go, why not. Poor Henna. She loves chocolate cake. I watch her put it down on the coffee table, eyeing it ruefully. Now I stare nakedly at Marcus, although I know I shouldn't.

Watch yourself, Polglaze. Don't give the game away.

> *"Lie there, lie there, you false-hearted man,*
> *Lie there instead of me.*
> *For six pretty maidens you have drownèd here,*
> *And the seventh has drownèd thee."*

I should probably not sing the last verse at all, because it is my intention to follow through with it tonight. I close my eyes and see my parents' house.

> *'She's mounted on the milk-white steed,*
> *And she's led the dappled grey,*
> *And she's rode till she came to her own father's hall*
> *An hour before it was day.'*

When I open my eyes, Mimi is staring at me, then looks away. Henna yawns and says her goodnights, making certain to hug everyone present before she leaves the room, so that no one will have any excuse to follow her up later. She closes the door to the living room as she leaves. Good move. Now she can carry her rucksack downstairs and hide it in the utility room by the back porch. I take my eyes away from the door and smile at Cliff, encouraging him to sing an old favourite which Marcus has suggested.

When the hands join each other on the clock on the wall at midnight, the others are still singing and drinking and smoking. I long for sleep – especially theirs. I will stay up late – why not? I have nothing else to do before the great escape. I'll keep a heavy-lidded eye on them. If I go to bed, I can't keep track of them. I will stay up as long as it takes to know they are all flagging and in bed themselves. I can do this.

At one o'clock they are still up. The whisky bottle is empty, the chocolate cake all eaten. Drita is flopped over the arm of the sofa, whispering to herself; Marcus is smiling far too much not to be stoned out of his head, and Cliff seems to be communicating something to Mimi with odd expressions. Then he gets up and walks over to Drita, helping her to her feet.

'I think we should all be heading up now,' says Mimi, looking directly at me. 'It's way past your bedtime, isn't it, Caitlin?'

I see what it is. Cliff can't go out without some unlocking going on, and she wants me out of the way first. I leap at the opportunity now, make an elaborate ritual of my goodnight hugs, and insist on taking a tray of empty glasses and bottles out to the kitchen. Mimi bristles.

'No, leave that. I can do that.'

'It's no problem.'

'Leave it. We'll do it tomorrow. Drita will do it.'

I glance at the clock: 1.15. In three quarters of an hour Kal will unlock the back door. They have to be gone from here. But even before I reach the top flight of stairs, I hear Marcus's goodnights to Cliff and the back door open and close. Then I pause and listen to Marcus walking Drita up the stairs to her room. I hover by my open bedroom door, breathing softly, hearing the bathroom door open and close and the toilet flush twice, waiting until the voices of Marcus and Mimi are blunted by the closing of their bedroom door; then I lie on my bed and watch the glowing hands of Granny Rostock's travel alarm as they turn slowly, ticking and tocking, towards the grand finale. No more doors open or close. At 1.50 the arms of the clock seem to be thrown up and out in a great big 'hooray!'

I listen and listen. I dare not move position or rustle the duvet for fear of missing a sound. At 2.15, no one has made a noise. At 2.30, all is quiet. If Kal has opened the door, he has done it noiselessly, but it's two flights down. Still, I wait. At 2.45 I get up and gently open Henna's bedroom door. She stands up from the bed, wearing her pyjamas. I nod at her, and she makes her way downstairs on silent foot. I long to go to the bathroom, but I must wait. The minutes go by. At 2.50 I whisper farewell to Granny's clock, stuff her handkerchief up my sleeve, check my pocket for my ten-pound note and tiptoe down to Daisy's room.

Daisy murmurs when I wake her gently.

'Ssssh! It's Caitlin, sweetheart. As quiet as a mouse – quiet as a mouse.' I picture her bewildered face in the dark and lean in close to whisper: 'We're going on our adventure. Going to the seaside with Henna.' As I speak, I pull her up to sitting, try to lift her to standing up on the bed. I coax her as quietly as I can. 'Just wrap your legs around me like a monkey.'

She does as she's told. I get as far as the door and turn back to the bed. It hurts to bend slightly, but I must. We can't forget Donkey.

Chapter Fifty-Eight

A dark figure is waiting by the back door. As we approach, it becomes clear that it's Henna, and she's taken the rucksack from the cupboard. I put Daisy down on the cold flagstone floor while I push down the door handle. It opens.

As soon as we troop through the porch, the gritty lino floor jolts me into realising that I was supposed to grab my Doc Martens from the hall, but I didn't. I feel around frantically for something to take with me, but it's useless in the dark, and I'm in danger of making too much noise. Henna is standing outside on the grass now, holding Daisy's hand, so I duck back into the utility room and feel for the old furry ankle slippers of Violeta's, which were stuffed under the counter the last time I was here. Then I close the kitchen door and the porch door quietly behind me, and we make our way to the far side of Mimi's office shed. Here, Henna pulls Daisy's shoes out of the rucksack and shoves them on her feet. I put on the slippers and feed Daisy's arms into a fleece from the rucksack. I'm impressed by their silence. They seem more organised than me, but they wait patiently for my lead, and follow me in the moonlit night up the path into the woods.

We don't start whispering until we get to Kal's place. The light in his bedroom is on and I wave to him, but I'm not sure he can see us. I beckon the girls through the little iron gate, which sobs on its hinges. The hall light suddenly flares right across the garden to the shed. We stop outside the front door and as we hesitate, it opens. Kal stands there, relieved and smiling, and welcomes us in.

At last we can speak, although we still whisper.

Kal says softly, 'Come in to the kitchen. I've made you some ciabatta rolls to take with you – for when you get peckish later.'

'Kal! That's so kind.'

'And there's a blanket for the girls.' He smiles at them each in turn: such a warm Kal-smile that they grin back shyly, confused perhaps to see that the ogre Marcus had conjured up for them is no such thing. 'Now, would you all like to use the bathroom – to get changed and everything?'

As soon as we're all fully organised, we troop out to the Land Rover, which is parked where it always is, in the clearing near the cottage. He produces the keys and clicks the doors unlocked. As he opens the driver's door, the car is flooded with light, and the girls clamber into the back as if they're going on a shopping trip.

'There's some cash in with the food so you can fill up with petrol, okay?'

'Oh, Kal!'

'Here,' he says as he leans in to put the keys in the ignition. 'Your carriage awaits!'

'You had the keys all along?'

'Yes.' He helps me up, as if I'm mounting a horse. 'I thought about what you said. About the girls' . . . um . . . safety and everything. I shouldn't have hesitated.'

'Thank you.'

I eye the dashboard. It looks suddenly very alien and complicated. I might as well be sitting in front of the controls to a spaceship.

'Oh,' he says, looking up at me from beside the car, 'and I bought you this – it's a burner. And my number's in it – see?' He hands me a mobile phone and shows me the screen. 'And this is your number. But if you have any problems – any problems at all – you ring me, okay?'

My throat is rock-hard with emotion. I want to embrace him,

but it's an awkward move from the Land Rover driving seat, and he'd probably back away, so I let the rock harden and the moment passes.

'Any time you're in Cornwall, look me up.'

'Of course. Now get going quickly.'

I turn to look at the girls as he slams the door. I twist the key in the ignition and the engine springs to life. It's an absurdly loud noise, crass and brutal in the stillness of the night. I take a deep breath, jiggling the gearstick. Neutral. Clutch in . . . first gear . . . clutch out . . . We lurch forward and stall. Daisy gives a little squeak.

'It's okay, I just let the clutch out too quickly. Don't worry.'

I try again. This time I put the gear in reverse, because I'll need to do a three-point turn to get out of here. I have rehearsed all of this in my head, but suddenly I can't seem to remember any of it. The dashboard is just a series of disjointed lights and figures without the car light on. It isn't supposed to look like this. How am I supposed to know where anything is?

The vehicle moves backwards a few feet, and I jam my foot on the brakes. As I take my feet off, the car stalls again. Dammit. Undaunted, I turn the wheel as far as I can to the right and ma-noeuvre into a forward arc for a few feet. By the time I get us heading up the track, we have stalled three times in all. I stay in first gear until we meet the main road and then clamp down hard on the brakes again.

'Are you okay with driving?' asks Henna, meekly.

'I'm fine. Just finding my feet again. It's fine.'

I need to signal. Which side is the signal arm? I push one arm down and the windscreen is squirted with water. Fucksake. Right. Not that one. I try the other one, and the familiar clicking of the indicator light comes on. I breathe. First gear, clutch up *slowly*. Handbrake off. We start to slip backwards. I brake again. Shit-a-brick. I've heard about holding the clutch on 'the bite', but I'm not convinced it'll work on a heavy vehicle like this. This is a monster. I can't hold it with my foot. What if we career back-wards down the track? It's steep. Oh God. We could hit a tree. *Ohgod-ohgod-ohfuck-ohshit.*

'Shall we sing a song?' from Daisy in the back, like Gretl in *The Sound of Music.*

'Maybe not yet,' says Henna. 'Caitlin needs to concentrate.' It sounds like an instruction.

I wish I could be more like Julie Andrews right now. Julie would know what to do. But it's not the Nazis who'll be coming if I make any more noise: it's Mimi and Marcus. Okay, I can do this. I can. I give little breaths through puckered lips, like someone trying to slow the contractions in birth. Okay. Clutch down, slip it into first gear, foot on the gas. Something else. What? Yes: turn the wheel. Okay, here we go. Clutch up slowly and keep foot on the gas. We ease at a snail's pace left into the main road. I'm so delighted that we stay in first gear for a hundred metres or so, until I can pluck up the courage to go into second. I've done it. It's very dark. *She leapt on his horse and she tore away.* The kerb is on my left. That is the kerb. Good. That is the kerb and this is the road and I'm in second gear and the engine is growling quite loudly but hey, we're going along. It's quite dark really. It should be a bit lighter. The road is bending oh fuck turn the wheel whoops not that much. Okay. Crisis over. I can do this.

'It might help to put the headlights on,' says Henna.

'Ah, yes.'

Headlights. Where is that? One of these arms. (Lovely Joan and the Crafty Maid didn't have any trouble operating a horse's reins.) I flick and push and pull, trying not to let the steering wheel swing a little as I do. The water is squirted again, the windscreen wipers come on. I flick that switch again and they speed up. And then light at last. A bright light. *Hooray.* But there's something wrong. It's flashing.

'Oh, God,' says Henna.

'Oh God,' says Daisy, copying her, presumably. Unless . . . Oh no. I look in my side mirror (for the first time – not good) and see it. A car behind us, flashing its headlights.

'Okay. We're just going slow.'

'What if it's . . .?'

'I'm going to speed up.' Not easy in second gear. I slip it into third – except it doesn't slip: it catches and grinds its teeth angrily. I panic. I brake. We are thrown forward and the car overtakes. 'It's okay,' I say. 'I'm just getting used to it.'

'It's stopped,' says Henna, a note of real terror in her voice.

'I know. But I'll get it going again. Don't worry.'

'No. It's stopped. The car in front.'

I peer out of the windscreen up ahead. There are two red tail lights, and a door opens and slams. The frantic windscreen wipers echo our pulse. In the moonlight, a dark figure is making its way towards us.

Chapter Fifty-Nine

'Run!' I open the driver's door, shouting back to the girls. 'Follow me!'

The man – it is a man – is running now. '*Wait! Wait!*'

Daisy is crying out to me, and all I can manage to do is to form a huddle with them in a ditch at the side of the road and squeeze my eyes shut, and the shame of letting them down is as sharp and sudden as a gunshot.

'Caitlin!' I open my eyes and dare to look at the figure standing now by the Land Rover. 'Caitlin, it's me – Kahlil.'

I let go of my breath, let go of the girls, and lie back in the cow parsley of the verge.

'Oh!' I get to my feet. 'What is it? What's happened?'

'I'm sorry to surprise you. But you can't drive like that. You won't get to Cornwall alive like that.'

'I beg to differ.' This is not strictly true. I totally agree with him.

'Look, I'm sorry. Please get in my car. I'll drive you down.'

'I don't think that's—'

'Let's do it!' says Henna, already ushering Daisy in the direction of Kal's car. Well, there's confidence for you. I don't blame her. She is simply choosing life over death/life-threatening injury.

Kal puts his hand on my shoulder. 'Please? Come on, before someone notices you're gone.'

He walks me to his car. The girls are already in the back, looking mightily relieved.

'What about the Land Rover? We can't just leave it there, can we?'

'No. It's better if it's back where it belongs. That'll make them think you're on foot. I'll drive it back to the house, but first I'm going to drive you back there, so you can wait in the house rather than on the road.'

I trust him, utterly. Not for one moment do I think he has any other plan than to keep us safe and drive us to Cornwall. I must make sure Mum lets him stay overnight, too. He can't go driving straight home. There's plenty of room in the barn.

'Isn't this breaking lockdown rules, though? You driving us?'

'Yes. I'm breaking the rules.'

When we turn into his drive – from the front entrance, which we've never used before – we consider staying in the car. But the drive has taken us to the side of the house near the front door, visible from the little gate in the wall.

'I need a wee,' says Daisy.

'Me, too.'

We all troop back into the house. I notice that Kal has his laptop by the door and a rucksack that wasn't there before.

'Stay in the kitchen. Don't answer the door,' he says as he leaves to pick up the Land Rover. 'It may take me fifteen or twenty minutes. Don't put any lights on.'

About twenty minutes later, we hear the Land Rover purr into its parking place. We're sitting at the table in the kitchen, lit only by moonlight. As our eyes adjust, the window shows a definite glow in the sky. The sun will rise before five o'clock, and it must be already half past three. The car door slams. The gate whines. Kal's footsteps approach until they crunch on the gravel by the front door.

Then voices.

Daisy grips my hand.

'Oh, it's you!' we hear Kal say.

What if Joe is back early? My pulse begins to hammer. We

don't move. We listen. The other voice is faint. It's a woman's voice. It's Mimi. It's getting closer. Kal's voice is getting further away. He has turned back, perhaps, trying to usher her away from the front door. But now her voice is closing in. We can't hear what she's saying, but Kal says, quite loudly: 'Yeah, I heard it, too, that's why I came out. But it was just a car turning round. Quite a big car – a four-wheel drive or something.'

'Okay. Only it sounded just like the Land Rover.' She's close now.

'Yeah. But it wasn't. It's still there. It often happens. Some driver decides to turn round and there's the little turning, so they end up coming down the track. I mean – not *often*, but sometimes.'

Her voice is right outside now. 'You're up late.' *Jesus*. It's like she's right next to the window.

'Should we hide under the table?' whispers Daisy.

I shake my head and whisper softly, 'No. Don't move. Don't make a sound.'

I know we would be better crouching under the windowsill, so that if she looked in, she wouldn't see us. The longer she stays chatting, the closer the sun creeps up to the horizon and the clearer the contours of the table and our shoulders will become. But if we move now, the single scraping of a chair leg will tell her there's someone here.

'I often work late. I work best at night.'

'And, of course, Joe's on night shift, isn't he?'

'That's right.'

'I'm sure I saw a figure walking about on the path, though.'

'Maybe he's back early. Maybe whoever turned round got out to take a leak. They sometimes do.'

'Maybe. Mind if I take a look round?'

Please, no. Kal. Stop her.

She knows. She knows we're gone. If she steps sideways from the front door, she'll be looking directly in at us, sitting at the table.

'I've already checked all around the house. I'm quite neurotic. There's really no one here.'

'Have you checked your car?' We can hear her crunch over the gravel. If she looks over at the kitchen window now, from the car, she will see us. She opens a car door. 'You know your car's open?'

'Yeah. We never bother to lock our cars up here. No one's going to steal my clapped-out car.'

'Well, you should be more careful.'

'Tell that to the friendly neighbourhood policeman.'

'Mind if I come in?'

Shit.

'Actually, Mimi, I'm sticking to social distancing. And I do need to get on. Joe will be back in a few hours and it's like a giant Labrador bounding in. There'll be loud music, bacon frying. Please. I need to work. Go home to bed.'

Wow.

There's a silence. I imagine it's a stunned silence. For a moment, I wonder if Daisy is going to shout out 'Mummy!' but she doesn't. She grips my hand even more tightly – as tightly as if the Nazis were coming for the von Trapp family.

'Well,' says Mimi, irritably, 'let me know if you hear any strange noises. Or if you see anyone hanging around. Also, you should know that our daughter Henna has stolen the car keys recently. Let us know straight away if you see her, won't you? She can't drive, and we're worried about her.'

'Oh, I'm so sorry. Yes, of course. Do you have a number I can ring you on?'

Nice one.

Another silence. I would love to see Mimi's face right now.

'Actually, no. Well, yes. You can use this number.'

'Let me just . . . okay. Right, then. I'll be sure to let you know. Nothing much gets past me up here.'

We hear her crunch away. Kal doesn't come in and close the door for a while – watching her, I imagine, to make sure she's gone.

'*Now* can we sing a song?' says Daisy.

'Not yet,' I whisper.

Henna leans in towards me and asks quietly, 'Why did she say I stole the keys?'

'Kal stole them. She must've assumed it was you because it happened the day you left.'

And even as I say it, I picture Marcus and Mimi on the stairs, and Mimi saying we could be released after 'they've turned up'. She meant the keys, not the couple who came for the baby. Of course, they would've had a spare set, but they thought we might have the keys to the Land Rover.

When Kal does come in, he tells us to stay sitting in the dark for a while, in case she's lurking somewhere.

'I'll go up to my room and pretend to work for ten minutes, okay?'

'You fielded that well.'

'Not sure if she clocked the bag of ciabatta rolls I just happened to be carrying in the dead of night: they were on the front seat.'

Fifteen minutes after Mimi's departure, at about 3.45, we bundle into Kal's little Ford Focus with his laptop and a couple of rucksacks. This time, as soon as we are through his front gate and onto the road, we start to sing.

Chapter Sixty

By the time we reach the motorway, both the girls are asleep in the back. Kal asks me how much they know.

'Henna, pretty much everything. Daisy, I'm not so sure. But they've been cruel to her, locking her up with us. I wouldn't be surprised if her loyalties are pretty confused. This is an adventure. A holiday in Cornwall. That's all we've said.'

'Right. And I imagine Henna needs no excuse to leave. God. I'm so sorry I hesitated about the keys. As soon as you'd gone last week, I knew I should just take them. You're lucky you escaped that place unscathed yourself.'

I stare at the road ahead, the tail lights of lorries lumbering in and out of lanes, the shapes of clouds pulled out across the horizon.

'Caitlin?'

'Yep. They are quite a duo.'

'You will report them to the police, won't you?'

'That's the plan. I just want to get these girls to my mum first. Get them somewhere safe. But, there's more to Marcus and Mimi than meets the eye. They're not just selling weed commercially on a grand scale. They're selling babies.' Kahlil doesn't say anything, but frowns at the road ahead and nods. 'I mean, that's not all. I think their friends Suze and Arrow are trafficking girls, and Mimi gets Marcus to impregnate them, with a promise of money and a trip home.'

'She lets her husband do that?'

'She encourages it. She has all their ovulation dates worked out. She had mine written down for him.'

His hands tighten around the wheel. 'You mean . . .? Did he . . .?'

'That's why I wanted to ring my surgery.' I can't look at him now. This is the one thing I have to tell him. I might as well get it over with while Daisy's asleep. I'm going to have to tell Mum anyway. I'd better get some practice in. 'I'm pregnant.'

'With his child?' He sounds horrified.

'Yes.'

'The bastard! Why didn't you tell me? The bastard! He raped you. My God, Caitlin, you have to go to the police straight away. I mean, as soon as we get to Cornwall. This is terrible.' He turns his head to look at me briefly, reaches over and squeezes my hand. Kahil, being reckless – for me. 'I'm so sorry.'

I could let him believe this. I could leave it here, the idea of my innocence, hanging in the air between us. But in the end, it's a veil. It's hiding me from him, and after all the deceit of the last three months, I need some honesty now. And anyway, innocence isn't the same as goodness. Being a victim wouldn't make me a good person. The longer I leave it, the worse it will be. I swivel my head and make out the slack features of the girls asleep in the encroaching dawn light. His whole idea of me will change. He will think I'm a slut.

'It wasn't rape.'

'Sorry?'

I stare at the dashboard. I can't bear to see the disappointment in his face.

'It wasn't rape. I wanted it. I enjoyed it.'

Oh fuck. Why did I say that? Because it was true. I may be ashamed of my bad judgement now, but I did enjoy it. It was wonderful. It was joyous – for my body, at least. It was pure lust fulfilled.

'Really?'

'Yes. I mean, I didn't know he was a total wanker when it happened. I didn't know he didn't give a toss about me, that he was just carrying out orders. I didn't know that. And I'm telling you, Kal, because I want something, some relationship with *someone*, to be real, to be true.' He is silent. 'I'd found out in Europe that my boyfriend had been lying to me, and it was shit, and I wanted something lovely to happen, and Marcus was lovely towards me, and I was really taken in, but that's not an excuse because I wanted something to *happen* and it did, and it was good, because girls like sex, too, girls can feel lust, too, and that's what it was, Kal, if I'm honest – and I want to be honest with you – it was pure lust. I loved it. My fault. My fault entirely.'

> *For what can be said when it's all said and done*
> *But that I fell in love with the roll of his drum?*

He moves his hands around on the wheel, adjusts his bum on the seat. He says nothing. I hear him sigh.

Then: 'Well, it wasn't your fault. It may have been consensual, but he lied to you. Sounds to me like he lied about everything. What was your crime?'

'I wanted sex.'

He snorts a little breathy laugh. 'Well, if that's a crime, we're all in trouble.'

I manage a smile. He drives on quietly.

'Your crime,' he says eventually, after about ten minutes, 'was bad taste. Very bad taste in men.'

We sit quietly, watching the sparsely populated motorway. We slip into an easy silence for fifty miles or so.

'They're not all bastards, you know,' he says.

'Who? Men?'

'Yeah. I mean, there are *good* men out there.'

325

'Yeah, but where *are* they?'

Kal is quiet for a while, watching the empty road ahead as if he needs to be alert for a pile-up. And then says, 'How are we doing for petrol?'

Chapter Sixty-One

'You know, what's really surprising to me, what I can't get my head around, is how I saw something that wasn't there. I swear, I really felt his interest in me, I really did experience something quite . . . overwhelming, quite different from anything I've felt before. Did I really just make it all up? Because now when I think of him, he just makes me shudder.'

'You did what we all do when we're in love. You saw what you wanted to see.'

I look sideways at him. *What we all do*. His profile is unchanged. He is still Kal: quiet, measured.

'Who was it with you?'

There's a long pause when I think he's not going to answer this.

'I moved into the cottage with her. She was the reason I rented the cottage – Izzy. And when she left, I took Joe in to help pay the rent. He just answered an advert. I'd never met him before.'

'Why did she leave?'

He takes in a long breath. 'She started seeing someone else. Someone more interesting and exciting, I think.'

'No! She said that?'

'No.' He laughs. 'But I remember that nutty phase you go through, when everything they say or do is interpreted in the best possible light.'

I think of Luke. 'Yeah. Like if they say something mildly interesting, they're a genius.'

'And if they tell a weak joke, they're hilarious.'

'If they write you a note, they're a poet.'

'If they say something cruel, they're just tired.'

'Yeah, and if they buy you cheap chocolates from the petrol station for your birthday, it's the most thoughtful present you've ever had.'

'Shit. And if they come home drunk with their dress on back to front, someone must've spiked their drink.'

'Yeah.'

I imagine Izzy coming home drunk and Kal making excuses for her. I imagine his disappointment and her lying to him. God, I hate Izzy. How could she? I'm not happy about her. Not happy about her at all. This is a Kal I haven't seen before, someone who's been hurt and lied to. If I ever meet her, I might have to slap her about a bit. Whatever was she thinking?

'It's like betrayal blindness,' I say.

'Is that a thing?'

'I think so.' I think of Luke, of Mum. 'It's like, because the things that you say to yourself are so closely linked to the things that you say out loud, that you just *daren't* think them – even in your innermost thoughts – or you might have to accept that they're real. You know you don't want to voice them, so it's just too dangerous to even *think* them. You just push the thoughts away, somewhere inaccessible. Well, *you* don't, your sort of head defence does it for you.'

'Your *head defence*?' He smiles. Then, catching a glimpse of my expression, he looks serious. 'I know what you mean. I think that's what I did.' He fixes his eyes on the road. 'You've thought about this before.'

In the back seat, I think the girls are awake, but I'm not sure. I won't say too much. I sit back and put my slippered feet up on the dashboard. It's not a pretty sight, the old second-hand slippers of Violeta's, a sort of dishcloth grey-beige. And my shins are wide and hairy. It's true, though. I have been thinking about this for a long time. Long before I met Luke. I've been picking away at it for years, how we know some things on an emotional level, and others we can put into words. And I think of Uncle Aaron, and how I didn't really know what happened until Mum sat me down and asked me about what Dani had said, asked me to say what had happened to me, and how she listened. And it only became real when I said it. And even as I said it, I knew Mum didn't want to hear that about Uncle Aaron being bad, because she liked him so much, and I knew Dad didn't want to believe it either, because he had let his brother babysit, confident we would be safe. Neither of them wanted to hear it, but they listened, and they believed me. And in believing me they set me free, although I have never told them that. Perhaps I should. Perhaps I will.

'Mum's a counsellor now. And she reckons that when you voice something for the first time, that can be when you actually know it for the first time. That's why talking is so important, so healing.'

He nods. I think the girls are listening. I wonder if Mum has talked to anyone. What with this pandemic, maybe she hasn't been able to get support from anyone about what's happened with Dad. There's a power in telling. I may need to remind her of that.

At Taunton Deane, we pull into the main service station. This may not be such a good idea; but he assures me no one is looking for his car.

I take the girls to the toilets, and we're shocked to see that the few people here are wearing masks. It's not compulsory yet, but even so, it makes us realise that this pandemic has barely touched our lives, except as an excuse to keep us away from the world. We could so easily have been making masks instead of knitting. When we get back to the car, we eat our ciabattas, and I share mine with him.

'What if they come after us?' asks Daisy.

'They won't,' says Henna. 'They don't know where Caitlin lives.'

I swallow hard. 'Don't worry.'

Kal waits for a tactful few seconds to pass before glancing at me. No doubt he is also thinking of the letter I gave Mimi to post, which is probably sitting in a drawer somewhere, displaying an address and postcode. And I wouldn't be surprised if Arrow had a satnav.

We have no water, so when Kal drives us to the petrol pumps, he says he'll get some when he pays.

'Kal's nice,' says Daisy, while he's gone. 'I like him.'

'Yeah,' says Henna. 'Anyone Marcus warns us off is bound to be nice. We should've guessed.'

We watch him walk towards us, not a confident, swanky walk, but at ease. *I know my love from his way of walking* . . . It's still awkward that I've told him I'd wanted sex. Perhaps he secretly disapproves of me. But there is something liberating about the revelation. Or maybe it's just this trip, this escape.

'Oh, damn,' he says, once he's strapped up. 'I forgot the water.'

'I'll go.'

'Okay, I'll move the car over there.' He points off to the left, where there are a few waiting bays.

I have to queue outside the petrol station shop. Only three people are allowed inside at a time. I've been longing to buy some little treats for the girls. I'll grab a girls' magazine for Daisy and an older one for Henna; and maybe a couple of bags of crisps and some snack bars. I have some of the cash in my hand, but I'll pay him back as soon as I can. A sudden wave of nausea slaps me as I think of greasy crisps, a reminder that I have all that to deal with yet: this pregnancy. A bit of Marcus inside me.

The automatic door of the shop opens at last, and it's my turn. Only I don't move. The woman who comes out of the door fiddles with taking off her mask and putting it in her bag. I'd know that profile anywhere. I stare at it, speechless. My stomach flips over.

'Caitlin!'

Chapter Sixty-Two

She stares at me, startled and incredulous, then rushes at me. Her arms grab and enclose me. I look to see if Kal can see me, but he has twisted round and appears to be talking to the girls in the back seat. A man behind me in the queue clears his throat, and I'm scuttled away towards a different waiting car, with a man in it. I glance back again at Kal's Ford Focus, but no one is looking my way.

She grabs me once more, and this time I let myself breathe in the sweet, remembered smell of her.

'Oh, thank God!' my mother says. 'Thank God!'

We stand for a while, still and holding on, faces pressed into necks, abandoning ourselves to closeness.

'You're wearing slippers.'

We both look at my feet.

'Yes. It's a long story. But what are you doing here?'

She explains how she decided to come and look for me when I didn't reply to their letters – when the only two letters from me seemed to have an address that didn't exist when they looked it up. She decided to drive around Gloucestershire and see if anyone knew an Amberside in Ribley.

'Who's driven you up here?'

She looks down, sheepishly. 'Me.'

'But you *hate* driving on motorways.' I can't remember the last time Mum drove on a motorway. She gets nervous joining the inside lane. Now I'm nervous. 'Where's Dad?'

She takes a deep breath and my heart gives a flutter. She's thrown him out. I glance at the car and there's an old guy in the passenger seat. I go around to the passenger side and check the back seat, which is empty. Then I hear my name, and see that the man looking out of the window at me, the skeletal man with sunken eyes, is my father.

'*Dad?*'

He smiles gratefully. 'Caitlin.'

It is a gravelly whisper, a voice that bears no resemblance to my dad's. The flesh around his mouth is so thin that the smile is almost skinless. He puts a bony hand out of the window, and then, remembering we are not supposed to touch, drops it back into his lap like something that doesn't belong to him.

'He's been ill,' says Mum. 'In hospital with the virus. Three weeks and two days on oxygen. We thought he'd die.'

I reach through the window and pick up the bunch of fingers I'm not supposed to touch.

'Dad . . .'

His eyes have welled up with tears, and his lips move again in the same rasping whisper: 'Thank Christ you're safe!'

For all my contempt, I'm transformed suddenly to a misty station in *The Railway Children*. *Daddy, my Daddy.* That was another book I only saw the film of.

'We need to go.' I turn, and Kahlil is at my shoulder. 'I can't leave the girls in the car.'

I introduce him to my parents, and his face lights up.

'I'm so pleased to meet you, Mrs Polglaze,' – he ducks to wave through the windscreen – 'Mr Polglaze.' He straightens up and says to Mum, 'Can I follow you? If you're driving home?'

'I'd rather follow you, if it's okay? I'll show you the exit you need on my map. But Caitlin knows the way after that.'

'I do,' I say.

Mum looks so relieved at not having to navigate any more, that it's only now I see how red and perspiring her face is, only now that the knuckle-clenching drive she has already endured becomes clear. She leans into the car for a map, her wide bottom sticking out of the driver's door.

'You go back to the girls, Caitlin,' says Kal.

'The girls?' My mother looks in the direction that Kal came from, as if we might be in charge of a school trip, impossible though that would be with all schools closed. She knows I've been tutoring two girls.

'But I haven't explained what happened.'

'I'll fill them in quickly,' says Kal. 'We'll have plenty of time to explain later. It's dangerous here.'

Back with the girls, I watch Kal with my mother. He is smiling and nodding. He leans forward, hesitantly. Two metres. It is supposed to be two metres. He frowns, and she frowns. She looks over in our direction. He's telling her about our escape. Then he's smiling again, and she is smiling and nodding. He takes one half of the map and they pore over it briefly together, their heads almost touching, breaking all the rules. Who'd have thought?

'Who are those people?' asks Daisy.

'That's my mummy. And the man in the car is . . .' *Daddy, my daddy* 'My dad.' I turn back to face the windscreen, so they can't see my face, which I don't trust. 'They came looking for us, and they stopped for the toilets like us.'

'Oh! They look nice.'

'Yes.' I think about this, briefly pondering Daisy's experiences of parenthood. 'Yes, they are. Very nice.'

My emotions are falling over themselves, my relief at seeing Mum tempered by seeing the frailty of Dad, and everything churned up by a sense of not yet being out of danger. Daisy asks me to sing a song, but I say it's too noisy on the motorway. She doesn't forget, though. As soon as we turn off the motorway, she leans forward.

'*Now* can we sing a song?' says Daisy. 'Will you sing us one?'

'Well, maybe it's time for "The Crafty Maid". You okay with that, Kal?' I ask.

'Go ahead.'

> *'Come listen awhile and I'll sing you a song,*
> *Of three merry gentlemen riding along.*
> *They met a fair maid, and unto her did say,*
> *"We're afraid this cold morning will do you some harm."*

> *"Oh no, kind sir," said the maid. "You're mistaken*
> *To think this cold morning will do me some harm.*
> *There's one thing I crave and that lies 'twixt your legs.*
> *If you give me that, it will keep me warm."*

'What do you think the man had between his legs?'

'Um . . . a blanket?' says Daisy.

'What do men usually have between their legs?' says Henna.

'A willy!'

'Well, you'd think so, wouldn't you,' I say. 'But that's not what she's after. It's "The Crafty Maid", and she's being crafty.'

I cast a sidelong look at Kal, to check he isn't shocked by all this talk of willies, but he's flicking his glance between the road and the side mirror, as if watching to see whether we are being followed by anyone other than my parents.

> *"Then since you do crave it, my dear, you shall have it,*
> *If you'll come with me to yonder green tree.*
> *Then since you do crave it, my dear, you shall have it,*
> *I'll make these two gentlemen witness to be."*

> *'So the gentlemen lighted and straightway she mounted,*
> *And looking the gentlemen hard in the face,*
> *Saying, "You knew not me meaning, you wrong understood me."*
> *And away she went galloping down the long lane.*

334

'Well . . . there's more, but that's the gist of it.'

'He thought she wanted his willy?' says Daisy.

'Yes, but she wanted his horse.'

'But why would she want his willy?'

'Exactly,' says Henna.

'Is that the end?'

'Well, more or less. Basically, they go after her, and his friend suggests offering her money for the horse, convinced she'll take it. But she's having none of it.

> *"Oh no, kind sir, you're vastly mistaken,*
> *If it is his loss, well, it is my gain.*
> *And you are a witness that he gave it to me."*
> *And away she went galloping over the plain.'*

Henna shifts slightly in the back seat.

'We stole Marcus's horse, didn't we?'

'We had a go. We're being lent another horse.'

Kal smiles.

'What horse?' says Daisy.

'There are horses near us in Cornwall,' I say. This must be true. There are bound to be some.

I keep hearing Dad's diminished voice again, in the passenger seat of our family car. I hadn't banked on his sorrowful eyes, or the feel of his limp fingers. I'm startled at the magnificence of my love for him, which is holding my swelling throat to ransom.

Not long after we leave the A30 and start to enter some country roads, Daisy says she needs the toilet, and so does Henna. I can see Kal is uneasy about stopping, and if I'm honest, so am I. When Marcus and Mimi find us gone, they'll know where we're likely to be heading. But it's another half-hour to go at least, so we pull over and wait for Mum to catch up with us.

'Everything okay?' asks Mum, getting out of her car.

'Loo stop. They need some bushes.'

'Oh, me, too! Will you look after Dad, Caitlin, while I go with them? He's fallen asleep.' She beams at Daisy and Henna. 'That all right, girls? We can keep a lookout for each other.'

The girls seem more than happy to go with her, so we wait by the cars. I lean down to Dad's window and see that his chair is semi-reclined and he is snoring peacefully. His mouth, half-open, makes his cheeks seem even more hollowed-out than before, and he looks like a skull with a thin covering of skin. I watch his chest rise and fall gently, grateful.

A nearby whistle startles me so much I jerk upwards. Kal puts his hand on my arm. The whistle comes again, just like Marcus's, and the pulse thunders in my head.

'Hey,' says Kal. 'It's just a dog walker.'

I look up the road and back, but there's no one. Then a man in a cagoule appears over a stile, carrying a dog lead. He whistles again as he comes towards us and a tiny dog skitters past him. He says hello as he passes, giving us a wide berth out of distancing etiquette.

'Hey, you're shaking,' says Kal. Then he says, 'Oh . . .' like a small groan of recognition.

'What?'

'I saw him whistle once, when I was walking along the ridge. He didn't see me. Then I spotted you joining him.' I put my hands over my face. 'I didn't realise then what it was for.' He shakes his head. 'What a shit.'

'Oh, God.'

I close my eyes. There's no escape now. Knowing Kal's mind is making its way through what followed the three whistles makes me feel grubby all over again. He must feel bad for mentioning it, because he looks at me and says, 'Hey. Listen, Polglaze: stop beating yourself up. But please, promise me one thing.'

'What?'

'That you will never let any man *whistle* for you, ever again.'

I smile, and so does he. And I promise.

'Donkey went as well!'

Daisy beams as she tells me this. I know this is Mum. I can just imagine her shielding them, back turned, as they crouch behind the bushes. I can guess that when they're done, she takes Donkey and places him in the grass, making sure he relieves himself as well.

I see the 'do not tumble-dry' logo on the tag sticking out at the neck of Mum's cardigan as she walks back along the grass verge to the car; I watch her wide goose-pimpled calves, her cracked red heels slapping against the sandals. And I am not ashamed of her.

Back in the car, Daisy says, 'Judy's really nice!' and Henna agrees with her.

It's strange. I've never heard anyone younger than me call her by her name.

Chapter Sixty-Three

A few days later, after we've arrived in Cornwall, Kal and I go back to Willerby in a police car. The detective on the case wants us to point out specific locations and to talk them through what happened. We visit the barn where Violeta died, the 'office' where Marcus took his women to get them pregnant, and Mimi's office – the first time I've been inside it properly. It was here that they had found my phone, in a drawer with several other phones belonging to girls who had disappeared – mostly girls from Eastern Europe who had come looking for work, and been taken on by Suze and Arrow in the sex trafficking business. Mimi's office was a treasure trove for the police: phones, bottles of fake 'pills', old packets of confiscated contraceptive pills dating back ten years or more, lists of menstruating days and 'fertile days' for each girl, and a laptop full of contacts for childless couples and emails about cash payments. It seems that her 'interest in genetics' was, after all, purely practical – about providing a baby that a couple could pass off as their own; so, more about their concerns than hers, which were entirely mercenary. The bottom drawer of her desk contained sixty thousand pounds in notes stuffed into a box of Kleenex tissues.

Everything looks familiar, but silent in a way it never used to be, even when we were locked away. There's a white tent around Violeta's grave and another around Thea's, and I shudder to think they might be digging them up for DNA evidence. No doubt they have proof now of the whereabouts of Violeta's baby. Further along, beyond the barn, three more white tents spring up before the end of our visit, as they've found evidence to suggest more bodies. The gorse continues to blossom in big yellow clouds, but the hawthorns are no longer in bloom. The birds are quieter, having built all their nests, but otherwise it's hard to see what's changed.

The polytunnels are another matter. After exhaustive inspection and photographing, all the plants have been taken away and destroyed, so that when we arrive there is nothing but a few rows of courgettes and strawberries. The few workers have disappeared, and there's no sign of Cliff. We're told he's been interviewed extensively by the police, and although he's been happy to dob in Mimi, he remained loyal at first to his old friend 'Mark'. In the end, though, when Marcus's office revealed evidence of the extent of his collaboration with her, and when he was told about Marcus's interference with Henna's sister, and his attempt with Henna, he conceded that Marcus had made mistakes, and he's been helping the police with their enquiries in exchange for not being an accessory to their darker crimes.

We're allowed to take a few of Henna's and Daisy's belongings (it's sad how little they had), and we visit the cottage so that Kahlil can collect the rest of his, which – most importantly – includes Filkins. He's already given notice on the rental, and he's keen not to meet Joe. In the end, though, Joe is there, remarkably chipper and jolly, presumably hoping we won't mention his connection with Marcus. Joe's enjoyment of an occasional spliff is possibly of little interest to the police under the circumstances, although we have no idea whether he's been investigated at any length.

Mum arranges for me to have a termination as soon as I tell her about Marcus and the pregnancy, and me not wanting it and everything. I spoke to her about it on the very first evening. I said I might choose to have a baby one day – who knows? But bringing a human being into the world seems a pretty important decision to me, and not one to be made haphazardly.

It's been amazing to see Dani again, and later on, Erin, too. The weirdest thing is, though, that all the time we've been worried about telling Mum what Dad has done, she already knew. She knew even before Dani told Erin. And the reason she knew was because Dad had told her straight away.

'He told me while Luke and Lotti were still here for the writers' retreat. He knew he'd been as drunk as a skunk, but he had an inkling of what had happened. He made no excuses for himself. He was ashamed.'

'He told you? When we were all still having those meals in the kitchen?'

'I'm glad it happened, in some ways. It was the moment he realised his drinking had to stop or else he would lose everything. Including me.'

'So you just forgave him? Shit, Mum. Just like that.'

'No. Not just like that. I made him sleep in the barn – until he got ill. Look, he didn't trust either Lotti or Luke afterwards. He felt he'd been "played", and when he saw Luke making a play for you, he was appalled. We were both worried sick about you going off to Italy with those two.'

While I was busy thinking how unsophisticated Mum was next to them, she *knew* – eventually – that they were patronising her, but said nothing. I remember how strongly she hadn't wanted me to go away with them, which I took to be all about limiting my freedom and insisting I get a degree; and even Dad, who usually supported me being independent, had seemed weirdly reluctant about the idea.

'Why didn't you *say* something to me?' I ask Mum.

'I did try.'

'You could've explained what a turd Luke was.'

'You'd have bought the tickets even quicker.'

'If you'd only said . . . I wouldn't have gone.'

This may not be strictly true.

'Oh, Caitie. You were in love.'

I make a puking sound. (How quickly I regress when I'm at home.) 'Well, at least I *can* fall in love. I don't think people like Marcus and Mimi – or even Luke – are capable of it.' She nods. 'Thank God I'm not in love now, though.'

This may not, strictly speaking, be true either.

'You should talk to Dad, love. Don't be too harsh. Hear him out.'

None of what she says excuses Dad, but the efforts he is making seem good for him, and they are certainly good for her.

I manage to get some time alone with him on one of his 'good' mornings, before everyone else is up. Mornings are best for him, as he struggles with speech later in the day. He's sitting in the garden, where Mum has walked him with his stick, at the edge of the tatty, unmown lawn.

'I think you have a bone to pick with me, don't you?' he asks when I join him.

'Well, yes,' I say. 'You could say that, you old self-indulgent Celt.'

He looks so fragile, then, his sunken eyes hooded and glistening. Apart from his voice, he sounds like my old Dad: honest and open. It seems like a harsh word might crack him, and he might never be mended again. So I say, 'But I really just want to understand.'

A trembling hand swivels over from the arm of his chair and reaches for mine. It feels like a bunch of runner beans.

'I'm not going to make excuses, Caitie, but I'll see what I can do.' He lets out a sigh. His speech is halting, breathy. 'Years back, when Mum and I found out about Uncle Aaron . . . when we found out . . . we were both torn apart. We both had this terrible, terrible guilt – and grief.' He closes his eyes tight for a moment, as if to shut out this painful memory, then opens them again, having discovered that it hasn't. He catches some breath. 'Mum dealt with the guilt better than me. I was pathetic. Weak. I turned to drink, as you can no doubt remember, but worse than ever. And then I turned insult into injury because . . . I refused to admit I was an addict, and of course I was no use to you girls or to Mum. No use at all . . . I simply added to everyone's problems.'

He's gasping. I give his hand a gentle squeeze, afraid it might fall apart.

'But Mum says you're making progress there. She says you stopped drinking after I left.'

'That's right. That's right. That was the one good thing I did – but the thing that prompted the decision was . . . well, you know what it was.'

'I only know what Erin said, and she only knew what Dani saw.'

He visibly winces, then. 'You see? I just compounded all the damage done by my . . . wretched brother. Instead of helping you girls, I made everything worse.' He takes a deep breath, as if to prepare himself for a dive into unknown water. 'But that was the turning point. That was my lowest possible ebb. Well, I know it happened, because I do have a vague recollection of it, but the thought that I could have allowed that to happen, and with people you liked . . . that was it for me. I told Judy straight away. I said, "This has to stop *now*. I have to stop drinking." And she was amazing . . . Your mother is amazing.'

'But . . . hang on . . . you mean you let Luke . . . ? You let him?'

'God, no. I was . . . so rat-arsed I was no good to anyone, but certainly not Luke. And the same goes for Lotti, by the way, before you ask. I mean, she did try. God. They were both very manipulative people, in their separate ways. No, wait – I take that back. That sounds like an excuse.'

'You don't think they were working as a team, then?'

'A team? Those two? They each thought they were God's gift to literature. They were as competitive as hell. And neither of them will ever get . . . anywhere.'

'But you "spotted" them. They were your new talent. I remember you said Luke's writing showed real promise.'

'It did. But the trouble with Luke – as I'm sure you've found out – is that—'

'He's always right.'

'You noticed.' He turns his head stiffly and smiles. I smile back. 'I knew you'd get there. He could never be published, because he would never allow an editor to suggest changes. He's just too . . . right. He lacks . . .'

'Talent?'

'No. He does have talent.' I'm disappointed to hear this. 'Humility. He lacks humility. He simply can't believe that he can improve on what he's written. So he'll never learn anything. And he doesn't have the . . . *patience* to work over a piece, stitch by stitch.'

'He thinks he can self-promote or buy his way into anything.'

'Well, he may be right – in a different field. He'd probably make a nicely corrupt politician.'

Still . . .

'But you *knew*. You knew all this and you let me go to Italy with him – and Lotti!'

He pulls his hand away and covers his face.

'Oh, I know, I know! That's the worst part of it. Watching you fall in love with that p-pompous little arsehole. Watching him woo you. The pair of them. P-parasitical little shits!'

It is weirdly soothing to hear him say that.

'What the fuck, Dad! Why didn't you *say* something. You could've at least *warned* me about him!'

'I'm sorry, Caitlin! I'm so sorry. I thought I could spare you from it. And you're smart. I knew you'd work those two out for yourself before too long. And you clearly did. But then . . . Erin told me in March that Dani had seen me with Lotti, and with . . . *him* . . . and that she'd rung you – and told you. God, Caitlin. I'm so sorry.' He's struggling, growing tired rapidly. He mislays words like socks or glasses, certain they're around somewhere, but not knowing where to look. 'I'd just come back from a . . . thing . . . in London when I heard, and I wanted to come out to Italy and explain, but then there were travel issues, then you said you were back in England, and . . . I got the virus. Then I was in hospital and a . . . chunk of life just seemed to disappear. When I came out of the . . . thingummy . . . the, um . . . induced coma, there were no visitors allowed, no one I recognised. I thought you'd all died in a disaster or something.'

I rub my thumb over the sun-warmed skin of Dad's hand, and lean into him, the old familiar smell of his jacket. How nearly this jacket could've been empty, hanging cold on a hook in the hallway.

'I've really screwed up, haven't I?' I say.

'You're telling *me* that?'

'I mean, getting involved with Marcus straight after Luke . . .'

'Oh, Caitlin.' He smiles his old, generous smile, eyes disappearing into the enormous stretch of it. 'Imagine . . . how dull life would be if we were right all the time. We'd never learn anything important, and there'd be no . . . stories to write.'

We sit quietly in the June sunshine, contemplating this. I'm glad he can't see my face.

After a while he says, 'You're so like your mother, you know.'

'Me?'

'Yes, you. You've got her wink, and her bursts of . . . dogged optimism.'

'Her best bits, then.'

'I like all her bits.'

'Stop there. Yuk, yuk. Gross.'

But I'm glad. Glad for Mum. When I next look, he has dozed off.

The girls have settled in quickly to life in Tremellick with us. Henna struck up an instant friendship with my sister Dani, and

344

they've become inseparable. The police also managed to trace her missing sister, Bryony, who was living with a bunch of homeless people in a hotel in Bournemouth which, like many hotels, took people off the street during the pandemic. Since then, she's been rehoused locally and has gone back to school to study for A-levels. She's hoping to become a social worker.

Since Dad was using Erin's bedroom, and Henna and Daisy were occupying mine, I took one room in the barn and Kal had the other. We share the living space there with Filkins, totally at ease in each other's company.

The tracing of Bryony has led to another small miracle. My father, long hostile to the idea of tracing his birth parents, has had a change of heart. Perhaps it was his near-death experience that made him yield to our encouragement at last. He says the illness taught him something important about life: *this is it* – this day, this moment.

And so's he grabbed the moment, and found his mother to be no longer alive, but his two sisters very much alive and both living on the south coast. They tell him that his mother, Paula, never stopped talking about her lost boy, and lit a candle for him every birthday. They've been searching for him for years, but assumed he didn't want to find them. Since then, he's been writing frantically: a new novel he started when he came out of hospital and found I was missing. It's about a missing girl. There are many stories about missing girls, but Mum – who is the only person he allows to read his first drafts – says this one is a corker. It's urgent and original and heartbreaking, she says. It's going to be a bestseller. Whatever it is, it's helped him turn a corner. He says he feels like a giant weight has been lifted from him, knowing his mother loved him. He no longer drinks heavily. There are still lapses, of course, but everyone helps him by steering him clear of the stuff. His new sisters bring him bottles of their elderflower cordial, and he says every day how precious life is.

*

In September the schools reopen and they all go back: Dani, Henna and Daisy. Daisy loves it straight away. She's meeting other children her age and can't wait for the time, when the pandemic's over, that she can bring them home to play. She and Henna have regular counselling sessions. Mum made sure of that, but the police have been really good, too.

The place is full of humour again now. One evening, when we were all eating and arguing and laughing together, Dad asked Henna how she was getting on with *Anna Karenina*. She said she would have to take issue with Tolstoy's opening paragraph.

'I don't think all happy families can be alike. This one's off the wall.'

We were in stitches, and Henna looked startled and pleased that an opinion of hers had had such an impact. I noticed Mum give her hand a squeeze.

That same autumn I get my application in for university. When I was busy getting through that ridiculous tutoring, I didn't realise – as I invented songs which made the girls laugh and came up with ways to make dull things a bit more fun – that I was actually quite enjoying it. I liked that I could help them, and that they trusted me. I'm not sure I've ever really helped anyone before. I didn't realise I'd made a decision until Mum asked me if I'd apply for uni now – looking defensive, as if I'd bite her head off for the reminder – and I said yes, because I've decided to be a teacher.

It seems to me that you don't necessarily get to the truth – or the way somewhere – by following the signposts, but by taking a back alley or a side gate that no one told you about.

Chapter Sixty-Four

May 2021

It's spring again in Gloucestershire, and we've come up to make a very important visit. Kahlil, Daisy, Henna and I walk a country lane not far from the old house, but we have no intention of visiting it. Instead, we pass between hedgerows thick with flowers, forget-me-nots, cow parsley and hawthorns clotted with creamy May blossom. The air is close with the heady reek of pollen. It's six o'clock, and the day is winding down to a snail's pace. We reach a signpost dappled with light from an overhanging beech tree. The bright green of everything is so new and exciting that Daisy gazes up at it, feet planted in the middle of the lane, remembering, perhaps, that other spring, those other days with the scent of this one, but less free.

Geoff is pleased to see us, and because we're now allowed to meet indoors, he invites us in for tea with his wife. We haven't met Sheila, but she is bright and ruddy, and delighted to be able to press her home-made biscuits on the girls.

'Well, come on, then,' says Geoff, getting up from his chair at last. 'Let's see if we can find those two young ladies you've been waiting to see, shall we?'

We follow him out of the farmhouse into the yard, and from there over a stile into a wide, sloping field. In it, small lambs race up and down like children, while their mothers graze quietly, offering the occasional deep bellow of protection. We follow him along the side of this field and up to a stile on the horizon.

There, ahead of us, is a flock of sheep grazing in the slanting sunlight. The sound of lamb bleats is everywhere in the quiet evening, but here the sheep have no lambs and their heads are down, nibbling frantically, as if last orders might be called at any moment.

'Your two are in there somewhere.'

'How can we tell where they are?' asks Daisy, looking anxious.

'You all go forward, look, and you girls call their names. I'll stay on this side of the stile, or else they'll think I've got sheep nuts for them or something, and then the whole lot of them'll come running and knock us flat.'

Henna laughs, and so do we, but Daisy goes for it. She's climbing over the stile and calling for Sausage as if it was yesterday. Henna joins in, quietly and self-consciously. A few sheep look up. Nothing happens. The summer evening paints a limpid green backdrop to the calling girls.

'They'll be a bit interested now,' says Geoff, keeping behind a bush, as Kal and I join the girls.

But they aren't. One distant sheep stares. It keeps on staring.

'Why don't these sheep have any lambs?' asks Daisy, sadly.

'They're still young. They'll have them next year.'

Then the staring ewe takes a few hesitant paces in our direction. It picks up speed. Now it's running full pelt at Daisy, and another sheep is running, too. As they get closer, it's clear that the first sheep has a wonky left ear.

'Sausage! My Sausage!'

Sausage nearly knocks Daisy over. The other sheep, clearly Freedom, barrels into Henna.

We're all laughing, astonished, and Kal asks, 'But how do they know? They haven't seen the girls for a year. How do they *know* after all this time, and from such a distance?'

The other sheep are looking curious now, and making their way over. Geoff leans over the stile and watches the girls hugging the sheep, clinging on and pressing their faces into their oily wool. We all watch them, and it's as if we know, we know just by watching them.

'I reckon there's no creature on earth forgets someone who's been kind to them.'

I always knew Geoff would have the answer, somehow. I knew when he first gave Henna the milk-replacer to measure out, that he had a magical simplicity to his philosophy, as simple as my mum's. He gave them something to care for, and he saved them.

A lot of people helped to convict Marcus and Mimi. Bryony, obviously, had her own story to tell, but Geoff had rung the police some days before we escaped, saying he was concerned about things. And the woman from the education service had reported concerns, too. So, by the time Mum rang the police, the evening after we arrived home, the pieces could be fitted together easily enough to suggest that Marcus and Mimi might need to be put away for a long time. It was Daisy, in the end, who put the nails in their coffins. She told the counsellor how she had been locked up and how scared she'd been. A DNA test proved that she was not related to either of them, but to Henna.

There was a news item showing Marcus and Mimi being led away from the house. Fortunately, the girls were in bed and we didn't watch the news for a week afterwards. But it would have intrigued Henna. Marcus walked away, smiling at the camera as if it was all a game, tall and childlike at the same time, inhabiting his body like a kid who'd been lent a dressing-up costume. Mimi looked like Bambi's mum again, elegant in her slouchy cashmere jumper, walking as if pulled upright by a string. No one would guess that she had been the one pulling all the strings. After that, it was just a slightly blurred mugshot of Marcus that appeared on news items, and a much older one of Mimi, in which she looked like she was wearing a wedding dress. They were married, after all, it turns out. But 'Mandy Stallard' had never been a doctor, nor had any medical training.

It seems that Mimi's mother died when she was born, and she was brought up chaotically by a drunken father. So she had no mother from whom to inherit a legacy of knitting, cooking, embroidery and self-neglect. She left school early and rapidly became a sex worker. I did wonder, when I read this in an article about her, whether all that cookery was her attempt to be motherly – although her dishes always looked as though they were intended to be photographed for an upmarket Sunday colour supplement, rather than to feed hungry mouths. In fact, I learned later that the police discovered a whole plan for a cookery book on her laptop, complete with photographs. I don't know why, but that made me well up a little. I think part of me still wanted to believe her lie that she was trying to save trafficked sex workers, and not exploit them.

Because of the pandemic, everything to do with the trial was delayed. When it did come round, although I was a witness, I learned most of the interesting details later from newspaper reports and television news items. We were all still hoping to find some answers, some new information that explained why two people who seemed so innocuous should set up such a brutal system of deceit and cruelty. Mimi, it seems, was the real force behind their business, both in turning the home-grown weed into a money-making empire, and in exploiting the local sex industry for the same purpose. She was, in the end, a Crafty Maid, although the crafty maids of song mostly used their guile to save themselves, whereas Mimi used men – and women – to her own ends.

And Marcus, well, I don't know. Perhaps she manipulated him more than anyone, or maybe that's just my own secret consolation. She saw a weakness in him and outsmarted him. I had loved how Marcus was curious about me, but now I realise that his interest was in something else. Marcus wanted to see how women worked; he wanted to prise them apart and see their cogs and wheels, to find out why his mother had acted as she did. And Mimi gave him the best gift of all: women to test out his theories, to see how easily they could be made to yield to their own lust, proving that women were not to be trusted. And didn't he, with every one he brought to her knees, get to pay back his mother for the way she had hurt him?

Of course, journalists were hungry for gory details, and there were plenty to keep them speculating. There were three other graves on the bank, hidden in among the gorse, testament to Mimi's lack of midwifery skills rather than any attempt to kill, it seems. Several girls did go home with a few thousand pounds in their pockets after delivering a healthy baby. None of this really surprises me. But there are two things that do.

Firstly, one of the female bodies found buried on the bank had a smashed-in skull, considered to have been from a blow with a heavy instrument. From dental records and DNA, she was identified as Marcus's mother. She had been lying in the ground for decades, and all the evidence suggests that she didn't 'leave' the community when Marcus was four, although she may well have had an affair with a carpenter. I can only imagine what effect this new revelation must've had on Marcus. In a strange way, I feel almost sorry for him – at least, for the four-year-old boy stuck inside him.

Thinking of all the pain Marcus and Mimi were dealt by their fathers, and all the love they didn't have from their mothers, makes me very sad. It's humbling. I don't think all happy families are alike, but they have things in common. How lucky I am to have the parents I do, flawed as they are. I feel their love like a great slab of Cornish granite jutting out into the sea. My waves crash against it, but it doesn't budge, just gets slightly smoother at the edges.

And there was one other thing – just a detail, really.

Cliff, whose late wife effectively brought Marcus up as her son when his own mother vanished, did remain pretty loyal to Marcus – if damning about Mimi – because Marcus was his friend's son.

But he must have been totally floored on hearing that Pete, Marcus's father, had most likely killed his own wife in a jealous rage. I have no way of knowing whether he accepted that hypothesis, but he must've been shocked by the discovery. I like to think he may have been unaware about the extent of Marcus's role in what was going on – especially with Henna. Still, when he gave his account in court, Cliff admitted to slashing the tyres of the Land Rover to prevent Marcus and Mimi from coming after me. When asked why, he said he knew I wanted to leave, and he had a soft spot for me because I had bandaged his foot once. He didn't know the girls were with me, but he hoped they were. When asked how he knew I had left, he explained how he couldn't sleep, and was alerted by a sound just outside his window. When he got up, there was no one, but he found something in the grass which must have belonged to me. He assumed I had taken the Land Rover, but later, he heard Mimi get up, saw her go up the path, and then come back. He heard her tell Marcus the Land Rover was still there. That was when he made his move. He went up to the woods where it was parked and slashed the two front tyres. Asked what he had found belonging to me, he said it was a handkerchief embroidered with the first letter of my name.

Eventually it was returned to me, and I still have it, the handkerchief my grandmother embroidered. I keep it in my bedside drawer, and take it out from time to time to touch the petals and to marvel at them.

Traditional Folk Songs Referenced

'Ned of the Hill'
'Jock of Hazeldean'
'Ploughman Laddies'
'Lovely Joan'
'Searching for Lambs'
'Bird in a Cage'
'The Bold Grenadier'
'Gathering Rushes'
'Let No Man Steal Your Thyme'
'I Wish, I Wish'
'The Unquiet Grave'
'Prince Heathen'
'A Week Before Easter/The False Bride'
'The Maid on the Shore'
'The Outlandish Knight'
'The Little Drummer'
'I Know my Love'
'The Crafty Maid'

Acknowledgements

The folk songs in this story came into my head as I was writing, and I apologise if the wording doesn't always fit with standard versions (although that is, I suppose, the nature of folk tradition). I would like to thank the many long-suffering singers from whom I collected scores of folk songs as a teenager, often copied out for me on pieces of napkin. Folk songs provide a wonderful snapshot of our shared social history, especially in regard to women, whose domestic circumstances have rarely been the stuff of history books. Women in folk songs fall in love, are betrayed, oppressed, beaten, murdered and *warned*. They show young women constantly negotiating their way around men. Occasionally, however, a woman challenges the expectations. These are the most interesting, as women escape danger and manage to turn the tables on those who would hurt them.

Thank you to my fabulous new editor, Leodora Darlington, for believing so heartily in this book; to wonderful assistant editor, Lucy Brem; to editorial assistant Sahil Javed, and all at Orion; to Francesca Pathak who first commissioned this novel and without whom it would never have been published.

To my indefatigable and lovely agent, Alice Lutyens, for always having my best interests at heart, and for rooting for me throughout.

To Hayley Hoskins, for writerly morning walks, and a constant supply of wisdom and mirth.

To Katie Jarvis, Caroline Sanderson and Katie Fforde for friendship and support over many years; to Caroline Montague and Melanie Golding for so much recent support.

To the many Gloucestershire writer friends for regular meet-ups, offloads and conversations throughout lockdown and beyond; to my book group friends for decades of stories and good company.

Above all, thank you to my cherished family: to Anna and Lucy and John. You are why I wake up in the morning and write.

Credits

Jane Bailey and Orion Fiction would like to thank everyone at Orion who worked on the publication of *Stay* in the UK.

Editorial
Leodora Darlington
Sahil Javed

Copy editor
Steve O'Gorman

Proof reader
Linda Joyce

Audio
Paul Stark
Jake Alderson

Contracts
Dan Herron
Ellie Bowker
Alyx Hurst

Design
Rachael Lancaster
Joanna Ridley

Editorial Management
Charlie Panayiotou
Jane Hughes
Bartley Shaw

Finance
Jasdip Nandra
Nick Gibson
Sue Baker

Marketing
Javerya Iqbal

Production
Ruth Sharvell

Publicity
Jenna Petts

Sales
Jen Wilson
Esther Waters
Victoria Laws
Toluwalope Ayo-Ajala
Rachael Hum
Ellie Kyrke-Smith
Sinead White
Georgina Cutler

Operations
Jo Jacobs
Dan Stevens

**If you loved *Stay*, don't miss Jane Bailey's
chilling previous novel . . .**

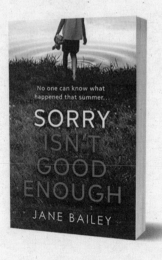

It is 1966, and things are changing in the close-knit Napier Road. Stephanie is 9 years old, and she has plans:

1. Get Jesus to heal her wonky foot
2. Escape her spiteful friend Dawn
3. Persuade her mum to love her

But everything changes when Stephanie strikes up a relationship with Mr Man, who always seems pleased to see her. When Dawn goes missing in the woods during the World Cup final, no one appears to know what happened to her – but more than one of them is lying.

May 1997. Stephanie has spent her life trying to bury the events of that terrible summer. But when a man starts following her on the train home from London, she realises the dark truth of what happened may have finally caught up with her . . .